CIRCLE
DARKNESS

NICHOLAS BELLA
AIMEE NICOLE WALKER

Circle of Darkness: Genesis Circle Book One
Copyright © 2017 Aimee Nicole Walker and Nicholas Bella

aimeenicolewalker@blogspot.com
nicholasbella.com

This is a work of fiction. Names, characters, places, and incidents either are the product of the author's imagination or are used fictitiously, and any resemblance to the actual person, living or dead, business establishments, events, or locales is entirely coincidental.

Cover art and interior images Jay Aheer of Simply Defined Art—www.jayscoversbydesign.com

Editing provided by Heidi Ryan of Amour the Line Editing www.facebook.com/amourthelineediting
Proofreading provided by Judy Zweifel of Judy's Proofreading—www.judysproofreading.com
Interior Design and Formatting provided by Stacey Ryan Blake of Champagne Book Design—http://www.champagnebookdesign.com/

All rights reserved. This book is licensed to the original publisher only.

This book contains sexually explicit material and is only intended for adult readers.

The authors acknowledge the copyrights and trademarked status and trademark owners of the following trademarks and copyrights mentioned in this work of fiction.

DEDICATION

We dedicate this book to our family, friends, and fans who love and support us unconditionally. Without you, D'Angelo and Angel wouldn't exist.

Prologue

Angel Bai

Seeing D'Angelo Kumar in my dreams was nothing new. In fact, he'd been a recurring star in both my daytime and nighttime fantasies more times than I could count since I'd first laid eyes on him in Martinelli's Italian restaurant where I worked as a waiter. Damn, the man was a walking, talking wet dream with medium brown skin stretched over the finest body ever put on the earth, inky-black hair he kept cut short in a fade, and light hazel eyes that stood out in stark contrast against his darker skin.

When he looked at me, it felt like he could see inside to the very heart of me. My fascination with him went beyond his looks too. He carried himself like a man who knew his place in the world—which was wherever he wanted it to be. He was both mesmerizing and mysterious, and I was inexplicably drawn to him.

I was used to people looking right through me like I didn't even exist, but not this guy. Our eyes connected the first time he sat at a table in my section, and I felt this unexplainable connection to him like I had never had with another person. It rattled me so much, I dropped his plate onto the table and nearly spilled his spaghetti and meatballs in his lap. I'd felt tears of humiliation welling in my eyes as I tried to scoop the spilled food off the table and back on the plate.

D'Angelo had placed his hand over mine to still me and I'd felt a buzz of awareness sizzle through me. I'd gasped and pulled my hand back in surprise. I'd held it up in front of me, half expecting it to look different or at least carry his mark on my flesh. I looked back at him and saw the same shock registered on his face. Then he closed his eyes and shook his head slightly before he reopened them. His usual mask of calm and cool was back in place so fast, I doubted my vision.

D'Angelo came to Martinelli's nearly every day that I worked after that. He always sat in my section, but that aloofness never faded from his face. He also couldn't seem to remember my damned name, either. No matter how many times I introduced myself to him as Angel, he called me Ansell. It rolled off his tongue in such a melodious way, I could almost convince myself that it was an endearment. I nearly googled it, but I was afraid it meant the exact opposite of a pet name and he was laughing at my obvious infatuation with him. There was no way he missed the way I blushed and stuttered in his presence, and it was equally doubtful that he didn't know the source of my discomfort. Yes, it was much better to pretend he had a pet name for me so I could continue fantasizing about him.

That night, it wasn't one of my usual visions of my legs wrapped around D'Angelo's waist while he powered in and out of me that had me jerking up out of my sleep with a pounding heart. My body was covered with a fine sheen of sweat from fear licking at my body rather than the flames of desire from the passionate kisses I normally dreamed about with him. My stomach pitched and rolled, threatening to spill its contents in a violent fashion. I wasn't sure if I was sick because of what I saw in my vision or from the way my brain pounded in my skull. I'd never had such a physically debilitating reaction to a vision before, and I couldn't help but wonder what had caused the change in me. It had to have been caused by what I saw in the vision because I had never in my life witnessed anything as scary.

"No!" I said out loud. "Please no." I shook my head vigorously to try to clear my mind of what I'd just seen and what it meant to the beautiful man with the hypnotic eyes. I wanted to believe it was just a bad dream and not a vision of things to come, but I knew better. I'd made that mistake before and it cost people their lives. As much as I hated it, I couldn't deny what I saw was a vision of things to come.

D'Angelo would break into someone's home to steal a cross made of a bluish-looking metal. It wasn't your everyday kind of cross either; it was sinister-looking rather than sacred. As he'd neared it, a blue light emanated from the cross and I watched in horror as D'Angelo writhed in agony as his soul was ripped from his body and absorbed by the cross. The only thing louder than my pounding heart was the sound of the beautiful man's tortured screams echoing in my mind.

Despite what people thought, a person couldn't live without their soul. I witnessed D'Angelo's death with my own eyes. The only thing I could do was try to prevent it.

Chapter One

D'Angelo Kumar

"Fucking humans are always getting themselves into some bullshit," I complained to my partner and best friend, Christian, as I looked at the featured item to be auctioned off that afternoon at Pilmer Auction House.

Christian was having his daily battle with the coffee machine when he paused to look up at me. "What do you mean?" He returned his attentions back to the machine. "Why won't this damn thing work for me?"

"Because you're a brute who doesn't know how to treat it with love and tenderness," Vixen said, then she walked over to him and took over. She pressed two buttons on the machine and it beeped into action. "See?"

Christian rolled his eyes. "Whatever. Thanks."

Vixen smirked, then flicked her pretty silvery bangs from her violet eyes. "No problem."

Christian smiled as he walked over to where I was sitting at the table. "What's going on?" he asked.

I pointed to the photo of what I clearly recognized as an ancient relic of the demon, Astaroth. Demonology was one of my favorite subjects in school, which was good considering the kind of school I had attended. Anyway, the Unholy Trinity of Astaroth, Beelzebul, and Lucifer was of a particular interest to me. Astaroth being one of twelve demigods in hell and Beelzebul being one of six hexigods. Of course, Lucifer was the first fallen angel. Hell was where they belonged and it was our job to make sure that was where they stayed. This relic being offered up for auction spelled out the worst kind of bad news.

Christian stroked his dark beard and his gray eyes narrowed as the seriousness of the situation took hold. "Is that what I fucking think it is?"

I nodded. "Yeah, and these dumb bastards are about to auction it off like it's some fucking coffee table topic starter. They have no idea what the hell that thing is. If they did, they never would have advertised it for sale."

Christian cocked an eyebrow. "Opening bid is five thousand dollars," he commented.

"Yeah, just goes to show you that they have no idea what the hell that thing really is." I got up from my chair and stretched my muscles.

"So, you're going to the auction?" Vixen asked.

"He has no choice. We can't let something like that get into the hands of someone who doesn't know what the hell they've just purchased," Christian said, retrieving his coffee now that it was finally brewed.

"Even worse, we can't let that relic get into the hands of someone who *does* know what the fuck it is," I pointed out.

"You better head out now. Pilmer Auction House is about a half an hour drive from here and the auction starts in an hour. Cutting it kind of close for this one, ain't cha?" Jinx asked.

I hadn't even realized she had been listening to our conversation, since she had been staring intensely at her beloved laptop through her rainbow bangs. She was a superb tech genius, but I was willing to bet she was over there playing some damn *World of Warcraft*. She'd been addicted to the game for the past six months and even her girlfriend, Vixen, was having trouble prying her from the game at times.

"Right you are," I said, then walked toward the elevator, snatching up my Jeep keys from the key rack nailed to the wall. "Is there a limit I'm allowed to spend to get this relic?" I had to ask Christian because he was my partner and it was his money that originally funded both our antique business and our legacy one. The legacy business meant saving people from the dark, ugly things the world didn't know existed. It was what we had been chosen and trained for. If you ever had a nightmare about a particular monster, trust me, that monster was real. Ghouls, demons, vampires, shapeshifters, witches, the boogeyman, trolls, goblins, evil fucking fairies, and cursed objects. All of it was our reality and our mission to eradicate.

On the surface, we looked like your legit antiques shop, and we were. But that was just another way for us to make money for weapons, food, and the lucrative salaries for ourselves and our female assistants. Above the shop was our real headquarters, housing the armory and living quarters. The place was a fortress, as we had a shit ton of wards up to keep the evil out. Although, if a monster dared to try to come up in here and start some shit, I'd be more than willing to fuck it up. I lived for this shit, killing demons and other nasties; Christian was a bit more reserved. It was a calling for him and a thrill ride for me.

Christian snorted. "The bidding starts at five grand... try not to go over one hundred. If it cost more than that, we're going to have to take some drastic measures."

I sighed. "If I have to pay that much for this—granted—priceless relic, I'll be pissed. Okay, I'm out." I stepped on the elevator when the doors opened and pressed the L1 button. I reached ground level in no time and made sure to lock up and reseal the wards with a few blessed words. The store was closed for the day, with it being Sunday and all. It was the one day of the week where we tried… emphasis on tried, to give ourselves a damn break. But alas, there I was, heading out to try to prevent what could potentially be a huge disaster.

I was walking towards my Jeep when I heard someone practically screaming my name. I turned to see the cute little waiter from Martinelli's rushing up behind me. What in the hell did he want?

He stopped short in front of me, huffing and puffing. "Oh… Oh thank god… I caught you," he panted. I was pretty curious as to what he wanted, it wasn't like I owed the restaurant he worked at a tab. Although, I found myself eating at Martinelli's quite often since he'd started working there. The food was damn good, but I did have to admit, I went on the days Ansell worked. Damn, he was cute as hell. But as much as I loved to gawk at him, he was holding me up from the serious shit.

"Umm, want to tell me what this is all about?" I asked. "I'm in a bit of a hurry."

"That's just it… I…" He paused and looked off to the side like he was hesitant to tell me something.

"Look, Ansell—"

"It's Angel," he snapped.

For the first time, I saw the fire blaze behind his beautiful brown eyes, which were a lovely feature from his Chinese-American heritage. He had many features that appealed to me that were flattering on him as well. But his eyes… those blew me away. And, well, his lips, too. I'd love to see them where they rightfully belonged—all over my body. I swore, the fantasies I'd had starring him left me with morning wood on several occasions and on the others… sticky sheets.

"I like Ansell more," I said, purposely ignoring his attempt to correct me. "Look, I'm really in a hurry, so if this can wait…" I let my voice trail off so he would get the hint.

"You're in danger," he blurted out.

I cocked an eyebrow. "In danger from what? What the hell are you talking about, and how did you find me anyway?"

"What do you mean, 'how'? You eat at Martinelli's more than I do. Besides, you always pay with your company account," Ansell said, pointing to the sign above our antique shop.

Well, okay, that made sense. "Fine. Now, about this so-called danger…"

"Look, you have to listen to me. I know what I'm about to tell you may sound far-fetched, but it's all true." He was looking up at me with eyes that were pleading for me to take him seriously, so I did.

"Tell me."

"Okay, I happen to have visions sometimes and when I have them this vividly, they usually come true," he began.

I laughed. "Did you dream about me and you in bed? Well, I could see why you'd be flustered."

He blinked in confusion, then rolled his eyes. "I'm not joking right now. Please pay attention."

"Then get to the fucking point," I snarled. He was holding me up and I didn't want to miss the auction over some bullshit-ass nightmare he'd had.

"Fine. I dreamt you were in danger. You were breaking into someone's house and some evil cross-looking relic was trying to steal your soul."

Okay, now that gave me cause for concern. The relic I was going to try to win in the auction this afternoon resembled a gothic cross, but it was the conjuring stone of Astaroth. The whole soul-stealing aspect was particularly noteworthy, because that relic required a thousand souls in order to open the portal to hell and bring Astaroth forth. Seeing as we lived in a world where I knew for a fact that the unexplained existed, I wasn't inclined to disregard his warning. Besides, there were just too many facts mixed up in his dream for me to ignore.

I placed my hand on his shoulder and felt that same stinging jolt

I had the first time I touched him, causing me to snatch my hand away. It felt like static shock and it was odd, because this was the second time it'd happened. "What the fuck was that?" My fingers were still tingling from the sensation.

He looked just as confused as I did. "I… I don't know. But I think it has something to do with why I had a vision of you. I… I mean, it was so vivid, like I was right there. I could feel your fear."

"So, in your vision, I was some bitch screaming for my life?" I didn't know why I'd said that, maybe it was because I tried not to let fear get in the way of my duty.

"Stop twisting my words. This… This thing was sucking your soul from your body. Of course you were afraid, afraid and helpless. That's why I had to warn and help you."

I could tell he really believed in this vision of his and he looked so cute with how passionate he was when telling me about it. So much so, I had to fight the urge to lean down and kiss those lips I'd been dreaming about for a month. *Keep your head in the game, D.* "Thanks, Ansell, for letting me know about your vision."

"Are you patronizing me?" he asked. His lips were pursed tightly, as if he were waiting for the other shoe to drop. Maybe he thought I'd laugh in his face and call him crazy. Well, that wasn't going to happen. Last week, I had to kill a slug demon that was killing utility workers in the sewer below Foster and Lane. So, yeah, no mockery here, buddy.

"I'm not patronizing you. I believe you. But I really do have to go," I told him. Although, I had to question if his vision was more like a vision/dream. Some truth mixed with fiction. Either way, I didn't have time to chat with him about it. I turned to climb inside my Jeep.

"Wait!"

I huffed. "What now?" As adorable and sexy as he was, he was annoying the hell out of me right then.

"Let me go with you. I need to protect you from what I saw in my vision." He brushed his asymmetrical bangs from his eyes as he looked up at me.

Okay, now this shit *was* hilarious. Ansell looked like he weighed a buck—soaking wet with clothes on. I didn't know what he saw in his dream, but there was no fucking way he was protecting me from a damned thing. Maybe from getting blue balls, but that was about it. I had been trained for the hard life and, according to my former headmaster, I'd been born for it. So, no featherweight-looking waif was about to muscle in on my territory, no matter how deliciously hot he looked.

"Now, that was the first thing you've said that is laughable. Look, I've got to go." With that, I closed my door and started my engine.

"Please don't go without me. I have to protect you, D'Angelo. You don't understand!" Ansell pleaded as he banged on my Jeep window, which pissed me off.

I backed up, which forced him to take several steps backwards, then I pulled away. I had to really put the pedal to the metal to cut into my travel time. Luckily, I had this persuasion powder Vixen had concocted. So, if I did happen to get pulled over by the police, I could blow the powder into their faces and make them let me go. Having a witch on the team was pretty damn helpful, that was for sure.

I couldn't help but think about what Ansell had said about the relic. No way would I let that bastard steal my soul. I was going to win it in the auction, take it back home, and lock it away with the other dangerous artifacts we'd acquired since Christian and I had started the Genesis Circle. Ansell had nothing to worry about. He could go back to dreaming about my sexy body instead of my grisly demise. I knew he had it bad for me. Every time I ate at Martinelli's, he could hardly take his eyes off of me. And that smile... damn that smile of his was something to behold. Okay, so maybe I had my eye on him, too. But I didn't do relationships and Ansell looked like the relationship type of guy.

He was the type that wanted the romance, the roses, the chocolates on the pillows, and the slow love-making in front of a roaring fire. That wasn't me. My lifestyle was too chaotic for such luxuries. Not to mention, I just wasn't the Prince Charming type of guy. I was more of the dashing rogue. Dashing in for some sweet booty and then roguing away. I wasn't boyfriend material, was all I was saying. So, I never made my move on him even though I really wanted to. The last thing I wanted was to do my thing, where I love them and leave them, and then have to deal with a pissed-off waiter at my favorite fucking restaurant spitting in my food. No, thank you.

As for my lifestyle, well, it was all business. The Genesis Circle had been Christian's idea. He wanted to carry on the work we used to do with the Chasseur Institute. The Institute was where we both attended school as youths. On the surface, the school looked like your pristine and elite educational powerhouse; boarding quarters that rivaled some people's apartments, state-of-the-art technology, every elective known to man from basketball to archery, and the best damned food you could eat. It was a school full of snobs, but within the student body, there were children who were deemed extraordinary. I was among them, every class grade had those who'd been chosen by our headmaster for special training.

That was how I learned about the other hidden creatures that resided in the world I thought I knew. The things that lived in the shadows and fed off human misery, fear, greed, and despair. Oh, and let's not forget flesh and blood, they ate that, too. Those of us who were handpicked to become hunters started our rigorous training as children or preteens. Let me be the first to say that there were no punches pulled, and as a kid, I'd hated my trainers. Hell, I wasn't all that fond of the school either, or was it my school mates? They teased me a lot growing up because I wasn't rich. I was only attending because I had been granted a full scholarship. At first, my mother didn't know why I was being offered the full ride. It wasn't like I'd had the best grades in the public school I'd been attending... and ditching from time to time.

The recruiter had convinced my mom I was just too advanced

and I needed to go to a school that understood my needs. Considering the school in question was Chasseur Institute, an all-boys school, she jumped at the opportunity to enroll me even though it meant I'd have to live there, which meant I had to move to another country all together. It didn't take the Powers That Be long at the school to enlist me for the noble work of eradicating evil. Like I said, the training was harsh, but necessary. It was also all covert. My mom never knew her son was being trained to be a warrior. And when you reached the age of sixteen, every last one of us who had survived or passed the training were tattooed with a special symbol that gave us remarkable abilities.

Through the power of our tattoos, true hunters could see the real faces of demons and other monsters that hid under human facades. We were also stronger than your average human. I'd say I had the strength of ten men. We could also heal pretty damn fast, which often came in handy in our line of work. A non-lethal stab wound might take an hour to heal as opposed to weeks. One more thing the tattoo did was awaken a dormant power that resided in every one of us. Mine was the whole heighten senses ability. I could see, hear, smell, and taste twenty times more than a normal human. So, believe me when I say that Martinelli's was a restaurant that should be honored to be my favorite, as I just didn't taste food… I experienced it.

Christian and I became best friends as children, and his special dormant ability was the power to see a person's deepest, darkest secrets. If you killed someone and didn't want anyone to know, then you'd better steer clear of him. We were both fine working as agents of the Institute until they decided to press us on the rules of their organization.

Of course, these were rules neither Christian nor I could abide by. They wanted us to find our mates and marry. That sounded all fine on paper, but in reality, the mates in question had to be of the opposite sex. See, every hunter was required to be straight. They were to mate with a female fated to be theirs, and procreate. One big happy hunter family. That was one sure way to keep the line of the hunters going. My parents weren't hunters, but someone in my family line had been at one point in the past. That was how the dormant gene passed on to me. Since my dad dumped my mom early on in my life, I never could ask him if anyone in his family was special or different.

As you could imagine, that presented a problem for Christian and me, since we were gay and in no way were we going to marry a woman just to procreate. The Institute viewed us as failures and abominations. They felt like we were betraying our oath and banished us. It was a bitch at first, to be cut off from the resources we needed to do the job we'd been born and bred for. Not to mention, the one place we'd called home for pretty much our entire lives. But we were tough sons of bitches and had persevered. That was how the Genesis Circle had been created.

We'd met Jinx and Vixen a year ago when we saved them from a cursed object. Trust Jinx to want the *Troll* collection. Well, one of the fuzzy-haired bastards was evil and tried to kill her and Vixen in their sleep by stealing their breaths. At the time it was happening, Jinx and Vixen had two other female roommates. Once they had died mysteriously, Father Thomas had recommended they see us. Good old Father Thomas. He was a true believer, as we'd saved him from a demon who'd tried to corrupt his faith and his soul a few years back.

All in all, we made some loyal and trustworthy connections and had a nice network of people we could go to for help… though, some of them weren't as trustworthy or loyal as Father Thomas, Vixen, and Jinx.

Ahhh, finally there. Good, I arrived just in time for the auction. Good thing it was a public event and not an invitation-only sort of affair. Although, our antiques business had quite the respectable reputation. I'd doubt they'd give me much trouble if I just showed up, wanting in on the action. I parked and climbed out of my Jeep, then headed inside, taking a seat towards the back.

CIRCLE OF DARKNESS

The auction room wasn't too crowded, only about thirty people in total. I scoped them out as discreetly as I could to see who might give me some trouble. Not everyone who came to this auction were millionaires or billionaires. Also, not all insanely rich people looked the part, but there was one guy in the back who did look the part. Late sixties, buggy eyes, pudgy gut, rubbery lips that looked like he had a botched collagen injection. It was all topped off with a horrible, bleached blond toupee that looked like a bird had made a nest on top of his head but thought it was too shoddy to lay its eggs in it, so it just left it there. You'd think with all the money he had, he'd go the distance regarding that toupee, but whatever. There was no accounting for taste. Of course, the same couldn't be said about his suit, it was immaculate and I knew it had to have cost at least ten grand.

I sat there in the last row adjacent to Mr. Money Bags with the wispy toupee for the first twenty minutes, waiting on the item I came for to finally be presented. I did see a kick-ass sword that I'd have loved to own, but it was already going for two hundred grand, seeing as it had once been wielded by the legendary warrior, Hans Von Hotzen, during the great wars of the medieval period. Sure wished I could have won that one. I was sitting there waiting and froze when I caught the very familiar scent of a certain sexy waif who was quickly becoming a nuisance to me. Mainly because I really wanted to feel his warm body pressed beneath mine as I slid my cock inside of him and saw his face light up with pleasure. But I was trying so hard to keep him at bay. I feared that if I got a taste of him, I might not want to let him go and, like I said, my life was too dangerous and that was why I wasn't boyfriend material.

"Oh, thank god I found you," Ansell said, sitting down next to me.

I looked at him. "How did you find me and what the fuck are you doing here?" I snapped.

"One of the chicks at the store told me. Besides, I've already told you, even if you don't want to believe me, I'm here to protect you."

I looked at what he was wearing. Skinny jeans, pink sneakers, and a white t-shirt with some cartoon character on it mouthing off a sassy slogan. I shook my head, chuckling. "I don't need your ninety-pound weakling ass to protect me."

"See, that's precisely why you do need me. Look, my dreams don't lie… I saw you dying and I'd never be able to live with myself if I didn't do everything I can to make sure that doesn't happen," he urged. "Oh, and I weigh more than ninety pounds, I'll have you know."

I was just about to rip him a new one when the relic I was waiting for was announced. "We'll talk later," I said, then turned all of my attention to the front. They had called the thing the Stellar Relic, claiming it came from Stellar Pilmer's private collection. The bidding started off at five thousand and I sat back and waited while others went into a bidding frenzy. Not too many people wanted the relic, only about five were going toe-to-toe for it. I wondered if they knew what it really was? Whatever the case, the assholes had jacked the price up to fifty thousand. Just when I thought it was about to die down and I could come in with the stealing bid, the bugged-eyed, toupee man in the gorgeous black suit with the silver tie raised his flag, and the bid upped to seventy-five thousand.

Damn, it was getting close to my limit. I decided to throw my bid into the mix. By now, the other bidders stopped participating and it was just the toupee guy in the suit and me going head-to-head.

"Geez, he must really want that cross," Ansell said.

"Which isn't good news for me," I grumbled, and then I raised my bid, hitting my limit. The guy in the suit paused and the auctioneer did the whole "going once, going twice" thing, and just when I thought that little baby was mine, that motherfucker in the suit chimed in.

"One-hundred fifty thousand dollars," he said with a wicked, self-satisfied grin, as if challenging me to one-up him. Luckily for him, I couldn't.

The bastard won the relic I came to get and now I had to figure out another way to acquire the damn thing.

Ansell frowned and looked at me. "It's all coming true. This must be why you were breaking into that house."

Well, I'd be damned... the thought had crossed my mind. Shit.

CHAPTER TWO

ANGEL

D'Angelo's expression could only be described as thunderous as he stared down at me. I found myself at a loss for words, which was a rarity for me. The entire encounter outside his antique shop, and then later at the auction house, seemed surreal. I would've thought I was dreaming, but the thundering of my heartbeat in my ears told me I was wide awake.

I expected the disbelief he showed me in the alley, but not for the reason he gave me. I thought he would laugh at me when I told him I'd had a vision and his life was in danger; instead, he laughed about my weight and ability to protect him. Okay, maybe I should've expected that part too because it wasn't like I hadn't been teased about my size my entire life. I weighed more than he thought, but I could tell by his expression that it wasn't the time to correct him.

"This is all your fucking fault," he said, seething.

My mouth popped open in shock. I could only stare at him

speechless for a few heartbeats, but it was long enough for him to rise angrily to his feet and walk away. It was what I'd needed to snap into action. I had to practically jog to catch up to his angry strides.

"My fault? How the hell do you figure that?" I demanded. Who did this sexy-as-sin jackass think he was?

D'Angelo ignored me and pulled his cell phone out of his pocket. "I lost the bid, Christian. Some dumb fuck outbid me." That wasn't my fault, but I guessed it was easier to blame me than being short on the funds needed to buy the evil relic. "What do you want me to do now? That's what I thought you were going to say, but there's a new development." D'Angelo looked over in my direction briefly on his way to his Jeep, letting me know that he was talking about me. "I'll call you back after I deal with it."

It? Had he just referred to me in such a callous way? I shouldn't have been surprised, but somehow, I was. Why I expected better treatment from him over anyone else, including my own flesh and blood, was beyond me. I had a moment where I contemplated that his fate with the creepy cross was well-earned, but it didn't last. Regardless of what he thought about me, he didn't deserve to have his very essence ripped from his body. There was goodness inside D'Angelo Kumar, even if it wasn't shown to me. I thought it was possible that he didn't even know it existed.

D'Angelo stopped and faced me once he disconnected his call and returned his phone to his pocket. "Tell me everything you saw about that library. I want you to tell me every fucking detail."

"No," I said stubbornly.

D'Angelo backed me up until I was pressed against the side of his Jeep. "Here I thought you wanted to help me." His voice was low and menacing, yet I was getting hard because it was the same voice he used in my sexy dreams. It didn't help when he pressed his body against mine. The electrical spark that only he could make me feel hummed beneath my skin. It sizzled through me at a lower voltage than the first time, but it was still enough to cause my synapses to misfire, leaving me muddled and dazed. D'Angelo's determination to get answers was temporarily distracted by the hardness he felt pressing against him.

"I do want to help you," I croaked.

"I can feel how badly you want to help me." D'Angelo smirked. I saw lust flare in his hazel eyes but it was extinguished so quickly, I knew I must've been mistaken. It was obvious that the man didn't mind playing dirty to get his way, either. He lowered his mouth until it hovered over mine. "Tell me everything you saw."

"You're just going to follow that man home and break into his house to steal that artifact once he's gone to sleep. I can't let you do it," I protested, but I sounded weak even to my own ears.

"No one 'lets' me do anything, Ansell. I do what I want, when I want, and how often I want to." *Were we still talking about retrieving that artifact?* "I don't make excuses for who I am or what I do, and I sure as fuck won't apologize." *Yeah, I'd definitely struck a nerve.* An idea occurred to me, one that could backfire, but it was the only hope I had of saving his life that night.

"Listen to you, sounding all 'badass' tonight." The air quotes and tone of voice made it sound like I was mocking him, when all I really wanted to do was distract him.

"Do you doubt my abilities, lightweight?" He would've moved closer if he could, but that would've required nudity, a condom, and lube—all things I was more than willing to produce, but not until after I saved his life.

"Another crack at my weight," I replied sarcastically. "What's next? Shoe size, the size of my hands, or better yet, my dick size?" I rolled my eyes dramatically. "I weigh more than you think, my shoes and hands are proportionate to my body, but my dick surely isn't." My boastful words and smug smile made it clear I was pretty damned pleased with my cock size.

"You're acting as if I don't feel your hard-on right now," D'Angelo said, reminding me of his proximity to my body. I could tell he wanted to say more, but his attention had returned to his mission of recovering the artifact. "I'm impressed about what you're packing, but that's not what I need right now." *Did that mean he might need it later?* "What. Did. You. See?"

I closed my eyes briefly to clear my mind of everything except the vision I'd seen. "You were all dressed in black," I said. "You were wearing a long-sleeved shirt, but not a Henley. It was a thicker, tighter knit material that looked made for battle; as if it could hold up to a knife fight. Your pants appeared to be a typical pair of black cargo pants, but they weren't. There were more pockets and loops to hold tools for cutting the wires to an alarm system and for scaling the side of a home to access the library through a second-story window."

D'Angelo snorted rudely.

"What was that for?" I asked him.

"Nothing. Quit jerking me around and finish telling me your story," D'Angelo said angrily, catching me off guard.

"I'm not jerking you around," I said defensively. "I'm telling you what I saw in my *vision*."

"Then you're embellishing because I don't own the clothing you described," he fired back.

"You will," I assured him. I gloated on the inside a bit because I realized my ploy to distract him long enough for the bidder to get away must've worked. I breathed a sigh of relief because D'Angelo Kumar wasn't going to die tonight. I could worry about another night later when I was home alone and could formulate a plan.

"Whatever," he said dismissively. "Tell me the rest."

"The guy lives in a huge stone home, more like a mansion, really. It's more of a gray stone instead of a beige." The irritated expression on his face said he didn't give two fucks what kind of house the dude lived in or the construction materials used to build it. "I'm going to assume the property is gated, but I'm not sure because my vision begins with you clipping the alarm wires and scaling the side of the home to a second-story window, as I previously mentioned."

"I doubt that, but I'll humor you, so get to the fucking part when I entered the home," he demanded hotly, obviously losing what little patience he had with me.

"Okay, okay," I said. D'Angelo was so focused on me, he didn't see the winning bidder exit the front of the auction house, and I certainly wasn't about to point it out to him. "The library was very opulent with floor-to-ceiling bookshelves, an ornately carved wet bar, and multiple sitting areas with leather furniture. It looked like an awesome space, and I bet there'd be a whiff of cigar or pipe tobacco in the air. I mean, this man has serious money—as you're obviously aware of since he easily outbid you."

"What happened once I was inside the home?" D'Angelo tersely asked through gritted teeth. The growl in his voice only made me harder, which I hadn't thought possible until it happened. If I wasn't careful, I would come in my jeans. The slight flaring of his nostrils told me he was aware of my reaction, at least on some level.

"There were several wooden pedestals with glass cases throughout the room with various treasures on display, but the one you were after was in the center of the room, as if it was his pride and joy," I told him.

"Can you describe any of the other artifacts the man had on display?" D'Angelo asked. I wasn't sure why, but I knew my answer was important to him.

"I'm sorry, but I can't," I replied, knowing that my answer disappointed him.

"It's okay," he said quickly. "Keep telling me what you do know, Ansell."

"As you approached the glass confinement, the gothic-looking cross began to vibrate a little. The closer you got, the more it shook, and the entire room rocked by the time you stood in front of it. Then this pale blue light started to form around the edges of it like wispy smoke and…" I had to stop a minute to catch my breath because reliving the moment was worse than experiencing it the first time.

D'Angelo's next move shocked me, more so than if had he kissed me. D'Angelo ran a finger softly across my cheekbone and said, "I'm going to be okay as long as you tell me what you know." The tender way he spoke caused me to reopen my eyes and refocus my energy on keeping him alive. Everything else would have to wait.

"The light got stronger and darker in color once you lifted the glass display case off the pedestal." My voice started to shake with the same intensity as the relic and my vision was blinded by the vibrancy of the light emanating from the evil device. "Someone outside my line of vision began chanting and the center of the cross opened. I watched as it ripped your soul from your body, D'Angelo. It wasn't quick, because you fought it, and because you struggled, this *thing* took its time torturing you. Your screams…"

I covered my ears as if that could stop me from hearing his pain and agony all over again as the relic sucked his life from him. It was so much more intense than the dream itself, but why? What had changed? Nausea came on me quick and sharp, and much stronger than the first time; my body broke out in sweat and dizziness washed over me. My heart pounded in my chest and I was both hot and cold everywhere and at the same time. My vision grew dark, and I realized I was on the verge of collapsing. I bucked my body until D'Angelo stepped back, only then could I breathe the air I needed into my lungs. I bent over and supported myself with my hands on my knees or else I would've fallen to the ground.

D'Angelo placed his hand on my back uncertainly, as if he wasn't used to offering comfort to someone. "Now I know to approach the thing from behind," he said, as if that made everything better. "I just need to…" His words broke off and I angled my head to get a glimpse of his face. "Son of a fucking bitch! You did this on purpose, didn't you? Oh my god! Are you faking right now to slow me down?"

I would've been celebrating inside had I not still been reeling from my reaction to telling him about the vision. It was almost as if I was in the moment with him, rather than seeing it in my mind. That was something that had never happened to me, and I couldn't wrap my head around it.

D'Angelo began to pace and curse while he dug his phone back out of his pocket. The farther he got away from me, the better I felt. *He* was the reason why I reacted differently to the vision, but what did it all mean?

"I need a backup plan. Following the guy home didn't pan out," D'Angelo practically snarled into the phone. The look he pinned me with while waiting to hear his next order was enough to make my insides quake again with fear. "It just didn't, Christian," he said in response to the question he was asked. "It's a long story and not one I want to get into right now," he said in frustration. "What? That's it? Just come back home?" *Home? Was Christian his lover?* "Yeah, fine. I'll be there as soon as I can and we'll figure out what to do next." D'Angelo hung up and turned to face me once he was done. "After I deal with you," he said to me.

I rose to my full height and waited for him to blast me with the anger I saw in his eyes. I swallowed hard, not knowing what the man was capable of and how far my stunt had pushed him. "I'm not sorry," I bravely—or stupidly—said. I clearly didn't know when to keep my lips shut.

"You're not, huh?" D'Angelo asked, marching toward me. "You saw what that thing is capable of, and yet, you hinder me when I try to stop it from falling into the wrong hands?" He didn't stop until he once again had me pressed into the side of his Jeep. "Do you know how many deaths you could be responsible for?"

"I know the one that I saved by telling him what I know the relic is capable of doing," I countered. "I also know that my vision wasn't going to come true tonight since you stated that you don't own the clothing I described."

"How many people will die before then?" D'Angelo demanded, knowing it was something I couldn't answer. "Those deaths will all be on you."

"They would've died anyway," I argued. "By saving you, I'm saving the world." I didn't know how the fuck I knew that, I just did. The same way I knew this wouldn't be the last time we argued about the relic.

"Is that what you really think?" he asked. The anger had faded some in his voice and I heard a hint of awe creeping in. D'Angelo placed his hand on my hip and I could feel the heat of his fingers through the denim of my jeans. It felt like he was about to brand me. "You think I'm that important to the world?"

"Yes," I whispered. My breath hitched in my throat when his hand slowly worked its way down the front of my jeans. Dear god, how had he gone from hopping mad to ready to fuck so quickly? The answer came when he reached inside my pocket and yanked out my keys instead of unzipping my pants and taking out my dick.

"Too damn bad you went to all that trouble for nothing," he said, turning away from me. "It was quite the show, Ansell."

"Damn it, D'Angelo, I'm not making any of this up." He didn't slow down to acknowledge me. "What are you doing?" I asked as I followed him to my car. It wasn't hard for him to figure out which one was mine since it was the least luxurious one in the customer parking lot.

"Making sure you don't follow me," he replied calmly. He unlocked my Honda Civic before he jerked the door open and reached in to pop the hood. "Stay the hell away from me, Angel." It was the first time he'd used my real name. I should've been over the moon, but I realized by his tone that there was a finality in the way he said it.

I stood frozen and watched as D'Angelo removed something off the engine of my car and pocketed it along with my keys. Why not just take my keys? Did he worry I had a spare key taped beneath my bumper or hidden in my wheel well like smart people do?

"You're going to leave me stranded here?" I asked in shock.

"You psychics never see the bad shit that happens to you," he smugly replied on his way to his Jeep. "Why is that?" Like I had the answer to that. It wasn't like he planned to stick around and debate it, either.

I watched in shock as he sped off after a smart-ass little beep and wave. I turned back toward my car, grateful that I could call for roadside assistance and wouldn't be stranded for too damned long. "Damn him!" I yelled, once I realized my cell phone was no longer in my pocket. That sexy son of a bitch had stolen it as well while he'd had me pinned to his Jeep.

Chapter Three

D'Angelo

"That little bastard!" I growled in frustration. I hated having my plans blown and I didn't like when things didn't go my way. Having Ansell there had thrown me off my game. Maybe I could have read the room better, maybe I could have intimidated my competition to the point where he wouldn't have fucking dared to raise the bet. None of that had gone into play as soon as I heard that soft voice of his telling me he was there to protect me.

Protect me from what? Just what in the hell did he think he could do? I faced danger every damn day, and let's not even bring up all of the hijinks that go down on Halloween. Where was he when a Kol'ksu goblin had nearly killed me three months ago? Probably waiting tables at some other restaurant, that was where he was. Since when did he decide to take up the mantle of being my savior? Saving lives was my job!

I was fuming as I drove back to the antiques store. All I could think about was what would that guy do with the relic he'd purchased? Did he know what it was? If he did, what were his plans? Who was he going to kill with it? If the thing absorbed souls like Ansell said he saw in his vision, how many souls would it need to bring forth Astaroth? Did this guy want to bring forth Astaroth or just use the relic to get rid of some undesirable people in his life? Or did he just think it looked wicked cool and wanted to show it off to friends and family? There were too many questions I didn't have the answers to.

What troubled me the most was Ansell's damned vision. How accurate was it? Was seeing my death something his subconscious created because he was worried for me? Hell, maybe I didn't even die in his vision. He did say he woke up before anything was final. Shit, I hated not knowing more about this situation. It probably wouldn't bother me so much if he had never told me about the vision. There was just something that took the fun out of life if you knew too much about your future. I was glad I wasn't a damn psychic.

The other thing that bothered me was how much attraction I felt for him. Not to mention the amount of attraction he felt for me. Granted, he was physically smaller than I was, but what I felt raging hard between his legs had been impressive. Still, getting involved with him more than I already had was bad news. I couldn't allow myself to get wrapped up in my feelings for him. Best to keep it platonic. I managed to find a parking space on the street instead of using our underground garage, and made my way inside our shop.

"Want to tell me what happened… in detail now?" Christian asked me the moment I entered the living room.

I plopped down in my chair and sighed heavily as I thought about how everything had gone to shit. "I got outbid by some rich bastard. Then I was interrupted by Ansell proclaiming that he was there to save me."

Christian cocked an eyebrow. "Come again?"

"Ansell totally distracted me and I didn't see the buyer leave the auction house."

"Ansell? The waiter from the restaurant? The one you've been jerking off to?" Christian asked with a look of confusion.

"Yeah, him. Did you have to mention I'd been wanking to him, though?"

He shrugged. "Just wanted to make sure we were talking about the same guy. His name is Angel, why do you call him Ansell? That's why I was confused."

"I like Ansell better."

"Okay, whatever. How did he distract you? I mean, you're normally all business when on a mission. Easily distracted isn't you," Christian stated.

I shook my head and ran my fingers over my hair. "It was the damnedest thing. Before I headed out to the auction house, Ansell stopped me, claiming he'd had a vision of me breaking into some guy's house to steal the relic in question. He said that I died in his vision, or at the very least, my soul was taken by the relic."

"You believe him?" Christian asked. He wasn't mocking, only curious as to how seriously I was taking the vision.

I shrugged. "The part about the relic was accurate. Don't know about the rest of his vision. For instance, he saw me wearing clothes I don't own, so, go figure." I leaned back, putting my feet on the cocktail table. "I do know one thing for sure. Vision or not, I have to get that relic."

Christian nodded. "That's why you were supposed to follow him."

I threw my hands up. "I would have, but Ansell used that moment to distract me like I told you."

"What did he do, bat his eyes at you?" Jinx asked upon entering the room with her cup of hot cocoa in her hands.

I snorted and rolled my eyes. "I'll have you know, I am not that easily distracted. It takes a lot more than a pretty boy batting his eyes at me to catch my attention."

"No, it doesn't. I've seen a pretty boy do less than that and you were on him all night until you got him home," Christian pointed out.

"When I'm on a mission, I'm not distracted. You know this... but Ansell was telling me about his vision in more detail and his cock was hard the—"

"Okay, that's a lot of information," Jinx said, holding her hand up.

I shrugged. "Well, you wanted to know how I got thrown off my game. I'm telling you, I had to keep my crotch from touching his body, because I was hard the whole time, too. Something about him really gets me going."

She giggled. "By the way I've seen you checking that guy out, I bet it didn't take much for him to gain your undivided attention."

"I can't quite put my finger on why I'm so attracted to him. Anyway, he was telling me about his vision. For instance, Jinx, I need for you to see what you can get on the guy who won the bid. Check to see if he has a two-story house with gray brick or stone walls. Find out his name and any other information." I gave her the description Ansell had given me of the home I break into in his vision. At the time that he was telling me, I didn't think those details were important. Turns out, they might be the key to locating this place. This guy might have multiple homes and we needed to be able to narrow it down.

"Can I get a 'please' and a 'thank you' with that?" Jinx asked, cocking one snarky eyebrow at me.

"Woman, if you don't get your ass on that computer and look up this information, I'll—"

"You'll do what? Not a damn thing, that's what," she shot back with a giggle.

"I'll sell your digital weapons to the first person to ask on *WOW*," I playfully threatened.

Her eyes grew wide. "You're crossing some lines now. That's dangerous territory you're stepping into," she jested... even though I knew she was mad crazy about that game and had a bunch of weapons, money, life, armor, and probably some charms and shit. I didn't bother with the game. I lived a real-life *World of Warcraft*.

I gave in and smiled sweetly at her. "Pretty please, with sugar on top?"

She grinned, baring her teeth. "See, that wasn't so bad, now was it?"

"My insides are burning," I joked.

"Oh geez, you're pathetic," Jinx laughed, then walked over to her expensive computer unit we'd purchased for her and took a seat. That thing had six screens, routers upon routers, and was even hooked up to satellites and police scanners. I knew she'd be able to find out everything I needed to know. If she couldn't, she'd at least be able to point me in the right direction.

"D'Angelo, time to get serious," Christian said.

I snorted. "When am I not serious?"

He made an off-handed gesture towards Jinx, indicating the little playful tit-for-tat that had just transpired between us, and I sighed.

"Fine. What's up?" I conceded. Jinx and I did fool around a lot, so he was right.

"I'm concerned about this vision. If Angel is a psychic, we can't disregard the part about you dying," Christian said.

"I'm not disregarding it. He told me everything that happened in his vision. I'm going to do my research on this relic, find out how it got to the Pilmer Auction House in the first place. The more I know about the relic, the better prepared I'll be," I stated.

"Okay, that's a good start, find out where it came from," Christian said.

Now that I thought about it, I wished I had stuck around the Pilmer Auction House to ask some questions before zooming back home. Damn! That fucking Angel had me all helter-skelter. I had to stay focused and not let him distract me anymore. I stood up and started walking towards the elevator.

"Where are you going?" Christian asked.

"Back to the auction house. I need to talk to the manager there and find out how they acquired the relic," I said.

"I'm surprised you didn't do that before you came home. Just how distracted did Angel have you?" he asked, but I knew it was more of a criticism. If nothing else, Christian was quite rigid. I thought he needed to get laid more than I did, but because of his ability to see people's darkest secrets... well, let's just say he didn't have the best date nights.

"I know... I fucked up. Won't happen again," I simply said. I didn't do the whole beating a dead horse thing. I messed up. I'd admit it and keep it moving. Christian got the message and didn't press.

I made the inconvenient trip back to the auction house, but I did stop off to grab something to eat along the way. When I got back there, I saw that Ansell and his car were both gone. Good, I didn't need him around, causing me trouble. I had a job to do. I climbed out of my Jeep and entered the auction house. I'd been there several times, making some nice, expensive purchases. So, I was familiar with the manager, Jeffrey Manners. I walked up to his assistant's desk and she smiled up at me.

"Welcome to Pilmer Auction House, how may I help you?" she inquired in a pleasant voice.

"I'd like to speak with Mr. Manners. Can you please let him know that D'Angelo Kumar of *Things of the Past Antiques* is here to see him?"

She nodded and made the call. I waited for the confirmation. "Yes, sir," she said before hanging up the telephone. She looked up at me again. "He'll be happy to see you in a few minutes. Feel free to have a seat if you like." She gestured to four very comfortable-looking chairs in the opposite corner of the room.

I thanked her and took a seat. It didn't take too long before Mr. Manners was ready to see me. I entered his office and took another seat. "Thank you," I said, making pleasantries before I might be forced to get nasty.

"My pleasure, Mr. Kumar. Now, how may I assist you this afternoon?"

"The relic that sold for one hundred fifty grand today… can you tell me how you came to possess it?" I asked, getting right to the point. They had called it the "Stellar Relic," which was the first name of the owner of the auction house, Stellar Pilmer. I found that curious because most artifacts that came to the auction house all had a point of origin. This one didn't, so they pretended like it came from Pilmer's personal stash, at least that was my hunch and my hunches were rarely wrong. My question seemed to make Mr. Manners a bit nervous as he sat back in his chair, clasping his hands together in his lap.

"I'm afraid I can't give out that sort of information on this item, sir," Mr. Manners said. Okay, he was about to make this difficult.

"Surely, you can give me some information. Was it acquired in an estate auction? Did the owner of Pilmer House get it in an excavation? Was it donated? These are simple questions, Mr. Manners," I said. I was trying to be polite, but if he didn't tell me what I wanted to hear… well, I had no problem being rude.

"Mr. Kumar, you have been a model client and we'd love to continue our business relationship with you, but I just can't give you that information," Mr. Manners said.

Okay, now I was pissed. Not only could I see that he was lying about not being able to give me the information I wanted, but I could smell and hear him lying. The sound of his heart beating faster the moment I first asked the question, coupled with the extra beads of sweat sprinkling his forehead were dead indicators. I might not be able to see a person's deepest, darkest secrets, but I could tell when someone was lying to me because of my heightened senses.

I was about to get physical with the man to get the information I needed, but then I remembered that I still had the persuasion powder Vixen had made for me. Perfect. I pulled the packet out of my pocket and leaned over his desk. "Mr. Manners, perhaps we can make a deal. Check this out."

His curiosity got the better of him and he leaned over to take a gander at what I had in the packet. When his face got close enough, I blew the powder at him and he coughed and sneezed a little, then fell back in his chair with a dazed look on his face. That meant it was working, but wouldn't last for long. Just long enough for me to get the answers I had come for.

"Mr. Manners, who is the buyer and where does he live?"

"I… I don't know who the buyer is, and he paid in cash," Mr. Manners said in a slow cadence because the powder was really working on him.

I hated that he couldn't even give me that information. That was highly unlikely, as every client had to at least have a file with this place. House rules. "No file was set up on this buyer at all?"

Mr. Manner shook his head. "I've never actually met the buyer before he attended the auction. But he gave us an additional hundred grand to keep the transaction private."

Well, fuck. Sometimes I hated greedy motherfuckers. "What can you tell me about the relic? Where did it come from?"

"That's just it," he said in a shaky voice, which meant the powder would be wearing off soon. "I don't know anything about it at all. It arrived at the House in a box, no return address," he said, then touched his temple and winced, as if confused.

"Can I see the box?"

He shook his head. "We threw it away."

Fucking hell. "So, you receive a mysterious item in a box and just decided to auction it off?"

He looked off to the side, then shrugged. "We had it authenticated. It was noted to be at least a thousand years old. Once Mr. Pilmer got the confirmation, he gave his approval to auction it. It's what we do, after all. We called it the Stellar Relic, just to give it a name, since no one has ever seen anything like it before."

Shit, sometimes I hated being right. Also, that just made my job that much easier… and by easier, I meant harder. "So, that's all you can tell me?"

He nodded. "That's all. To be honest, the thing creeped me out."

I arched an eyebrow. "How so?"

"Well, I felt sick around it, so did everyone else."

"And you still decided to auction it off?" I was pissed off about that.

He shrugged. "It just gave us the heebie-jeebies. I think it was all mental anyway."

Ahhh, good old denial. Worked every time and left you fucked up in the process. "Why the low starting bid if you appraised it at least a thousand years old?"

"I… it was supposed to start at five hundred grand, that's what Mr. Pilmer wanted, but… I… I don't remember why it was switched," he said. And this time, the confusion displayed on his face had nothing to do with the powder. He really couldn't remember why they lowered the price. Shit, at half a mil, there was no way I was going to win it. Someone wanted this little relic to have a guaranteed sale, that was for sure. I was wondering who had gotten to Mr. Manners before the auction to have him lower the price.

"Do you remember talking to anyone about the relic prior to you listing it for auction?" I asked.

"No… Excuse me, why are you asking me these questions?" he asked. Okay, that meant my powder spell had worn off and he was back to being himself.

Again, I felt annoyed because I knew this shit went deeper down the rabbit hole. "I want to thank you for taking the time out of your day to answer my questions. I hope we can continue to do business in the future."

He smiled because he didn't remember me blowing the powder in his face. "Of course, Mr. Kumar. We are always looking forward to working with you." He rose and shook my hand when I extended my own, and when he released it, I turned and left his office. I drove back home to see if Jinx had come up with anything since I was still batting zero. Sure, I had some information, like I knew for a fact that other forces were involved with this auction. Nothing was random. But I still had to figure out who was involved and where to start looking.

"Any luck?" Christian asked me when I stepped off the elevator, as he happened to be walking by with his cup of coffee on his way to the den.

I followed beside him. "Not really. Relic arrived in an unmarked box, they sold it to the buyer who didn't leave his information and paid in cash," I said. "Also, I'm pretty certain a person with mental abilities visited the auction house prior to the relic being listed because it was supposed to go for way more money. Originally, it was supposed to start at half a mil, but was lowered to just five grand."

We entered the den and sat down on the comfy sofas adorning the room with the eighty-six-inch screen television that was my happy place whenever I wasn't out kicking demon and monster ass. We also had all of the modern gaming systems too, because shit, we liked to unwind just like everyone else.

"And Jeffrey doesn't remember who he spoke to that wanted the bid lowered," I said, bringing him up to date.

"Damn, someone wanted that relic to be purchased at a cheap price," Christian commented.

"Not only that, but they made sure to have a buyer lined up. I don't think I was ever going to win the bid on that damn relic," I added.

"And the House didn't have a file on the buyer?" Christian asked, still surprised by that fact.

I shook my head. "Said the buyer paid an extra one hundred grand to keep it secret."

"I can't believe Mr. Manners or Stellar would jeopardize the integrity of the Pilmer House for money, as if they don't get enough," Christian said with a distasteful sneer.

I shrugged. "Greed will do that to you."

"You have a guest," Jinx said when she poked her head into the den. "I'll bring him in." With that, she walked away.

I already knew who the guest was. I recognized the scent of Ansell and felt both annoyed and seduced by his presence. Because of him, I lost what little lead I had on the guy who bought the fucking relic. I got that he was worried about me, which was kind of sweet, but I couldn't put my life before the lives of millions, maybe even billions. That was what I wasn't sure he understood. I turned to face him when he walked in behind Jinx.

"I told you, I don't need your protection."

Ansell stood there with a frown on his face. "Yes, you do. You're just too damned arrogant to think you don't. Oh, and I need a hundred and fifty dollars to pay for the tow truck you forced me to use. And I want my cell phone and car keys back too. That was really dirty and low down of you to leave me stranded like that, you asshole."

I smirked, because damn, I liked them feisty!

Chapter Four

Angel

Was that a hint of respect I saw in D'Angelo's eyes? The day before, it would've meant something to me, but not after the stunt he pulled at the auction house. The man who introduced himself as Christian chuckled at the silent standoff waging between his partner and me.

"Give me back my phone *and* keys," I amended, using a tone I thought was pretty badass. The smirk on D'Angelo's face said otherwise.

"Or what?" D'Angelo's words matched the bravado that oozed out of his pores. "You going to take me down?" He pulled my cell phone from his back pocket and held it up in front of him, wiggling it a little as if to spur me into action.

Before I could respond, a woman entered the room. Her features were dainty and petite, reminding me of the fairy painting my best friend had hanging in her living room. I almost expected to see pointy ears poking out of her silvery pixie haircut instead of ordinary shell-shaped ones. She was completely unaware of my presence or the tension in the room. Her excitement was palpable and practically vibrating off her.

"You guys won't believe the bargain I found online for some new duds for when you're out in the field. These could save your—" She screeched to a halt when she looked up and saw me. She tipped her head to the side and raked her gaze up and down my body. I had never seen eyes the color of hers before; they weren't blue or purple, but both. Violet was the color that came to mind. "Well, hello," she said with a friendly smile before she looked at Christian and D'Angelo. "I didn't know we were expecting a guest tonight."

"We didn't know either, Vixen," Christian said to her with a shrug.

I noticed D'Angelo's eyes never left the stack of clothing that Vixen held in her hand during the exchange. Christian noticed it too and his chuckle must've snapped D'Angelo back from where his mind had gone. D'Angelo looked sharply at me and said, "He's not staying, Vix."

"But why not?" she asked with a pout. "He's so adorable."

"It's doubtful that he's housebroken," D'Angelo said with a sneer. Any hint of respect I'd seen shimmering in his eyes was gone, and in its place, was a complex mixture of emotions that I couldn't name. Of course, he blinked and they were gone.

D'Angelo's words shouldn't have hurt me, but they did. I'd been treated like a mongrel my entire life; had, in fact, been called that to my face by both strangers and people who should've loved me unconditionally. I didn't know why I expected different treatment from D'Angelo. Did I think a little sizzle between us would make him see me in a different light than everyone else? I stopped being that naïve years ago.

D'Angelo approached me with my phone out in front of him. "Take this and leave. Don't come back here, Angel." I avoided touching his hand as I took the phone from him because I didn't want to risk having another reaction to him; twice was enough. I also tried not to stare longingly at his back when he turned and walked away from me. *Why did his opinion of me matter so much? Why couldn't I just flip my normal switch and ignore him?*

"I thought you liked to call him Ansell?" Christian asked in confusion.

"They can mean pretty much the same thing," said the woman with the rainbow-colored hair that escorted me into the den. She walked directly to me and extended her hand to me in greeting. "I'm Jinx."

"Hi," I said shyly, shaking her hand.

"I see that you've already met D'Angelo, so let me introduce you to the rest of the crew," she offered cheerfully, although I didn't know why she bothered.

"No introductions, Jinx," D'Angelo said angrily, still with his back to me. "He's not staying."

"What's your problem, man?" Christian asked. He shook his head in disbelief before he looked at me. "I'm Christian."

"I'm Vixen." The fae-like woman wiggled her fingers in greeting. She looked around the room in confusion. "I feel like I've missed something important while I was out. What's going on?"

"Nothing," D'Angelo said.

"Oh, it's something, all right," Jinx said, then snickered.

"Let me guess," I said to Vixen. "I bet those shirts look like ordinary, lightweight V-neck Henleys, but they're actually fortified with a kind of metal thread that makes it harder to penetrate with a knife and maybe even slows down a bullet. I bet those cargo pants have extra pockets in them to hold tools that a regular tradesman wouldn't need."

"How the hell did you know that?" Vixen asked me. "I didn't tell anyone about finding these clothes."

"Fuck!" D'Angelo swore, but he turned and faced me once again.

"I can take it from here, Angel. Thank you for what you're trying to do, but I don't need you." *Another phrase I was used to hearing.*

"What the hell is going on? D, it's not like you to be so damn rude," Vixen asked, looking and sounding surprised. It was obvious I brought out the best in him.

"I'll fill you in once *he's* gone," D'Angelo said firmly.

Christian, Vixen, and Jinx looked at me sympathetically and their kindness was nearly as painful as D'Angelo's coldness. It was a glimpse at something I have wanted my whole life but still remained out of reach. Acceptance.

D'Angelo's eyes widened a little in surprise when I walked toward him. Maybe he expected me to run from him like a timid little mouse or maybe he was surprised to see the determination in my eyes.

"I'll gladly get out of your way, but there's one little problem," I said, looking into hazel eyes that appraised me suspiciously.

"What's that?"

"You still have my car keys," I answered. "I very well can't leave without them and I sure as fuck can't afford another tow bill." I held my hand out in front of me, palm up. "I'm not going anywhere until you pay me back the money I used to hire a tow truck. Some of us are barely scraping by."

D'Angelo looked shocked and slightly embarrassed that he had forgotten he still had them. He reached into his pocket and pulled them out. I expected him to drop them in my hand and walk away, but instead, he set them in my hand. The tips of his fingers brushed against my palm and I felt a pulsating energy rush through me. I had to get out of there because I knew what was about to happen, although I couldn't figure out why.

"I don't have any cash on me right now," he said gruffly.

"I'll get it from petty cash," Vixen volunteered. "How much did the tow cost you?" She gasped when I told her the amount, then she shook her head disappointingly at D'Angelo. "I'll be right back, cutie." She practically skipped out of the room. I wished I could bottle up her vibrancy and save it for a rainy day or use it as a post-vision cure.

I'd been having visions ever since I'd hit puberty, but they always came to me in my dreams. I had never had a vision while awake, but then again, what happened to me in the parking lot at the auction house had been a new experience also. Something had changed—or rather, someone had changed me. I knew I needed to get the hell out of there as fast as I could. I couldn't bear the thought of them seeing me in such a vulnerable state after the way D'Angelo rejected me and my offer to help. Sometimes, you just had to know when to pull up the stakes and leave. It was definitely one of those times.

I curled my fingers tightly over my keys and shouldered past D'Angelo. "See you around." *Not if I could help it*, I thought to myself.

Vixen walked into the room just as I reached the doorway. She held my money out to me. I grabbed it quickly and tried to go around her.

"Let me walk you out," Jinx offered from behind me.

I waved her off. I didn't want anyone to see what I was about to experience. My vision started to darken around the edges and my blood roared in my ears. I felt like I was about to lose consciousness and I wanted to make it to my car before that happened.

"Angel, wait," I heard D'Angelo call out from behind me. I just kept walking because I needed to be as far from him as I could get. If he said anything more after that, I didn't hear it because my heartbeat became an angry bass drum thumping in my ear until it drowned out the sound of everything else around me.

"Please," I prayed, although I wasn't sure who I was asking help from. God? I was pretty sure he'd given up on me like everyone else had. I just needed to make it to my car so I could have my vision, recover, and go home.

I stumbled out the front door of the antique shop, looking like I was drunk. The blackness had invaded my vision until only a pinprick of light remained. I could just make out the shape of my vehicle and continued to stumble toward it, hoping to just make it there. It felt like I was looking through a magnifying glass, because distance was distorted. I couldn't tell if I was two feet from my car or twenty, but regardless, I wasn't going to make it.

I put my hands out in front of me, hoping to break my fall as I fell blindly to the ground. I felt the pain of the asphalt busting open my chin and forehead, along with the crunch of my nose breaking before the warmth of my blood gushed out beneath me. I swore I heard D'Angelo shouting my name. He sounded concerned, but I was certain it was the tiny part of me that still clung to the hope that maybe that flash of heat I saw in his eyes when he pressed against me was real and not a figment of my imagination.

"Ansell!" I had to be imagining it because he no longer called me that. Then there was nothing but darkness.

Next thing I knew, I was sitting in the front passenger seat of a luxury car, a Mercedes to be exact since I saw the logo on the glovebox in front of me. I looked to the left of me and saw it was the guy from the auction house—the one who outbid D'Angelo. There were many people I wouldn't mind riding shotgun with, but this creepy bastard wasn't one of them.

His bulging eyes were looking ahead, but it didn't seem like he was really there. You know, like when someone checks out mentally when they are right in front of you. He gave me that vibe. He swiped his tongue eagerly over his fat, fleshy fish lips before he grinned wickedly. A person didn't need to be psychic to know he was up to no good.

I decided to quit fixating on the creepiness of the auction guy and pay attention to where we were headed. He drove through urban streets until he took an exit for a freeway. He was heading to an area of the state that was as foreign to this poor boy as a third world country. He took the exit for Highland Heights, which was one of the wealthiest areas outside of Chicago. The homes were old money, huge properties behind stone walls and iron gates—the kind that were passed down through the generations like royals handed down their crowns.

I committed each turn and every street name to memory so I could retrace our steps. D'Angelo wasn't going to give up on his plan to retrieve the relic, which meant that I needed to make myself valuable to him. He might've scoffed at my ability to protect him, but I knew I was the only chance he had. Maybe I couldn't lift boulders off him or some He-Man macho shit, but knowledge was power.

The man pulled into a driveway and stopped at a set of fancy iron gates. I expected him to open the gates from inside the car, but he pulled up and stopped at a keypad instead. He rolled down the window and the wind caught the ends of his ridiculous toupee as he leaned out to enter the code. I leaned over as well to see the numbers he entered so I could share them with D'Angelo. 6-9-5-8-2.

Darkness creeped in on me again and I knew I was going to lose him. As frightened as I was to be with the man, I was even more afraid of not knowing what he was planning, but I was powerless to control my visions. I couldn't make them go away and I couldn't hang on to them longer when I wanted to know more. It wasn't long before my vision once again faded to black.

✦

"He's coming around," I heard a soft, feminine voice say. "Get back and stop crowding him. Let him breathe."

"When did you get so damn bossy, Vixen?" D'Angelo asked.

"Someone needs to hold you accountable," she said snarkily.

"You think you can take me on, Pixie Dust? I can fit you in my pocket," he fired back, but I noticed the affection in his voice.

"Fun size," she said. I didn't have to see her to know that she was waggling her brows at him.

"I can attest to that," Jinx said, not bothering to keep the lechery out of her voice.

"Damn, he's going to be hurting for a few days. He took one hell of a header onto the pavement," Christian added. "He might need to go to the E.R. to rule out a concussion."

Vixen scoffed. "Really, Christian? I'm sitting right here. I think I can handle these little scrapes, the broken nose, and a concussion."

"He's human," Christian countered. *Human? What the fuck were they?*

I probably should've let them know I was conscious the minute I came to instead of eavesdropping on their conversation, but I liked hearing them banter back and forth. I knew as soon as I opened my eyes, D'Angelo would throw me out on my ass. In fact, I was shocked that he had brought me inside. I could tell by the soft surface beneath my aching body that I had been placed on a bed or a sofa. Did that mean D'Angelo had carried me? I figured it was more likely that he dragged me inside by my hair while bitching the entire time.

"I can still handle whatever minor ailments he might have," Vixen said. "His wrist looks a little swollen too from where it was pinned between his body and the concrete. It's either sprained or broken. Either way, I'll fix him right up."

"Honey, how will you explain it to him?" Jinx asked. "We can't risk him telling people about us."

"He has psychic visions, Jinx, one that included seeing an ancient artifact come to life and suck the soul out of numb nuts over there. I think he's aware that people exist with certain *skills* in this world."

"I'm not sure he has anyone to tell," D'Angelo said. "He gives the impression that he's kind of a loner." *Wow. I thought his opinion of me couldn't get any worse than it already was. I was so wrong.*

"He sure is cute," Vixen said.

"We're not keeping him," the rest of the group said at once.

"He's a human being with a free mind and free will," Jinx told her girlfriend, or at least I thought they were a couple. "We don't just get to decide that he stays." My heart actually ached with the possibility that anyone could want me enough to keep me.

"He needs us," Vixen said softly, "and I'm pretty sure we need him too." I felt a cool hand push my bangs off my face and it was all I could do to not lean into her touch, which might've tipped her off that I was awake and listening.

"Let's get out of here and let him rest," Christian said. "We'll check back on him later and maybe feed the guy before we send him home. He looks like he could stand to eat a few BLTs." *Again with my weight.*

The room was quiet and I thought that I was all alone. I was exhausted from the vision I'd had and my body ached from head to toe as if I'd been hit by a semi-truck. I felt comfortable and safe, two things that had eluded me for a very long time, and I wasn't eager to part with them. A soft sigh escaped my swollen lips as I nestled further into the blankets.

"I knew you were awake, Ansell." The warm, dark voice in my ear made me shiver.

I slowly opened my eyes and turned my head in the direction of his voice. Two things stood out in stark clarity to me: I saw genuine concern for me in his uniquely colored eyes and he had gone back to using my pet name.

"This is all your fault," I said through lips that felt swollen and cracked. I was sure that I must've looked terrible.

D'Angelo looked shocked at the way I responded to his statement. "My fault?"

"Yes, you!" Fuck! My face hurt when I tried to talk, but I had shit I needed to tell him before the others returned. "You've touched me a total of three times and each time you've triggered a vision. The visions, and the side effects afterward, keep getting stronger the more you touch me. Before you, I only had the visions in my dreams! I don't know why it's happening, but I know it's true. You're screwing up something inside me."

D'Angelo shook his head like he couldn't believe it. *Couldn't or didn't want to?* "I'll take you home after you've had a chance to recover a bit."

I didn't want to leave him and the others yet, so I said the one thing that guaranteed they'd keep me, if only for a little while. "I know where the man and the artifact are," I told him.

Chapter Five

D'Angelo

"You're a sneaky one, I see. First, you convince Jinx to bring you to our office, which she knows is off-limits. Then you somehow injure yourself by tripping on nothing. But if that's not enough, you eavesdropped on our conversation," I said, letting him know that I was onto his ass. "And now you claim to know the exact information we're looking for. How convenient."

Ansell rolled over onto his side so he could get a better look at me. "First off, I didn't do anything sneaky to get Jinx to let me into your 'secret office,'" he said, complete with air quotes. "I just told her you owed me money. She took one look at the tow truck releasing my car and must have known I was telling the truth. She told me to follow her. I had no idea where she was taking me. Secondly, I didn't just trip over nothing. Something is happening to me and I can't explain it. I had a vision and that's why I fell out. And as far as it being convenient… well, that's something that should please you. I have information you need. Now, are you going to continue to be an asshole and act like you don't need me, or are you going to accept my help?"

Okay, I had to admit, he was feistier than I thought. Back at the restaurant, I never would have believed he could speak to me like he was doing now. Either he really believed he could help me or… shit… did he feel closer to me? I couldn't allow him to get close. He wasn't prepared for what my world offered. I had to keep him at bay, regardless of how much I wanted to wrap him up in my arms and kiss those luscious lips of his. It was getting harder and harder to resist my attraction to him, but I had to. I had to in order to keep him safe. Time to embrace the asshole he thought I was.

"Another vision, eh? Just what are you going to claim you saw this time? Me crying in a corner?"

He snorted and then winced as he touched his aching temple. "Don't be a dick."

"Hey, I wasn't the one eavesdropping," I stated, cocking an eyebrow.

Ansell smirked and looked off to the side. Yeah, I knew his ass was guilty of something. He returned his gaze back to me and there was something in his eyes that spoke to me, or at least they were trying to, but I couldn't quite figure it out. "Okay, so you've got me there."

"What all did you hear?" I crossed my arms over my chest as I waited for his reply. I knew he'd had to have gotten an earful. Fucking Vixen was so eager to flex her witchy healing skills.

I saw the pain Ansell felt when he tried to shift on the sofa and he moaned. I reached out quickly to help him get more comfortable. He looked up at me with those gorgeous eyes and I felt something deep inside of me tingle. I knew he was sassy and… god, he was beautiful. Totally my type, but I felt something else drawing me to him other than my desire to feel what his insides felt like, and not in a violent way. The kind I was so familiar with when I'd punch a hole in some monster's chest. No, the way I wanted to feel Ansell's insides was by sliding my cock inside his tight hole and making him cry my name out in the heat of bliss-filled passion.

What the hell? Get your shit together, D. I couldn't have those kinds of thoughts right then, and especially not with Ansell. "Feel better?" I asked as I fluffed the pillow behind him.

He nodded. "Thank you."

I gave him a curt nod, then returned to my chair. "Okay, back to my question. How much did you hear?"

He frowned. "You're all business."

"Ansell…"

"I heard enough to know that Vixen thinks she can heal me," he said. "What is that all about?"

I sighed heavily. See, this was why we couldn't let outsiders inside the inner sanctum. "That's all you need to know."

"No, it's not," Ansell said, then he tried to sit up, but cried out in pain.

"You better take it easy," Christian said from the doorway. I knew he was standing on the other side of the door. Not only could I hear his heart beating, but I could smell his cologne a mile away. Having heightened senses had its moments, like now… or when I was out in the field. Not so much in other environments.

"I was wondering how long you were going to eavesdrop," I remarked. I guessed everyone was just super curious today.

"I wanted to see just how you were going to treat our guest. You can be uncouth at times," Christian joked as he made his way into the room. He took the seat beside mine.

"I'm not going to beat him up and toss him out, if that's what you're thinking," I snapped.

"I'm thinking we need to hear him out," Christian shot back, then turned his attention to Ansell. "Why don't you tell us about your vision."

Just then, Vixen and Jinx entered, both were carrying some

herbs with them that I knew Vixen was going to use to work a spell in order to heal Ansell.

"Yeah, tell us about this vision," Jinx said.

Angel looked at them, then back at me as if he was unsure if he should. I shrugged and he rolled his eyes, then looked at the others. "From what I overheard earlier, it sounds like you all believed me when I said that I have visions."

"We do," Christian said. "We have experience with things other people would write off as... unbelievable. So, please, tell us."

"Okay, I had one of D'Angelo dying," he said.

"Hey, you don't know that. You didn't actually see me die in your vision," I stated.

He turned to me, then winced again as he swayed. "Oh god, that hurts," he moaned.

"Can I heal him now, please?" Vixen snapped.

"Fine," I said, giving in. "But he needs to not remember that you healed him."

"I think we're beyond the whole erasing his memory thing. If he's having visions of you that are coming true, or are about to, then he's already seen shit he can't explain," Christian said.

I could tell by the look on Ansell's face that he had more questions, because he looked confused as hell. As much as I wanted to prove my point that we... that *I* didn't need Ansell's help, I could tell they weren't about to let it go. So, I just sat back and let Vixen do her thing.

"Angel, try to remain calm. Like you, Vixen here has some special abilities. She's going to heal you of your injuries," Christian explained in his smooth-as-silk voice. He was the charmer between the two of us. The petals of the rose to my thorny stem. Not only could he sugarcoat some shit for you, but he'd add honey, too. Not me... I was a direct, to-the-point kind of guy, and according to Jinx... maybe a little tactless. But, whatever.

"Al—all right," Ansell said. He was still very confused and

looking almost like a deer caught in the headlights.

"I do have some pretty awesome skills, if I may say so myself," Vixen said as she began to mix up a potion.

"What are you doing?" Ansell asked.

"I'm a witch," Vixen stated.

"You're a human that happens to be linked to a witch's amulet. We still don't know how dangerous that thing is, or how much power you should be drawing from it," I said.

"I'll be fine, stop worrying," Vixen shot back.

But I did worry. Three months ago, we were fighting a very powerful witch who'd killed her sister in order to syphon her powers and combine them with her own. We were attacked by the witch while trying to trap her. Christian had managed to kill the witch, and all that was left was her amulet. Before either Christian or I could stop Vixen, she had picked it up. That was when the amulet chose her and bonded itself to her soul.

She could draw power from it, make potions and cast spells, but we didn't know nearly enough about it to keep testing its capabilities. I don't know, maybe I was the paranoid one, because Christian seemed perfectly at ease with her stretching her magical legs, so to speak. He felt that if she could master it, she could be helpful to our missions. I couldn't deny that she was even more helpful since acquiring it. But still, it had belonged to an evil witch. Who was to say that amulet didn't make her that way? Let's just say, I was remaining cautious.

We all watched as Vixen mixed the potion and then chanted something, which made the potion stir and smoke. With a wicked smile, she extended the cup to Ansell. "Okay, drink up."

He backed away from the smoldering brew, like any person with an ounce of good sense would do. "Ummm, I don't think so."

"Trust me, it will heal you," Vixen said.

Ansell looked at her, the cup, and then to me, as if he had wanted my confirmation. *Did he trust me that much? I really hadn't given him any reason to.* I nodded, because it seemed like he was waiting for me to chime in and give him the thumbs-up.

"O—okay," he said, then he reached out tentatively, taking the cup from her hands. "Will this burn? Is it poison?"

She shook her head. "It won't burn. And I put vanilla extract in it for flavor. Go on, drink up. You want us to trust you, so you have to start trusting us."

That seemed to put a spark in him and he tipped the glass cup to his lips. Oooh, those lips—Damn it… I had to get my mind back on track! I watched him sip the drink like he was afraid it was going to burn his mouth. I could tell by his perked-up eyebrows and the delightful "umm" sound he made that he was surprised by the taste.

"Are you feeling better?" Vixen asked.

Ansell nodded. "Wow, this stuff works fast!"

"Yeah, I've perfected my ingredients. Dealing with these guys, I needed to come up with something to heal all of the boo-boos Jinx and I got," Vixen said.

I huffed. "Can we not pour out all of our damn secrets to a total stranger?" I complained. I mean, why in the fuck was everyone so lax around Ansell?

"I think you're a bit too uptight, to be honest, D," Christian said. "As far as I'm concerned, Angel is a client of ours. We have to get to the bottom of why he's having visions of your death."

"And before you try to say that my visions aren't anything you should worry about, I did predict everything up till this point. Even the outfit you're going to be wearing," Ansell pointed out. "I really wish you'd take me seriously, D'Angelo."

I sat back in my chair, running my finger over my eyebrow. "Listen, it's not that I don't take you seriously—"

"Then what the hell is it?" he asked, his pretty brown eyes staring at me with all of the concern he must have been feeling.

"It's just that I'm no stranger to danger, Ansell."

"So, we're back to using Ansell, I see," he said, irritated.

I smirked. "Seems like you like it. Besides, I like the way Ansell sounds flowing off my tongue."

"By the way you've been staring at him, I'm sure his name isn't the only thing you want of Angel's... oh sorry, Ansell's, on your tongue," Jinx teased.

Well, she wasn't lying. But still, I had to play it cool, so I rolled my eyes at her. "Anyway, getting back to what I was saying, taking on life-threatening missions is just what we do."

"What do you mean by that? What do you do?" Ansell asked as he looked at each of us, waiting to see who was going to answer him first.

"We save people from things other people don't believe exist."

Ansell frowned. "Like what?"

Christian motioned to the empty cup Ansell held in his hand. "You saw for yourself that magic exists. Your injury is now completely healed. Then there's the matter of your visions where you see the relic killing D'Angelo. We deal with the threats that hide in the shadows and prey on the innocent."

"L—like vampires, witches, and boogeymen?" Ansell asked.

Christian nodded. "Exactly."

I snorted. "He's not going to believe that."

"Don't you tell me what *I'm* willing to believe," Ansell snapped. "All my life, I've felt like I was different. I've always been able to see visions and have been too afraid to say anything about it because people treat me differently once they know what I can do. They treat me like some sort of freak. I've faced discrimination on all fronts from my nationality to my ability, so I know what it's like to not fit the norm. Don't just cast me aside like I couldn't possibly understand."

I felt everyone's eyes on me, especially since Ansell had just chewed me out... and if I was being honest, I'd had it coming. I was so pissed that he had been in my way, I hadn't thought about how I'd been treating him. Sure, I wanted to keep him at bay, but I had been cruel, like leaving him stranded. In retrospect… that had been a dick move.

"Okay, you're right. I shouldn't have said that. You think you can take the truth about who we are and what we do, fine. I'll tell you why I don't need your help. I've faced off with vampires, werewolves, trolls, goblins, witches, demons, you name it, and I'm still here kicking ass and taking names. You claim you want to protect me, but all you have done is hinder what it is that I have to do. Because of you, I missed my opportunity to get the relic from that guy." I stood up, towering over him while he looked at me. "Did it ever occur to you that because you interfered, you're the one who's putting me in danger?"

He looked up at me, mouth slightly open, and his bottom lip trembling. "I… I don't want you to get hurt. I… I just know what I saw. My visions always came true in the past because I never did anything to stop them. Even when I tried and told people, they didn't do anything and horrible stuff happened. This time, I wasn't just going to sit back."

I couldn't let those soft brown eyes throw me off my game. Not again. I had to be honest with him, even if it hurt. "Don't think I don't get it. I do. But, it's you who doesn't understand. My life…" I shook my head. "I can't put it above protecting the world. I can't be too afraid to do what needs to be done. I can't let your fear stop me. Now, I'm going to this guy's mansion, vision or no vision, and I'm getting that fucking relic. You are going to stay out of my way."

I hoped that put things into perspective for him.

"Before we get off track completely, I'd like to know what this latest vision was, and you should want to know this information, too, D," Christian stated.

"Fine. Tell us, Ansell, what did you see?" I asked, looking down at him.

He swallowed what looked like impending tears, then began to tell us about the vision he had before he fell out. Apparently, he had more details to offer, like the city the mansion was in and the password I'd need to get past the security gate… if his vision was that true or accurate. I wasn't willing to disregard it. I would use that code, and if it worked… well, let's just say, I'd be a lot more cautious.

"That's remarkable detail," Christian said, then he leaned back in his chair. "This concerns me, D. I don't think you should go alone. I think you should take Angel with you."

I turned to him. "Are you shitting me?" I'd just spent all of this time telling Ansell I didn't need him at my side, and here was my partner betraying me.

He shook his head. "I'm serious, and you know it."

"How is his coming along with me going to be helpful? The last vision he had made him pass out and damn near kill himself," I stated.

"I don't know why I had that vision while I was awake. It's been happening more and more since…" Ansell trailed off and looked off to the side again.

"Since what?" I asked.

"Since I've been in contact with you," he said.

I scoffed. "You've always been in contact with me."

"But you've never touched before, I bet," Vixen said. "I noticed something flash between you two the last time we ate at Martinelli's. It was like a spark in the air, like a connection was made. That's probably why he just started having visions of you."

"Hmmm, that does make sense. Maybe the more time you spend together, the stronger that link grows," Christian speculated, then he turned to Vixen. "V, please look into that a bit more, will you? You know how I don't like not knowing what I need to know."

"Sure, I'd like to see what it all means, too." Vixen looked at Ansell. "I've never met anyone who can see the future."

"Like I was saying, you should stick together. If he can see what's coming, you may be able to avoid danger," Christian said. I knew he was just trying to look out for me, but I wasn't too keen on working with someone completely new to the world I lived in.

"Really, with me having to carry him on my back like a baby because he can't stay conscious long enough to tell me what he's seen?" I fussed.

"Fuck you!" Ansell snapped. "You may think you can handle this all on your own, but I know you need me. Why else would I be having the visions? I'm going with you whether you like it or not."

"Oooh, I like him," Jinx said.

"Is that why you let him into our secret office?" I asked.

"Yep. He told me he had a vision of you dying and wanted to protect you. Plus, he said you owed him a hundred fifty dollars for towing fees." Jinx shrugged. "I don't know. I just got a great vibe off of him. You know I have amazing intuition."

"Listen, I'm all for Angel joining you this time. D'Angelo, just suck it up like a big boy. You're working with a partner and that's that," Christian said.

I frowned. "You're not the boss of me, Christian."

"No, but I'm your best friend, and I don't want to see your pride get you killed, you stubborn ass," he shot back.

"Me either," Vixen and Jinx said together.

I looked at Ansell and his petite frame and tried to imagine what it would be like for me to go on this mission with such a lightweight. All hunters were expertly trained and had the muscle mass to get the job done, on top of being supernaturally strong. Jinx and Vixen had been training with us, so even though they were pixie petite, they both packed a punch. Vixen even had the magic elements on her side. Ansell… well, he almost spilled my meal in my lap and had fumbled with it so bad, I'd thought he was going to burst into tears. I didn't see him as being reliable backup, was all I was saying.

He shrugged. "You already know how I feel."

"Fine. I don't like it, but it seems that you won't let it go. So, you're coming with me. Don't get in my way, and if you pass out, I'm leaving you on the ground and completing my mission. Do you understand?" I asked him.

"I get that you're this badass monster killer, but you don't have to be so mean to me," Ansell said.

I started to toss him another one of my comebacks, but when I saw that I'd hurt his feelings, I decided not to. "I'm not trying to be mean, I'm just not someone who's—"

"Tactful," Jinx supplied.

Again, I rolled my eyes. "I'm just all about business, like you said. I get the job done at any cost because I know what's on the line. I can't risk you holding me back, because that relic is dangerous in the wrong hands. It's not a mistake that that guy won it today. I don't think I was ever going to be able to outbid him. Maybe he knows more about that relic than we do, and having that knowledge makes me uncomfortable. So, as long as you know that about me, then we can do this."

Ansell placed the cup on the coffee table and stood up. "I won't get in your way."

I nodded. "Good."

"Okay, if you're going to do this, at least let me make something for you just in case you have another vision. We don't want you passing out. That's bad news for both you and D'Angelo. It would leave you vulnerable," Vixen said.

"What are you going to make?" Ansell asked.

"I'm going to make an anti-unconscious spell and put it in something you can wear that will keep you from passing out," she explained.

"Great idea," Ansell beamed.

"Well, it looks like everyone has things they need to be doing," I said. "I'm going to get my tools together." I walked out of the room to get dressed in the outfit Jinx had purchased that eerily resembled the clothes Ansell said I'd be wearing. A part of me almost decided against wearing it, but shit… it was perfect and had plenty of pockets to place things I needed. So, it was what it was. I didn't know what else to expect tonight. When I went on missions with a partner or partners, it was always with Christian and/or the girls. Never with a novice, and definitely never with a novice that I was extremely attracted to. I didn't want Ansell hurt, but he wasn't going to let it go. So, I was going to try my best to keep him safe. Damn, what the hell was I getting myself into?

Chapter Six

Angel

I tried hard not to take D'Angelo's attitude toward me personally. He seemed to be genuinely concerned for my safety, which contrasted with his surly, abrupt attitude toward me up to that point. I tried even harder not to make too much of the fact that I was riding shotgun with him on a mission. I half expected him to toss me in the trunk instead of allowing me to sit beside him on the plush leather passenger seat. The biggest challenge of the night was trying to keep my physical reactions to his nearness under control. The smell of his body wash or aftershave in such a tight space was making me light-headed and my dick…

"What's wrong with you?" D'Angelo asked abrasively.

"What do you mean?" I asked in confusion. "What did I do now?"

"You're moaning over there," D'Angelo replied, almost in disgust. "You're still hurt, aren't you? I knew I should've left you at my home for Vixen to fuss over, Ansell. It's not too late, you know. I can drop you off at your home and…"

"No," I said vehemently, cutting him off. He needed me, regardless of what he thought about my abilities. Besides, the leaking roof I lived under could never be called a home. "I'm not in any pain."

"Then why are you moaning?" he demanded. I felt my face flushing hotly in the darkness of his Jeep. "Ohhh," D'Angelo said smugly.

I could tell by his voice that he was remembering the way my body reacted to him earlier that evening when he'd pressed me up against the side of his Jeep. I hoped that my embarrassment would deflate my semi-erection, but I had no such luck. My body—namely Cockzilla—liked the fact that he was aware of how much I wanted him.

"Thank you for highlighting another reason why I shouldn't have brought you along with me," he said in a growl. "We need clear minds on this mission, Ansell. Too much is at risk."

"Why do you keep calling me that?" I asked. Anger was the only emotion strong enough to defuse the fire the man stoked inside me, so I clung to it like a life raft.

"It means God's protection," D'Angelo said calmly. "To me, that's what angels represent. They're meant to watch over us and protect us." His words shocked me into silence, but only for a few seconds.

"It's good that you admit you need me," I purred. *Where the hell had that throaty voice come from?* Oh my god, it sounded like I was flirting with him. I didn't flirt with guys. I didn't know how. I…

"Let's not get carried away," D'Angelo said firmly, popping the little balloon of happiness inside me. "I only need you to get me past the gate and into the house."

"I already gave you the code," I said defensively.

"I'm just making sure you weren't dicking me around out of fear for my safety. I'll be perfectly fine now that I know what the relic is capable of doing to me," D'Angelo replied confidently.

"I know one of the things it's capable of doing," I rebutted.

"What's the likelihood that some demon relic can only perform one trick?" I looked over at D'Angelo then to judge his reaction. The lights from his dashboard illuminated him enough that I could see a tiny bit of his confidence falter, but it was short lived.

"You're only going to get in the way and get me killed," D'Angelo said, but his voice was devoid of the menace I expected. At that point, I knew we'd have to agree to disagree because neither of us was willing to budge on our stances. "Which exit do I take again?" he asked, reminding me of why I was with him.

"Highland Heights," I told him.

"That's coming up next," D'Angelo said sharply. "Then it's show time."

"You sound excited about the prospect," I said, watching him for a reaction.

"It's what I do, and I'm very good at it," he said smugly. D'Angelo glanced at me quickly and smiled crookedly. "I happen to excel in *everything* I do."

"Not cool," I told him as my dick started to harden even more at his taunting. I didn't need him to tell me how good he was in bed. It was something you could sense about a person, although I was certain that some people disguised their sexual prowess, not that I had firsthand experience or anything. "You're supposed to keep me focused on our mission and not your performance in bed."

"*My* mission, Ansell," D'Angelo corrected. "Besides, I get the idea that you don't need any encouragement from me when it comes to fantasizing about my sexual abilities. Seems to me, you have that down to an art already."

Anger was my friend and it wrapped my soul like a warm coat on a cold winter's day. It was better to focus on that than the humiliation that coursed through my body. It took me years to get over being ashamed of my attraction to men, but right then, I was ashamed of my attraction to just one of them. I faced forward and looked out the windshield, and my only interaction for the rest of the drive was to guide him through the turns once we left the highway.

"Do I use the code and possibly trip an alert that tips the bastard off or do I climb the fence and sneak in from behind?" D'Angelo asked as he slowly drove past the mansion. I could tell he was reasoning things out loud rather than asking my opinion. He was clear about his opinion on my inability to assist him beyond gaining access to the property. "Driveway is too well lit," D'Angelo commented further. "I'm going to need an alternate access point and I'd bet Christian's left nut that a place like this has a service driveway."

"I have a bad feeling about this," I said, pushing my hurt and disappointment aside to focus on keeping D'Angelo alive.

"Are you having another vision?" D'Angelo almost sounded hopeful.

"No, it's just that something feels off about the situation to me," I replied.

"I'm not going to pretend to have all the answers, Ansell. I just know I can't let fear of the unknown hold me back because too much is at stake," D'Angelo said. "Aha!" he exclaimed. "I knew it." D'Angelo turned onto a gravel driveway that was surrounded by dense woods on both sides. He kept driving until the rear of the mansion came into view. He put his Jeep in park and stared out the window quietly for several long moments. I kept my eyes on his face and witnessed him swallow hard. "You saw me climb *this* structure? Are you sure?"

"Oh my god! That's what you were snorting about outside the auction house. You're afraid of heights." It was quite nice to know that the guy felt human emotions like fear.

"I'm not afraid," D'Angelo replied dryly. "I just believe in working smarter, not harder." He tapped his head and said, "Sometimes your most important weapon is your brain. If the code from your vision opens the service gate then I'd bet a day's wages that it also opens a service door at the rear or side of the house. It would be *smarter* for me to attempt that than climb up the side of a building that high."

My lips quirked up in a half smile. He wasn't fooling me one damn bit.

"Okay, I'm going to leave my ride parked right here under the cover of the trees and make the rest of the trip on foot."

"D'Angelo…"

"Save it, Ansell," he snarled. Then he blew out a frustrated breath as if he regretted his harsh tone or was digging deep for patience. I figured it was the latter until he reached over and gently touched his fingers to the side of my face that had sported nasty cuts and scrapes until I took the healing potion. "I can tell that you genuinely care about my safety and I honestly appreciate your concern. If you really want to help me, then you need to stay here where I know you'll be safe. I'm at a greater risk of getting hurt if I have to split my focus between watching your back and retrieving the relic. I could force you to stay here with a restraining spell, but I don't want to do that. I want you to trust that I know what I'm doing, and I want to trust that you'll listen when I say it's best for me if you remain behind."

I wanted to believe that the pleading I saw in his eyes and the gentleness in his touch was genuine and not a ploy to get me to listen to him, but I knew better. I knew as soon as he got his way, he'd revert to the same guy I'd met earlier that night, but that didn't stop me from giving in to him. There was truth in what he said because I had zero experience in the field of… anything.

"Okay, D'Angelo. You win," I said and waited for the sneer to return to his face. Instead, he rewarded me with a smile, I mean a real smile that showed his perfect, white teeth. Then he brushed his thumb over my bottom lip, causing my heart to pound harder in my chest. "You like that, don't you?" He leaned closer as if he were going to kiss me. Instead, he stopped before his lips touched mine. "I can hear your heartbeat and smell your desire for me."

My fingers twitched from the need to reach out and touch him, too. What if it was my last… *No! I wouldn't go there.* Instead of leaning into him, I pulled away. "You better get going," I told him. "Remember to…" The rest of my words were cut off when he pressed his lips to mine for a brief kiss. He looked as surprised as I was that he had kissed me.

"This is why you have to stay far away from me," D'Angelo said gruffly. *Did he mean permanently or just on that mission?*

"Be careful," I told him when he reached into the back seat and pulled out the ancient, leather-bound case that Vixen had chanted a spell over before we left.

"I'll be back before you can get bored," he said cockily before he left the car.

I watched him stealthily approach the service gate and debated on praying for the code not to work. I realized it was a futile thing to pray for since he'd just use the front gate or scale the iron fence. I didn't know a lot about D'Angelo, but I was certain he wouldn't be dissuaded from his mission that night, or any other. D'Angelo gave me a thumbs-up when the access code worked. My pulse thundered in my throat as I watched him walk through the open gates and disappear out of sight.

"He'll be okay. He'll be okay. He'll be… oh fuck." The nausea I'd experienced earlier rolled over me. Vixen had given me an amethyst amulet on a leather cord to wear around my neck to protect me from losing consciousness like I had earlier. I gripped it hard and closed my eyes until the sensation faded. I expected a vision to immediately follow but it never came, so I chalked it up to a case of nerves. I sat staring at the mansion for the longest time with my heart in my throat, looking for any sign that D'Angelo was okay.

I looked at the display on my phone and realized that fifteen minutes had lapsed. I had no idea how long it took to scale the side of a mansion, enter through a second-story library window, and retrieve the evil relic, but something felt off to me again. I didn't need a vision to know that D'Angelo was in trouble. I just inexplicably felt it in my soul.

I got out of the Jeep and started running as fast as I could in the direction that I thought he took. Man, I'd never scaled an indoor rock climbing wall for sport, let alone the side of a building, so I hoped D'Angelo's theory played out. I found a rear door with an exterior keypad and held my breath as I entered the code from my vision. Sure enough, the red light turned green and I pulled open the door. The feeling that D'Angelo was in danger grew stronger once I entered the home. I ignored the fear and explored my way through the first floor until I found a wide, curving staircase that led to the second story.

I was midway up the steps when I heard wicked laughter echoing and bouncing off the marble steps and landing above me. The laughter was followed by a chanting in a language I didn't recognize. Fear slid down my spine like someone trailed a cold finger down my back. I was spurred to run faster when the second story lit up with an eerie blue light and I heard D'Angelo groan in pain.

I ran as fast as I could toward the light, which was coming from beneath the bottom of a set of ornate double doors. I burst into the library and found D'Angelo completely at the mercy of the cross just like in my vision, except the angle was different in real time. In my vision, I stood behind the cross and saw it suck D'Angelo's soul. In reality, I entered from the side and saw that the buyer from the auction held the relic in his hand and was responsible for the eerie chanting that brought it to life.

D'Angelo was paralyzed and unable to move, yet I could tell he was fighting the demonic powers with his force of will. His body shook violently and the anguished groans coming through his gritted teeth tore my heart in two. D'Angelo's face morphed into an expression of pure agony as the cross battled him for his soul. *He doesn't have much time left.* As soon as the thought crossed my mind, I saw D'Angelo's soul start to break loose from his body.

In my vision, D'Angelo's soul left his body in the form of a wispy, ghost-like replica of his body. It floated toward the cross, which seemed to take delight in ripping his essence out one inch at a time rather than all at once. I looked around the room frantically for something to help save him, but nothing jumped out at me. By the time I looked back at D'Angelo, the head and shoulders of his soul had been pulled free from his body. *Wow, it had seemed slower in my vision.*

The buyer paused his chanting and looked at the relic with a startled expression on his face. The light shimmered for a few seconds, then retracted inside the cross. I didn't stop to think of the consequences because there wasn't time. I just tackled the buyer as hard as I could and knocked him to the ground. I watched in stunned disbelief as D'Angelo's soul returned to his body as I crawled over to where he had collapsed in agony. He stared up at me in shock for a few seconds before he said, "I told you to wait in the car." His voice was thick and a little slow like I'd expect it to be first thing in the morning.

"I couldn't stay behind because I knew something was wrong," I told him. "I couldn't just sit there and do nothing while you were in danger." D'Angelo said nothing; he lay beneath me and blinked in shock over the turn of events, or perhaps a brain injury from his head hitting the marble floor. "Okay, looks like this mission is all on me." I rose to my feet and saw that the cross was gone.

"Fuck!"

"Not now, Ansell," D'Angelo slurred.

"It's gone, D'Angelo, and so is the buyer."

D'Angelo winced in pain as he slowly rose to his feet. He looked weak and I worried that he might lose consciousness.

"Loop your arm around my neck and let's get going. We need to get back to the antique store and figure out what to do next."

"I don't need help," D'Angelo said, swaying on his feet. "I heal fast."

"Of course, you don't need my help," I lied. "It's for me."

"You're not fooling me," D'Angelo said, but he looped his arm around my neck and leaned into me anyway. "I have something better for you to do with those lips than smart off to me." He sounded more drunk than hurt.

"Really?" I asked. "I wasn't aware that you gave my lips any thought."

"Too much," D'Angelo confessed.

I wanted to pump him for information while his guard was down, but that felt wrong. Instead, I focused on putting one foot in front of the other and making sure D'Angelo stayed conscious so I could get him to the Jeep without calling for backup. He looked lean, but he weighed a fuck ton. It felt like it took an hour to get him to his Jeep.

"Keys?" I asked when I opened the passenger door for him.

"Front right pocket," he said, then snickered a bit because there were at least five pockets on the right front side of his pants. I found the keys, then buckled his seatbelt before I got behind the wheel. "Do you really want to know why I call you Ansell?" His voice got even heavier and I knew he was about to fade away at any minute.

It was wrong to take advantage of him, but I couldn't help myself. "Yes."

"Your name is too similar to mine and I wanted to be clear it was your name I was calling when I came. Only narcissists shout their own name while jerking off."

I turned my head quickly to look at him. Surely, I had heard him wrong. I was going to ask him to repeat himself, but his head dropped forward slowly until his chin touched his chest. I wasn't sure if I should drive him to the nearest hospital or home to Vixen. I checked his pulse at his wrist and it felt steady, so I decided Vixen would be his best option.

I smiled when I turned the ignition to start the engine and said, "You're going to be horrified if you remember what you just confessed."

Chapter Seven

D'Angelo

I started to slowly come to and realized I was in a vehicle. My vehicle, and on the wrong side of it… the passenger side. Who the fuck was driving? Oh yeah, that was right, it was Ansell. Damn, what the fuck had happened? My head throbbed, which was unusual, because I didn't get sick. My vision was a bit blurry and my stomach was doing flip-flops, summersaults, and triple lay-ups.

"Pull over," I demanded as I felt a violent wave of nausea wash over me.

The Jeep slowed as it eased to the side of the road and even before the wheels stopped, I was flinging the door open. My stomach lurched and I vomited my last meal all over the graveled pavement below. I could feel Ansell rubbing my back as he tried to comfort me in one of my least sexiest moments. I was tough as hell, but here I was dizzy, sick, and weak from whatever the fuck that cross did to me.

I spit the last of the bile on the ground and sat back in the seat, letting the cool, nighttime air refresh me. I just sat there with my eyes closed, waiting for the nausea to pass. Another wave hit me and I leaned over again, letting it all out. Ansell patted my back, which in some strange way did make me feel better. Once more, I sat back and tried to let the horrible fucking sensation run its course.

"Are you better now?" Ansell asked in his soft, sweet voice.

I shook my head. "Not yet."

To his credit, he didn't say anything else. Just let me sit in silence until I felt better. My headache wasn't as intense, but at least the nausea went on about its business and left me the hell alone. I reached into my glove compartment and pulled out a tiny bottle of mouthwash and a napkin. I wiped my face, sloshed some mouthwash around, spit it out, and then wiped my face again. That would have to do. I closed the Jeep door and motioned for him to continue on. Ansell started the engine and we were off.

"What happened back there?" he asked.

As much as I hated eating a plate of crow, I was man enough to own up to my own mistakes. "You were right, I was wrong. That's what happened."

I cut my gaze to him to see if he was going to smile or gloat, but his expression was still one of concern. "The relic was trying to steal your soul. I was so afraid that my vision was coming true. I… I didn't know what to do, so I just tackled that guy when he paused his chanting. I'm so sorry he got away."

Jesus. "Ansell, you took a big chance even putting yourself in the same room with us. I would have hated for my own arrogance to have gotten you killed."

He tossed me a glance. "What do you mean by that?"

"We had no way of knowing if putting yourself in proximity of that cross would trap you in its vortex. You took a big risk to save me. Thank you. But please, don't do that again."

"I didn't think about that. I just—"

"I know. You acted. Sometimes, all you have is a rash thought when in the field. You hope it works out like it did tonight, sometimes it does and there are times when it doesn't. At least we now know that the relic only takes the souls that are nearby when it's activated by the spell. That's something we'll have to keep in mind. I hate that the son of a bitch got away," I said, wishing I hadn't been on my way out of my mortal coil of existence at the time. I could have ended this had I paid more attention to Ansell's visions.

"I'm just glad I was there," Ansell said.

I nodded. "You saved my life, so it turns out that I did need you." I rubbed my temples, which were still throbbing. "God, this fucking headache."

"We should be back at your place soon so Vixen can fix you up," Ansell said.

"It's not as bad as it was when I first woke up. This was brought on by supernatural forces, so I guess I have to deal with it as such," I said. I hated feeling sick.

"Was that guy there when you walked into the room?" Ansell asked.

I shook my head. "I didn't see or even sense anyone when I first entered; everything was going smoothly. I reached for the cross, which was just sitting out there on display in the library, like you said it would be. That's when I became paralyzed. The pain that coursed through me was more agonizing than anything I'd ever felt in my life. I felt it trying to steal my soul. When I fell to the floor, that's when he appeared to step out of the shadows, and then he picked up the cross and continued to chant the spell."

"He used magic to hide himself?" Ansell asked.

"Yeah, a pretty powerful cloaking spell, because even with my heightened senses, I didn't know he was there. I remember thinking, just before I reached for the damn relic, that this was a little too easy. Had a normal human being…" I stopped talking right then, not sure if I wanted to tell Ansell everything about myself.

"What? Wait, you have heightened senses? And what do you

mean by 'a normal human being'?" Ansell pressed.

"Let's just say, had you been caught by the relic, you wouldn't have been able to fight it as long as I did," I clarified.

"Okay, but what did you mean by a normal human and heightened senses? Aren't you human?" he asked, not letting my slip-up slink away silently.

Technically yes, but there were other aspects to what made me a hunter. "We don't need to get into that."

He huffed. "Listen, I just saved your life back there… just like I told you I would," he said.

I scoffed. "Oh, here comes the 'I told you so.' I was wondering how long it would take you to start gloating," I snapped.

He veered my Jeep to the side of the road and slammed on the brakes.

"Easy, damn it!" I fussed.

Ansell put the Jeep in park, then turned to fully face me. "You listen to me, D'Angelo fucking Kumar. I'm not gloating… I don't need to gloat. All I've ever wanted to do was help you, but you were too pigheaded and full of yourself and what you were capable of to appreciate what I was capable of. You went against everyone's good advice into that mansion and almost made my vision come true." He huffed and took a deep breath before continuing. "I just hope from this point on that you stop treating me as if I'm some nuisance and start treating me as your partner. Because I'm not going to leave your side, not until we get this damn relic. This is not up for debate."

I wanted to have a comeback, but I didn't. He was tearing into me and I didn't have a fucking leg to stand on because he was right. I didn't like being wrong… especially when I knew what the hell I was talking about.

"I'm waiting," he said.

"On one condition," I said.

"What's that?"

"I call the shots."

"You called the shots before and look what happened. Not gloating, just pointing out facts." Ansell held his hands up as if in defense.

"I mean that I will call the shots as a team. Instead of making you wait in the car, you'll be by my side… but I need for you to follow my lead."

"Okay, I agree to listen to your expertise. Will you listen to mine?" he asked. "Because, I don't want to have to say I told you so again. By the way, *that* was me gloating."

I looked at him. He was a lot sassier than I thought. "You're very different than you are at work."

"At work, I have to do my job and service customers like you. But if I warn a customer that they might want to stay away from Martinelli's Spicy Shrimp Pasta if they suffer from heartburn, but they don't listen… I have to keep my 'I told you so' face to myself. But they know. With you… I can be completely honest. Something tells me you appreciate that," Ansell said.

I had to admit, I was seeing a side of him I didn't realize he had in him. Honestly, I wondered if he even knew he could be this assertive. He seemed like such a meek guy at the restaurant, but I wasn't seeing any of that now. I actually found it enticing, he turned me on… oh shit! My memory was coming back to me and I said some things I wished I hadn't said to him after he saved my life.

"Are you going to take my advice?" he asked again, pulling me out of my embarrassing recollection.

"Yes. We'll be partners," I conceded. "Umm, can we not get into how south everything went in there when we get back to the others?"

Ansell smirked and tossed me a knowing look. "You *were* quite out of it."

"Yeah, ummm, you need to forget that bullshit I said back there, too."

He giggled. "Oh, about how you jerked off to me and why you call me 'Ansell'?"

Shit!

"Yeah, just forget that I ever said that." I wished I could go back in time and change a lot about how this night had gone.

"Sorry, no can do. Those words are burned into my brain now. But as for the others, I'll just let you tell the story of why we don't have the cross," Ansell said, then he put the Jeep in drive and we were off again.

"I take it things didn't go according to plan. You look like shit took a shit on you," Christian said when we entered the living room.

I shook my head. "I felt that way, too. Turns out, his vision was accurate in every uncanny detail."

Christian tensed as he rose from the chair, walking toward me. "Did you almost die?" he asked, his brows creased with concern.

I was laid out on the sofa and he squatted down next to me. Ansell took a seat in the chair across from the sofa. "Yeah," I admitted.

"Holy shit," Christian gasped and covered his mouth for a few seconds. "Even with Ansell by your side?" He turned to look at Ansell.

Ansell shook his head. "I'm the reason he's still alive, though."

I didn't want to admit how badly I'd fucked up, but there was really no point in hiding it. "He wasn't by my side, Chris. I told him to stay in the Jeep for his own protection. I went in there and discovered the cross had been activated. I got close to it and it nearly took my soul. The longer that thing is active, the more powerful it will get. Soon, its range will grow broader and once the spell starts, those that are in its trap will die," I said.

Christian frowned as he looked at me.

"Before you start to bitch at me about my pride, let me just say, lesson learned. Now, can you get Vixen to come in here and concoct something for me that will get rid of this fucking headache that is showing no signs of going away?" I asked.

"Fine. This is our top priority, now. We didn't get any useful information from the auction house, so that was a dead end. You need to go back to that mansion and gather intel on the buyer, find out his name, any other properties he might have, where he works, etc. We need to know more about him," Christian said.

"I could use your help on this," I pointed out. I meant, like damn, I'd nearly died.

He rose to his full height of six-three. "I'm not sure if I'll be much help; I have my own mission that just fell into my lap. Got a call from Father Danelli from Italy. A child's been kidnapped and, according to the good Father, this kid is special. Apparently, the girl was born on the first day of January."

I held up my hand. "Say no more." A missing kid was as serious a threat to the safety of our world as this relic was. Children were used in all kinds of evil-ass rituals where the sacrifice of innocence was necessary. And children born on the first of the months seemed to be of particular interest to demons. Looked like it was going to be just Ansell and me on this one.

Christian nodded. "I'm happy you're alive. Now, please try to stay that way."

I nodded. "Trust me, I have no intentions of feeling that shit ever again."

"Good. Listen, I've got to go."

"Yeah, yeah... take care of business." I knew he was on his way out anyway when I came home because he had his jacket on. Also, the packed suitcase by the elevator was another dead giveaway. I forced myself to sit up long enough for him to give me a hug, then he left. I didn't like him going alone on his mission, but this time, it couldn't be avoided.

I sat back and rubbed my eyes, thinking about how fucked up our lives were sometimes. But when we saved people, it all made it worthwhile to not be able to live a normal life. Some people said ignorance was bliss. But I was more of the party that believed knowledge was power. However, there were some days when I wished I had bliss.

"Are you feeling any better?" Ansell asked me.

I opened one eye and looked at him. "Just a little." I stretched out on the sofa just as Vixen came in carrying a cup.

"Heard you were all kinds of jacked up. I hope this helps. I'm not used to having to come up with this remedy for you guys. You never get sick," she said.

I sat up enough to drink the contents of the cup she gave me. I prayed the shit worked, because this headache was taking me completely out of the fight.

"That reminds me…" Ansell began. "What makes you so much more different than a normal human?" *Well, I see he wasn't letting that go.*

Vixen looked at me and I looked at her. "Oh, I'm not touching that question with a ten-foot pole. That's all yours." She took the now empty cup from me and left the room.

I was thanking my lucky stars that the potion she'd given me was actually working. The throbbing in my head that felt like two men were banging my temples with sledgehammers was fading to the size of little hammers. I lay back down on the sofa and looked at Ansell.

"It's a long story, but I'll give you the Cliffs Notes version," I said, then took a deep breath. "As children, we were trained at the Chasseur Institute to be hunters. Once we reached a certain age, they gave us this special tattoo that is supposed to protect us, as well as bring out our inner innate abilities that we were born with." I unzipped my vest and lifted up my black shirt so he could see my tattoo of the *Mark of Abrafo* on my left pec. It was an intricate pentagram that had other sigils designed inside of it.

Ansell slid from the chair and crawled over to me to take a closer look at the tattoo. Of course, seeing him on his hands and knees crawling towards me did things to my cock and balls that had the beast between my legs stirring awake. Oh yeah, I was starting to feel much better!

"This is beautiful," he said as he reached out, touching it. "Oohh."

He snatched his hand back and looked up at me with a red face. Yeah, I'd felt it too, that little jolt. I'd been feeling it all day. I knew that little shock wasn't the only reason why he was red in the face, though.

I winked. "Like those muscles you're feeling?" I asked, seeing as his gaze had gone from one of amazement to one of lust.

"I was just admiring the ink work," he said, still blushing. But he stood up and walked back to his chair, sitting down. "Okay, go on."

I shrugged, then pulled my shirt down. "Not much to tell with the Cliffs Notes version. The tattoo gives Chris and me the ability to see demons for what they are even when they are hiding behind human faces or in human bodies." I held my hand up, because I could see the confusion on Angel's face. "What I mean by that, because I can see the follow-up question forming on your face, is some demons are powerful enough to enter this world and they don't need to take possession of a human's body. They can do a glamour or transform into human form. We can see them easily. Others who have taken full possession of a human, we can see their demonic faces morphing with their human facades."

"Oh man, that is so creepy. I'd hate to have to see demon faces everywhere," Ansell said, and the look in his gorgeous amber eyes told me that he actually felt sorry that I had to witness such horribleness.

"It's okay, don't feel sorry for me. Though, I don't care to have to see a demon's face in any capacity, but I like knowing what I'm dealing with. Some people ask for it and have sold their souls willingly, and therefore, in their world… and ours, it's a fair trade."

"Who would do that?"

"People desperate enough to want to change their lives for what they think is the other side of the grass. Some people don't believe in souls, or they actually do worship chaos and evil, so to have their bodies taken over, well, that's like an honor to them."

"Fucking weirdos," Ansell commented under his breath. Of course, I heard him loud and clear.

"I don't disagree. Anyway, to continue, we have enhanced

strength and healing abilities. In addition to that, each one of us has a unique ability that we can use. For me, I have heightened senses. I can see, hear, smell, and taste on a magnified level. That's the best way I can describe it."

Ansell's face seemed to blossom with excitement when I said that. "Oh wow! That's so cool. No wonder why you thought you didn't need my help. You're human, but like a superhuman," he said with a wide grin.

I smiled. "Yeah, but you're special too. Seeing the future to the exact detail… that's a marvel."

Again, Ansell blushed and my cock twitched. Thank goodness these cargo pants had room in the crotch area. I was also wearing a cup, so it kept my partner-in-lust contained. "You can stay if you want," I said.

"I'd like that, thank you. The girls seem really nice. Are they Genesis Circle members too?" he asked.

"Yes, but they didn't come from the Institute like Chris and I did. They were living a normal life when the abnormal damn near killed them. Jinx likes Troll dolls. Turns out, a real troll was masquerading as one of them and had stolen the life force of two of their roommates and was working on Vixen next. It was going to save Jinx for last. They thought their house was possessed and were afraid to stay there. Couldn't blame them. Two roommates die, and then you feel like you're next. Yeah, I'd get the fuck out of there, too. They went to a friend of ours, Father Thomas, hoping to get him to perform an exorcism, so he checked it out. He saw that it wasn't a possession, but figured it might be something else. That's when he contacted us."

"Holy shit, that's terrifying. What happened?" Ansell asked. I could tell he was riveted by the story, because his beautiful amber eyes were as wide as saucers as I spoke. It was so fucking charming.

I continued. "Well, Chris and I went to investigate. With our vision, we were able to spot the culprit. It doesn't just work on demons, but any monster using glamour tricks. That little bastard was fast, too. His little ass ran all around that apartment. But Chris and I finally caught it and killed it. That's when our two lovely ladies realized that there was a world beyond the one they were familiar with. After that, they wanted to help us. At first, Chris and I were wholeheartedly against it, but Jinx and Vixen are a lot like you. Persistent as fuck and …"

Ansell leaned forward. "And?"

"Adorable as hell," I added with a wink, and he blushed. "They won us over, like you did. So, they joined the team. Jinx is a wiz with the computers and after one of our missions where Vixen came into contact with the amulet you see around her neck, she got promoted to our resident witch. So, that's the short version of that. They've been so helpful and are like family now, I can't see life without them. As for you and me, well, I'm going to bed," I said, rising from the sofa. "Be sad to go alone… unless you want to join me?" I wiggled my eyebrows. By the look on his face… he was definitely giving it some thought. Hmmm, I wondered what he was going to do.

Chapter Eight

ANGEL

Surely, *he didn't mean what I thought he did.* I narrowed my eyes and studied his expression, looking for any sign that he was teasing me. Did I want to join him? Hell yes, but the last thing I wanted was to agree only to have him laugh at me.

D'Angelo walked—more like prowled—over to where I sat in the chair. I tipped my head back to maintain eye contact with him. His eyes appeared to have darkened with some type of emotion. I thought it could be lust, but I couldn't be sure since I had no experience to fall back on. "I know for a fact that you're curious about my other superhuman talents." His voice was as smooth and rich as some of the expensive liquors I'd sampled at the restaurant. And like with the booze, warmth spread throughout my body until I felt slightly buzzed.

"Uh…" *Real smooth, dumb ass.*

"I think we both know where this is heading, Ansell." D'Angelo slid his hand around the back of my neck. I wanted to close my eyes to break the spell he had cast on me, but I couldn't look away from his mesmerizing stare. "I can also tell that you're not ready yet."

His words had the same effect as pouring a bucket of ice water over my head. I pulled free from his grasp and rose to my feet, forcing him to take a half step back. "What the hell does that mean?" I demanded to know.

D'Angelo's sultry smile turned into one of pure amusement. "You look like a pissed-off kitten." He reached forward to touch me again, but I raised my hand to block him. "It's adorable." *It was the label every man wanted to wear. Not.*

"Don't call me that," I said in a low growl.

"Or you'll do what, exactly?" D'Angelo challenged. "Scratch my eyes out?" He chuckled darkly. "Baby, I have better things for you to do with your fingernails, such as raking them down my back while I make you mine." D'Angelo's expression turned from seductive to stunned in a heartbeat, like he couldn't believe the words that came out of his mouth. I could see him erecting his shield in front of me and I wasn't about to let that happen. For better or worse, we'd gotten past his indifferent phase and I wasn't going back.

"There you go confusing me again," I managed to stammer out. "You've flirted and you've kissed me, then pulled back each time. Why do you do that?"

"That wasn't a kiss," D'Angelo said, shaking his head.

"That's not an answer to my question. And what do you mean by it not being a kiss? You pressed your lips against mine. That's a kiss," I argued.

"You've never really been kissed before or you'd know what I meant," D'Angelo said, stepping forward and closing the slight distance he'd put between us. "Close your eyes, Ansell."

I swallowed hard to dislodge the lump of emotion stuck in my throat. "What? No!"

"You can trust me," D'Angelo said tenderly, and fuck if I didn't do exactly what he said. "That's my good guardian angel."

"Don't make me regret this," I warned, pretending that he hadn't just seen the way my body visibly trembled.

D'Angelo placed both his hands on my neck and circled his thumbs comfortingly over my pulse points. "Tell me how I kissed you in your fantasies."

I was too turned on to be mortified. I happily pulled my favorite fantasy of the two of us out of my spank bank catalog and let my mind and senses completely engage. D'Angelo and I were sitting naked in the middle of a large, antique bed with a massive, intricately carved headboard. It was a rich, dark wood that gave it a masculine feel. Mahogany, maybe. Well, D'Angelo was sitting in the middle of the bed and I was sitting on his lap. "Naked," I said honestly, earning a dark chuckle.

"Beyond that," D'Angelo said encouragingly. "What stands out to you the most?"

Better and more real than any porn scene, I watched D'Angelo's hands slide into my hair and hold my head still for his kiss. *Kiss?* No, it was more like a possession. D'Angelo's tongue teased at my lips until mine parted to grant him access. He didn't just shove his tongue into my mouth either, he eased the tip of his tongue inside my mouth to tease mine.

"Oh," I heard myself saying out loud.

"I'm going to need you to share with the rest of the class, Ansell," D'Angelo purred. "I can't read your beautiful mind." It was the first time anyone had every referred to me as beautiful in any way. I ate it up like a starved man. "What am I doing to you in your fantasy?"

"You're teasing me with the tip of your tongue before you suck mine into your mouth," I whispered hoarsely.

"Now, we're talking, baby. What about my hands? Where are they?" D'Angelo prompted.

"One is fisting my hair on the back of my head and the other is… Oh!" I gasped out loud because the image that played out behind my eyelids wasn't the same as it had always been. Before, D'Angelo had kept one hand on my neck while he fisted my hair with the other, but that wasn't what I saw. *Why would my fantasy shift like that?*

"Tell me." D'Angelo's command was more like a growl. "Where's my other hand, Ansell?"

I swallowed hard, then said, "It's caressing the cheeks of my ass and then you're sliding your middle finger along the crack and teasing my hole." My eyes jerked open in shock at the startling difference between my two fantasies.

D'Angelo lowered his head until his lips hovered above mine. "Do you see the difference between what happened briefly in the car and in your fantasy? Did you see that I kissed you with more than just my lips?" he asked. "Tell me how it was different."

"You kissed me with your entire body," I answered. "I felt you everywhere."

"You seem rattled, but not necessarily in a good way," D'Angelo said, removing his hands and moving back to give me a bit of space. "Did I scare you?"

"No." He didn't scare me; the drastic changes in my fantasy did.

"Something is wrong and I need you to tell me," D'Angelo insisted. His brow furrowed in concern as he waited for a response.

I wasn't sure how to say it without sounding lame. I thought my prior fantasies were heated and erotic, but the newest version took that up a few hundred notches. It highlighted just how inexperienced I was and I felt my cheeks turn pink in embarrassment.

"That blush is going to be the death of me," D'Angelo purred. "What's wrong?" he asked once more. I told him without pausing to think about it any further. D'Angelo's eyes narrowed as he thought about what I said, then his lips spread into a sexy grin. "Those aren't fantasies, my Ansell, they're premonitions."

"How do you know?" I asked stubbornly.

"Do you want me to prove it to you?" D'Angelo asked without missing a beat.

"Yes, I think I do."

I didn't know what I expected D'Angelo to do, but him grabbing my hand and pulling me down a long hallway until we reached the last bedroom wasn't it. D'Angelo twisted the knob and pushed open the door dramatically before he flipped a switch, bathing the room in soft light.

"Oh my god!" It was the same huge, ornate bed from my fantasies, complete with the opulent-looking emerald-green comforter. In my dreams, it was shoved to the foot of the bed to reveal luxurious ivory sheets that tangled around our bodies.

"Am I right?" D'Angelo asked. I could tell by the tone of his voice that he knew the answer.

"Yes," I whispered.

"You weren't fantasizing about me all this time; you were having visions about me. Tonight, your visions gave you more detail because we connected."

"Were all of them visions?" I asked in a stupefied voice.

"There's only one way to find out," D'Angelo replied, turning to face me in the doorway of his bedroom. "I can't allow it to happen until after we retrieve Astaroth's cross. I need all of my focus to be on finding and destroying it, not taking your ass on every available surface I can find."

"You're not helping," I told him dryly.

"You're right, I'm not," he admitted.

"That's twice tonight that you said I was right."

"It's after midnight now, so technically, I told you on different days," D'Angelo said smartly. His statement came across as a ploy to focus our conversation on something other than sex, which was hard to do with his big, inviting bed nearby.

He was right that we needed to stay focused—more him than me—so I decided to take one for the team, so to speak. "I'm going to head on home," I said, taking a step back.

"No, you're not," D'Angelo said firmly. "The buyer might know who you are by now and I won't risk him hurting you, so you're stuck with me—all of us," he corrected, "until this is over."

It didn't feel like being stuck, it felt like the greatest miracle to ever happen to me. I couldn't express that to him without sounding like a complete loser. I had no idea where things were going with D'Angelo, beyond the obvious, and baring my soul to him was entirely different than baring my ass.

"I can't stay with you," I told him.

"Guest room is the next door back. It's never been used before, so you can be the first," D'Angelo said, cocking his head to the side. "How appropriate." He led me back into the hallway and to the guest room. I knew he was referring to my virginal status without actually mentioning it. I could've challenged him on that; just because I knew nothing about kissing didn't mean I hadn't been fucked. But I wasn't wasting my energy on stupid statements that would only be proved as lies later.

"How long do you think it will take to track down the cross?" I asked.

"I like your eagerness," D'Angelo said, stopping at the room next to his.

"I have a job that expects me to show up," I said in explanation. "I can't just disappear and hope they'll save my job for me."

"We'll think of something tomorrow," D'Angelo said confidently. "We both need to get some sleep because we have a big day ahead of us tomorrow."

"Okay," I told him. I knew it would be next to impossible for me to sleep that night, but I had to try.

"I'll see you in the morning," D'Angelo said, backing up. The lustful look from earlier returned as if he liked the idea of me sharing a space with him. "I'm really going to look forward to making your dreams come true, Ansell."

I didn't even attempt to hide the way my body trembled from his words. My brain told me to go inside that room and shut the door, but my heart and body urged me to jump him right there in the hallway. It was obvious he wouldn't put up much of a fight. Then again, I didn't want him to have any regrets, so I did the wisest thing.

"Goodnight, D'Angelo," I said softly before I shut myself in the room. It felt like his warm chuckle floated down the hallway, penetrated the thick door, and wrapped around my cock. "So much for sleep," I mumbled.

I undressed and got beneath the sheets anyway, knowing it would be futile. I tried everything I could think of to fall asleep from counting sheep to meditation but nothing worked. My mind was spinning and my dick was harder than it had ever been. I tried conjuring up the least sexy things I could think of to get my dick to go to sleep, but it was ready to pull an all-nighter.

I tossed and turned until I couldn't take it anymore. I shoved the sheets and blankets to my knees and reached for my leaking cock. I growled in frustration as I smeared my pre-cum along my shaft, using it as lubricant to stroke up and down. Knowing D'Angelo was in the next room only turned me on more. I reached between my legs and teased my hole with my middle finger while I jerked harder and faster, wishing it was his hand on my cock and his finger teasing my pucker. I covered my face with the spare pillow to muffle the cries of ecstasy when I shot my load all over my chest.

I wasn't embarrassed about my need to come, but I also didn't feel the need to broadcast it. I cleaned myself off in the attached bathroom, then climbed back beneath the sheets. I was relieved when I felt my eyes get heavy and my body relax because I knew sleep was finally around the corner.

It felt like only twenty minutes had passed when I felt the edge of the bed shake. My eyes flew open and I saw D'Angelo standing next to the bed with a cup of coffee in one hand and a black lacquered box in the other. I thought he looked well-rested except for the scowl he wore on his face.

"I smell your cum," he growled. I thought he was angry until I saw his nostrils flare and his eyes dilate.

"Is that cup of coffee for me or did you just bring it in here to tease me?" I asked, feeling bold. D'Angelo was about to learn that I wasn't a morning person. "Better yet, why don't you let me sleep for more than an hour before we head out on a mission."

"An hour," D'Angelo scoffed. "It's almost noon."

"The hell you say," I declared, jackknifing into a sitting position. I picked up my cell phone off the nightstand, but it had died sometime during the night since I didn't have my charger on me.

"All that jerking off must've helped you sleep a lot better than I did," D'Angelo groused as he pushed the cup of coffee toward me.

"Am I to believe that you didn't jerk off last night?" I asked, doubtful.

"You don't have to believe it, but it's the truth. I'm saving it all up for you, Ansell. I have wicked plans for you," he said. His sensual threats only heightened my awareness of the fact I was naked beneath the blankets and responding to both his words and his scent. Absent was the embarrassment I would've normally felt because accepting that I was going to be with him made me braver.

"What's in the box?" I asked, looking to change the subject. I took a sip of the sweet, vanilla-flavored coffee and wondered how he knew it was my favorite.

"Butt plugs," D'Angelo said cheerfully.

I had just taken my second sip of coffee and spit it out all over the blankets, which was slightly better than choking on it. I looked at the mess I'd made, then pinned D'Angelo with a dirty look. "Really?" I asked irritably.

"Why would I joke about something as serious as butt plugs?" he asked.

"Could you say it any louder? Maybe not everyone on your team knows about your little goody box," I said. "Unless you make it a habit of bringing home v-v…"

"Virgins," D'Angelo supplied for me. "It's not a dirty word. The answer is I've never brought anyone home until you, but technically, you came to me."

"As if I had a choice," I snapped. "You just happened to have that lying around?" I nodded to the box.

"No, I went out and bought it this morning when I realized we were going to need them," D'Angelo said calmly, as if he were discussing a new pair of shoes. "If your visions have been as vivid as your blushing indicates, then you know damn well that I'm hung."

"And modest," I added.

"Nah, that's not my style," he retorted, then placed the box on the bed. "We'll start using these tonight to get you ready. There are five different sizes and we can use a different one each night."

"I thought you said no hanky-panky while we search for the cross?" I reminded D'Angelo.

"We'll have that relic long before then," he said confidently. "In fact, I need you to get up and get dressed because there's a debriefing in thirty minutes. Jinx has a lead."

D'Angelo set the box of butt plugs on my nightstand, then winked before he left the room. I sat there for a few minutes, staring at the black box and wondering if I'd somehow fallen down a rabbit hole.

Chapter Nine

D'Angelo

When I got up this morning, I told myself to back down on Ansell. I was D'Angelo and I didn't do relationships. That our attraction was just temporary. But no matter what bullshit I kept telling myself, none of it mattered. I felt different around Ansell, I always had, but now… that feeling had become intense. When I was around him, my body ignited with desire and all I seemed to be able to think about was his luscious lips on mine. His arms and legs wrapped around my body while I made love to him against the wall, or in the bed, on the counter… the back of my Jeep. Damn it! My thoughts were running rampant and all were about what I wanted to do to him.

It didn't help calm me down knowing that he was a virgin. His body was no man's land, as in no man had ever been where I wanted to be. I knew he wanted me just as much as I wanted him, and it seemed as if Ansell had been saving himself for me. I didn't even know why I felt that way, exactly. Sure, I'd known him for a little while because of the restaurant, but recently, I just felt connected to him in ways I'd never felt connected to any other person.

And that feeling was strong as hell, too. So strong in fact, that I woke up extra early, before everyone else, to shop for a little something special for Ansell. While I was in the sex shop looking for the best butt plugs for Ansell, there were several guys there giving me all the signals. Normally, I would have picked one and had him crying out in pleasure in the bathroom of the store. But none of their flirtatious stares had any effect on me. Shit, I didn't know whether to panic or not about that. Those guys were hot, but I just wasn't interested. The only person who was on my mind was Ansell. He was the one I had to have. He was mine.

On the drive back, my dick had grown hard thinking about Ansell and the face he'd make once I was sliding inside his perfect, cherry hole. I wanted to pull over and jerk off, but I didn't. I'd been battling that urge since last night when I could hardly get any sleep because of my erection. Eventually, I willed the beast back into slumber, but it wasn't easy. I was all good until I walked into Ansell's bedroom when I got back to wake him up and give him the coffee.

I could smell his dried cum on the sheets and it took everything I had not to yank those covers off of him and give him the real thing. I had to take several deep breaths before I woke him up. He looked so cute when opening his eyes… I could see myself happily waking up to him every day. That was relationship shit right there, and I wasn't so sure how I felt about that. I wasn't as afraid of the aspect of being with someone as I had been in the past. Still, I didn't really understand what it all meant.

Anyway, I left him alone to get himself together and I was making myself my own cup of coffee, with lots of cream and sugar. "Mmmmm," I moaned after taking my first sip.

"That's not coffee anymore, it's a hot milkshake," Vixen said, taking the coffee pot from the machine and pouring herself a cup.

"No one asked you for your input," I teased as I lightly nudged her with my elbow.

She giggled and put the coffee pot back. "I'm just saying."

"It's a bitter drink, I like things that taste sweet on my tongue," I pointed out, and then instantly regretted it once Vixen gave me a knowing, teasing look.

"Yeah, I bet," she joked.

"And I knew you wouldn't miss an opportunity to exploit it," I retorted.

She punched me in my arm. "Exactly. I wouldn't be me if I had just left that one lying out there."

I laughed and shook my head. "Okay, back to the point. What did your girlfriend come up with last night? She said she had a lead."

Vixen shrugged. "She didn't tell me, either. Just wanted us all to meet in the living room in…" she paused and looked at her watch, "three minutes."

"It'll just be the four of us," I said. Christian was already gone. I hoped he was having some success on his case. No telling what evil was being worked up with that child being kidnapped. Sometimes, I really fucking hated monsters. Not all of them were bad, of course. Some of them really wanted to just live their lives and not start a ruckus. But a bunch who broke the rules needed to be killed good and proper.

"I'll meet you in the living room. Not sure if Ansell knows the way," I said. I really didn't give him any grand tour last night. I was so shocked by his fantasy and how accurately he had described my bedroom and how much I liked to grab ass when I kissed, I wanted to prove to him that his dream was another one of his premonitions. Now that I thought about it, that was just one more thing that made me want him more, knowing that it was damn near guaranteed that we would be rumpling my sheets someday.

"I'm surprised you boys actually slept in different rooms. I can feel the sparks literally flying off you two, the chemistry between you is that strong," Vixen said.

I cocked an eyebrow. "You can? What do you make of it?" I was curious as hell, and maybe our resident witch could shine some light on what was happening between Ansell and me.

She shrugged. "I just get this vibe when you two are together. It feels like metaphysical pieces of a puzzle coming together, and it gets stronger each time you two are close. Maybe it's because you're both lusting after each other like crazy. Why don't you just fuck and get it over with?"

"Thank you for that insight," I said with a heavy, sarcastic tone.

"Just saying," she quipped. "See you in a bit." She walked out of the kitchen and I made my way to the guest room to gather Ansell.

This time, I knocked on the door. He opened it a few seconds later and was fully dressed. "Hey, you ready?" I asked. Damn, he was so fucking fine. I was almost resenting this damn case because it was preventing me from shoving him back to the bed and staking my claim. Instead, I had to keep it together. That relic was active and there was no telling how many souls it had taken already.

"Yes, let's go."

I led him to the living room, but I did give him a mini tour, pointing to doors, both open and closed, and telling him what they were. So, now at least, he knew where the kitchen, den, dining room, and extra bathrooms were. We entered the spacious living room with its comfortable suede seating. Jinx was sitting in one of the chairs with her legs crossed and Vixen was lounging on the chaise. I gestured to the sofa and Ansell joined me as we took our seats.

"Okay, Jinx, we're all here. What's up?" I asked.

"Not good news." She began, which I had expected. "Sixteen people were all found dead in a diner in the Bradenhurst neighborhood. It was as if it happened instantly."

"Holy shit," I snarled.

"Oh my god," Ansell gasped.

"Sixteen deaths?" Vixen frowned, and I knew her heart was

aching for all of those innocent lives. She shook her head and sighed.

I was pretty sure this was the work of the relic. I knew a lot about that artifact, but not everything. I didn't know where it had been hidden all of this time, or I would have found the damn thing and destroyed it. I did know that it wasn't empty. Almost a thousand years ago, a demon had tried to free Astaroth and had given the relic five hundred sixty-four souls before a hunter put an end to it. The details about the relic's whereabouts had been lost. Out of sight, out of mind, I guessed. But now, it was very much in my sights and on my mind. It was trying to make me number five hundred sixty-five last night, but that was a bust. It was time for me to put in some serious effort. Because now that it had been activated again, it was going to be able to absorb more and more souls at one time until it reached one thousand.

"So, they all just dropped dead in mid-activity?" I asked, getting more of a picture of what happened. I was sure the police and medics were perplexed as hell. They probably thought it was some gas leak or terrorist poison attack. Sometimes, it was best to let them think the plausible in order to keep the implausible (though very real), like demons and magic, away from public knowledge.

Jinx nodded. "I've been monitoring police activity and hospitals to see if any alarms go off. That was a pretty big one. It's said that people were still eating and the cook was still cooking when they just all suddenly died at the same time. The coroner's initial report is pretty exact on when it all went down, which was two fifteen this morning. They couldn't find any immediate cause of death. Of course, they are going to be checking for gas leaks or poison, stuff like that."

Just as I suspected. "I guess he wanted to test the limits of the relic's power and doing so when very little people would have been in that twenty-four-hour diner was the perfect opportunity."

"I'm surprised it had that many people in it at that time. Must be a popular place," Jinx said. "It's so sad. I hate that those people died."

"Yeah, me too. Listen, keep me posted on any other mysterious deaths," I said, rising to my feet.

"Okay. Where are you going?" she asked.

"Back to that damn mansion to see what I can find."

"What if he's there?" Vixen asked.

"I hope he is. But I doubt it. Not if he's out collecting souls for that relic," I said. "Once I'm done at the mansion, there are a few monsters I need to visit. Some of them have their ears to the ground and might be able to give me some answers… even if I have to beat it out of them."

"Being the tech genius that I am, I managed to gather some information on that address you went to last night. The house belongs to a Mr. Regis Maxfield. He owns several other properties, some in the city and surrounding suburbs, and others in other states and countries. He owns a pharmaceutical company, and get this, this asshole likes jacking up the prices of life-saving medicine to hundreds and even thousands of dollars, making it harder for people to afford them," Jinx said.

Vixen sneered. "Ugh, it's no wonder he's neck deep in demon shit."

Well, her computer skills just made my life a bit easier. "What is the name of his company?" I asked.

"Lifesource Pharmaceutical," she said. "It's a billion-dollar industry."

I nodded. "Of course. I'm still going to his mansion to see if I can find out anything else that you can't gather on the computer. I want to see if he has any other dangerous relics. He might have taken them with him, but I need to know for sure."

"I'm surprised he didn't have security guards, seeing as he can certainly afford it," Jinx said.

I nodded. "Frankly, I was too. Especially since his system was so damned advance, I had to call you for help. And it still took me over ten minutes to disable it and the subsequent alarms, which was annoying as fuck. Once I was inside the library, I realized why there was so much security. He had a lot of pricy artwork in there."

That was what had taken me so damned long. The password Ansell saw in his vision only went to the gate and service side door. The security system outside of his library needed voice and facial recognition. It was a monster in and of itself to disable. It took me longer to get inside and that was probably why Ansell started to worry and came in to check on me. Thank god he had, because I might not be here today otherwise.

"Well, I'm about to see what I can gather. Let me know if he goes to work today. I'd love to be able to catch him at his job," I said.

"I'm coming with you," Ansell said.

"Yeah, partners… but remember what we discussed," I reminded him.

He nodded. "Yeah, yeah… you're in charge. Can we swing by my apartment for some clean clothes first?"

With me with him, maybe we could stop by his house for a quick minute. Just enough for him to pack a bag of things he would need, then we were going back out to Highland Heights. I was certain the owner wasn't home. Had I not been so fucked up last night, I would have gathered this intel then and done a more thorough search. But if he was home… fingers crossed… his ass was mine.

"Sure, you need to gather a few things anyway. I was serious about you staying here. If you're going to be my partner, you need to stay someplace safe. This is our headquarters, so it's warded off against monsters and demons."

"Wow!" Ansell gasped, then released a long, shuddering breath. "I know you said these things exist, it's just hearing you say it so matter-of-factly, just… I don't know… made it seem more real and threatening."

I nodded. "It is real and so is their threat. My world is a very dangerous one, Ansell. That's why I fought so hard to keep you out of it. But now that you are in it, I will fight hard to keep you safe. So, no more Martinelli's, at least until we solve this crime. I'll talk to your boss, don't worry."

"And tell him what?" Ansell asked with a curious expression.

"I'll think of something." I didn't want to tell him that I might pay Mr. Martinelli off and if that didn't work… I wasn't opposed to issuing a few well-meaning threats. "For now, we need to get back to your apartment, so let's go."

"Okay, I guess my little meeting is adjourned," Jinx said.

"Babe, I love you, but the next time you have so little information, can you just send a text? I got up early for this," Vixen complained.

Jinx huffed. "I woke you up at eleven o'clock."

Vixen rolled her eyes. "Yeah, that's early for me."

"Sorry, geez, I just wanted everyone to be on the same page," Jinx said in her defense.

Of course, I knew it was because she wanted to feel like she was contributing and a part of the team, and truth be told, she did. Jinx was the only one amongst us who didn't have powers. But what she had was something we didn't. Mad fucking computer skills. That was special in my book. Although, I did have to agree with her girlfriend on this matter. I just didn't say anything. I looked at Ansell and motioned for him to follow me.

"Which one of you ladies will be minding the store?" I asked.

"I put a sign up saying we'll reopen at two. I'm going down there now. Breathe," Vixen said.

"Okay, we still need to run that business, too," I teased. They knew the drill. Vixen flipped me off and I snorted. "Catch you later," I said, and led Ansell to the elevator.

"What kind of monsters are we going to question?" Ansell asked, and I could tell by the tone of his voice that he was excited and frightened by the prospect.

"A demon named Gregor and a vampire, who's more annoying than the demon, if you can believe it, named Lorcán Kennedy. They should be able to tell me something," I said.

"Oh shit… okay. Man, I am totally going to let you take the lead,"

Ansell said.

"Good." The doors opened and we walked off. We made our way through our antique store and checked the sign Vixen had put up. I decided to leave it alone. She'd be taking it down soon. Ansell and I climbed into my Jeep, which luckily had only one ticket on the windshield. I looked at it, then back to Ansell.

He smiled sweetly at me and shrugged a shoulder. "I'm sorry."

I sighed. "For the future, baby…" *Yeah, I called you baby, and look at you blushing.* I loved it. "Park in the underground garage." Street parking was annoying and expensive.

He nodded. "I will."

I slipped the ticket in the glove compartment. "Okay, so… where do you live?"

Chapter Ten

Angel

I realized I hadn't really thought it all the way through before I asked D'Angelo to take me by my apartment. While it was true that I needed clothes and my phone charger, I didn't want him to see the squalor that I lived in.

"Was that a difficult question?" D'Angelo asked when I didn't respond right away.

"You know, it makes no sense for us both to go to my apartment. Why don't you go ahead and interview the demon and vampire while I gather some things? I can meet you back here when we're both finished." It amazed me that I was so calm about learning of the existence of demons, vampires, and witches, but perhaps my psychic ability made it possible for me to believe that other phenomenon existed in the world too.

"Are you afraid of being around supernatural beings or don't you want me to know where you live?" D'Angelo asked. *Damn him and his intuitiveness.* "I can promise you that you'll be safe with me by your side and that I'll never show up at your place uninvited or at least without notice."

"Neither," I replied honestly. I wasn't afraid of the interviews today because I knew D'Angelo would have my back and I wasn't worried about him dropping by unannounced.

D'Angelo pursed his lips in concentration and studied my expression, looking for clues to what I was thinking. "Then what is it, because I can tell something is bothering you?"

"So now you're a psychic too?" I asked childishly.

"I don't need to be a psychic to know you're worried about something." D'Angelo reached over and ran his thumb over my bottom lip. "You've nearly chewed your lip off, and I have big plans for that mouth. I'm going to want to feel those plush lips moving up and down—"

"Weren't you the one who insisted we stay focused?" I asked, cutting him off before he could finish. He was much more adept at hiding his emotions than I was, and I needed his help to keep my head in the game.

"The quicker we solve this case and get the relic back, the quicker I get to claim your tight ass," D'Angelo said in a voice that was roughened by lust. "You might say that I'm motivated."

"I thought you said you were going to stretch my ass over a five-day period; one plug per night." I didn't want to wait five days to feel him inside me. I had already waited a lifetime. It felt like a cruel form of punishment to be near him twenty-four hours a day, knowing that what I wanted was just out of reach.

"That was my plan," D'Angelo agreed, nodding his head.

"Was? You've changed your mind?" I asked, hopeful.

"That depends on a few things," he replied coyly. I could tell by the wicked smile on his face that he was enjoying my torment.

I took the bait without hesitation. "Such as?"

"First, how well your ass stretches. Just how greedy and eager will it be to know my cock?" *Pretty damn greedy and eager.*

"What else?" I questioned. "You said, 'a few things,' which implies more than one. What else besides my needy, greedy hole will hold you back? Oh, the case," I said, answering my own question. "You said that we needed to wait until after we retrieved the relic before we—"

"That might backfire," D'Angelo said, cutting me off.

The desire I saw in his hazel eyes thrilled me and made me brave. If he could be brutally honest, then so could I. "I hesitated because I'm ashamed of where I live and I don't want you to think less of me."

"I'd never be so shallow, Ansell. I come from very humble beginnings and I know better than to judge a man by his material possessions," D'Angelo replied sincerely. "I only care about what's in here," he placed his hand on my heart, "and here," he said, stroking a finger across my temple.

"Maybe my pants, too?" I asked, feeling sassy.

D'Angelo smiled crookedly before he said, "I also care greatly about what's in your pants. I don't care about the condition of your apartment or your lack of worldly goods. So, how about we get this show on the road?"

"Okay," I agreed, but I still had my reservations.

"Great," D'Angelo said, turning his key in the ignition. "Besides, how bad could it be?"

※

"It's pretty bad," D'Angelo said once he was standing in the center of my one-room apartment. He looked at the water stains on the ceiling, the peeling paint on the walls, and the carpet that was so filthy, one had no guess at the original color.

I was about to respond to him—probably in the form of an apology—when my door banged open.

"Where the hell have you been?" an angry female voice demanded to know. "And who the fuck is this?"

D'Angelo and I turned around to face the irate woman standing in the doorway. Megan "Meggie" Monahan was the only friend I had in the entire world. We'd become instant friends the day I moved in. Neither of us had any family to speak of—none that would claim us anyway—so we formed our own little family.

"I called your phone at least a dozen times when you didn't come home last night. I was five minutes away from filing a missing persons report," she said angrily. "Where have you been?"

"I'm sorry I worried you, Meggie," I said. "I ran into a little bit of trouble last night and had to stay over at my... uh, friend's house and didn't have my charger. My phone died and I didn't know you were looking for me. How'd you even know I was missing?" It wasn't like we kept the same hours. I worked mostly during the day as a waiter at Martinelli's and she worked nights as a waitress at a bar aptly named The Dive. "What were you doing home?"

"I got fired," she said calmly. "Some douche nozzle customer thought he could put his hands on me anytime he wanted. I let him know that I didn't approve by driving my knee into his balls. The bar manager decided I wasn't a good fit." Meggie shrugged like it wasn't a big deal, but I saw the stress lines around her eyes and mouth. "So, are you going to introduce me to your new *friend*?" I caught the slight change in her voice. She was all kinds of curious, but also cautious. Life had taught us to be that way.

D'Angelo closed the distance and held out his hand. Meggie giggled softly when she shook his hand. Her caution didn't stand a chance against D'Angelo's charm. "I'm D'Angelo Kumar." He studied her closely and I wondered what he thought of my petite friend, who wasn't much taller than five foot four. Her curly, red hair hung riotously over her shoulder and her green eyes appeared to be larger than normal as she took in D'Angelo up close. I understood completely why her breath sighed slowly through her parted lips.

"Megan Monahan," she replied, a soft blush spreading across her cheeks. Meggie broke eye contact with D'Angelo and looked at me.

"How long have you guys known each other?"

"A while," D'Angelo answered vaguely. "Ansell is going to be staying with me for a while, so we're here to grab a few things."

Meggie turned her attention back to D'Angelo. She placed her hands on her hips and straightened her spine. "Ansell? Who the hell is Ansell?"

"That's the nickname I've given him," D'Angelo replied calmly, but this was a man who battled demons for a living. "Do you care to tell her why I call you that, Ansell?"

"No," I squeaked. "Look, Meggie, I'm not sure how long I'll be gone. I'll call you tonight and explain." D'Angelo raised his brow, silently questioning how much I was going to tell my friend. Thankfully, I had an entire day to come up with a plausible explanation. I sure as hell couldn't tell her the truth. She didn't know about my psychic ability. I had learned a long time ago not to trust anyone with the truth. D'Angelo was the one exception, which seemed to be the case when it came to several things.

Meggie walked to me and searched my eyes. "I don't like this, Angel. If you're in some kind of trouble…"

"He's not in trouble," D'Angelo answered.

"I'm not talking to *you*," Meggie said firmly. "He's more than capable of talking for himself."

"I'm not in any trouble," I assured her. "I promise you that everything will be okay." I meant what I said, even though there was no possible way for me to know things would work in my favor.

"You promise to call me?" Meggie asked softly.

"I promise. Are you going to be okay though?" Neither of us could afford to leave our jobs. As shitty as our apartments were, it was a vast improvement over homelessness—something both Meggie and I knew firsthand.

"Yeah, I just need to find a new job soon," Meggie replied. "Preferably one where people aren't grabbing my ass or breasts."

"We're hiring," D'Angelo said suddenly.

"You are?" Meggie and I asked at the same time.

"Who is 'we' and what kind of job are we talking about here?" Meggie asked, suspicious.

"I own an antique shop with a partner and we're looking for another sales associate," D'Angelo said. "I need to free Allison's time up to search for more artifacts, which she can't do if she's manning the shop all the time." *Allison? Who the hell was Allison?*

"I appreciate your offer, but I know nothing about antiques," Meggie said, her shoulders slumping forward in disappointment.

"You don't have to be an expert," D'Angelo explained. "The antiques are catalogued with very detailed descriptions. If a customer asks for more information, you only need to type the item number in our computer system and it will bring up everything we know about the origin of it. You just need to be personable and reliable," he told her. "Feel like giving it a shot?"

"I don't know," Meggie said hesitantly. "Don't you want to talk it over with your partner first? My ego can't take getting fired before I'm actually hired."

"Christian has his hands full right now and we trust one another's judgment. Tell you what," D'Angelo pulled a card out of his wallet and handed it to her, "stop by and see Allison this afternoon. I'll give her a call to let her know to expect you. She can show you around and you can make an informed decision on whether you want to work there or not."

"This is really nice of you," Meggie said. "Why would you do this for me?"

"You're important to Ansell," D'Angelo said in a matter-of-fact way that allowed no argument.

Meggie tapped the card to her lips while she thought about her response. "Thank you, D'Angelo. Please tell Allison that I'll be there in an hour." She looked at me and pinned me with her no-nonsense look. "Call me tonight or I'll hunt you down."

"I will." I kissed her cheek and shooed her to her apartment to get ready. I shut the door behind her and asked, "Who the hell is Allison?"

"Jinx," D'Angelo said.

"Oh," I replied. Jinx suited her so well, I couldn't imagine her going by any other name. "I guess that Vixen is a nickname too."

D'Angelo nodded and said, "Her real name is Vanessa."

"I appreciate what you're doing for Meggie. She's got a heart that's a hundred times her size. It's been just the two of us for a while now and…"

"Hey," D'Angelo said softly, cutting me off. "You don't need to thank me. We really need Jinx out of the showroom and in front of her computer. I hope this works out for everyone." D'Angelo tilted his head toward the raggedy dresser I had tucked in the corner of the room that doubled as a television stand. "Grab some clothes and your charger so we can get going. Big plans, remember?"

My face flushed with heat. *As if I could forget.* It took me an embarrassingly short period of time to pack a few changes of clothes and my phone charger. My bathroom at his house had a new toothbrush and plenty of grooming products.

"This should do it," I said, zipping up my duffle bag.

"That's not much," D'Angelo noted. He looked over at my open dresser that still had plenty of folded items in the drawer.

"I'll be coming back here when the mission is over," I told him.

"Yeah," D'Angelo agreed, but he didn't sound happy about it. "Ready?" he asked, looking eager to get back on the road.

"As I'll ever be to hunt down demons," I answered dryly.

The drive to the buyer's mansion was made in complete silence except for when D'Angelo called Jinx to let her know that Meggie was coming to meet with her about the position he had created for her that day.

"Yes!" Jinx's voice sounded jubilant through the stereo speakers. "You guys are going to be outnumbered."

"How do you figure?" D'Angelo asked.

"Three gals versus two guys," she fired back.

"We have Angel, so that makes it three against three," D'Angelo shot back. He made it sound like my position with them might be more than temporary. I was afraid to hope.

"Ohhh, we get to keep him after all," Jinx said excitedly.

"One day at a time," D'Angelo said firmly, backtracking a little bit. "I'll call you with any information I find at the mansion."

"Be careful, guys," Jinx said.

"We will," D'Angelo said before he disconnected the call.

I kept my eyes on the scenery through the windshield rather than chance a look at D'Angelo. My stomach was already in knots and I worried what would happen if his mask of indifference returned when he looked at me. Worrying wouldn't prevent or fix anything, so I spent the rest of the ride trying to come up with a reasonable explanation of why I had to miss work until the buyer was caught. I couldn't say that I was sick because they'd require an excuse from my doctor to keep my job. Everyone knew I was estranged from my family, so saying that I had to return to California for a death in the family wasn't going to work. Even if they bought it, I risked someone seeing me around town while we hunted relics and demons.

I was so busy with my thoughts, I didn't realize we had arrived back at Regis Maxfield's mansion until D'Angelo called my name. I turned to look at him and was happy to see concern etched on his face instead of a blank mask.

"Clear your mind of everything except our mission," he said firmly, but not harshly. "We're going in there to see if we can find any clues as to where Regis might've gone with the cross. It wasn't likely he returned after he vanished."

"Got it," I said, nodding my head.

D'Angelo was so confident of that fact, he pulled right up to the rear of the house after opening the gates. The back door was open like we had left it. He jerked to a stop once we entered the kitchen. I suspected he was tapping into his super powers to see if he detected anything out of the norm. "Okay, let's see what we can find."

Nothing on the first level looked disturbed or out of place, except that all the mirrors we came across had been smashed. "He can't stand the sight of himself," D'Angelo said as we made our way up the grand staircase.

D'Angelo didn't say much when he approached the wooden pedestal where the relic had been the previous night. The wood was pitted and burned where the cross had sat. "I better get a sample of this ash." I noticed that his hand shook slightly when he scraped a sample into a plastic baggie, and who could blame him? He had been just minutes from death the last time he stood there.

It wasn't so much his actions or his words that alerted me to the fact that he was more shaken than he let on. It was the connection I felt to him, which seemed to grow stronger every minute. It was the creepiest feeling I'd ever felt, yet it was also the most amazing. I had never felt tethered to another person in my entire life and I wanted that connection with D'Angelo more than anything.

I reached for his hand and squeezed it briefly before I left D'Angelo to collect his samples while I searched the large desk. We already knew his identity, so I was focused on clues as to where he might be hiding, like evidence of another house he owned, but all I found were pamphlets and brochures for various plastic surgery procedures from several different plastic surgeons. At first, I discounted them until I came across a picture of him in his younger days standing next to a woman wearing a wedding dress. The glass in the frame was shattered like he had smashed it against his desk or threw it against the wall.

Regis was much better-looking in his younger years, healthier too. I had to wonder if he blamed his physical appearance for whatever event had caused him to smash his wedding photo. Had his wife left him for a younger man?

"I might have something."

"Do you know where he went?" D'Angelo asked.

"No, but I think his motive is more personal than simple greed." D'Angelo looked up and I showed him the pamphlets and smashed picture frame. "This probably explains the shattered mirrors."

"True," D'Angelo said as he joined me at the desk. "Motive might help us predict this bastard's move, but I'd love to know where he's hiding or find a cell phone bill with his number on it."

We searched every square inch of that desk, but didn't turn up his cell phone number or any proof that he owned another home. We did find a credit card statement that D'Angelo hoped Jinx could use to track his activity and help us locate him. I learned that my... D'Angelo was gifted at cracking safes. If his superhuman strength wasn't enough to rip the door right off its hinges, then he pressed his ear against the metal door and used his superhuman hearing to crack it.

I was completely turned on by the intense look of concentration on his face when he listened to the inner workings of the lock while he slowly turned the dial. I was certain he'd wear that same look once he had me pinned beneath him. *Focus, Ansell.* Hell, even I was starting to think of myself as Ansell instead of Angel. There would be times where I could relax and think about the sexual delights that awaited me, but standing in a demon's playground—which was what the room felt like to me—wasn't one of them.

"Aha," D'Angelo said triumphantly, then turned the handle to open the safe. "I still have it."

"Was there any doubt on your part?" I asked.

"Not really," he confided with a cocky grin before he focused on the contents of the safe. "Well, look what we have here. The Soul of Agenta," he said reverently. D'Angelo bit his lip and narrowed his eyes while he thought about his discovery. "Now I have you, Regis Maxfield."

I walked over to the safe so I could see what he'd found. It was an amulet with a shiny black stone. I could tell there was something gray inside the stone, but I couldn't make out what it was before D'Angelo slid it inside a black velvet pouch. D'Angelo found stacks of cash that he also pocketed.

"This trip paid off big time," D'Angelo said, rising to his feet. "I think I know what good ole Regis is up to. You did good today, Ansell," he said affectionately. "Ready to meet a demon and a vampire?"

"Is he the sparkly kind?" I asked, hopeful.

"Definitely not," D'Angelo said after he had a good laugh. "Please don't mention that to him, either."

"Not a fan?" I asked.

"No."

"Fine. Are there any other rules I need to know?" I asked, curious.

"A few," he told me. "I'll fill you in on the way."

Chapter Eleven

D'Angelo

I knew we weren't going to find Regis Maxfield at home. He'd probably never return to that place now that we knew about it. At least, not until he was done doing whatever it was he was planning. At least, it wasn't a complete bust searching the mansion. He ran out of it so fast last night, he didn't get a chance to clear out his safe that was located behind one of his expensive paintings in the library. Imagine my surprise when I found the *Soul of Agenta* sitting there among several stacks of hundred-dollar bills, which I also took. Shit, he owed me for damn near killing me last night.

Ansell and I climbed back into my Jeep and headed off to see Gregor first. Hopefully, by the time we were done talking with the demon, the vampire might be friendlier even though we'd be interrupting his sleep. I handed Ansell the artifact, which was nicely concealed in a black velvet pouch.

"What's this?" Ansell asked. "You said the name, but didn't tell what it is. I mean, should I even be holding it?"

"I wouldn't have given it to you if it wasn't safe," I said, wanting to put him at ease. "What it is, is an artifact that is used to turn a human into a monster or demon."

"Oh shit. Fuck that, I'm not holding on to this thing," Ansell said, then he opened the glove compartment of my Jeep and pushed the artifact in past some papers and closed the door. "That's better."

"You didn't trust me when I said you were safe?" I asked.

"I trust you, I just don't trust that thing. It's creepy. I mean, you just told me that relic turns people into demons. You'll have to forgive me if I don't want to hold it in my lap," Ansell said.

I laughed. "Yeah, I see your point." I shrugged. "I guess I'm just used to all of this shit."

"So, do you think he's trying to turn himself into a demon?" Ansell asked.

"Not sure what the fuck this guy is up to. The more answers I have to those questions, the better. Then I'll know what I'm fully up against." I sighed. "The fact that he has that relic leads me to believe he thought he had the relic to transfer his soul into another body of his choosing. If he tried to work that spell with the wrong relic, well, he may very well have left himself open to a demon or monster mutation. Spells are very specific and you need all of the correct ingredients, sigils, and artifacts if you want them to work properly."

"Think maybe that's why his face was messed up?"

I snorted. "Naw, that was just hack surgery right there. I hope he didn't pay the doctor for that botched shit. Fact is, I'm not sure what is going on. I didn't see a demon inside him when he stepped out of the shadows. Of course, I was also out of my mind with delirium and recuperating from nearly dying, so I can't really trust my skills or what I think I know at this point."

"Well, we'll get some clues today, I'm sure. Speaking of questions that need answers, what about my job?" Ansell asked.

"Ahhh, yeah, sorry. Umm, you're no longer employed there," I said.

His eyes bulged as he looked at me. "What? You said you'd help me out, what the fuck."

"I did. You hated working there. Yeah, the food was great, but the pay is shit. Besides, it's safer if you work with me or the girls at the shop. I want to know you're safe."

Ansell looked like he wanted to fuss some more, but then he sat back in the seat and sighed. "I did hate working there," he admitted. He looked at me again, brows creased with confusion. "How the hell did you make that happen?"

I shrugged. "It was a simple thing. I had Jinx call your job and I spoke into her computer, but it was your voice that came out. So, your boss thought it was actually you calling to quit."

Ansell pouted.

"I thought you'd be happy about that." Now, I was confused. I knew I might have crossed a line, but I was also very confident that I had done the right thing.

Ansell shrugged. "I don't know… I feel kind of robbed of the opportunity to quit that place myself."

I nodded, seeing where he was coming from. "If it's any consolation, I told him to kiss my ass when he told me that you weren't that good of a waiter."

He whined, "Aww man, now I really wish I could have told him that myself."

"Sorry, I wasn't intending to go the whole, 'I quit' route. But when he started giving me grief over sick days and shit, I lost my temper and just said, 'fuck it,' Jinx did record everything, so you can listen and laugh over it later," I said, hoping that would make him feel better. I really hadn't planned on handling Ansell's job the way I had, but in the end, I felt it would be better if he was with me.

Ansell nodded. "I'd love to listen to it. Thanks for that. I'd rather work at the shop anyway. Hey, now that I think about it, is working at the shop going to be safe for me and my friend?"

"The shop is warded against demons and the like, so… yeah, it's safe. That's one of the reasons I want you there." I was relieved that he was happy about what I'd done.

"What about when she leaves?" Ansell said. "I mean, the whole point of me staying there is because what we're working on can get dangerous. I'm sure monsters know where you all might live, they just can't get in there. I don't want anything to happen to my friend."

Damn, I hadn't thought about that when I offered the job. Jinx and Vixen and on occasion, Chris and I, worked the shop, but it was mainly the girls who kept it running. But they also lived on location. They knew about what we were, and were prepared if or when shit got ugly. Megan didn't know about any of it. I guess I was going to have to run a few things by the others.

"I honestly didn't think about that, Ansell. I'm pretty good at reading a room and could tell that she was someone you cared a great deal for. She was down and out and I just saw the opportunity to help and possibly…" I let my voice trail off because I was about to say something I couldn't take back.

"Possibly?" Ansell asked, looking at me.

I sighed. "You're like a dog with a bone at times, do you know that?"

"You gave me the bone, I'm not going to let you take it away."

I smirked when he said that, because like it always seemed to do when I was around him, my mind went straight to the gutter. "I haven't given you the bone yet."

He blushed, but I could tell he wasn't going to be distracted by lust. "Stop it… god." He looked away, but his face grew even redder.

"What? I'm just stating a fact."

"Well, how about answering my questions," he said, turning back to me.

I sighed. "Fine. Damn. Maybe if she was working there, you'd want to stick around." I shrugged. "I don't have many weaknesses… at least, I don't think so… but impulsiveness is one of them. I tend to act out passionately without fully thinking things through. Sometimes that works perfectly in my favor, sometimes it doesn't."

I threw a glance his way, but couldn't completely read the expression on his face. Was he happy that I wanted him to stick around? Or did that make him nervous? I wanted so badly to just stop the car and kiss him, but I wanted to get the job done and we still had a lot to discuss.

Instead of wondering what he was thinking, I just decided to ask him. "What are you thinking?"

"That you want me to stick around," he said.

"Do... do you want to?" I asked.

Damn, why was I so nervous right then? Geez, I was acting like some blushing girl. We hadn't even had sex. Sure, we'd both flirted like crazy, especially on my part, but neither of us even knew if we'd want to be around each other after we did. I mean, what if I wasn't cut out for a relationship? What if my world proved to be too dangerous for Ansell and he didn't want to stick around?

He looked at me and smiled. "I... I think I do."

With those words, my mental ramblings came to a halt. I smiled at that, because there was hope. "Let's not worry about all that, now. But you're right about your friend. I'll have to run this by Chris and the girls, but maybe she can stay with us. Or maybe she might not want to and she'll go home. We can put a ward up on her apartment as some safety measure. It won't be as powerful as the one we have at the store, because we own that property. She's just renting, so it's a ward that can be broken by the right spell. However, it's something, which is better than nothing."

"I'm not sure about all that. I think if she works at the shop, she should know what she's getting herself into. And if she decides she doesn't want that level of danger, then that's that," Ansell said.

I nodded. "Fair enough."

"I'll talk to her about it."

"All right."

"I appreciate you wanting to help and," he smiled, "keep me close."

I rolled my eyes and turned my head, so he couldn't see me grinning like a fool.

"I see you grinning," Ansell smirked, busting me out.

"Okay, you caught me in a happy moment."

He giggled, then sighed blissfully. "Hey, I have another question. Why did you think they'd be looking for me? Or is it that you just wanted me to spend the night?"

I tossed him a look and saw him giving me a sly expression before I turned my gaze back to traffic. "Honestly, I was worried he would be able to track you down since you touched him. He's no stranger to dark arts, and with the right spell, he might have been able to locate you since you two had that connection when you tackled him. I wasn't willing to take the chance of you getting hurt. That's why I wanted you to stay with us. At least, until all of this is over," I said, even though I wasn't sure what was going to happen between Ansell and me when this case was over.

"Ahhh, I see. Good call. Damn, I can't believe all of this was going on under my nose all of these years," he mused.

I nodded. "It's important to keep the truth from people. Can you imagine what would happen if the world found out?"

Ansell shook his head. "I don't want to imagine."

"Tell me about it. Okay, first things first that you should know. We have rules we have to abide by. Both hunters and the monsters. The most important one is no killing of innocents. No humans can be permanently harmed—"

"But humans can be harmed?" Ansell interjected.

"In a manner of speaking, yes. For instance, vampires have to feed. So, they are allowed to feed on humans as long as they leave them alive. Vampires who obey that rule get to keep on existing. Those who don't go on the endangered species lists. Vampires tend to obey that rule. It keeps the hunters out of their lives and they get to live free. They are also pretty good at policing that rule themselves," I said.

"Meaning?"

"Well, some monsters have their own society and they run it with iron fists. For example, vampires, witches, and werewolves have kingdoms known as sovereigns, covens, and packs. They like to keep track of their own and if they have a rogue, they like to hunt them on their own. They tend to show us proof the rogue has been dealt with, and that keeps the peace," I said.

"Wow, how long have monsters and demons existed?" Ansell asked.

"For thousands of years."

"Who made up the rules?"

"The place where I was trained. The Chasseur Institute. They are one of the oldest schools in existence on the surface and that makes them highly prestigious. But the sole purpose of the school is to find the best and brightest, those children who have innate abilities, and train them to be executioners, if you will. To hunt down evil and eradicate it. A thousand years ago, the school's hunters were quite busy killing things, but they were also dying as well. It was a complete bloodbath. The monsters that didn't want to be hunted decided to call a truce, if you will. So, that's how the rules came into play."

"Were the hunters winning?" Ansell asked.

"Both sides were taking major hits. And even demons and monsters that weren't doing any harm were targeted. They were the ones who stood up and made the first move towards a peaceful coexistence. Truth is, I think in the end, the hunters may have lost that war. For every vampire we can kill, another hundred can be made. So, the Institute thought it best to hear them out, seeing as it could help save the lives of their hunters as well." I pulled into the parking lot of a metalwork shop and killed the engine. "The demons, vampires, witches, werewolves, skin walkers, shape-changers, and some demons sat down with the council that controls the Chasseur Institute and they came up with a plan. Those with structure, we let them police their own, and in doing so, they protect the humans. For the stragglers, like goblins, ghouls, and rogues that escape their nets, well, that's where we come in. So, that's how the first two laws came into effect."

"Holy shit, that is a wild story. I can't believe it's actually true. What are the other rules?" Ansell asked.

"No opening portals, no casting spells that do harm. No possessing human bodies that are occupied by human souls," I said.

"So, the person has to already be dead?"

I nodded. "And not murdered by a demon or demonic associate. So, it has to be a regular human death that the demon had nothing to do with. Also, the demon entering this plane has to be approved by both the Institute and the demonic council."

"Why would the Institute ever agree to have a demon enter this plane?"

"Trust me, it's not a decision they are happy with, just as the Demonic Council isn't pleased with the arrangement or rules set up. But the truth is, some demons aren't evil. A lot of them are assholes, but not necessarily malicious. They can also be helpful to humans, so that's why the Institute agreed," I informed him.

Ansell shook his head in disbelief. "A nice demon… is there such a thing?"

"Nice would be stretching it," I said with a chuckle.

"So, do demon have their own hunters?"

"Yeah, but they aren't nearly as interested in stopping demons from breaking the laws. They like to leave that in our hands, which is why we're in this situation now. That's why I'm touching base with Gregor. He's a lower level demon, but he's a part of their community. He might also be able to tell me something."

"Why don't we just go to the Council?" Ansell asked.

"I don't trust demons that damn much… or at all, really. Not to mention, they don't have a location. You have to conjure them all into one place and they hate that. Out of all of the monsters who made the pact of peace, the demons are the ones who break it the most and they are the ones we have to watch more than the others," I said.

"Seems like they have a lot of leeway," Ansell pointed out.

I shrugged. "Witches can cast spells, but they can do no harm to humans. So, healing spells, a little lust spell, nothing that causes major chaos or mischief. That goes for some monsters and demons that feed off of causing trouble. No human can be killed or seriously harmed. The beings that don't want to play along, well, those are the ones that get hunted."

"So, you're saying that it's basically impossible to get rid of all evil, so working out this peace is the next best thing?" Ansell asked.

"That's pretty much exactly what I'm saying. Even if we were to try to open a portal to get rid of every monster or demon on this plane… a spell of that magnitude would only leave this earth vulnerable to more of them coming through, as portals are open both ways. We'd never want to risk that, because there is a huge chance it wouldn't work and only make things worse. Right now, people live in this world with little to no knowledge these beings even exist. We want to keep it like that," I said.

Ansell nodded and looked out of the window. "Where are we?"

"Gregor's Metalworks. He owns it," I said, then climbed out of my Jeep. Ansell did the same, and then followed me inside.

"How can I hel—oh, it's you," Gregor said as he came around the metal sculpture he'd been polishing.

"Nice to see you too, Gregor," I said sarcastically as I approached him.

"I can't say the same, you bastard," Gregor retorted. "What do you want?"

To every human eye, he would look like one of them. Blond hair, blue eyes, about five-ten and had a swimmer's build. He probably got laid a lot and the human was none the wiser that they were fucking a demon. However, from what I'd heard, the human was the lucky one. I didn't care, really, as long as the human was left unharmed. Demons could give them all the orgasms they wanted. Getting back to perceptions. Humans saw only the human face. But the hunters of the Chasseur Institute and I, we could see his true demon face, and it wasn't anything pretty.

And what I meant by see his true demon face, when I used my vision to expose them, I saw the full demon since no human soul was repressed inside the body. So, I could see his spindly-looking body dressed in human clothes. His leathery skin was black and his limbs were long, as were his toes and fingers. His claws looked dangerous too, and they were also black. His face was another nightmare. Red eyes, along with several tiny horns that lined his forehead. His ears were long and pointed at the tips. His nose resembled that of a skeleton, that non-existent. His lips were thin and they covered his razor-sharp teeth that cluttered his mouth. Yeah, he was a fugly son of a bitch, and I was ready to switch back to my rose-colored vision, which I did. Now, I could see what Ansell was seeing.

"Hmmm, what do I want?" I pursed my lips, faking contemplation.

"My time is for paying customers, so if you're not interested in one of my fine sculptures…" Gregor said, indicating that he'd rather like me to leave.

"No, but you can answer some of my questions. Can we go in the back?"

He sighed, then turned to his employee. "Jake, mind the store, will ya?"

"Sure, Mr. Henson," Jake replied with a grin.

"Thanks," Gregor said, then led us into the back towards his office. Once inside, he shut the door. "I don't know anything about anything."

"I haven't even asked you a question yet, you prick," I said.

"Look, I'm a low-level demon here. If something big is going down—"

"Then you might know something about it. Don't give me that

lower level bullshit, Gregor. I know just how significant your role is," I said.

"I make shit, D'Angelo. No one comes to me unless they want a weapon of some kind," Gregor said, which was true. He was a demonic blacksmith with a skill for crafting weapons that were extraordinary. Demons came to him, and hunters as part of the peace pact. I had several demonic weapons in our arsenal that bared his signature.

"What do you want to know?" he asked, finally dropping the act that was starting to piss me off. "Just know that I might not be able to help you."

"What can you tell me about the relic, the *Stone of Astaroth*?"

He whistled. "That's a nasty piece of business, there."

"Tell me something I don't already know."

"You're an asshole," Gregor shot back.

I growled, and he laughed. "See, I knew you didn't know that. You still think you're an ace guy."

"Go fuck yourself. I'm losing my patience," I warned.

"Well, I'm not breaking the laws, so you can lose all the patience you want, buddy."

"I may not be able to kill you, Gregor, but do you really want to see my bad side? Like you said, I'm an asshole," I asked, cocking one eyebrow. I flexed my fist and watched closely as his eyes traveled down to see how tense my body was. I was ready to spring into action if he kept bullshitting me.

He held up his hands. "Calm down. You don't have to get physical."

"That's good to know 'cause you're ugly as fuck," I stated.

He huffed. "That's not nice."

I shrugged. "Maybe, but it's true. Demons aren't a handsome bunch."

He rolled his eyes. "Look, I don't know much, I swear."

"Tell me what you do know about this relic."

"Do you have the relic?"

I shook my head. "No, which is why I'm asking questions about it."

Gregor nodded. "I did hear about some human going around asking questions about how to transfer his soul into another body. The only reason I brought that up is because the demonic demigod and warlord, Astaroth, has the power to do that. So, maybe that guy has the relic."

Oh, he had the relic, all right, but now things were starting to make some sense to me. "Do you know who he went to for answers?"

Gregor shrugged. "The typical places, you know? Most humans don't think we exist, and those who do tend to get so excited when they discover the goth bar they've been wanting to visit may actually be patronized by a demon or two, or even a witch. They don't know about the real places that our kind usually hang out at."

"Except vampire bars," Ansell blurted out. I turned to look at him and give him a reprimanding expression, but he gave me a sweet smile that melted away whatever anger I might have had. He was just trying to help, and I did say he was my partner. "Sorry," he mouthed. I nodded, then returned my attention back to Gregor.

"Boyfriend?" Gregor asked, not that Ansell had his attention.

"Not your business, back to the subject," I said.

Gregor sighed. "Well, I would say check the vampire clubs. Or that book store, the Witches' Brew. A few humans know that the book club isn't your typical 'book club.'" He made air quotes.

"That's all you can tell me?" I asked.

He nodded. "Yeah, like I said, I've just been minding my own business, but when I do go to my hangouts, which… by the way, was Hypnotic, I hear things others say."

Hypnotic was the second location on my investigation trip. It was a dance club owned by the vampire, Lorcán Kennedy, Regent of Sector Dios in the kingdom of Nero, also known as Chicago. He was young for a regent, as most were at least a thousand and older… but he was badass and had earned the position. I wasn't looking forward

CIRCLE OF DARKNESS

to going there, because Lorcán was one evasive and arrogant bastard. But if whispers were heard there, then all the more reason for me to interrupt that bastard's day rest.

"If you hear anything else, call me. I mean it," I said.

"Don't worry, I will. I'd rather be on your good side than bad," Gregor said, then opened the door to his office.

I walked out and Ansell followed behind me. It wasn't until we got in the Jeep that he broke the silence.

"Are you mad at me for speaking in there?" he asked.

"I was at first, but I have to realize that we're partners. If you think of something I didn't, I have to allow you to voice it. I'm just so used to doing this alone," I said.

"Don't you work with Christian a lot?" Ansell asked.

"Only when the case is bigger than what I can handle. Most of the time, we're out there doing our own things, like now. He's on a case dealing with a missing child. We can't always be there for each other, so we have to be tough enough to handle things on our own," I said. I patted his thigh. "It was a good question. Sorry if I overreacted back there." I felt like I was the one who needed to apologize.

"I know you said that you were in control," Ansell said.

"Yeah, but we are also partners. I have to learn to work with you. If you think of something that you believe will be helpful info, go on and ask them. But if it gets tense, I'll step in," I said.

He nodded once. "Gotcha."

"Okay, he told me a lot without really telling me a lot," I said.

"What do you mean? We already knew Regis had the relic."

I started the Jeep and put it in reverse. "Yeah, but now I know his motivation. He wants Astaroth to grant him his wish of being younger, which is something that Astaroth can do. However, demons of his level normally don't play fair."

"Meaning?"

I put the Jeep in drive and started towards Hypnotic. "Say you want to be young again. A demon like Astaroth will grant your wish, only instead of being twenty-one again, your ass is now twenty-one days old. Maybe he turns you into a twenty-one-day-old embryo. If he's in a good mood, he might give you what you want, or he might fuck you over. That's the risk humans take when they make deals with demons."

"Damn, that's so messed up. I feel like I'm getting the craziest crash course ever," Ansell said.

"That's because you are. I'm dumping a lot on you, because we're in this together and these are things you need to know," I said, then continued. "If this idiot was using the *Soul of Agenta* to try to switch bodies, then he really fucked up. What he needed was the *Eye of Ezel*, which we happen to have back at home. Because it can switch souls, it's an extremely dangerous relic. Unfortunately, there are at least two more out there."

"Oh, that's a good thing, right, that he didn't have the right relic? That means he'll need to come to you for something," Ansell said.

I nodded. "That's my hope. That's if he doesn't bring Astaroth here first. That demon may not need the relic in order to fulfill the deal. I want to let the word get out that I have the *Eye of Ezel*. If Regis still wants it, he may take the bait. If so, I can put an end to this before matters get to shit-hitting-fan level."

"What can you tell me about Lorcán?" Ansell asked.

"He's a pain-in-the-ass vampire who's been helpful in the past. I don't deal with him often, because, like I said, the vamps tend to handle their own business. If I get wind of a human-vampire related death, I let him know. He's the regent of the area. It's his job to keep an eye out on vampire activity in this city. He makes sure no vampires are made without his permission and that newborns aren't abandoned by their sires. He also makes certain new vampires are made at some point, and if there's a rogue, he handles it."

"Wait a minute, they are still allowed to make vampires?" Ansell asked and he looked pissed.

I nodded. "Only if people want it. The Chasseur Institute decided a long time ago that you couldn't stop people from doing what they want to do. So, if they make that conscious decision to become a vampire, or witch or werewolf, etcetera, then that's on them. I mean, if they wanted us to hunt down every human who switched sides, Vixen would be on their hit list. Both sides had to compromise." I wanted him to understand the world we lived in, both the light and dark sides of it. When I mentioned Vixen's name, he seemed to calm down a little, and that was good. I guess he was starting to understand.

"I see your point… it's just… I hate that they can make more monsters," he said.

I nodded. "Yeah, me too, but it is what it is. As long as they keep it together, I go on about my business, Chris, as well. Of course, he doesn't like them even more than me. He has never met Lorcán, probably because he'd be too tempted to chop off his head if they were ever in the same room together."

Ansell arched both eyebrows inquisitively. "Oh really? Why?"

I sighed. "A long, ugly history with vampires. His entire family was killed by vampires. Mom, father, sister, and brother. He is the sole survivor and beneficiary of the family fortune."

Ansell gasped. "Oh my god! That's so sad, no wonder he hates vampires. I'd hate them too." The look of anguish on his face proved that he was horrified. He really didn't know Chris that well, or much at all, but he was hurt by the knowledge of what happened to his family. That just made me like Ansell even more. He was empathetic.

I nodded. "Yeah, it was rough for him going through all that shit. I think the police still have him as their suspect even though they had no evidence he had anything to do with it. Chris really is one of the strongest guys I know. I mean, on top of that horrible shit happening to him, a vampire almost took him out when we were teenagers. It was our first mission. I was to stand back and only step in if or when it looked like he couldn't succeed on his own. The vampire was clever, and we both underestimated him. He bit Chris, and would have killed him had I not intervened. He just has a distrust of them."

"Shit, I don't blame him. I'd be scared of them, too. They've pretty much stolen everything from him. He has no family now because of them."

"Distrust, not fear," I corrected. "He hates them to his very core, but he doesn't fear them."

"Sorry," he said with a slight pout that made him look so fucking hot. I loved how he poked out that bottom lip. Mmmm, I was going to get it soon. "Didn't meant to imply that he was scared of them. I am, though."

"And you should be, because you have common sense. And it's okay about Chris." I just didn't want him thinking Christian was afraid to deal with the vampires. So not true. He'd fuck one up one of these days. We weren't kids anymore. It was just that he didn't care to be in their presence.

"Thanks."

"No biggie. Besides, you look so fucking cute when you pout," I said, giving into my lust for just this moment. I grabbed him by the back of his head and leaned over, kissing him deeply. I wanted to show him what a real kiss felt like and to give him a little taste of what was to come… and hopefully cum. I devoured his mouth, claiming him as mine, and he gave himself to me, moaning the whole time. I didn't want to, but I had to pull away. The people behind me were beeping because the light had changed.

"What… what was that?" he asked as if he were out of breath. I knew he was because I'd stolen it away.

"That, my Ansell… was a kiss," I said, then sped off. The erection I got kissing him was worth it to see the look on his face and his own tent in his pants. I couldn't wait to be inside of him. Shit… depending on how he took to the first butt plug, we might be good to go. I didn't know if I could hold off for five days. Shit, five minutes was starting to become a challenge. I didn't want to rush things with Ansell. I wanted him to enjoy every second of it. I also didn't know what was going to happen with us afterward. Shit, maybe that was why I kept wanting to focus on the case and derailed us getting together every time we got into the mood. Granted, the case was insanely important, but I also felt that Ansell was too. Shit, I knew it was inevitable, he already had a vision about us entangled in my bed. But what happens to us afterward? That was what… that was what scared me. I wanted him so badly; at times, he was all I could think about. But then, I was afraid of what those feelings meant. I'd never had them before.

Fuck! I needed to clear my mind. Again. I didn't say anything else on the ride over and neither did he. It didn't take us long to get to Hypnotic, which was a trendy club with mirrored walls on the outside that the patrons loved to look at themselves in.

"Is he going to be mad that we're waking him up?" Ansell asked as he kept step with me as I walked towards the side door.

"Oh yeah, but I don't give a shit. Vampires can be up during the day, they just don't like to. They aren't as powerful during the day either, a lot of their abilities don't work or don't work as well. So, night is their time to shine, so to speak. But, I need some answers from him," I said, then I banged hard as hell on the door several times until it opened. Standing on the other side with a very agitated expression on his face was Stephan, Lorcán's day watcher.

"What the fuck, man? Why are you here, and at this time of day?" Stephan asked.

"I'm here on official business, so go wake up your master," I said as I pushed my way past him and walked inside.

He snarled as Ansell followed in behind me. "He's not going to be happy you're here," Stephan said.

"Do I look like I care? I wouldn't be here if it wasn't important." I pointed to one of the many black leather booths in the place. "I'll just sit here until you get him." I sat down and Ansell took the seat beside me.

Stephan crossed his arms over his chest as he approached my booth. "You fucking hunters are habitual line steppers. One day, he might not be so friendly."

"And when that day comes, I won't be so nice," I shot back. I watched as his jaw tightened, but he refrained from giving me any more veiled threats.

"Wait here and don't touch shit." Stephan pointed to the bar. "That's not open, so don't make yourselves at home."

"I wouldn't dream of drinking your cheap, watered-down liquor. I'm sure he keeps the good stuff for himself," I said.

Stephan rolled his eyes, then turned, walking away from us. I knew he was heading upstairs to where his master slept and I sat back and turned to Ansell. "So, any questions?"

He nodded. "Lots. First, day watcher?"

"Yeah, a vampire of Lorcán's stature would no doubt have a daytime protector," I said. "Don't let his looks fool you, he's a deadly bastard. I only know that because I've seen Stephan in action. A team of rogue hunters came here to attack Lorcán during the day. They never made it past Stephan. Of course, I got wind of it and came to warn him just in time right before they attacked the place."

"Really, okay… so what happened to the hunters?" Ansell asked. He looked so excited to be learning all of this information.

"Like with monsters who break the rules, they died. We have to be fair all around. We aren't supposed to hunt and kill monsters without just cause. We have to have proof that a law was broken before we can carry out executions. Lorcán obeys the rules. He keeps the other vampires in line. I was honor bound to warn him of the attack and assist. Now, I can take Stephan, but let's just say, I wouldn't leave unscathed," I said, giving credit where credit was due. Sure, he looked like a fop at times with his extravagant fashion sense, but he'd take off his Armani and the Rolex to whoop some ass. God forbid if you made him break a sweat or force his heavily product-styled ginger hair out of place. He also didn't take kindly to people making fun of his freckles. I had to admit, Stephan was a looker with his bright blue eyes and well-toned body. I wondered if Lorcán and he ever fucked.

I'd be surprised if they didn't. Considering he was his day watcher, the two pretty much went hand in hand with bedmate, too.

"I'm confused," Ansell said out of the blue.

I frowned. "Confused about what?"

"Why would a vampire have a human watching over them?"

I snorted. "Oh, because he's no regular human. He feeds on Lorcán's blood, which makes him powerful as hell and gives him long-lasting life. For as long as I've known Lorcán, which—granted—has only been about three years, Stephan has been his day watcher. For all I know, Stephan might be over a hundred years old."

"Okay, wow... when you said your world was dangerous and that there was a lot to learn, you weren't joking," Ansell said, shaking his head again. I was sure he was feeling overwhelmed by the amount of info he was getting, although I knew he believed every word I said.

"You have no idea," I stated. I looked up when the elevator doors opened on the second level. I watched as Lorcán stepped off, yawning. Stephan was trailing behind him.

"Oh my!" Ansell gasped, and I tossed him a look. "Sorry, but he's hot."

"Not better than me."

"Ehh," he teased with a waggle of his hand as if to say, *maybe*.

I laughed, then turned to meet Lorcán as he approached wearing black satin pajama pants and a robe—untied. I did have to admit, he was gorgeous. Not all vampires had model looks, but he did. You could clearly see his Mexican and Irish heritage in his sun-kissed, tanned skin, piercing green eyes, narrow nose, perfectly lined jaw, and killer body. Yeah, I really couldn't fault Ansell for looking. He better just know who he belonged to. I'd already laid claim on my Ansell.

"Why are you here?" Lorcán asked, his Hispanic accent a little groggy and thick.

"I need some answers about a guy who may have come here looking for a transference spell," I said.

He stood with his hands on his hips. Stephan stood behind him with his hands still crossed over his chest. "This idiot sounds very familiar. What do I get in return for helping?"

"My gratitude," I shot back.

"Which is worth shit. How about a cup of your blood? I bet hunter's blood—correction, the blood of a Chasseur hunter is the elixir of all elixirs," Lorcán said. "We both know your lot are not like the run-of-the-mill hunters."

I scoffed. This was why I hated having to be bothered with this bastard. "For a cup of my blood, motherfucker, you better deliver me the man yourself. Then, and only maybe then, we could talk about me opening a vein."

I watched his gaze sharpen, then he smirked. "One day, I will taste such a delicacy."

"Is that a threat?" I asked, rising to my feet. I was about an inch taller than him, making Lorcán six-feet even.

He shook his head. "Not a threat. Just one day, you or your partner will need my help at any cost and you already know my price. For now, I'll tell you what I can. If only to keep the peace between our two factions. The man's name is Regis Maxfield. He came to me, had heard that I was the real thing, a vampire. Apparently, the demons at Hellfire have loose lips."

He walked over to Stephan, grabbing a handful of the ginger's hair, then yanked it back, revealing the thick, bluish veins in Stephan's neck. He struck, sinking his fangs deeply into the man's artery. I heard Ansell gasp, but I put my hand on his shoulder, steadying him. Vampires liked all the human emotions: fear, lust, anger, etc… It helped whet their appetite. Meanwhile, Stephan was on cloud nine, moaning and rubbing his body along Lorcán's as the vampire fed from him. I bet the feeling was euphoric, at least, that was what I heard. Even Christian admitted to it feeling exceptionally good that one time he'd been bitten.

Once he'd gotten his fill, he released Stephan, licking the wounds closed. He turned his attention back to me. I bet he wanted to see if I was affected by his public feeding, but it was nothing I hadn't seen before.

"Are you done? Can we get back to the reason why I'm here?" I asked.

He chuckled as he ran his tongue over his bottom lip, licking up the smear of blood on it. "Sure. I was a bit parched, not used to waking up so early. Anyway, he came to me, begging for me to turn him into a vampire once he was young again, because he wants immortality and doesn't care about the cost. I told him that I wasn't interested and sent him on his way."

"Why weren't you interested?" I was curious as to why he'd turn down a man who was obviously rich as hell. Regis, especially if he managed to get himself into a younger body, could be beneficial to Lorcán's vampire sovereign.

"Old, vile, disgusting thing. His desperation was repulsive to me... and his botched plastic surgery." He shivered as he thought back to Regis, then scoffed. "I would suggest you go to Hellfire. Someone there told him to contact the demon, Orcal, in order to help him become younger. From what I've heard of that demon, he was banished to hell and is a minion of the demigod, Astaroth. As you know, demons never do anything for free," Lorcán said. "Now, that's all I know. If you will." He gestured toward the side door we came in through.

I caught the hint. "I'm sure we'll see each other again."

He smiled, revealing just a hint of fang. "Don't we always."

I let him have the last word, because if I didn't, we might be talking way into the sunset with him trying to get the last word in. I gestured for Ansell to follow me and we were out of there.

"Wow, I can't believe I was just in a room with a real-life vampire. Oh my god!" Ansell blurted out enthusiastically before we could get back to my Jeep.

"Yeah, as you can see, he put on a show for you. I'm sure he read your mind and saw that you were a virgin—"

"What?!" Ansell exclaimed.

I chuckled. "A virgin to this world," I said, completing my thought. "But hey, if you were thinking about that other virgin status of yours in there… he may have read that, too." I turned, taking him into my arms, and grabbed a handful of that ass I'd been licking my lips at since we'd been together. "This is mine, so no sharing."

Ansell smiled and I couldn't help myself. I had to kiss him again. Once more, I made him weak in the knees and I loved it. Maybe Vixen was right, every time I touched Ansell, I never wanted to let him go. That connection between us that came to life with a spark just drew me closer to him. I wondered if he felt the same way. For now, I let him go, because we had a demon bar to go to. For the most part, none of the heavy hitters hung out at the Hellfire bar. Maybe it was too tawdry for their tastes, who the fuck knows.

"Where to now?" Ansell asked as we climbed into my Jeep.

"Hellfire. Maybe you can ask the questions, just to get your feet wet. I'll have your back, this time," I said. It was about time he saw and truly experienced what this was all about. If we were going to have a future after that special night, then it was time we made sure that could come true, too.

Chapter Twelve

Angel

"Me?" I asked D'Angelo nervously. "I'd have no idea where to begin." I was blown away that he was willing to trust me with such an important task, but I wasn't ready for it. *Was I?*

"What do we know so far?" D'Angelo patiently asked me while he started his Jeep and pulled out of the parking spot.

"Regis wants to be young again and he's wheeling and dealing to make that happen," I replied. "He needs the assistance of a demon named Orcal, but rumor has it that he's been banished to hell to be a minion for Astaroth, the soul snatcher," I said.

"See, you're getting it," D'Angelo said, competently navigating through traffic. "What worries you most about questioning the demons?"

"I don't understand the demon hierarchy," I answered. "I don't want to mess up."

"We'll get into all of that later back at home," D'Angelo said. "Right now, just trust the instincts you're honing without realizing it and ask the questions we need answered. Remember," D'Angelo reached over and squeezed my thigh comfortingly, "I'll be right there with you."

"Okay. I can do this," I said, not sure which of us I was trying to convince.

"Of course, you can," D'Angelo responded confidently.

Luckily, the drive from Hypnotic to Hellfire was quick, which meant I didn't have enough time to talk myself out of my newfound confidence. I walked tall beside D'Angelo and my poise stayed with me until every person—or demon, rather—looked at us when we walked into the bar. I stopped in my tracks and tried to calmly assess the situation. I drew on D'Angelo's strength behind me. I felt the pressure of his strong hand on my lower back.

"You've got this, Ansell."

"I didn't expect to see so many people here at this time of day," I said quietly. Human bars and clubs were never packed with patrons that early in the evening. Admittedly, I lost track of time in all the excitement, but it couldn't have been much later than five o'clock when we arrived at Hellfire. Some of the patrons even rose to their feet when they saw us like they expected trouble. "They look very unhappy to see us."

"They're unhappy to see me," D'Angelo said. I noted a hint of pride in his voice. "Remember, just because we agree to play nice doesn't mean we like or respect one another."

One man looked particularly nervous to see D'Angelo inside his favorite watering hole. The slender man swallowed hard and turned an unpleasant shade of white. "What'd you do to him?" I asked D'Angelo.

"He had answers I needed about some rogue witches wreaking havoc and didn't want to give them up. Turned out he was intimately involved with one of the witches and was afraid of what she'd do to his dick if she ever found out he talked about her or her coven," D'Angelo told me.

"And you somehow convinced him to talk with his dick on the line?"

"Well, I convinced him to roll the dice on the witch," D'Angelo answered smugly. "It was easy to do when I had a death grip on the man's cock. With me, losing his dick was a given; with her, he stood a fighting chance at keeping it."

"I can see why that tactic worked," I commented, trying to keep my jealousy of D'Angelo touching another dude's dick out of my voice. I had no right to be jealous; I knew damn well the man wasn't virginal like me.

"It wasn't about pleasure, Ansell," he practically purred in my ear. "He had answers that I needed. It was business." Though it might've been true, I still didn't like it.

The man tending bar stood to his full height and flipped the white towel over his shoulder. "What do you want, hunter?" His voice was rough and gravelly and it sent shivers of dread down my spine. I couldn't believe that D'Angelo expected *me* to get information out of badass demons.

"Information only, Barron." D'Angelo held both of his hands up, signaling that he'd come in peace. I missed the warmth from his hand, but his faith in my abilities kept me calm and focused.

"We don't have answers," said a blond man wearing a battered, black leather jacket. He rose from his stool and nodded his head to the door behind us. "Get on out of here."

"Keep your cool, Will," Barron warned. "Go ahead and ask your questions, hunter."

"Which one of you told Regis Maxfield about the demon, Orcal?" I boldly asked.

"Who the fuck is this punk? He's no fucking executioner and we don't owe him a fucking thing," the hostile man named Will said. I received the resistance I expected, but I didn't let that stop me.

D'Angelo believed in me and it was time I believed in myself. I raked my eyes up and down his body dispassionately, so he knew his badass routine didn't shake me a bit. The ultimate badass stood next to me and I instinctively knew that Will was no match for D'Angelo.

"You're going to answer every question he asks," D'Angelo said, his voice having dropped to a low growl.

"Or what?" Will asked, clearly looking to push his luck.

A vision hit me fast and swift, catching me off guard. The closer I got physically to D'Angelo, the easier my visions came to me. Sure, it could've been the enchantment in the amulet that Vixen hung around my neck, but I knew the source of the magic came from the man beside me. As if sensing the change in my body, D'Angelo moved closer to me to offer protection in case my vision left me vulnerable to an attack. Already, we were an amazing team, and I was excited to see what we could do once I got some training.

"I have the answers we need," I told D'Angelo as my vision played out behind my closed eyes. "Fonzy over there," I said, using the name of a popular television character who wore a black leather jacket and acted tough, "is the one who told Regis how he can turn back the time on aging."

"I don't know what the fuck this weird-ass is talking about," Will argued, but he sounded a little nervous to me. I blocked out his blathering and focused on my vision.

"He was wearing that stupid leather jacket that night too, but he wore a Rolling Stones T-shirt instead of the classic '50s white one he's wearing now. There was a band doing a cover of 'Closer' by Nine Inch Nails. Barron wasn't behind the bar; a bald man who looked like Mr. Clean was serving drinks." Will gasped and I knew my vision was dead-on. I opened my eyes and found him watching me in fear. "You told Regis Maxfield to summon the demon, Orcal, with the Soul of Agenta. You even told him where he could find it, Will."

"I…"

"Don't bother lying to me," I snapped. I saw the truth of my words in his eyes and it emboldened me to push on. "How many hundreds were in that stack he handed you? Ten? Fifteen? Were the lives of dozens of people worth it to you?" I thought about how close I came to losing D'Angelo and I was ready to rip that man apart on my own. "You are responsible for the lives already lost and the ones who'll die for your greed."

Will took a step toward me but two burly-looking bouncers seized him by his arms. "You're not going anywhere," one of them said harshly to Will, who began to fight in earnest. "You better save your fight for when you go in front of the council."

"No," Will said, struggling to get free. "They'll sentence me to death. Barron, you can't let them do this to me. I have a good explanation."

Barron watched dispassionately as the bouncers dragged Will toward a door at the front of the bar. He didn't appear to be fazed by the man crying and begging for his help. He resumed wiping down the bar as if it was an everyday occurrence.

Will kicked out and hit one the bouncers in the nuts just as they reached the door. Turns out, demon nuts hurt just as badly as human ones when they're racked. It was the break that Will needed and he jerked away from one of his captors when he doubled over in pain. Will rounded on the second bouncer, prepared to strike, but his face connected with the meaty fist of the other man before he could act first. Will fell unconscious to the ground in a heap at the bouncer's feet.

"I ought to kick him in his puny nuts to see how he likes it," the wounded bouncer said once he was able to stand.

"Nah," the second bouncer said, "wait until he's conscious again so you know he feels the sting."

"Good idea."

Each bouncer grabbed one of Will's arms and dragged him through the door.

Barron turned and looked at me, not D'Angelo, when the

bouncers and Will were gone. "Did you get the information you needed?"

"I have one question," D'Angelo said before I could respond. Barron turned his attention to him and he asked, "Can you confirm that Orcal crossed the plane? Did you feel him?"

Barron responded with a slight nod of the head before he returned to wiping down the bar in front of him.

"That'll be all then. Let's head home," D'Angelo said softly from beside me.

Home was something I'd never had and the thought that D'Angelo could be my home excited me even more than the prospect of knowing him physically. In all my fantasies of D'Angelo, I never imagined what would happen *after* the loving was over between us. I could chalk that up to not being very imaginative, or I could accept the fact that I knew my heart couldn't handle seeing something I'd always craved but would never have for myself.

D'Angelo and I hadn't discussed what would happen between us once the case was solved. I sensed his hesitation to let me go and heard the growing affection in his words when he'd confessed the reasons he offered the job to Meggie. Even though I'd seen and heard the proof, a large part of me was still afraid to believe. Face down demons in a bar? Sure, no problem. Chance my heart to the only man I wanted to belong to, the only one whose rejection I couldn't endure? I wasn't sure I was strong or brave enough.

The thrill of my first successful interrogation spiked my already high level of lust. I boldly grabbed a fistful of D'Angelo's shirt when we got in his Jeep and pulled him to me for a kiss. I tasted his surprise, but that soon gave way to desire. I tried to climb the console that separated us, but D'Angelo placed a hand on my chest and gently pushed back until we broke our kiss.

"I want you," I told D'Angelo. "Now."

"Baby, we talked about this," D'Angelo said soothingly.

"I don't want to wait for days. I need you tonight."

"I'll take care of you when we get home, Ansell. I promise." D'Angelo turned away from me and started the ignition. I placed my hand on his leg and began stroking the length of his thigh.

※

Peals of feminine laughter and a delicious aroma of Italian food greeted us when we returned home. My stomach growled loudly as I sniffed the air.

D'Angelo chuckled, then threaded his fingers with mine and pulled me toward the kitchen. "I think our sexy time will have to wait a little bit. It seems you have a visitor?"

"Me?" I asked, but then I recognized my best friend's throaty laugh. "Meggie!" I exclaimed. I found her in the kitchen, sitting at the table with Jinx and Vixen. Her long red locks were pinned in a messy bun on top of her head and the relaxed smile on her face was one I'd never seen in the years I'd known her. It seemed to me that I wasn't the only one benefiting from time spent beneath their roof.

"Hi, honey," she said happily when she looked up from her massive plate of spaghetti. She had always been able to eat ten times her weight in pasta. "This is the best spaghetti I've ever had. You must eat some."

"Better than Martinelli's?" I asked her.

"Yes, but don't tell Mario that I said that." She waved her hand toward the empty place setting beside her. "Sit down and eat. Tell me about your day. Did you shake down demons for information?"

I stood staring at her in shock. I had told D'Angelo that I would tell Meggie the truth about the circumstances that I—we—found ourselves in so she could decide what she wanted to do, but I was prepared to ease her into it.

"The girls briefed me on the situation," she said calmly. "They knew you'd try to handle me with kid gloves and I really don't need it."

"It's a lot to take in," I told her. "Demons, witches, vampires, and superhuman beings who fight the big baddies in the world. You seem to have handled the news admirably well."

"The wine has helped," she said, holding up a nearly empty wineglass. "Look, Angel," she began softly, "I appreciate the way you want to protect me because no one else has ever cared to try, but I'm a big girl and I can take care of myself. Besides, I've had plenty of run-ins with humans vile enough to make these demons look like fluffy kittens."

I knew that Meggie had been through a lot, but nothing she had endured would compare to what would happen if a demon decided to rip her to shreds. I could tell that she'd made up her mind, and like me, felt comfortable and safe for the first time in a very long time, if ever. I wouldn't take that away from her.

My response was to walk to her and drop a kiss on her forehead before I sat beside her. I didn't realize how hungry I was until I inhaled the smells of Italian food. I heaped food onto my plate while D'Angelo chuckled in the seat beside me.

"It's good that you're loading up on some carbs, Ansell. You're going to need them," he said low enough so only I heard him.

My hand shook slightly as I brought the fork to my mouth. I was so tempted to set it back down and demand that D'Angelo take me upstairs right then. I knew firsthand how well spaghetti reheated, but one of the ladies went to the trouble of feeding us and it would be rude not to appreciate their efforts.

"Oh. My. God," I said with a mouthful of food.

"Right?" Meggie asked. "Best I've ever had."

"That's what she said," Vixen said, nodding toward Jinx.

"You got that right," Jinx said emphatically, causing Vixen's cheeks to flush.

"What did you learn today?" Vixen asked, changing the subject.

I listened to D'Angelo tell the girls what we had discovered, even though most of it went over my head. It didn't help that D'Angelo traced my thigh teasingly beneath the table as he talked like I'd done to him as he drove home. So far, I understood that Regis got the name of the demon who could change him back to a younger version of himself, but possibly used the wrong relic to attempt it. The Soul of Agenta would open Regis up for demon possession, not give him the youth he craved. We knew Orcal crossed over and suspected that he has had Regis doing his dirty work for him.

"Lorcán mentioned that there were rumors that Orcal had been banished to hell to be Astaroth's bitch, but I don't know that for sure. It seems likely since Orcal, through Regis, gained the Stone of Astaroth and is collecting souls," D'Angelo said.

Jinx placed her delicate hand to her neck and said, "That's some dangerous shit."

"It is," D'Angelo confirmed. "But, I know how to lure Regis out of hiding. We have what he needs to regain his youth."

"We do?" Vixen asked.

"The Eye of Ezel," D'Angelo told her. "We'll use it to draw him out once we find him. Let's hope his greed will lead us to Orcal."

"Do you have any idea why Orcal was banished to hell?" Jinx asked.

"Orcal tried to free Astaroth a few centuries ago and that's how the relic had five hundred sixty-four souls inside it already. Orcal was taken out by a hunter by the name of Bart Nappenstern before he could collect the one thousand souls needed," D'Angelo told them. "He's a demon and his motivation is simple: avoid a trip back to hell where he belongs.

"Do you have any single men around here?" Meggie piped up, changing the subject. "It's clear that you two are in love," she gestured between Vixen and Jinx before looking at D'Angelo and me. "It's clear the two of you are heading toward something. Am I going to be overhearing headboards hitting the wall all night long with no one to wear out my frustrations on?"

"Nah, the walls are made of thick concrete to protect us from a demon attack," Jinx told her. "Christian is the only other team member, but he's gay like us."

Meggie let out a long-suffering sigh. "Fine. Maybe you'll recruit a new member who'll rock my socks."

"One never knows," Jinx responded.

"I do sometimes," I said jokingly, earning laughs from everyone but Meggie.

She pointed her fork at me and scowled. "I'm going to need an explanation why you didn't trust me with the truth about your abilities. Not tonight," she amended quickly. "I can see you have plans." Jinx and Vixen whistled and catcalled from the opposite side of the table. Jinx winked lecherously at me while Vixen grinned from ear to ear.

I felt the skin on my face flush hot with embarrassment over the teasing my friends gave me. It was the most awkward moment of my life until D'Angelo took my fork from my hand and set it on top of my plate.

"We need to go now. I can't take another second of that blushing." D'Angelo rose from his chair and pulled mine back from the table. He reached for my hand and pulled me to my feet, then tugged me out of the room without so much as a goodnight to the girls.

"D'Angelo," I said in horror. "They're all going to know what we're about to do."

"And this bothers you?"

I thought about it for a whole two seconds. Did it bother me? "Nope."

⁂

We made a quick trip into my bedroom long enough to retrieve the black box containing the butt plugs from my nightstand. "You'll be staying with me tonight," D'Angelo said. Somehow, he made those words sound slightly threatening. "You don't get to come again until I do."

"So, in like ten minutes," I said hopefully.

D'Angelo didn't slow down until we reached the privacy of his room. "This is only day one of five," he said.

"Just kill me now then," I whined. It felt like an evil fever took over my body and left me aching everywhere—partly because of my raging desire to be with him and partly because of the secret I'd been keeping all day long.

"Give me a few days and you'll die from pleasure," D'Angelo said confidently as he set the box on his bed. "Maybe we can speed things up a bit by skipping the smallest plug. Hell, if you ever fingered your own ass then you'd…" D'Angelo's words died in his throat when he flipped open the box and saw that a plug was already missing. "What have you done?" he asked me.

"I fast-tracked my anal training," I told him smartly. I pointed down to where the second from the largest plug was missing from the box. "I decided waiting five days wasn't acceptable to me. I can't be sure that I'll live that long."

"Ansell," D'Angelo admonished at hearing my words.

"None of us can be sure we'll be here the next minute, let alone five days." I pulled my T-shirt over my head and toed off my shoes. "It's been a little uncomfortable at times today, but all I had to do was think of how amazing it would feel to have you inside me to change my discomfort into wanting."

D'Angelo just stood there staring at me until I reached for the zipper to my jeans. He knocked my hand away so he could take over the task. D'Angelo's smoldering eyes never left mine as he slowly eased the zipper down. I wondered if the sound of the metal scraping along the teeth was louder to him with his enhanced hearing. Or, was he able to drown the sound out to focus on a different sound, like the wild pounding of my heart.

"You could've hurt yourself," he admonished softly, but he didn't sound very angry. The hungry look in his eyes told me he wasn't mad at me; it was more like mad to have me.

"I was made for you," I told him as he pushed my jeans down to my ankles. I stepped out of them and pointed to my erection tenting the front of my black briefs. "I'm obviously excited about the idea of us, not afraid." D'Angelo released a long, shaky breath and I knew his surrender was near. "I *need* this, D'Angelo. I *need* you."

I had no idea where the hell my courage to seduce and push him came from, but I embraced it. Maybe it was because of the uncanny connection that grew between us or perhaps it was the raw hunger I saw in his eyes. As wild as he looked in that moment with his flaring nostrils and hard breathing, I knew with complete certainty that the only true pain would come when we separated after our joining was over.

D'Angelo hadn't been inside me yet, but I already resented the moment he would withdraw from my body. I knew without a doubt that I'd ache to have him fill me again as soon as possible, yet beneath the lust boiling in my blood was a yearning for a deeper connection than I could ever fathom before I met him. He made me feel stronger, braver, and hornier than I'd ever felt in my life.

In fact, I didn't wait for him to make the next move. I pushed my briefs down my legs so that I stood in front of him naked and wanting. I had zero experience to fall back on, but I'd seen enough visions of the two of us to know what he liked. Yes, I knew he was hung, uncut, and would love me playing with his foreskin. I also knew that he craved my ass like a drug he couldn't get enough of to please him. I proudly turned so he could get his first look at my bare ass. D'Angelo's breath hissed between his lips seconds before I felt the warmth of his hand on a rounded cheek.

"Perfection," he whispered darkly as he traced his finger over the curve of my ass. "I'm going to own it and every part of you, Ansell."

"Yes." My whisper sounded like both a plea and a promise.

"Let's make you comfortable," D'Angelo said. He placed both hands on my shoulders and turned me to face him. "Get on my bed and lie down on your stomach." His no-nonsense tone sent chills dancing down my spine.

I did what he commanded and listened to the sounds of him undressing behind me. "I wanted to watch you undress," I said with a pout.

"Next time, you can undress me," D'Angelo replied. "I'm hanging on to my control by a thread and if you put your hands on my body, then I worry that thread will snap and I'll hurt you."

"You'd never," I told D'Angelo. I felt the bed dip under his weight and the heat rolling off his body as he straddled my thighs. His heavy erection felt hot against my bare flesh.

"Never intentionally," D'Angelo agreed. "Unfortunately, some pain will be necessary, but I promise you the pleasure will make up for it. I'll never take this gift for granted." He placed both of his hands on my ass cheeks and began to knead them. "I don't care what it costs me, Ansell. I'm going to make this night magical for you."

I had no doubt about that. D'Angelo moved his large hands around to massage every inch of my skin. When he got closer to my crack, I felt the plug move inside me. It nudged the bundle of nerves that sent pleasure screaming through my body. That alone was almost enough to make me come.

I moaned loud and proud, not bothering to temper my response to the things he made me feel and need. My legs were captured between his stronger ones, but I spread mine a little farther, invitingly. I desperately wanted him to replace the plug with his cock, to know what it really felt like to be coveted and desired by another living soul.

"I can feel how close you are to coming, Ansell. I can smell it, too." I felt the sticky, wet heat of my pre-cum on my stomach and loved that he could smell my desire for him.

I pressed against his hands, seeking more. "D'Angelo," I pleaded softly. His first response was a rumbling chuckle that made all the hair on my body stand up and his second response was to grip the handle of the butt plug that protruded from my ass. "Please."

"So needy," D'Angelo admonished playfully.

"Yessss," I hissed between my teeth when he pushed on the plug a little more, aiming it at my prostate gland. My ass clenched the plug tightly.

D'Angelo leaned over my back and pressed kisses between my shoulder blades, then worked his way down my spine. Each kiss or flick of his tongue against my goose-pebbled flesh caused my ass to clench and quiver with need. "Mmmm, look at that pucker." D'Angelo traced my stretched opening with his finger first, then his tongue.

"D'Angelo!" In all the visions I'd ever had, his tongue teasing my crinkled hole wasn't one of them.

"Damn, I'm going to need to make you yell my name more often." D'Angelo's threat sounded like a purred promise to my ears.

"Please do," I said, the thick lust in my voice rendered it unrecognizable to my ears.

My confidence only faltered briefly when D'Angelo slowly removed the plug from my ass, but then he soothed the stinging sensation with gentle flicks of his tongue. My gasp of surprise was met with the sexiest declaration ever spoken. "Nothing about you will ever be off-limits to me. There will never be a part of you that I don't want to taste and know intimately."

D'Angelo lifted off me and I heard him fumbling around in the drawer of the table beside his bed. He found what he needed quickly and returned to me. "Roll over, Ansell."

I did so immediately and got my first look at his naked body in real life. My eyes feasted on the defined muscles in his arms and upper chest before they trailed lower to take in his cut abs and happy trail that led to the promise land. D'Angelo's thick dick hung proudly between his legs and I swallowed hard because I was going to need to stretch a hell of a lot more to accommodate that.

"It's not too late to change your mind," D'Angelo said tenderly. "We can wait and…"

"No, I want you now," I demanded. I reached for his cock, but he blocked my hands.

"Put your hands over your head and keep them there. I'm having a hard enough time behaving as it is," D'Angelo warned.

"Behave? Fuck that," I said, but I raised my hands above my head anyway. I regretted it immediately, because I had the strongest urge to trace my fingers over the intricate tattoo of a pentagram inside a circle on his chest. It was like it called to me, but I decided to wait until after D'Angelo claimed me. I'd have plenty of time to lick and touch it later.

My eyes shifted down to where D'Angelo rolled a condom down the length of his erection. I told myself to just relax and breathe because he wouldn't hurt me anymore than necessary. D'Angelo growled in pleasure when he pushed my legs back to expose myself more to him.

"Mine," he said while slicking my hole with oiled fingers. "All mine."

"Yours," I agreed, somehow knowing that I'd never give that part of me to another man for as long as I lived. Only D'Angelo.

I shook with anticipation—and a little fear—when D'Angelo leaned over me and pressed the tip of his dick against my opening. I saw the question in his light gaze and my words failed me. I nodded my head that I was certain I wanted him.

"D'Angelo!" I cried out when the head of his dick penetrated my virgin passage. He stopped and allowed me time to adjust to his girth before he inched a little further. Sweat popped up all over my body; I was burning hot and freezing cold at the same time as he continued to push inside until he was fully sheathed inside my body.

Something happened then that defied reason and logic, but I was living in a world with vampires, demons, witches, and hunters. Nothing should've shocked me at that point, but the shimmering lightness I felt in my soul right then did. It got stronger until it felt like my entire being was alight with the purest love. I think I would've levitated right off the bed had I not been tethered to D'Angelo.

D'Angelo's lips parted and he gasped softly. "Do you feel that, Ansell?"

"What's happening?" I asked in astonishment. I'd had orgasms before and this euphoric feeling far surpassed an orgasm.

D'Angelo lowered himself on top of me, threaded his fingers through mine over my head, and kissed me with a passionate promise I didn't know existed in the world. He pulled back after several long moments and smiled down at me with eyes alight with wonder. "Our souls have bonded, Ansell. You're my mate."

Chapter Thirteen

D'Angelo

I had heard others describe how amazing the mating bond felt. The connection of minds, bodies, and souls. It seemed like an earth-shattering experience... one Christian and I never thought we'd feel because we were gay. Everyone at the Institute was straight and the bonding ritual between mates was as important to the mission as it was to the relationship. More hunters could be born from their union. Humans with amazing abilities from both of their parents. It was one of the strong points of the Institute. Homosexuality was extremely rare among the chosen and once they found out that Christian and I were both gay, we were cast out. That was why we had formed the Genesis Circle.

The moment I saw Ansell, I knew there was something about him that drew me to him. But I was afraid to act on impulse where he was concerned. What could I have offered him other than a fantastic lay before I disappeared from his life? That was what the others

I'd had sex with received. My life was so dangerous, I didn't want to let my feelings for Ansell bring him into my world. So, I told myself that we weren't meant for each other. I kept him at bay… but it would seem that I never had the right to keep him away from me. Fate made that decision for the both of us. Apparently, there was someone out there for me. I wasn't destined to die without ever knowing what love felt like. I now knew what it meant to have someone in my life who'd always be there for me no matter what, and I'd always be there for him.

I released his fingers, freeing his hands as I pushed deeper into Ansell. Our bodies shuddered as the pleasure of our lovemaking rippled through us with such an intensity, I could barely hold off. I looked down at him, our eyes locking, and all I saw was the most beautiful being in the world. There was almost a light surrounding him and I wanted to cry because I was so happy. So complete. This one union was making everything else I'd ever known feel empty. This was what it was supposed to feel like when two people shared their bodies with each other.

"Oh god," I gasped as the ecstasy took hold of me again. My body actually shuddered with pleasure, if such a thing could be described.

"D'Angelo," Ansell purred, and I knew he was experiencing the same thing. A true union.

I loved the way his face flushed as I grazed his prostate. Every time his fingers brushed along my flesh, my body ignited with a new level of passion. I wanted all of him, every fiber of his body belonged to me, and vice versa. We were both smiling at each other and loving the sheer ecstasy we shared. I slid my hands up the length of his arms until I reached his hands and our fingers interlocked as I rocked back and forth on top of him, pumping my cock inside of his luscious body. His precious gift to me.

"Oh… oohhh," Ansell moaned, and it was the most lovely sound I'd ever heard. I leaned down, kissing him, and he returned my affection wholeheartedly. I lost track of time and everything else as we made love. Finally, the moment came when both of us felt the ultimate bliss of our union. My muscles tensed as the sensation rolled through me like a tsunami. I cried out and roared as my orgasm shook my body to my core. I could hear Ansell's loud moans and groans as he spasmed beneath me. The muscles in his thighs tightened around my waist and it was the sexiest thing I'd ever experienced.

Afterward, my limbs felt like spaghetti and I collapsed on top of Ansell, both of our chests heaving against each other. Neither of us could really move after what we'd just done. And lying there, on top of him, still inside of him, felt so perfect... I really didn't want to move.

"Baby... air is becoming an issue," Ansell squeezed out.

I chuckled and pulled back, only to flop down beside him, my hand still on his waist. It was as if I wanted that connection we shared while we had sex to never go away. I didn't want to be apart from him ever again. I loved the way our bodies sparked whenever we touched. It was all making sense, though, that spark wasn't a mated thing, it was just something special that Ansell and I shared. I knew that now.

"Whew, that was amazing!" Ansell beamed. "Is it always like that?"

I smiled. "Not ever, in my experience. I mean, I've enjoyed sex a great deal, but it's never felt like that."

"Is it because we're mated?" he asked.

I nodded. "Yeah." I brushed my fingers over his cheek, then leaned over, kissing him again. "I've never felt this connected with anyone in my life."

Ansell smiled widely, showing off all his pearly whites. "Me either. I never want this feeling to end."

"We're mated now, baby. At least now I know why we were so drawn to each other. We each were born for the other," I said as I brushed his bangs from his beautiful amber eyes.

"What does that even mean?" Ansell asked.

I propped myself up on my elbow and took a deep breath. "All right, ummm, remember when I told you that we were all chosen as children to be hunters?"

"Yeah." Ansell began to trace the dragon tattoo I had on my shoulder with his finger as he listened to me. I loved how he was biting his bottom lip as he gazed at me.

"Well, some hunters are born into the Institute because of mated unions between members. It's actually pretty rare for a hunter to find their mate, and it's only been documented cases of it being male and female. All of the hunters, be them male or female, are all straight. Once they passed the test and receive the tattoo, then they are expected to fullfill their duties under the rules of the Institute. They report to and live at the Institute for males or the one for females. Because Christian and I were gay, we were banished from the Institute."

"Holy shit… that's horrible. Those assholes," Ansell growled, and I smirked because it was so cute to see him pissed off, especially that little winkle in his brow.

"Yeah, that's what we thought too when they kicked us out. But of course, we were already indoctrinated, so to speak. We had the tattoos, knew the rules, and had the training. We also knew the truth about what was out there, so we created the Genesis Circle and carried out our sworn duties," I said.

"Do—I mean, did they try to stop you?" Ansell asked as he traced the intricacies of my other tattoo, my *Mark of Abrafo*, with his finger. I shivered a little as his soft touch sent tingles throughout my body. He looked up at me, smiled, then continued to trace my tattoo. Damn, he was so sweet and sexy.

I shook my head. "No, they didn't try to stop us. In spite of the Institute being the big kahuna, so to speak, of hunters… they know that other hunters are out there, and frankly, they could use the help. However, they did cut us off from their resources. So, if we catch ourselves in a pickle, we can't count on them for help."

"Uppity sons of bitches!" Ansell snapped.

"Yeah, pretty much." I laughed. "But getting back to the story. We were taught that homosexuality was a sin and, therefore, there could be no mates for any homosexual hunters and they were not worthy of the *Mark of Abrafo*. Christian and I knew we were different, but were too scared to say anything for fear that they'd kick us out. So, we kept quiet, took to the training, and when it came to the tattoo ceremony, I remember being terrified, thinking my flesh wouldn't be able to take the mark."

"Why?" Ansell asked as he continued to trace it.

"Because it's imbued with the blood of Christ and all other hunters before us."

Ansell's finger froze on one of the points on the mark and looked up at me. "Are you serious?"

I nodded. "Yes. It's a blessed mark, Ansell. That is why we can see the evil of demons for what they are regardless of their human faces. It's also the thing that gives us our strength and healing ability. It brings forth our own innate abilities. A child born of male and female mates can have more than one innate ability. Those children born into the Institute are stronger than those of us whose parents do not possess any abilities, like mine."

"Oh my god, so Jesus really did exist," Ansell said, and by how awe-inspired his words came out, I could tell he was still processing the information.

"Yes. Well, anyway, Christian and I pretended—"

"Wait, hold on. I'm sorry, but that's just not something you can gloss over like that," Ansell said.

I chuckled. "Sorry. I'm just so used to that knowledge, I have to remember you're still all new to this. Any questions?"

"Do they have any documents or real paintings of him?"

"One of his disciples started the church as a way to bring people to the light and train holy knights to fight against demons. Of course, the story of Jesus being betrayed by Judas is well known, but what isn't is that demon possession and influence played its part. Before Jesus died, his faithful disciple, Nathanael, captured his blood in a jar as he hung from the cross and it was used in a magic ritual to give power and abilities to the holy knights. This was two thousand years ago, and over time, the Institute was created to carry on the righteous, holy mission," I said, giving Ansell another crash course in my history.

"This is blowing my mind," Ansell said as he put his fingers to his temple. "You actually have a tattoo on your body that was made from the blood of Jesus Christ."

I nodded. "And every hunter after has placed a few drops of their blood into the jar. Chris and I did the day we received our tattoos."

Ansell looked up at me as a single tear rolled down his check. "You're a blessed holy knight. Are you sure we're really mated? I mean… I'm just a waiter—"

I cut him off right there with my finger to his mouth. "Jesus was a carpenter. Coming from humble beginnings isn't anything to feel ashamed about. But more importantly, you are so much more than a waiter, Ansell. You are a prophet, as you have the gift of sight. Even more important than that, is that you are and were born to walk this earth by my side as my mate. Don't ever doubt that or us again. I won't let you." Again, I grabbed him by the back of his head and pulled him to me for a kiss I knew would shake him to his soul. When I felt his cock harden against my thigh, I knew I'd succeeded. He needed to know how much he meant to me. I pulled away and looked at him, and he was grinning like a dope.

"Okay, I'm convinced."

I laughed. "Good. Okay, do you want me to continue with the other part of my story?"

He nodded. "Yeah, I just had to hear about the whole Jesus thing. I mean… wow!"

"Yeah, I was awestruck like you when I first found out. As for the Institute, Christian and I pretended to be straight for as long as we could, until neither of us could continue to live a lie. We confessed, and they promptly sent us on our way when we refused to mate with women. That was five years ago, and I couldn't be happier, because as it turns out… homosexuals *can* have mates. We can find love and we are worthy and blessed just like any other human. You have no idea what this means to me, Ansell."

"Actually, baby, I do."

I smiled, because it was the second time he'd called me baby, and I liked that shit. However, I wasn't so smitten that I didn't hear what he was saying. Apparently, my baby had a rough life, too.

"I can't see anyone ever mistreating you," I said, pulling him closer to me. Then I thought about how mean I was towards him earlier. Of course, it was coming from a place that didn't want to see him hurt, but I could have been nicer. I was glad he forgave me. Maybe he did that because he understood me better than anyone else did, even Christian, who was like my brother from another mother. I kissed the top of his head. "I'm so sorry for ever being cruel to you, Ansell."

He kissed my pec. "It's okay. I know why you were. You just wanted to protect me. But I wanted to protect you, so no matter how mean you were, I was never going to let you push me away."

I held him tighter, because now I knew he was my gift in life, and I was his. "I know. Thank you." I kissed his forhead again, and this time, he lifted his face up toward me and pressed his lips to mine. It was one of the best kisses I've ever had and I could only hope for more.

"So, we're mated?" Ansell asked, retrospectively.

"Yeah, that might explain why you have been experiencing stronger and more exact visions while being around me. My senses have grown stronger being around you," I said.

Ansell frowned. "How strong?"

I laughed. "I can still smell your cum from last night on your fingers, stomach, and cock even though you took a shower."

"Oh my god!" he gasped, appalled as he covered his face with his hands.

Awww, he looked too adorable right then. I pulled his hands

from his face, which was bright red at the moment. "Don't be shy. I like the way it smells on you. Makes me all kinds of… mmmm." I ended in a lusty growl because I was starting to feel my desire rising for an encore. No doubt, I was going to be making love to him again.

"I'm so embarrassed," he whined.

"Don't be. I'm just saying, we make each other the best versions of ourselves. That's what mates do, and I'm just so happy that we found each other, and in a restaurant, no less," I said. I thought back to when I'd first laid eyes on him. Who knew he was mine? The thought made me smile, but then I remembered what he said about his life and I wanted to know more.

"What you're saying makes a lot of sense. I was wondering why things were so different for me since meeting you. I mean, I even felt drawn to work at Martinelli's, so that's why I applied for a job there. I was in need of cash, too, so I didn't think much of it. They were hiring and it all worked out. But I had no idea how amazing things would fall into place," Ansell said.

"Finding your demon-hunting, stubborn mate over a plate of pasta and sauce?" I joked.

He laughed. "Yeah."

"That makes two of us. Now, I've told you a lot about me, I want to hear your tale, Ansell." He looked up at me with those beautiful eyes that held so much emotion and pain, I almost regretted asking, but I wanted to know more about my mate. But maybe I could let him tell me when he was ready. "Umm, if you're not ready to open up about your past, Ansell, you don't have to." I hoped that would give him comfort. Not everyone was ready to share. Hell, the only reason why I was so open was because he needed to know the truth about my world so he could be prepared. Knowledge was power, and considering what we were hunting, we needed a full arsenal. Anyway, I'd let it be his decision.

Chapter Fourteen

Angel

Typically, I didn't talk much about myself. In fact, I'd probably prefer to have a nail driven under my fingernail rather than talk about my past. Honestly, the nail would hurt so much less than rehashing the many ways I'd disappointed people in my life. Meggie was the only one I felt comfortable baring my soul to until D'Angelo came along. Truthfully, Meggie didn't know half of what I'd been through.

"I want to tell you everything, D."

"You have nothing to fear from me, Ansell. Ever."

I nodded because I knew he was right. There had always been a physical chemistry between us whenever we were in the same room, but that paled in comparison to the emotional connection I felt with him once we bonded. D'Angelo was my mate, my partner for life, and I instinctively knew that I could trust him with every piece of me—even the ones that others rejected.

"My father died in a work-related accident when I was an infant. My American mother never felt welcome in my father's Chinese family. She said that they never tried to know her or accept her into their lives, but I doubt she made it easy for them, nor do I think she tried to meet them halfway." I shook my head in disgust. "Apparently, losing their only son at the ripe old age of twenty-five wasn't punishment enough in my mom's eyes, because she packed our bags and we boarded a Greyhound bus for Chicago in the middle of the night. She told me that they didn't want me anyway, so why bother sticking around. I figured she was right because they never tried to locate me."

"I'm sorry, baby," D'Angelo said, reaching for me.

"My mother didn't talk about my father unless it was to run his family down. She'd tell me over and over how they didn't love me, but it was okay because she loved me enough for ten families. I believed her, D'Angelo. I thought she was the most amazing person in the world and I would have her love no matter what life threw at me, but it turned out to be nothing but lies. She didn't love me either." My voice cracked and tears filled my eyes as I relived the moment when my mother realized that I was different.

"Did she reject you because of your sexuality?" D'Angelo asked softly.

"No," I replied. "She was totally fine with the fact that I liked boys. In fact, she pointed cute ones out to me."

"What the hell caused her to turn on you?" D'Angelo asked.

"She thought my visions were the work of the devil," I told him. "I'll never forget the horrified look in her eyes when she realized my nightmare was actually a premonition."

"How old were you?" D'Angelo asked.

"Thirteen," I replied. "I had a vivid dream where the neighbor's dog broke his leash and ran out into the street. Mr. Barton chased him and ended up being the one getting hit by a car, instead of the dog. The sounds of his bones breaking and his cries of agony felt so real to me. I remember waking in a cold sweat with a pounding heart and the signs that I was going to be sick. My mother found me curled around the toilet as I wretched repeatedly. She rubbed my back and wiped my brow with a damp cloth while telling me I was going to be okay. D, I knew that night that I would never be 'okay' ever again. I knew that something was really wrong with me."

I closed my eyes briefly and took a deep breath to center myself so I could tell him something I'd never told anyone. "I told my mom all about my *dream* between broken sobs. She assured me it was just a bad dream and told me that everything would be okay. You should've seen the fear in her eyes when my vision came true the next afternoon. My own mother was terrified of me, D. She locked me in my bedroom until she could figure out what to do with me."

"Baby," D'Angelo said softly. "Come here."

I went to him without hesitation and reveled in the feel of his strong arms holding me tight against him. "Her solution was exorcism." D'Angelo's body stiffened but he remained silent. "She brought in a priest who tried to excise the demon out of me. I was starved, beaten, and then abandoned when they realized there was no hope for me." My body trembled hard as I remembered the way my stomach cramped from hunger and how my lips dried until they cracked and bled. "I could feel the sting of the priest's belt against the back of my legs as he tried to beat the evil out of me. My throat burned from screaming and pleading for my mother to help me, but she never came. She didn't love me like she said she did, D." Hot tears raced down my cheeks when it became too hard to hold them back. "I entered the foster care system on my fourteenth birthday."

"I don't know what to say, Ansell. I want to hunt them down and make them pay for what they did to you," he growled angrily in my ear. "No one will ever hurt you like that again. Do you hear me?" I saw the fierce protectiveness in his eyes, plus an emotion I never thought I'd see again: love. With D'Angelo, there were no conditions I had to meet, no hoops for me to jump through to be worthy of his devotion.

I was made for him.

Everything I'd experienced in my past—every bruise, broken promise, and tear—led me to D'Angelo. With that knowledge came power, and with that power came the realization that my past couldn't hurt me anymore. I overcame hate and torture and would gladly embrace the acceptance and love my mate offered to me.

"D'Angelo, I l-l..." My words trailed off as my insecurities resurfaced.

D'Angelo covered my lips with his finger. "I don't need words to know how you feel." He rolled me to my back and leaned over me. "Let our bodies do the talking."

I thought I was prepared for the fireworks D'Angelo ignited inside me when he pressed his lips to mine, but I wasn't. I became aware of my body in ways I'd never experienced before, not even when our bodies joined the first time. I felt and heard my heart thundering in my chest, my blood racing through my veins, and my skin was so sensitive, I could feel every single one of my hair follicles.

D'Angelo broke our kiss and raised his head so he could look into my eyes. I saw the same awe in his gaze that I felt in my soul. He smiled crookedly and said, "That's never going to get old."

"Never," I agreed.

D'Angelo opened his mouth to say something else, but he was interrupted by pounding on his bedroom door.

"D!" Vixen said frantically through the door. "We have a serious situation and we need you downstairs."

"Probably just a big, hairy spider," D'Angelo said to me, but I saw the worry in his eyes. Vixen wasn't the kind of woman who rattled easily. I didn't know her very well, but I knew that much at least. "Why don't you stay here all snuggled in bed and I'll be right back after I..."

"Bring Angel with you to the round table. Jinx is trying to track down Christian. We're going to need all hands on deck to fight this bastard," Vixen said fiercely.

"Be right there," D'Angelo told her.

We dressed quickly and headed down to the situation room. I figured Christian's office was the hub of activity, but I was wrong. One entire wall was nothing but computers and television monitors. The computers were scrolling data so fast, it was impossible for the human eye to keep up, and the television monitors appeared to be tuned in to news broadcasts streaming from all over the word. I expected to see large glass cases housing superhero costumes when I looked around.

Jinx was already downstairs manning one of the computer terminals when we entered the room. I had no idea what the hell was going on, but I could tell by her rigid posture that she was as upset as her girlfriend. The only person missing was Meggie, who must've been sleeping upstairs.

"Over here, guys," Vixen said, gesturing to a polished conference table. "I have a fresh coffee brewing for you to take on the road with you."

D'Angelo pressed his hand at the small of my back and guided me to the table. "What happened, V?" he asked worriedly.

"It's bad, D'Angelo." Her voice broke and tears welled in her eyes. "It's one of the worst demon attacks in recent times."

"Regis?" he asked her.

"Has to be," Vixen replied. "Jinx is printing off details from multiple sources so we can try to rule out fact from fiction before we hit the scene. Here she comes now."

"Guys, it's bad," Jinx said, passing out the papers she printed.

My heart stuttered to a painful stop when I glanced down and saw the headline: **127 Dead in Movie Theater.**

Authorities on the scene aren't saying much, but a suicide pact isn't being ruled out since all the deaths occurred in one of the ten theaters located in the multi-level, twenty-thousand-square-foot facility. The particular movie theater where the deaths occurred was showing a movie on Wall Street greed and corruption and one source is speculating that the movie goers were making a political statement.

"It's not a political statement," I said out loud once I finished reading the paragraph.

"Definitely not," Jinx said. This had Regis written all over it. We needed to find him and shut him down before he killed anyone else. The more souls the relic claimed, the hungrier and more demanding it would get.

"I called Christian three times, but got his voicemail each time," Vixen said. "I can't help but think he's avoiding us and I don't know why. It feels like he's struggling with something by himself rather than letting us help him."

"I'm sure Chris is just fine, Vix. Maybe he's close to wrapping up his case and needs to put one hundred percent of his focus there, or he's just not in cell range right now. Either way, he'll call you as soon as he can. In the meantime, I'll head over to the theater and see what I can learn from the authorities on site."

It sounded a lot like D'Angelo didn't plan on taking me with him. "Don't you mean that we'll head over to the theater and see what we can learn from the authorities?" I asked him.

D'Angelo breathed deeply. I couldn't tell if it was to buy him a bit of time or if he wanted to find the right words to say to me. Regardless, I was positive I wouldn't like the words that left his lips. "Ansell, I need you to stay here with the girls." Yep, I was right. I hated it.

"Girls?" Vixen and Jinx asked at the same time. I wasn't the only one who disagreed with D'Angelo's assessment.

"We're women," Jinx corrected.

"Very capable women," Vixen added. "One of us knows magic that can shrink your…"

"Whoa!" D'Angelo said, holding up his hand to stop her. "No offense intended, ladies. I wasn't asking Angel to stay and protect you. I was asking him to stay here so he can rest and be safe." D'Angelo then turned and looked at me with earnest, pleading eyes. "I haven't slept much these past days, and I need my senses to be sharp. I can't afford to make mistakes right now, Ansell. Please stay here and rest while I do some initial investigating. There won't be much I can learn with the place crawling with investigators anyway. I can at least interview some witnesses and find out if any demons are present. You can go back with me later to do a more thorough investigation."

I would've been pissed off by his attitude just twenty-four hours prior, but I knew better than to question his judgment. If he said he should do it alone, then I'd believe him. He wasn't trying to demean me, he was trying to be practical and safe. I was a danger to him until I could learn how to handle my new heightened senses and physical reaction to him.

"I'll do it," I told him.

I saw the relief in his expression even though his body remained coiled with tension. "Thank you, Ansell." Was he thanking me for agreeing or for not putting up a fight first? D'Angelo rose to his feet, then cupped my chin and tilted my head back so he could look into my eyes. "I won't be long, so keep the bed warm for me." D'Angelo lowered his head and kissed me softly before he walked away.

"Wait, don't you want some of the coffee I made you?" Vixen asked.

"I'd rather drink gasoline and chase it down with a match. Don't you drink it either, Ansell," D'Angelo said before he left the room.

"My coffee isn't that bad," she said with a pout.

"Honey, it's stronger than demon piss," Jinx said affectionately. "How about I whip us up some hot cocoa because no one is going to just head back to bed and fall asleep."

"True dat," I replied.

Meggie was already in the kitchen whipping up her homemade hot chocolate at the stove. "I figured whatever had you pounding on doors in the middle of the night was pretty serious," she said. "Hot cocoa never hurts."

"It smells so good," Jinx said.

"Almost as good as my coffee," Vixen countered saucily.

"Lifesaver," I said after my first sip of the heavenly potion. "You always knew just when I needed it."

"You're not the only one who can sense things, I guess," Meggie said, grinning. "So, it's not likely that you'll be getting back to sleep anytime soon with your honey out there investigating. Now would be a great time for you to tell me why in the hell you never told me about your psychic abilities."

"It's a long story," I told Meggie.

Jinx, Vixen, and Meggie placed their elbows on the table and leaned in simultaneously like they were following a script. Who knew, maybe life was a giant play and we were nothing more than scripted characters.

"We've got plenty of time," Jinx said softly.

I unburdened my soul for the second time that night. I found that it was much easier to get through the second time, and I wondered if keeping it bottled up inside for so long had done more damage than good. The ladies didn't coddle me and I didn't see pity in their eyes; I saw respect, love, and admiration.

I was finally home.

CHAPTER FIFTEEN

D'Angelo

I felt so honored that Ansell opened up to me the way he did. I knew it couldn't have been easy for him to tell me about his past. I couldn't imagine what life was like for him, to lose his family at such a young age because of abandonment. My mother gave me to the Institute when I was ten because she wanted to give me a better life. My father had deserted us and my mother did the best she could with a fifth-grade education and an honest job as a cashier. We were on welfare and living from paycheck to paycheck. The day the recruiter came to our apartment, my mother saw an opportunity for me that she didn't have. I didn't feel abandoned by her, she took the time to explain to me her reasons. Sure, I was mad because I didn't want to leave her, but I was going to an academy that would provide everything I needed to succeed.

She didn't know the real purpose of the academy, because as its front, most of the students that went to Chasseur Institute did go off to lead normal, successful lives. That was what gave the school its reputation. Only those few chosen with innate abilities went on to become hunters. But I couldn't complain, my job was noble, I spoke ten languages fluently, had amazing fighting skills, supernatural powers, and had a diploma from one of the most elite schools in the world. My life has amounted to something, which was all my mom wanted for me. I did get to visit with her on holidays and breaks, but I had to keep the secret of the school… well… a secret. I cherished those moments when I could astonish my mother with the things I knew. Seeing her son bloom never left her with regret. She died when I was sixteen from cancer, and I got to attend her funeral, the memory still stinging for me.

As for Ansell's mother, she didn't deserve him. Just because you could procreate, didn't mean you should. A parent should never abandon their child. She let fear and ignorance tear her away from a boy who needed love, understanding, and compassion from the person he trusted most in this world. That, I couldn't forgive. Well, he would never feel that loneliness again if I had anything to do with it.

I hated having to leave him, especially after rocking his world between the sheets. I'd been wanting to do that since the first moment I laid eyes on him. Fuck this Regis bitch for pulling this evil shit and ruining my night! I was tired as hell, but I needed to get on the scene and do a little investigating. Maybe I could try to sense if there was any demonic residue, so to speak, from the relic. It didn't take me too long to get to the theater, it was about a half hour drive from my home. There were a lot of cop cars there, ambulances, coroner vans, and of course, nosey ass onlookers. Not to mention, the multiple media outlets all clamoring for a story.

I got as close as I could before the cops blocked me. I knew they would, I just wanted to catch a scent, really, and I did. I could smell the relic and its power. The strong scent of sulfur was in the air, and it burned my nostrils. Rotten eggs that had been rotting for days was something that couldn't be mistaken for anything else. Well, other than rotten eggs, but I knew that wasn't the case. There was also an invisible aura hovering in the air, like a reddish hue that only I could see because of my heightened senses. Demons could see it, too, because it meant that another demon had been in the area. Was Regis working with a demon? Probably. I didn't get a chance to see the hue at the diner, too much time had gone by. But it was bright red, which meant the relic was very close to getting the souls it wanted. That meant the demonic demigod would be able to enter this world soon.

I needed to find Regis, and that meant the only person who I knew for sure had met with the man was that bastard-ass vampire, Lorcán. I was going to need him to lure Regis to me, and I had just the relic to do the trick. If Regis wanted to be in another body—a younger body, he was going to need the *Eye of Ezel*. I was going to need Lorcán to get in contact with Regis to let him know he had a seller interested in making a deal.

In the meantime, I did my part as a nosey onlooker and asked some of the others if they'd seen anything. Of course, no one had any information to give me. They were either just walking by the theater and saw the commotion and got curious, or they were in the theater, just not in the same screen room where the mass deaths took place. There was speculation of a terrorist attack, like at the diner. With the use of poison gas. Then people came up with a serial killer that was poisoning people in public places. The panic was starting to rise and it would only get worse for the world if Astaroth came through.

At least I knew now that a demon was involved. Back at the mansion, when I was first attacked, there was no scent of sulfur or demonic hue, which came when a demonic spell was used. Which meant Regis had knowledge of demon magic in order to work that spell. However, seeing the hue now, smelling the sulfur meant either Regis was working with Orcal, or maybe Orcal was running the show from Regis' body. I'll find out for sure if I could lure him to where I wanted. I needed to get back to Ansell. If I went to the club without him, he'd think I didn't trust him or didn't want him with me. And I'd never let him wonder if that was the case. He was my partner now, in everything. I knew that the moment our bond link solidified. I drove home and caught up with Jinx and Vixen in the kitchen.

"Did you sense anything?" Jinx asked.

I nodded as I opened the refrigerator and pulled out an energy boost drink. I needed the caffeine overload to keep my eyes open right now. "That relic is close to getting what it wants. It took over a hundred souls tonight, but it can take more. I think one or two more activations and the demon will come through. I'm heading out again to Lorcán's club."

"Ooh, Lorcán," Vixen purred.

"Watch it, missy," Jinx hissed.

Vixen shrugged. "What? I'm just saying he's pretty freaking hot." She walked over to Jinx, wrapping her arms around her waist and kissing her on the cheek. "Don't worry, I'm strictly pussy."

"Oookay," I said, breaking up that little kitty cat fest. "Fact is, I want to use the *Eye of Ezel* to lure this bastard to me. Once we have him, it should stop the killing. I can get the relic from him and avoid a demonic disaster."

"Please do, go on, get moving," Vixen said, then she turned her head, returning the kiss Jinx gave to her.

I downed the drink in my hand, letting the caffeine do its job.

"You could have had my coffee if you needed a boost," Vixen said.

"I have enough hair on my chest, thank you," I remarked.

"Shut up," she retorted with a flash of her middle finger.

I chuckled. Vixen's coffee was a wicked potion of black crude sludge that was stronger than a thousand-proof whiskey. I had no idea what she put in the concoction, but I made the mistake of taking a sip one day and was up for thirty-six hours jacking off, playing video games, running on the treadmill, dancing to music that wasn't playing, and a whole bunch of other shit just because I had too much energy to burn. Thanks, but no, thanks. She was always making it, too. I avoided it like the plague, so did Jinx. In fact, Christian was the only one who seemed to appreciate her coffee.

I walked out of the room and into my bedroom where Meggie was sitting on the bed, legs folded, talking to Ansell. "I thought I told you to get some rest."

Ansell snorted. "Like I could sleep without you next to me ever again."

Awww, I had to smile at that. "You're going to make me blush."

He smiled. "I'd like to see that. Besides, if I was asleep, I bet you were going to wake me up, right?"

Well, he had a point there. "Yeah, so are you ready to go?"

"Sure, where are we going?" he asked as he climbed out of bed.

"To Hypnotic, Lorcán's dance club. Should be teeming with patrons about now," I said.

"Ooh, can I come?" Meggie asked.

I cocked an eyebrow. "Any other day… well, I'd still advise against it. It's a vampire bar, Meggie. Vamps are allowed to feed on humans. They also have the ability to control you mentally and make you give them your blood. Walking into a club, especially knowingly, means you're accepting those unspoken, unwritten terms. The only thing they can't do is kill you, but you're still taking a huge risk. I wouldn't recommend it. Another reason why I'm going to have to deny you is because we're on a mission to stop this asshole Regis from killing a few hundred more people. We're not going to party."

When I said that, I saw recognition of how dangerous our situation was come into her expression and she nodded. "I see. Okay, please be safe."

I nodded, and nodded my head for Ansell to follow me.

"See you later, Meggie." He kissed her cheek and both of them followed me out of the bedroom. By the time Ansell and I were on the elevator, I could hear Meggie talking with Vixen and Jinx. The elevator door closed and in no time, Ansell and I were climbing inside my Jeep.

"Do you think he will help us?" Ansell asked.

"His ass better. But you never know with monsters. Some of them are cooperative and some are straight-up assholes. Lorcán can be both depending on how he's feeling." I told Ansell what I'd learned at the crime scene, bringing him up to speed on what was going on. "As much as I'd love to have passionate sex with you again, we have to put that on the back burner until we catch this son of a bitch."

"Oh definitely," Ansell agreed. "But I don't regret having had sex with you, D."

I looked over at him and smiled at his wide grin. "Me either. It was meant to be, so it happened. Fate put us on this path and I'm happy to walk with you side by side. The only thing I regret is how foolish and stubborn I was being before by trying to push you away. We could have been bumping bodies." I laughed.

Ansell chuckled as he shook his head. "Thank goodness I wouldn't let you push me away."

I reached over, taking his hand into my own, squeezing it a little. Too much and I could break his bones, I was that strong. "Thank goodness."

⸙

We pulled into a parking spot at Hypnotic and climbed out. It was one of the few nightclubs that had its own parking garage, which Lorcán charged for. It was pretty packed with cars, so I knew the club had to be booming. I could hear the music violating the speakers as we walked towards the elevator. Just a loud thumping and drumming of erratic rhythm from pop music. I hit the only button I could, which was the ground floor indicated by the little "star" by the "G." There were two levels to the garage and they were P1 and P2. We were parked in P2. This wasn't the elevator Lorcán used. His would have had a button to access his home, which was over the nightclub.

I'd never been inside his home, but I was guessing it was pretty luxurious. He looked like the type to be materialistic. The elevator doors opened and the loud music damn near blasted us back against the wall. Damn, it was obnoxious as hell, especially for someone with heightened senses. I had to tune them down or suffer. I stepped off the elevator and Ansell followed me. It took me a few minutes to locate Lorcán. He was in his VIP section with his manservant, Stephan, and several humans, along with two other vampires, who looked to be feeding. Of course, to the casual patron, they might have thought that the couple was just making out, doing a little necking. I was sure some of the people here knew what was going on and hoped to be picked one day to be fed on. Some people, I just didn't get.

I cut my way through the sea of people gyrating and copping feels towards his section and was stopped by the vampire bodyguard that protected the red velvet entrance. I looked past him to Lorcán and saw the high-ranking vampire roll his eyes, but he knew the business.

"Klaus, let them through," Lorcán called out. Even over the loud music, the vampire didn't have to yell, but Klaus heard him perfectly and so did I. Klaus stepped aside and unlatched the rope so Ansell and I could ascend the five red-carpeted stairs that had a gold rail lining them. There were aesthetically pleasing red and black satin curtains hanging from the ceiling, I guess to provide privacy for when they wanted to feed and not make a spectacle of themselves like the two who were now licking their bloody lips clean. The sofas and chairs looked very comfy with the expensive Italian leather and nice glass cocktail and end tables. I wondered how much he charged to rent out the VIP section?

"What can I do for you this time?" Lorcán asked once I was near. He had his arm around a pretty blond guy with bee-stung lips meant for sucking cock. Of course, I wasn't interested in anyone but Ansell, but I had no problem admiring. As for the vampire himself, gone were the satin pajamas from earlier. Now, he was wearing a badass charcoal suit with a black shirt and tie. The black patent leather shoes were shiny enough to see your reflection in. The jacket was left open in that casual way, making him look like he was too cool for school and shit. His hair was slicked back and parted, not tousled, and that gave him a commanding appearance. His green eyes were watching Ansell and me carefully.

"We need to speak privately," I said.

Again, Lorcán released a long sigh and motioned for the others to leave.

"What business does a rejected Chasseur hunter have with our regent?" one of the vampires asked.

"Not any of yours," I snapped.

His human meal ticket was looking like he had just experienced the best high and orgasm of his life. There weren't any puncture wounds on his neck, so that meant the vamps were covering their tracks. As for the vampire who was now challenging me, he was tall, average-looking with brown hair, blue eyes, and a snarl on his face as he stared up at me. I also caught the unmistakable sound of a menacing growl. Vampires were hard to kill, but I had the right tools to do the trick. I always kept a blessed knife on me; this time, it was strapped to my left calf.

"Don't growl at me, motherfucker," I warned.

His sneer grew wider and I saw his fangs popping through. "Or what?"

I cocked an eyebrow. "Well, if you're feeling froggy… jump, bitch." The tension in the room was pretty thick and I could sense Ansell's fear. But I knew I had to be tough with this lot. Lorcán seemed to be studying me, but I could see that he was intrigued.

"Dennis, Farris, leave," Lorcán said, with a nonchalant wave of his hand.

This time, neither vampire gave any feedback. They just got their asses up and walked out of the area, taking the three humans with them. Of course, I looked up and saw Stephan sitting in one of the chairs in the back.

"He stays," Lorcán stated in his resolution before I could even mention the lagger oner.

"Fine." I knew when to press and when to relent. Lorcán obviously held Stephan in high regard, so I let it go.

With everyone out of the VIP section, he pushed a button that was inset in the armrest of the sofa and two sets of glass doors began to close, shutting out the noise from the rest of the club. That was pretty cool.

"Is the glass see-through?" Ansell asked.

Lorcán shook his head. "We can see out, but they can't see in. You wanted to talk privately."

I sat down on the opposite love seat and Ansell sat down with me. "I need for you to contact Regis Maxfield. I've got something he wants and I'm willing to make a deal with him."

Lorcán raised a cocky eyebrow. "Since when do vampires do the bidding of the Genesis Circle?"

I sighed, because this was the game I hated playing with these fucking monsters.

"Lives are at stake," Ansell said. "We need your help."

Lorcán's green gaze panned over to Ansell and I felt a powerful need to protect him from the vampire's eyes and whatever else. "Lives are always at stake. Don't you know someone somewhere is dying right now, either by natural causes or violence? That's what's wrong with you humans, you think because your lives are so fragile that it should be of some importance to us."

"You feed on humans, need us to survive, you'd think you'd see the relevance of protecting humans," I said.

"A handful of humans can keep us going forever. Why do you think vampires don't overpopulate? *Our* survival is the only thing I hold in regard," Lorcán said.

I sighed heavily again. "What's this shit, Lorcán? Are you still pissed that I interrupted your day nap? What the fuck is it going to take to get you to do the right thing?"

I was annoyed as hell right about now. I hated having to deal with this ornery-ass motherfucker. He controlled the Chicago district, which was known as Sector Dios to him. That meant his word was law. Sure, he had to obey and carry out the edict of his vampire king, Nero, but he had his own rules the vampires had to abide by. So, calling him an arrogant bastard went without saying. He was also the one who approved new vampires being made and who had to keep all of the vampires in line. He had soldiers who helped him keep order, but it was all his responsibility. That was a lot of power for a vampire as young as him to have. It made me wonder just why he was so damned special, but I never asked.

Lorcán smirked. "Am I frustrating you, hunter?" His Spanish accent was particularly grating at the moment, so yeah.

"You're pissing me off because I'm trying to save lives and you're over here bullshitting as you always do," I snapped.

Ansell put his hand on my shoulder and I immediately felt his calming influence come over me. "Perhaps we can each relax and work something out," he said. I could tell he was nervous, especially addressing a real-life vampire that he just learned existed, but he was keeping it together really well.

"I'm listening," Lorcán said.

"This Regis will unleash the demon, Astaroth, onto this world if we don't stop him."

When he mentioned Astaroth's name, I saw Lorcán's eyes narrow in recognition.

"Demons and vampires don't play well, that's no surprise." Lorcán's smirk melded into a frown and his total composure changed from lofty superiority to all business as he uncrossed his long legs and leaned forward, resting his elbows on his knees, and clasping his hands together. "This demon is extremely powerful. I've never met him, but I've heard tales of the last time he did walk this earth. Pompeii was a thriving city before he was raised."

"I thought that was because of volcanic eruption," Ansell stated.

Lorcán shook his head. "Demonic powers. They are dangerous

and keeping the most powerful ones in hell is everyone's duty. So, I will help you. What do you need from me?"

Well, I'll be damned. Okay, well, maybe my hot-headed approach wasn't always the best way to get things done. Seemed like Ansell's sensible method worked wonders even on a vampire like Lorcán. I was learning from my mate… not that I thought I would change much. This was me, but I could keep my mouth shut like I did and let him do the talking from time to time. We could be good cop, bad cop.

Okay, now it was time for me to take over. "Regis wanted to be a vampire, right?"

Lorcán nodded. "He did, but I'm allowed to permit so many procreations a year. Some must be done to keep our ranks strong. He was too repulsive to me to warrant my approval."

A simple "yes" would have sufficed, but okay. "I'm sure he left you contact information in case you changed your mind, right?"

Lorcán frowned. "He did, but I didn't keep it. My decision was made."

"I still have it, sir," Stephan said.

Lorcán turned to him. "Why'd you keep it?"

"He was rich, you know how the king likes to recruit influential people into the ranks. You might have changed your mind," Stephan said.

Lorcán turned back around, lips pursed. Yeah, he had nice lips, too. I wondered if it was his looks that Nero took favor to and if that was the reason Lorcán was promoted?

"That is true. But I still think I might have passed on this guy. Anyway, yes, apparently, I still have his contact info," Lorcán said.

"Well, can you please contact him, let him know you've changed your mind. You'll turn him, but if he wants to be in a younger body, he'll need the *Eye of Ezel*. Let him know you have a dealer willing to make a deal in mind that has the relic he needs and you're willing to meet him tonight."

Lorcán snorted. "Even if I was going to approve his initiation, I'd never do it myself. Wouldn't want to put my lips on his flesh."

"He doesn't need to know that."

"I wasn't going to tell him, calm down." Lorcán rolled his eyes again. "Stephan, fetch me this idiot's information."

Stephan stood up and left like a well-trained… manservant and walked off to do his master's bidding.

"What is he using to kill people?" Lorcán asked while we waited.

"The *Stone of Astaroth*. It needs so many souls before the doorway can open and Astaroth can walk through its portal. Once it reaches a thousand souls, all hell will break loose. So far, by my calculation, and from what I know, he has seven hundred three. He only needs two hundred ninety-seven more before that happens," I said. I wanted to add, *this was why I didn't have time to play "stroke your cock" games with you*, but I didn't. I was learning from my mate.

Lorcán licked his lips and nodded. "I see the urgency." He looked up when Stephan returned with the business card Regis had left and handed it to him. Pulling out his cell phone, he called. I tuned my super hearing so I could listen to both sides of the conversation. The telephone rang and rang until the voicemail came on. Lorcán hissed and ended the call. "Fucking hate voicemail."

"If he doesn't answer, I'll need you to leave him the message," I said.

"And I will, but let's give him a chance to answer, shall we?" Lorcán gave me an exasperated look.

Stephan chuckled, but didn't say anything. Humans like him were complete sycophants in my eyes. They would give their lives to their vampire masters if the vampire asked for it. They worshipped the bloodstained ground these monsters walked on and I just didn't see the appeal. Was their bite that damn orgasmic? Yeah, Lorcán was hot, but the fact that he had fangs and would drink my blood kept me at bay. Other vampires weren't even lookers like him, but they still had humans clinging to them like *Reynolds Wrap*. I just didn't get it.

We waited about five minutes, but Regis didn't return the call. Sure, it was going on twelve midnight, but he'd just gotten through killing a bunch of people about three hours ago, so I was sure he was still awake. Lorcán called him again and still didn't get an answer. This time, he left the message and hung up.

"You're free to wait here until I close to see if he ever returns my call," Lorcán offered.

I was exhausted as fuck, but I wasn't going to miss my opportunity to catch this bastard. "Thank you," I said.

"I won't be waiting in here with you, you're boring," Lorcán simply said, then he rose and left the VIP section with his boy toy in tow.

"I hate his ass," I said. I wasn't sure if I really hated him, but extremely disliked would be a good assessment.

"He doesn't seem too bad… for a vampire, I guess," Ansell said.

"You caught him post-treaty. I'm guessing he was hell on two legs before that. He's only a little over one hundred sixty years old and he's a regent. The youngest I know of is six hundred, and that's the exception. The rule of thumb is the thousand-year mark and a vampire can become a regent. See where I'm going?" I asked.

"I think so. You're wondering how powerful Lorcán really is," Ansell said.

I nodded. "What does he have that other vampires don't? There's too much I don't know about him."

"At least he was willing to help," Ansell pointed out.

"Yeah, after you talked some sense into him. That was pretty neat. Already, we're making a great team."

"Good cop, bad, psycho, crazy batshit cop?" he taunted.

I laughed. "If I wasn't so tired, I'd do things to you."

"Oh no you won't. Not in this club," Ansell warned.

Well, it wouldn't be my first time getting freaky in a public place, but it would be Ansell's. If he wasn't comfortable, I would never force him. I smirked. "God willing, if we survive this demon shit… I'm going to put a dent in my mattress in the shape of your ass."

He grinned. "That, I do look forward to."

I felt myself being shaken awake by strong hands and I opened my eyes. It was Lorcán standing over me, still dressed in his slick-ass nightclub suit. "He never called me back and I'm going to bed. You can see yourselves out."

I blinked a little and looked around. Ansell was out cold on the love seat, his legs draped over the armrest. I had lain on the sofa to catch some shuteye while he was supposed to keep watch. What a pair we made. The club was closed, the music was turned off, and Lorcán looked annoyed as fuck.

I sat up and wiped my eyes. "Thanks, Lorcán. If he does contact you—"

"Don't worry, I'll let you know."

He turned and walked out of the VIP area and made his way upstairs towards the elevator that led to his home. But, now I was wondering what he had going down on the second level of his club. That was a question to be answered on another day. Stephan was standing at the velvet rope waiting to see us out. I decided not to wake Ansell up. Instead, I picked him up from the love seat and carried him to my Jeep and put him inside. Once he was safely strapped in, I headed home. Once home, I checked with Jinx to see if there were any more murders, mass or otherwise. She gave me a list of individual homicides, but nothing like the theater. Maybe, the relic could only take so many souls a night in one swoop. If that was the case, maybe that worked in our favor, but it still put us on a clock. I needed to get to Regis. But one thing was making me curious about all of this… why were the murders happening only at night? What was the restriction? So many questions, so zero answers.

I laid Ansell down on the bed and climbed in with him. I wasn't going to be any good to this investigation if I was dead on arrival. I needed to sleep and that was what I did.

CHAPTER SIXTEEN

ANGEL

I was having the most incredible dream about morning blow jobs with D'Angelo when something woke me. I struggled to stay asleep so I could finish my dream and hear the sounds that D'Angelo made when he came. I wanted to hear his throaty growls at least once a day for the rest of my life. Then I thought, why dream about it when I could live it? I stretched my arms over my head and arched my back off the mattress as I came fully awake and aware of my surroundings.

I'd slept better than I had in... I couldn't actually recall a time I'd slept better in my life. Exhaustion and stress from the case caught up to me and knocked me out, but knowing I was safe with D'Angelo made it possible for me to rest peacefully. If I didn't know better, I would've thought I had died, but my morning erection reminded me that I was very much alive. I became aware of exactly what brought me out of a deep sleep when I felt D'Angelo's finger tracing a path from my inner thigh to my taint.

I turned my head and found him propped on his elbow, watching me. D'Angelo smiled broadly and said, "Good morning."

"I have a feeling it's about to become a great morning." My voice was still heavy with sleep and gravely with lust. I spread my legs to give him better access to whatever parts of me he wanted. D'Angelo was my mate and pleasing him felt as natural to me as breathing. I'd never withhold anything from him—not my body, my heart, or my soul. I had a momentary flash of guilt that I hadn't said the three magic words to him yet, but he had said that words weren't necessary. He had reminded me that he could feel my emotions and how much he meant to me, just as I could see what I meant to him.

"I hope you slept well, Ansell. We have a long, busy day ahead of us," he whispered as he lowered his lips closer to mine. D'Angelo slid his finger lower and circled my pucker.

"We do?" I asked, trying to grasp a train of thought other than how badly I wanted to feel D'Angelo inside me again. My brain had gone from muddled with sleep to fogged with lust. As soon as I asked the question, I remembered that I'd fallen asleep at Hypnotic when I was supposed to play lookout while D'Angelo rested. I slapped my forehead and groused, "I can't believe I fell asleep in the club. Some partner I am."

"You're an amazing partner," D'Angelo replied. "Look how you calmly stepped in and took care of the situation between me and Lorcán. You knew the right things to say to calm me down and get Lorcán on board with my plan. Let me tell you something; that's no easy feat. Lorcán is a tough nut."

D'Angelo's hand never stopped moving the entire time he spoke. He continued to drag his finger between my taint and my pucker, and back again. I wondered just how easily he'd be able to focus and talk if I had my hands on him. I decided to test my theory. I wrapped my hand around his leaking erection and began slowly stroking up and down. I'd never jacked another guy off before, so I just did what felt right to me. Yeah, I saw D's eyes widen in surprise when I added a sexy little twist when I reached the head of his dick before I slid my hand back down to his base. I smiled because I was getting to him too. "Does that mean you guys set something up before we left the club?"

A broken hiss slipped from his lips, but his hand never faltered from teasing me. "Nope," D'Angelo casually replied like I wasn't pumping his dick. He lowered his head and began kissing along my collarbone. "We're waiting on Regis to return Lorcán's call and set something up." My balls drew tight against my body when D'Angelo moved his hand to my cock and began stroking me at the same pace as I jacked him.

I tried to play it cool like I wasn't about to bust a nut all over my stomach. "So, what's our next step in the investigation?"

"First, you're going to quit pretending that you don't want to straddle my head and fuck my face, then we're going to eat something besides liquid protein for breakfast before we set out to do a bit of investigating." I wasn't aware that straddling D'Angelo's face was an option, but I couldn't think of anything else after he spoke the words. D'Angelo rolled to his back and said, "Come here."

D'Angelo made me feel bold and brave. I didn't second-guess my instincts around him; I acted. I got to my knees, but instead of facing the headboard, I turned and straddled his head so I could suck his dick at the same time he sucked mine.

"So fucking sexy," D said as he lapped at the leaking cum from my slit. "Mmmmm." He drove me wild by teasing the sensitive spot beneath the crown with his tongue.

"D'Angelo!" I wanted to make him as crazy as he made me. I lowered my head and took his dick straight to the back of my throat and swallowed around the head.

D'Angelo gripped my ass with both hands and sucked my cock into his mouth. My guttural moans were muffled from having a mouthful of cock, but I was certain that he heard my pleasure loud and clear. I reached between D's legs and massaged his firm balls at the same time he reached for mine.

Sucking, slurping, and moaning echoed around the room as we pleasured one another. I tried to pull out of his mouth when I was about to come, but D'Angelo wouldn't let me. He gripped my ass harder and worked my cock faster. I felt the way his body stiffened beneath mine and knew he was right there with me. I wanted to taste him every bit as bad as he wanted me, so I sucked harder and faster.

We came together, loud and hard. I collapsed beside him once the last ripple of pleasure had left my body, and then sucked much needed oxygen into my lungs. D'Angelo swatted my ass playfully and said, "That's step one, baby."

"Do you have room service around here?" I teased because I wasn't sure my legs would support the trip down to the kitchen for the non-liquid protein part of our morning. And as for investigating, I doubted I'd be able to form a coherent thought after coming my brains out.

"We're going to work on your stamina," D'Angelo said teasingly. "I'll start you on a training program that will make it possible for you to come one minute and execute demons the next." I raised up and quirked a brow at him. The smile slid from his face and the humor faded from his eyes. "All teasing aside, I do need to train you if you're going to share a life with me. Danger is always just around the corner for me and I need to know that you'll be able to handle yourself. It doesn't seem fair, and I feel like you've been forced into a reality that you didn't want."

"You're not forcing me to do anything, D," I said tenderly. "I was made for you. For once in my life, I belong to someone who wants me. It's the most amazing feeling in the world. I'm going to learn to do whatever it takes to be your partner in all aspects of our life. I'll learn to swing a sword, kick some ass, and anything else."

D'Angelo snorted. "Okay, Buffy." I was happy to see his humor return, so I didn't call him out on his remark. "Your first training session starts as soon as we get cleaned up."

"Yeah? Swords?" I asked excitedly.

"Food one-oh-one," D'Angelo said. "I wasn't joking about fueling for a long day. You can't always swing through a drive-thru when you're out in the field. The right foods will keep you going."

"I could eat," I replied casually. I had never been so hungry in all my life. It was baffling how quickly my life was changing from an obscure, unwanted waiter to a man with a bonded mate and a bright future—even if it would be bone-chilling scary at times.

"Look at you two lovebirds," Jinx said when we walked into the kitchen. "Heck, I didn't expect to see you guys until noon."

"Murder scenes to investigate and demons to trap," D'Angelo said in his matter-of-fact, no-bullshit way. "Time to fuel up and head out."

"One step ahead of you," she said. "I made a big breakfast and stashed it in the warming drawer."

Vixen's coffee might've smelled scary, but she could cook like a pro. We ate our weight in fluffy scrambled eggs, crispy bacon, and thick pancakes. I eyed the coffee suspiciously until D took a drink and gave me a nod that it was all clear.

"I saw that," Vixen said in a huff.

"Wasn't trying to hide it from you," D'Angelo countered.

"Good morning," Meggie said when she entered the room. "What smells so damn good? Please tell me there's a gym inside this big ole place because I want to stay fit and trim for when I meet my mate."

"Huge, kick-ass gym," Jinx said. "I'll be working out later if you want to join me."

"Thanks, J." I thought it was awesome how easily Meggie clicked with the Circle members she'd met. Christian seemed stoic and more reserved in comparison to Jinx and Vixen, so I wasn't sure how well he'd take to her. I was confident in her ability to win him over, though.

"Despite your comments about my coffee," Vix said, "I have something I want to give you guys." She opened her hand to reveal two rings with onyx stones. "They've been enchanted with a cloaking spell to help you maneuver around without anyone knowing you're there. The spell only lasts for an hour after you slip it on your fingers, so don't put it on until the very last minute."

"This is cooler than *Harry Potter*," Meggie whispered in awe.

"This is a little flashy, couldn't you have picked a less showy piece of jewelry? You know how I feel about rings," D'Angelo said.

"I bet you wear a flashy ring after you and Angel have your bonding ceremony, so you might as well get used to wearing one," Vixen countered.

"Bonding ceremony?" I asked.

"Sounds kinky," Meggie said, almost sounding hopeful. "Do you mate publicly under a full moon or something?"

"Of course not. Don't be a perv, Meggie," I told my friend. Then I realized I had no fucking clue what a bonding ceremony entailed. I turned to D'Angelo and said, "Right?"

D cupped the back of my head and pulled me to him for a kiss. "You're so fucking adorable, I could eat you."

"You already did," I whispered softly enough that only he could hear it.

"It's more or less a wedding of sorts. We'll recite vows, exchange rings, and our union will be blessed by a high priest or priestess, and we'll have a feast like a wedding reception. The differences are the ceremonies that lead up to the big day, but we'll talk about them closer to that time." He narrowed his eyes and looked at Meggie. "We don't sacrifice animals for the feast." Meggie held her hands up in defeat, but I saw humor sparkling in her eyes. "It's purely ceremonial and doesn't impact our bond. It has no legal recognition in our world, but it's a lovely tradition that honors the bond and commitment we share."

"One that you never thought would happen for you," I said. I didn't need to be psychic to see how important the ceremony was to D'Angelo. "I'd be honored to exchange vows and rings with you."

"Party!" Jinx said excitedly. "So, a week from tonight?" she asked.

"Let's solve this case first so we can really relax and enjoy the special occasion," D'Angelo said. He never took his smoldering eyes off me.

"Like I said before," Vixen said, pulling our attention back to her, "you might as well get used to the feel of a ring on your finger."

"Why can't they go in there wearing suits and waving around fake FBI badges?" Meggie asked out of the blue.

"This isn't an episode of *Supernatural*, Meg," I teased. She rolled her eyes dramatically. "You're no fun."

D'Angelo and I smiled at one another, then pocketed our rings before we tucked back into our breakfasts. Meggie wasn't the only one who would need to find the gym, and fast.

✣

The movie theater complex was still crawling with investigators from both local and federal branches when we arrived. There were a dozen or more vans from news outlets parked outside the perimeter and reporters milling about with their cameramen looking for an exclusive soundbite or video clip they could share on their network.

We couldn't just roll on into the parking lot, slip the rings on our fingers, and exit the vehicle. Let's be real. Car doors that opened and shut on their own would draw too much attention to us and that was the last thing we wanted or needed. We used the chaos and crowd excitement to our advantage by joining the crowd at the fringes and slowly making our way toward the news vans that were parked close together on the far end.

"Okay, a few things to go over before we go inside," D'Angelo said as we stepped between two of the news vans without being noticed. "A cloaking spell means that they can't see us, but they can hear us. We need to be completely silent and communicate with our hands."

"No talking and use my hands to communicate. Got it."

"Is your ringer off on your cell phone?" D'Angelo asked.

I checked my phone and nodded. "Let's do this." I sounded much calmer than I felt. I was half-convinced that the cops and investigators would be able to hear my thundering heart when we entered the theaters.

"You're going to be amazing," D said, reminding me that he could feel all my emotions. It was just what I needed to calm myself down. I couldn't let myself be a distraction to him.

D'Angelo slipped his ring on first. It was the weirdest fucking thing I'd ever seen. One minute he was there and the next he vanished into thin air. I admit that I panicked a little bit before I slid the enchanted ring on my finger and found D'Angelo was still standing in front of me. I knew we didn't have much time, but I stood on my tiptoes and kissed him anyway.

D'Angelo smiled when I pulled back from him and tipped his head to the side, indicating that we needed to head to the theater. It was the weirdest damn thing to walk up on someone who had no idea you were there. I'd heard people talk about feeling invisible, and I had even felt that before, but it was nothing like the real thing. I followed D's lead when he ducked beneath the crime scene tape, then entered the open door at the front of the movie theater complex.

Even though the complex had many theaters inside, it wasn't hard to figure out the one where the slayings had occurred. We followed behind a man wearing a blue jacket with FBI printed on the back and he led us to the right theater. The room was crawling with crime scene investigators collecting evidence to take back to their labs. I had no idea what the hell we were looking for and I doubted that Regis had left an obvious clue that would lead us to wherever he was hiding, but I figured D'Angelo wanted a backup plan in case the one with Lorcán went tits up.

I saw something on the floor that broke my heart. It looked like a school ID for a teacher who appeared to be in her late twenties. She smiled happily in the photo, and I just knew that she was loved by her students. Although I didn't know it for sure, I suspected that Allison Flannigan was one of Regis' victims.

I had the strangest urge to pick the ID up to see what school she worked at and started to do so, but D'Angelo placed his hand on my arm to stop me. He pointed at two police detectives standing off to the side not more than six feet away—one a Hispanic male and the other an African American female. The female detective wasn't looking in our direction, but the male detective was looking right at us. I sucked in a breath and D immediately placed his hand on my back to calm me.

"What has you so spooked, Miguel?" the female detective asked.

"I can't say for sure, Carlotta," he replied as he narrowed his eyes speculatively.

"Partner, your hairs are standing straight up on your arm. You're freaking me out," she said.

"Something is here in this theater with us. I feel it," he said.

"Evil clearly paid a visit," his partner replied, looking around the room like she was trying to see what her partner felt.

"True, but this is something else. I can't say for sure if it's good or bad. It feels like a little bit of both."

"The chief is gesturing for us to come over there," Carlotta said. "Maybe they've finally found something useful."

We gave them a wide berth, but followed behind them. I jerked to a stop when I felt the warning signs that I was about to have a vision. D'Angelo stopped too and looked at me in concern. He must've seen the panic in my eyes because he pulled me to him and held me tight as the vision hit me like a ton of bricks. I bit my lip to keep from crying out when I saw what that bastard Regis had planned next. I had to be dreaming because surely evil like that didn't truly exist in the world. I felt hot tears pouring down my face as my vision played out cruelly in vivid color.

D'Angelo silently led me outside and we backtracked over to the vans and made sure we were alone before we slipped the rings off our fingers. We said nothing until we reached the safety of the Jeep. "Baby, what did you see?" D'Angelo asked. His brow furrowed in a deep V with the concern he felt for me.

"Regis' next target is a large crowd of children," I whispered brokenly. "There looks to be hundreds of them gathered excitedly outside their school. One minute they're happy, innocent children and the next, they're lifeless bodies. We have to stop him."

"Do you know where? Did you see the name of the school? What triggered the vision?" D'Angelo sounded as panicked as I felt when he fired one question after the other at me.

"I saw a teacher's ID badge on the floor in the theater. I saw her name was Allison Flannigan, but I didn't see which school she worked at. The kids in my vision wore uniforms and there was a crest embroidered on the sweater vests. I'm pretty certain it was a private school," I told him.

"Your abilities are getting stronger, Ansell. We'll go back home and you can describe the crest and uniforms to Jinx. Between the teacher's name and description of the crest, she's sure to find it. We will stop him, baby. I promise." I knew it was a promise he couldn't guarantee under the circumstances, but it still helped me shove aside my fear and focus on the mission.

"We have to, D'Angelo."

"Are you feeling okay? Do you need…" He was cut off by an incoming call through his Bluetooth feature through his radio. "It's Lorcán," he told me. "Lorcán, tell me you have good news. We know what Regis is planning next, and we have to stop him before he can carry it out. Don't bother giving me any of your usual bullshit, either."

"Well, I'm not calling you at this ungodly hour to exchange recipes," Lorcán said snidely. I looked at the clock and saw it was noon, but I guessed that was early for a vampire. "Stephan woke me when the evil rotter returned my call. Guess you're getting your wish, he'll be here shortly."

CHAPTER SEVENTEEN

D'Angelo

"If he gets there before we do, I need you to keep him there, Lorcán. Ansell and I are on our way," I said. My body was charged up at the fact that he'd heard back from Regis. I just needed to get back home to grab two artifacts. One would help me convince Regis to exorcise the demon from his body, which was the *Eye of Ezel*. The other was going to trap the fucking demon for good once he was out. And that was the *Orb of Orleander*. Exorcising a demon was no easy feat. The evil bastards liked to anchor in deep and not let go when it was time for evacuation. This would be a delicate process and I needed all the right tools.

"I'll have you know, I'm not thrilled about having to lose sleep over this case of yours," Lorcán pointed out.

"It's not like this isn't your case, too. The guy came to you first and if Astaroth is freed, literally, all hell will break loose. I know you don't want that. I'm sure your sovereign will reward you for your dedication and sacrifice to protecting his kingdom," I said, putting things in another perspective for Lorcán, the testy bloodsucking son of a bitch.

"Stop trying to sell it to me, I know how serious this situation is. Just get your ass here." With that, he ended the call.

I looked at Ansell. "There isn't anything more we can gather here. I'm sure they'll find that ID. There was something off about that cop, but I can't put my finger on it. I think he sensed us there."

"Maybe he's psychic like me," Ansell said.

I shrugged a shoulder. "Maybe. Let's go." I put the jeep in drive and pulled out. I drove as fast as I could without attracting the police all the way home. I explained to Ansell what I wanted to do and what we were going to need to get the job done. Ansell was on board and I called Vixen ahead of time so she could have the stuff ready. I didn't want to risk Regis leaving Lorcán's club. If the demon was inside of him, his actions could be very unpredictable. If the demon was his partner, well… same thing, but I wouldn't know until we met.

I pulled up to the shop and Ansell stayed in the car while I ran inside to get the materials. Vixen was standing at the front desk and when she saw me, she reached under the desk and handed me the box with my holy water, holy oil, salt, and two artifacts.

"Is this all you'll need?" she asked me discreetly, as we did have several customers browsing our store.

"Please tell me Jinx is finished working on that cloaking device. I think we're going to need it," I said.

"Yeah, she just finished updating the software or whatever you call it about forty minutes ago. She's been bragging about it since, talking about how amazing it is and how she's the world's greatest genius." Vixen rolled her eyes with a smirk. "I'll go and get it."

"Thanks." I minded the store while she fetched the cloaking device Jinx had been working on for the past three months. Unlike the rings, which only hid our physical forms, the device literally cloaked the physical forms, interactions, and sounds, making it look like the people being cloaked weren't even there. It was her idea in case we ever had to take on a bad guy in public and didn't want anyone to see. As long as we were within its range, which was about a hundred-foot radius, give or take, no one would be any the wiser to what was really going down.

Both women came back, and Jinx had a little box with a shiny-looking crystal in it. I guessed that was needed to cast the reflection or whatever. I wasn't sure how it worked, so I listened intently as Jinx explained it to me. I took the box from her and examined it.

"You are a genius if this works," I said.

She scoffed. "If? Please, don't insult me. Of course it works. I've already tested it. Only one downfall. It lasts about fifteen minutes before the cloak comes down. I'm going to have to work on that to improve it. But that's the window of time you'll have."

I nodded and put it in the box with my other items. "Okay. That will have to do."

"Anything else you need?" Vixen asked.

I nodded. "Try to contact Christian again."

"I've been trying, and I still can't reach him. I'm starting to get worried," she said with a frown.

I sighed. Not being able to contact Christian for so many days wasn't unusual, but it wasn't any less nerve-wracking, either. He liked to do things on his own more than I did, which was why I found it so odd that he was pressuring me to work with Ansell. Maybe he saw something I didn't and he knew Ansell was my mate. Christian did have the ability to read a person's deepest secret, dark or otherwise. Perhaps he was reading ours and saw how attracted Ansell was to me, and me to Ansell. Regardless, he should have contacted us by now, I didn't care even if it was by carrier pigeon!

"Keep trying," I told Vixen, then took the box and left. I put the box in Ansell's lap. "Hold tight to this."

"Hey, wait. You have a bad habit of putting shit in my lap that is dangerous," he pointed out.

I smirked because he was right. "It's fine. We'll need those," I said, hopefully easing his anxiety. He needed to know I'd never do anything that would harm him.

He smiled. "I know. I was just messing with you."

I shook my head and climbed in behind the wheel. I was speeding to Lorcán's club when my cell ringing interrupted the music playing through the speakers. I hit the "speak" button on my steering wheel.

"Yeah?" I could hear Christian's voice, but it was coming from my pocket. "What the fuck? Damn Bluetooth acting up again," I grumbled and reached into my pocket, removing my cell. I switched to "private mode" and answered. "Hey, man, what's up? Can you hear me now?"

"Yeah. I see you've been trying to reach me, what's up?" Christian asked, like we'd only been trying to reach his ass for the past hour instead of for the past twenty-four.

"Where are you?" I asked, since I figured he was okay. He didn't seem to have any urgency in his voice, though that could be deceiving. Christian was great at compartmentalizing.

"I'm in Beijing now, I was in Afghanistan before. Those mountains block cell phone reception like a bitch. I took down one of the monsters killing those kids, but the other escaped. I've got great intel that he's in Beijing. It's a Nephilim, and one that's trying to raise his father from hell by using the blood of innocents. I managed to steal the blood he's collected, so now he'll need more."

Well, shit, it sounded like Christian had his hands full, so he wouldn't be heading back home anytime soon to help us. Good news was, I knew he was closing in. He was one determined motherfucker. He was like a dog with a bone. His jaws locked around that bad boy if you tried to take it from him. I decided I was going to let him get back to business, but I was happy to hear from him.

"Keep me updated, okay. Don't be a fucking ghost again. And call Vixen, the girls have been worried sick about your ass," I said.

"I will, take care," Christian said, then he ended the call.

"Christian okay?" Ansell asked.

I looked at him; god, he was so perfectly beautiful in every way. How someone couldn't appreciate his kind spirit was beyond me. I loved everything about him, his cute, slender nose that ended with a button-like shape at the tip. His soft lips that begged for my kiss, and his warm amber eyes that looked at me with so much compassion, trust, and love. I was born to be with him and I wanted to always hold him close to me. I was happy to say goodbye to those days of bed hopping with strange men. Ansell and me forever. I needed to carve that into a tree somewhere.

"Yeah, it was Christian," I answered finally. I could tell he was starting to get curious. He didn't know that I was just lost in the vision of him. "He's close to closing the case. So, he won't be able to help us."

"What's he working on?"

"Turns out it was a Nephilim that was killing those children."

Ansell shook his head. "A what?"

"You've got a lot to learn. I can't wait to teach you everything. For now, here's the Cliffs Notes version. Nephilims are children born of higher beings that have been rejected from heaven. So, demons, but only the most powerful of demons."

"You mean like a fallen angel?"

I nodded. "Exactly."

"Holy shit! So angels are real?" Ansell asked, his voice going up an octave in his excitement.

"Yes. Though they don't come to earth often. However, I think you can summon one, but it's hard as hell. It would require someone willing to give themselves over as the vessel and the killing of a high-level demon to even get their attention. Angels are God's warriors, so they only recognize a warrior of their own caliber. They also don't care for humans, they're an arrogant bunch. Even after you've done those things to try to summon one, they'll only come if they want to. Demons are different, they love to break out of hell. After certain seals are broken, big baddies can be set free, like the claiming of a thousand souls from the relic will release Astaroth. Now, he's bad news, but he's not a fallen angel turned demon. However, he is the son of one. If Astaroth decides to release his father or mother, I can't imagine what would happen."

"So, one of these fallen angels got out and had a baby?" Ansell asked. I could tell he was absorbing all of the information I was giving him. There was so much of it.

"A Nephilim is the offspring of a demigod, which is the offspring of a hexigod. The hexigod is the fallen angel. If there's one thing that can bring an angel to earth, it's when fallen angels, known as hexigods, are released from their prisons in hell. I've never personally faced off with a hexigod, but from what I've heard, they are damn near impossible to kill with what we work with on this plane," I said, hoping to put things into perspective for Ansell. "Astaroth is a demigod."

"Is Orcal a Nephilim?" Ansell asked.

I shook my head. "Not according to data collected back then when he tried to pull this stunt centuries ago. He's just an upper level demon, which is a pain in the ass enough, trust me."

"I guess that's a silver lining."

"Yeah." I continued to update him on my partner. "So, this Nephilim that Christian is tracking down wants his daddy back."

"Are Nephilim's evil?" Ansell asked.

"Not necessarily. They have a great capacity to be both good and/or evil, just like humans. Their fathers may be big boss demons, but their mothers are still human with morals. Nephilims are immortal and powerful, but they can be killed too, with blessed weapons like what we have, or by another Nephilim. I've even known vampires to kill one."

"Vampires are that powerful?" Ansell asked as if shocked by the information.

I nodded. "It's a reason why they're arrogant like that bastard Lorcán. The only way to kill one is to pierce their hearts with a blessed weapon. Or decapitation, sunlight, or fire. But even if you try to decapitate one, you'll need a blessed weapon. Their bones are very hard to break or slice through with normal weapons. It's almost impossible unless you have super strength. That's why most human slayers use fire. That's also why most vampires have human bodyguards to protect them during the day."

"Wow," Ansell puffed out. I could tell he was developing a little more respect for Lorcán. The vampire whose club I was only five minutes away from now.

I decided to continue. "Vampires are a pain in the ass to deal with if you're trying to take one down. They are fast, strong, have mental powers where they can glamour you or read your mind. The older they are, the more powerful all of their abilities grow. Those guys become regents, eventually, like around millennia. They need to be that old to be able to handle the challenges of that coveted role, such as disobedient vampires. I wonder just how special or strong Lorcán is for why he's a regent at such a young age. It's really nagging me."

"He's like a hundred fifty, right?" Ansell asked.

I nodded. "A bit over that."

His eyes widened. "And that's young to you?"

I nodded. "Again, for a regent, yeah. But Lorcán has been a regent for the past ninety-eight years, which means he got the position at only sixty-nine years old."

"Ooh, now I see what you mean. Well, now *I'm* curious as to how badass he is," Ansell said.

"We're here. I just hope that son of a bitch, Regis, is here too." I pulled into a parking spot in the garage and climbed out. I helped Ansell climb out too, as he was holding the box. The elevator was disabled. I figured because the club was closed. So we walked around to the side door like before. I knocked on the door twice before it opened. Stephan was standing on the opposite side, dressed in a pair of black jeans and a white satin button-down shirt with an interesting pattern on it. I couldn't say it was my style, but he claimed to be into men's fashion, so I kept my mouth shut.

"'Bout time you got here," he said, as if he had better things to do. Motherfucker was probably just standing in the room watching Lorcán sleep and rubbing his nipples. I could smell his lust for Lorcán whenever I was in their presence. I wondered if the desire was mutual. Didn't seem that way. Lorcán only seemed to want Stephan's blood and servitude.

"Where's Lorcán?" I asked, not even wanting to respond to his snide remark. I was all about business right now. Both Ansell and I stepped into the club and looked around.

"He's in the VIP area with Mr. Maxfield's tasteless-dressing ass. You two should get along fabulously," he said, throwing that little insult in at the end.

Again, I didn't take the bait. Stephan was as insufferable as his master, in my opinion, but I needed Lorcán, so I'd play nice.... for now. I walked over to the VIP section with both Ansell and Stephan behind me. My body was so tense, I swore I felt like my muscles were wound up tight like a coil ready to spring into action. As we approached the area, I saw Lorcán sitting on the sofa with one leg crossed over the other. He was wearing a white satin bathrobe and satin pajama pants. His slippers were black, though. Pompous ass. Again, he didn't look too pleased to have to be awake during the day, but tough shit. The other man with him, who I could only see from behind, I presumed to be Mr. Regis Maxfield. As I came around, I saw that it was Regis and he was sitting in the chair, fidgeting as it were.

Just by looking at the man, I couldn't see if there was a demon inside of him, but I felt something was off about him. I took a few steps closer towards him and stopped in my tracks. In the reflection of the glass walls, I saw it. The demon that was hiding deep inside

Regis' body. I'd never seen anything like this before. Just how in the hell was this demon riding passenger inside his body? Either a demon killed the human and took full control, or the human soul was trapped until it died. Either way, the demon was behind the wheel and, therefore, I could always see it.

This was uncharted territory for me. It was as if his features and Mr. Maxfield's features were blended, making the human's features appear distorted… demonic in the reflection. I could see little horns protruding from his forehead, fanged teeth in his mouth, and a snout-like nose, but the rest were still human features. I cleared my throat and continued forward as if I hadn't noticed it. I was going to have to feel my way through this one.

"Took you long enough," Lorcán complained.

"We came as quickly as we could," I responded as we walked up the stairs.

Lorcán arched an eyebrow as he looked at me, then at Ansell. I didn't have his ability to read minds, but I knew what the bastard was thinking.

"Sorry to disappoint, but we were all business, Lorcán."

He sighed and shrugged. "Too bad for you, then."

Vampires had a great sense of smell, but nothing like a werewolf, or even mine. I could still smell the scent of my cum on Ansell and his on me, but obviously Lorcán couldn't. Now, if it were blood, well, that was another story. Vampires could smell a drop of blood a mile away.

"Speaking of business, Lorcán tells me you have something I want," Mr. Maxfield interjected.

"I have something you need." I took the seat opposite Mr. Maxfield, whom I'd call Regis, for now. Ansell sat down next to Lorcán, who gave my mate a lingering look. One that, on any other day, would have sent me into violent action… or at least, would have caused me to make a comment or two about keeping his fucking eyes to himself. Or something like that. But this was serious and not the time to throw around my machismo. I looked at Regis. "Let's not beat around the bush, you made the mistake a lot of novice humans make when they encounter demons. You made a deal with one."

"How do you kn—"

"I know things, it's my job to know them. So, when a demon tries to get you to kill hundreds of people, I like to be there to put an end to it."

Mr. Maxfield scoffed. "I have nothing to do with those deaths."

I smirked. "Come now, Mr. Maxfield, you are in possession of the *Stone of Astaroth* and you did have the *Soul of Agenta*. These are very dangerous relics. Especially in the hands of a clueless human."

Regis gritted his teeth and rose to his feet. "I had nothing to do with those deaths!"

Ansell reached out, touching Regis' arm. "Please, we only want to help you. Hear us out."

Regis gave my mate an angry glare and snatched his arm away. "I came here to purchase whatever artifact you said you were selling. Not to be accused of murder! You've got some balls, buddy."

"Sit down, Regis, or I'll put you down," I snapped. It was time to take off the kid gloves. This son of a bitch was denying what we all knew to be the truth. I didn't have time for his bullshit. Especially if he was planning on killing a bunch of kids.

With the tone of my voice and the threat behind my words, he seemed to reconsider his stance of leaving and sat back down in the chair. Lorcán chuckled, then yawned. Perhaps he was bored and entertained at the same time, who knew with him. I turned my attention back to Regis.

"Listen, I know the demon is inside of you. Did that happen when you used the *Soul of Agenta*?"

He looked around like he was contemplating on lying, but then he sighed and nodded. "Yes."

"You were trying to put your soul into another human? What about his soul?" Ansell asked.

Regis held his hands up. "He was a criminal. Had killed his wife, but was never convicted due to lack of evidence. So, save your judgement. I was going to do great things with his body. He didn't deserve his youth or looks."

"Regardless," I interjected because I didn't want to get off topic. "You need the *Eye of Ezel* in order to transfer your soul into that of the younger body. If that's what the demon promised you, I can help with that. Besides, with the *Eye of Ezel*, you don't need a living being, just a fresh vessel." I really had little to no intentions of getting this man into a younger body if I could help it. But if I had no other choice, I was going to visit the morgue to see if I could find him a newly dead corpse. No one alive, that was for sure. Thing was, I needed him to believe me so he'd allow me to perform the exorcism. It was easier to extract the demon if the human host wasn't fighting the exorcism.

I could tell I had his undivided attention now. The rage was melting from his expression and he was looking thoughtful, as if he were trying to figure things out. "You claim to have this *Eye of* ..."

"*Ezel*," I supplied. "It was the real relic you were looking for, but were fooled into purchasing the *Soul of Agenta*. Whatever ritual you used to try to put your soul into another body was corrupted by that relic. That is how the demon breached the two worlds and entered into ours using your body." I was able to put two-and-two together now that I knew he botched his spell with the wrong relic. That was why I couldn't fully see the demon, who I assumed was Orcal. They were sharing one body, and perhaps Regis was still in full control. Highly irregular.

Regis frowned. "Two worlds?"

"Ours and hell," Lorcán stated. "When you fucked up your ritual, you opened a gateway to hell large enough for a demon to get through. A minion of Astaroth, to be more exact. Your body was used as a conduit, and that is why you are possessed. I would suggest you take my friend's advice, accept his help and free yourself of that demon nuisance."

I had to admit, I wasn't expecting that from Lorcán. He seemed to know a lot about the demonic world in order to explain that much to Regis. I guess I needed to give vampires, or maybe just him, a little more credit. In any case, Regis definitely had something to think about now.

He looked at me. "The man whose body I was going to take is imprisoned in my mansion."

"The one in Highland Heights?" Ansell asked.

Regis shook his head. "No, I have another mansion in New Hillshire, two hours' travel time from here. I can have my people bring him so that we can perform the ritual. But that still doesn't solve the other thing the demon promised me."

"First off, we don't need to use a living human. I can get you one," I said.

"A healthy body? See, because I know this guy is healthy and free of bullet and knife holes. If we do this, we're doing it with the body I chose. You don't have to like it, but it's my choice," Regis said, being stubborn on the matter. "Besides, I've already set up everything financially for this body. After my dear father dies, his son will inherit his fortune. His son being me, in my new body."

Ansell shook his head in disgust. "I was wondering if you were going to kill him, because if you switched bodies, he'd be you and then what? You are one diabo—"

"Fine," I said, cutting Ansell off because I could tell he wanted to rip Regis a new asshole. We needed this dude to trust us. Again, I didn't plan on giving into his demands, but he needed to think that I would. The good thing about this conversation… at least he stopped denying the truth. Now, we could get down to business. "We'll do it your way. About this other thing the demon promised you, what was it?"

"Immortality and power. He promised me these things if…"

His voice trailed off as if he'd caught himself before revealing too much. But, that only made me curious as to what he was trying to hide. "What did you promise to him for the things you wanted?"

Regis' face became somber and he averted his gaze so as to not have to look me in the eye. "I... I couldn't kill. He wanted four hundred thirty-six souls to feed to the *Stone of Astaroth*. I... I just couldn't kill all those people."

"You were going to kill that guy," Ansell pointed out.

"That was one asshole who deserved to die. Remember, he killed his wife. Trust me, he did it," Regis said in his defense.

"You must have gotten over that, because you did kill, and now that thing only needs two hundred ninety-seven more souls. All it takes is one more time at the right location for that to happen." I thought about the school. There would be teachers, parents picking up kids, and children. More than enough souls for that relic to absorb and release Astaroth. Jesus Christ! Sometimes, I wished the world was really like most people believed it to be. Free of monsters and demons and the ever-present threat of hell on earth.

"I didn't kill those people," Regis continued to protest.

"Then who the fuck did?" I asked. He was really testing my patience with this bullshit.

"Look, let's just say that I wasn't there when shit went down." Regis was as vague as he could be.

"What about when you tried to kill me at your mansion that night?" I confronted.

"I knew you two looked familiar!" Regis blurted out.

"Yeah, yeah, we've met. So, explain yourself," I snapped.

He shook his head. "I... I was just doing what Orcal told me to do. I saw what was happening to you and..." He looked off to the side.

I cocked an eyebrow. "And?"

"It freaked me the hell out. So, I stopped chanting, but then this guy over here..." he pointed to Ansell, "tackled me, so I ran."

I was starting to put the pieces together. I was also right in assuming Orcal was the demon sitting cozy inside Regis.

"I see," Lorcán said. Apparently, he was coming to the same conclusion I had. "You wanted what the demon promised, but didn't have what it took to carry out your end of the bargain, so you gave the demon possession over your body."

"That explains why the killings only happened at night. That's when the demon takes over, right?" I asked.

Again, Regis averted his gaze as if he was too ashamed to admit the truth. I shook my head, disgusted by how far and how fucking low he was willing to go to get what he wanted. Still, I needed him to believe that I wanted to help him achieve his goals. Really, I wanted to get that bastard-ass demon out of his body and then lock Regis in a human jail for murder. Of course, the confession he gave may end up putting him in a mental institute instead. Bottom line was, he was dangerous and didn't need to be free. Maybe, just maybe the Institute would find someplace to put him. If not, well, I wasn't opposed to taking out a human threat. I didn't like making a habit of killing humans, but for ones this dangerous, I always made the exception.

"You want immortality and power?" I asked.

Regis looked at me and nodded. "And eternal youth."

"Here's the deal. We switch your soul into the body you want using the *Eye of Ezel*, then Lorcán has agreed to give you both immortality and power," I said.

"Oh really?" Regis turned toward Lorcán. "So, you've changed your mind? Because when I came to you first, you were very clear that I wasn't worthy of vampire blood."

Lorcán shrugged. "Financially, you are worthy. Perhaps I was too hasty in my decision before."

I had to admit, Lorcán was a great liar. I knew he didn't want to turn Regis into a vampire. I knew he wouldn't, too. If his fangs entered Regis' flesh, he was going to drain that human dry as a bone. Of course, that would be against the law, but I might make an exception, like I said. I was watching Ansell and he was totally absorbing everything he was seeing and hearing. He was learning how things went in my world. I was seeing how sometimes we had to use deception to save lives. I hoped he didn't think differently of me, knowing I was lying to Regis. To Ansell's credit, he was playing along.

Regis pursed his lips, obviously weighing his options. He could refuse our offer and go with whatever the demon had promised him. Or he could screw the demon out of the deal and take a chance on us.

"Will it hurt?" Regis asked.

"Most likely, yes. You've given the demon partial possession of your body. It's not going to want to leave. It will hurt like hell to exorcise it from your body. Now that I know the demon's name, it will be a little easier." There was power in knowing a demon's name when it came to controlling, exorcising, or conjuring one.

Regis sighed and nodded. "I never wanted to hurt anyone innocent. I thought I didn't have a choice. Being a vampire, will I have to kill people?" He was looking at Lorcán now.

Lorcán cocked an eyebrow. "Killing humans is forbidden. Feed, not kill."

Regis exhaled a deep breath, as if he were relieved by that information. "Okay, that's good. Will it take long?"

I shook my head. "No, once I set everything up and say the magic words… this demon will be sent back to hell and you'll have your body again. Then we can do the transformation for you."

"I need to ask, why are you willing to help me?" Regis asked me.

I didn't have a good answer for that. Outside of the truth. I wanted to get rid of the demon and save the world.

"Because, my sovereign wants you to be a part of our people. Like I said, financially, you are worthy. Our blood is sacred and we are very particular about who receives it. You want to be young, you already have a body on standby. This is a win-win situation, Mr. Maxfield," Lorcán said, taking over. "My friend here is someone I contacted to assist us, as he is an expert in the field of demonology."

Thank goodness he stepped up and gave this man a believable

lie. Time to add to it. "Lorcán wants to turn you. I want to stop the demon, that's why I broke into your house. I knew that relic was bad news. In any case, you get what you want. We all get what we want. So, are you ready?" I asked, putting things into perspective.

He took a few seconds to think about it, then nodded. "Yes."

"Good. Okay." Finally, progress. Maybe I could prevent Ansell's vision from coming true. I wasn't surprised that Orcal was involved. It was either going to be Orcal, Remer, or Eve. Those were the known minion demons of Astaroth. The only ones powerful enough to bring forth their master. Remer was actually a Nephilim, Astaroth's son, but he was trapped in hell, too.

"What does this ritual entail?' Lorcán asked.

"I'll need to bind Regis in a demon cell, so to speak."

"Does that mean you'll be painting shit on my floors?" he asked.

I looked at his lovely non-slip floor in the dancing area and the marble flooring in the seating areas of his club. Perhaps, I could do him a solid and do this in the parking garage or in the basement. Once I began the exorcism, the demonic seal would set fire and char the spot I painted it on. I decided to explain that to Lorcán, who frowned.

"I will make sure to send you the bill to have my floor replaced," he said, then added, "We'll do this in one of the rooms upstairs."

Ohhh, I was about to find out what happens on the second floor. Or maybe I was going to see where he lived.

"Follow me." Lorcán rose from the sofa and we all did the same, then followed him up the stairs and onto the elevator to the third floor. Oh well, I guess I wasn't about to see where he lived because there were obviously three more stories to this place. We walked off the elevator and he led us to a room that had some bondage gear all around it. Chains with cuffs connected to red velvet walls. Chains dangled from the ceiling with hooks. I could smell blood on the floor even though none could be seen. There were cages, bondage tables, and chairs strategically placed around the room, along with

St. Andrew's crosses.

I looked at Lorcán. "Should I even ask what this room is used for?"

I looked at Ansell, and he was being very careful not to touch anything, or let anything touch him. But I could tell he was curious by how he was looking at everything.

Lorcán chuckled. "Some vampires have particular tastes. I assure you, Mr. Kumar, no human was killed in this room. As a matter of fact, I think whatever you're going to sear into my floor would fit in this room. It would only add to the ambiance."

I shook my head. I didn't want to imagine what vampires or humans were doing in this room. Pain and sex didn't match well in my book. I was all about pleasure, giving and receiving. I didn't say any more on the subject. I just walked over to Ansell and pulled out a jug from the box he was holding.

"I'll teach you how do to this too, okay?" I told him.

"For now, I'll just watch you," Ansell said.

I nodded, leaned over, kissing his forehead, then I stepped away towards the middle of the room. The floor was black marble with gold flecks. The room was nicely decorated, you know, if you took out the BDSM shit. I might do a little light spanking, but couldn't really see myself doing the hardcore stuff that this room lent itself to.

I opened the jar and poured the holy oil in a circle first, then walked back over to the box, removing a paint brush. Getting the sigils right was essential in working any spell. One wrong design and you could be totally fucked. I dipped the brush in the oil and painted each intricate design carefully until the seal was complete.

"All right, now I need for you, Regis, to stand in the middle," I instructed.

Regis hesitated, but eventually, he did move to the middle of the seal. I supposed he really wanted to get rid of the demon more than following through with the deal he had made with the thing. He still didn't know if he could trust us. But maybe he wasn't a hundred percent sure he could trust the demon, either. The lesser of two evils, I guess that was what Lorcán and I were to him. I'd take whatever I could get at this point.

I looked at Lorcán and Ansell. "Once I start, I cannot be interrupted, no matter what happens. Okay?" Lorcán nodded. I looked at Ansell, who hadn't given me confirmation yet. "Okay?"

"I don't want you hurt," he said, then put the box down to give me a hug. I hugged him back, trying not to squeeze him too hard. He didn't have the super strength that I did. I didn't want to break him, even though I wanted to hold him as hard as I could just to feel him closer to me.

I released him. "The demon will lash out, so you should stay a safe distance away. I have to do this. It's what I was born to do. I need to make sure you understand this, Ansell, and you won't try to interfere." I was studying his worried face and hating that he was even in this position. But this was our world, and we both had to get used to it and get used to feeling worried about the other. I was so accustomed to just looking out for number one on these missions. Now, I had to look out for two.

Ansell nodded finally. "Be careful."

"I will." I smiled, then motioned for him to stand back farther.

Lorcán took him by the arm and moved him to the far corner of the room, and then he stood in front of him. If I didn't know any better, it would seem the vampire wasn't as heartless as I thought he was. Perhaps there was more to him than I suspected. Now, I was even more curious about who Lorcán really was than before.

I put the jug and brush back into the box and then pulled out some rosary beads, one for me to hold and the other to go around Regis' neck. I knew the exorcism spell by heart for this level of demon. There were nine levels of demons, just like there were nine levels of hell. And you had to use the right spell according to the level of demon or you were sure to fail the exorcism. We had to study each spell every day for six months in the Institute, and every once in a while, they gave us a pop quiz to make sure we remembered.

I knew all nine spells like I knew my name. Of course, the ninth level spell could only weaken the demon. The ninth level was a hexigod, they didn't possess humans, didn't need to. You just couldn't shove them back into hell with a few words. You could bind them temporarily until you could call an angel to finish the task. As for demigods, they didn't need to possess humans either. But the eighth-level spell along with the *Orb of Orleander* would trap the demon and then you could send him back to hell using the Orb as a landline, so to speak, with another spell.

But that was a lesson for another day. I had to stay focused on this particular task. Orcal was a seventh-level demon and I began my exorcism, saying the words that would first call the demon forth, then as I continued, it would force the demon back to hell. As I said the words, I could see Regis' body start to twitch. Initially, it was small movements, then he began to shake more violently. His eyes rolled up inside his head and he began to foam at the mouth. All signs that the demon was fighting me. That was why it was so important to make sure the human was willing. I was going to get enough opposition from the demon side of this. I sprinkled more holy water on Regis' body as I spoke the spell and he thrashed his body from side to side, snarling and growling in an inhuman voice. I could see out of the corner of my eye, Ansell clinging to Lorcán's back as he watched in a mixture of fear and awe.

"Fu…fuck… you… hunter," Regis said in a voice that was much raspier and gravelly than his own. I knew then that the demon was surfacing. I could even see his true face better hidden behind his human façade.

I continued to say the words, I couldn't break the spell's sequence. Regis' body began to convulse, his arms flailing about as his legs seemed to spasm in some grotesque dance. This demon was really fighting. It didn't help that Regis had not only allowed himself to be possessed in the first place, but he'd given the damn thing permission to take control of his body. This was going to be an ugly exorcism.

Regis' face twisted into a horrible mask as the demon's features became more prominent. Red eyes, yellow sharp teeth, and its pug nose with its flaring nostrils. "He… he's mine!"

The demon growled, then I felt an invisible force lash out at me, sending me crashing against the wall of chains. The metal clinked behind the impact of my body and I refused to break the spell even though my body throbbed from the pain. I steadied myself and approached the demon again. The demon yelled, its foul breath beating me in the face, making me want to gag. It was hot and putrid like you'd expect a demon's breath to smell. I was sure the whole room was filled with the rancid scent. Still, I continued to say the words.

I was nearing the end of the exorcism and starting to worry, because it seemed as though the demon was getting stronger. I had to continue, though. I couldn't stop, because once you started, if you did stop for whatever reason, you left a two-way portal open that was unchecked. Anything could travel from hell into our world on that level or a being could accidentally be sucked into Orcal's level of hell. And level seven was a real nasty place to be.

Again, the demon cursed at me, growled and hissed, but I continued until the last word was free of my lips, and that was when Regis' body fell to the floor in a crumpled heap. His body was literally dripping with sweat and his chest heaved as he slumped there in the confines of the seal. Something was wrong, very wrong. I needed to see Regis' face, because this hadn't gone down like I had expected.

"Regis?" I asked and slightly shook his shoulder.

Regis slapped my hand away hard enough to snap the bones in my wrist. I felt the instant pain shoot up my arm as my wrist went limp. Again, he sent another blast of power, which thrust Lorcán, Ansell, and me back against the walls with such force, it rattled my body and knocked the air out of my lungs. My head smashed against the chains, giving me a nice dose of dizziness. I slid to the floor, my vision blurred. I watched through a cloudy veil as Regis rose to his feet. His face was still human, but I could clearly see Orcal's demonic features now. Somehow, Regis was now gone and Orcal had claimed full control of the human vessel. The demon smiled at me, then said something in his language that I could loosely translate into "freedom" and "break." After he said his words, the entire building began to shake like we were experiencing an earthquake. Just then, the floor cracked where I'd painted the seal, thus breaking it.

My wrist was on fire and I had to wait until my bones healed in order to use it again. Still, I had to do something. I struggled to my feet, trying to keep my balance as the building continued to shake.

Regis laughed as he stepped out of the seal and approached me. "Hunters… you think you're stronger than us. Smarter than us. Boy, I have lived eons before your little Institute even existed. I walked the earth long before your Christ bled for your sins. It is his blood that gives you the abilities you have. None of which are a match for me or my master, Astaroth. He will rise, and when he does, you better pray you're already dead."

I pulled my blessed knife from my back sheath and it was a struggle, because the demon was asserting his power over me, over all of us, actually. Ansell and Lorcán were both plastered against the walls by a force, keeping them immobile. The demon looked down, seeing my knife, as I knew he would. I felt like I was moving in slow motion, even though I was trying as hard as I could to attack this son of a bitch.

The demon laughed. "I don't think so, little hunter." He grinned, showing off his teeth. Human in the front, but I could see his demon fangs behind the human mask. Again, I was blasted against the St. Andrew's cross. My head slammed against the hard wood of the cross before I fell to the floor. My head took another blow when it clashed with the hard marble tile. That was when everything went black.

"Please, baby... please wake up."

The sound of Ansell's strained voice began to draw me out of my state of unconsciousness. I slowly opened my eyes and became aware of a throbbing headache, followed by a violent wave of nausea. I gagged and, before I knew it, I spewed my stomach contents on the floor in front of me. Ansell was rubbing my back as I puked.

"Gross," I heard Stephan say.

I was in too bad of shape to give his bitch ass a comeback. I dry heaved a little, then swallowed hard, trying to calm my stomach down. I laid my head down on Ansell's lap and let him rub the throbbing pain from my skull with his gentle, loving fingers.

"Are you okay?" I asked him. My words were barely a whisper, but I needed to know that he was unharmed.

"Yes, I'm not hurt, badly that is. I've got a few bruises. We'd all be dead if Lorcán hadn't used his fire on that demon. Too bad he got away. Good news is, I know where he's going. I had a vision. Baby, I need you. Please be okay."

The sound of tears and pain in his voice was almost too much for me to bear. I forced the cobwebs out of my mind and sat up. That fucking demon was stronger than anything I'd faced before. Not to mention, he was a slick one. In retrospect, I could see now why my exorcism didn't work.

Hold the fuck up? Did I hear Ansell correctly? Lorcán used *his fire*? Last I remembered, before my head got smashed into a wall, was that both he and Ansell were pinned against the wall by the demon's powers. I needed clarification.

"What did you mean by Lorcán used his fire?" I asked Ansell.

"He means, I have the ability to conjure fire. And that's all you need to know," Lorcán supplied with a bit of attitude. "Lucky for you that I do, because that demon was going to kill you with your own blade after you were knocked unconscious."

I looked up at him, shocked. Well, I believed my mystery had been solved. All this time, I'd been wondering how in the hell he got to be a regent at such a young age. If a vampire could control fire… that made him one deadly son of a bitch. Having that question answered only opened the door to a dozen more questions, like how in the fuck did he have the ability to control or conjure fire? I wanted to ask him, but that was going to have to be a conversation for another day. Even though I doubted he'd tell me. Rather than test my luck, I got back to the situation at hand and its dire importance. I needed to let them know what happened and why the spell went wrong.

"Orcal had used the time when he was in control of Regis' body to bind himself to the vessel like an anchor. That's a rare spell and it doesn't always work. But his possession was so odd, it did work. In the event that Regis died, he'd take over. When I tried to get rid of him, the sheer force of the exorcism destroyed Regis' soul. It was as if the spell had reversed because of the counter spell the demon put on the body. If I had known beforehand that the demon had done that, I would have tried to lock the demon down in Regis' body first, making the body a sort of prison for the demon. Then I would have killed Regis, because at that point, I had no other choice."

"Kill him, but wouldn't that have still freed the demon?" Ansell asked.

I shook my head a little, because I was still seeing stars. "Death by fire spell, seventh-level exorcism, would have destroyed the vessel and the demon would have been sent back to hell that way too. I try not to kill humans if I can help it, but had I known that Regis was doomed, I would have done that instead. Now, we have to track down this fucking demon."

It really was a shame that Lorcán couldn't have taken Orcal out with his fire. It would have saved me the trouble, for once.

"But you're injured," Ansell said, pointing to my obviously broken right wrist.

I groaned and winced when I cradled it. "It's healing. Feels more like a fracture now than fully broken." Of course, I still couldn't use it fully.

"When?" Lorcán asked.

"In about twenty-four hours. Maybe a little less, but I need Vixen to whip up one of her potions."

"We don't have time for that. You've been out for ten minutes. The demon probably has its souls by now. Especially since he's no longer bound by Regis and the deal he made that only allowed him control at night," Lorcán said, then he walked over towards me. "Drink my blood."

"The fuck I will," I snapped.

"The fuck you better, if you want to stop this demon. Look, it will heal you instantly and give you added strength… for a bit. You won't be bound to me. All you need is a little," Lorcán explained. "Instead of acting like an uninformed child, be grateful I'm willing to share my blood with you at all."

Well, I guess he had a point there. I really did need to get back into the fight. And that wasn't going to happen with me all banged the fuck up. Time to man the fuck up and bottom's up on this vamp blood. Something I didn't think I'd ever be doing, by the way.

Lorcán bit into his wrist and extended it to me. He licked his own blood from his lips as his fangs receded. I looked at his wrist with the two bleeding holes. God, this was so gross and wrong. Had I still been in the Institute, they'd surely kick me out for doing something like this. But since they kicked me out for sucking cock, fuck 'em. Neither Christian nor I had to follow their rules anymore. We made our own. I took his wrist and put my mouth on the wounds, and sucked. It wasn't like anything I had expected. It was actually very fucking good. Damn, it was good! My cock throbbed instantly and was hard enough to hammer nails into stone. Jesus Christ, no wonder so many humans wanted to be around them… demons and other monsters too!

"Okay, that's enough," Lorcán said, then he snatched his wrist and his beautiful, delicious blood from me.

I had to catch myself from reaching out and grabbing his wrist and forcing it back to my mouth at all costs. My chest was heaving and I wanted to fuck like there was no tomorrow. But shit, if I didn't get myself together and fast, there might not be a tomorrow. My wrist was healed completely, the throbbing and nausea was gone. I felt revitalized and stronger. Yeah, they were a great drug. I also saw why they policed themselves as strongly as they did. If the world knew how amazing vampire blood was… oh shit… things would get really ugly.

"Thanks, Lorcán," I said as I rose to my feet. I helped Ansell to his feet. I thought about Ansell's vision and how the kids were going to be killed during the day. Before this failed exorcism, Orcal only had control of Regis' body at night. Now, he was free to kill at will. My exorcism allowed that to happen. I wish my baby's vision could have given me that detail, but it is what it is. This is all new territory. For now, we had a demon to kill.

"The demon took your knife," Ansell said.

"I have more weapons in the Jeep. We need to go." I kissed him quickly. If I survived this mission, I was going to make love to him all day and night. I was going to put up a "do not ever fucking disturb" sign on my door and just ravage him. That was if we both survived.

"Take Stephan with you," Lorcán offered.

"I'm going with them?" Stephan asked, shocked by Lorcán's command.

"Yes, you have my blood and can offer the aid in my stead."

"But, what about you? I need to protect you," Stephan argued.

"If we don't stop this demon, you won't be able to protect me. Now, do as I've commanded. Go," Lorcán ordered.

Stephan ceased whatever protest he wanted to give and nodded.

"Um," Ansell said, catching everyone's attention. "I don't mean to be rude or anything, I really don't. But that demon rendered you kind of powerless, Lorcán. How can your human servant help us?"

"How dare you," Stephan snarled. I watched him ball his hands into fists, as if he were going to lash out at Ansell.

"Touch him and see what a real hunter can do," I warned.

"Enough!" Lorcán belted out, getting everyone's attention. "To answer your rude question, whether it was intended that way or not, during the day, vampires aren't as strong. That is why we require daytime protection. I am willing to offer you mine in order to stop this demon. Remember, don't look gift horses in their mouths or I might not be so helpful in the future, especially when it means putting myself and my businesses at risk."

"Thank you," I said, hopefully putting an end to a potentially unnecessary squabble.

"I really didn't mean to offend," Ansell said, then picked up the box with our stuff in it.

"I know, baby. Let's let this go. We've got to catch this demon," I said, then walked out of the badly damaged room. Ansell and Stephan followed me. I was sure Lorcán was going to send us one hell of a bill. I wasted no time getting down to my Jeep. Stephan did a little grumbling, but kept it to a minimum. I looked at Ansell, who was sitting in the passenger seat with the box in his lap. "Okay, baby. You said you had a vision. What did you see and where are we going?"

Chapter Eighteen

Angel

I heard Stephan snort at D'Angelo's term of endearment, but I ignored him. I knew the situation was dire—hell, I'd seen the aftermath of that demon's visit to the school in my vision—but all I could think about right then was how lucky I was that my mate was still alive. Yes, we had serious work to do, but I wasn't going another minute without telling him how I felt about him.

"I love you, D'Angelo," I blurted. I felt my cheeks heat with embarrassment for the way I handled my declaration.

I wouldn't say the tension faded from D, but a sweet smile spread slowly across his lips. "I love you too, Ansell. I'll show you when we get back home."

"Oh, for fuck's sake," Stephan snarled from the back seat. "I didn't agree to this soap opera bullshit. Suck his dick if you must because I wouldn't mind seeing that, but save that lovey-dovey crap for when we kill that motherfucking demon. Damn, D'Angelo, I thought you were more badass than this."

"Shut the fuck up, blood bag," D'Angelo snarled at Stephan without taking his eyes away from mine. He offered me another smile before he looked at our unhappy sidekick in the back seat. I looked too and saw that Stephan's face was almost as red as his hair, which made the freckles stick out on his nose. The fiery flash I saw in his light blue eyes told me he was ready to tangle with D'Angelo. D didn't seem too worried about it, though. "You should be so lucky to have a mate to share your life with, but you're too busy holding out hope that Lorcán will see you as something other than an appetizer."

"You don't know what the fuck you're talking about," Stephan said, but his voice didn't sound as confident as his words.

It was obvious to anyone who looked at the two men that Stephan was in love with Lorcán, but the vampire didn't return his human's feelings. I finally knew what it felt like to love and be loved, and I felt bad for anyone who didn't get to experience that amazing feeling for themselves. Apparently, I hadn't learned to hide my feelings because Stephan took one look at me and flipped me off.

"Someone still acts like he's in the third grade when he doesn't like what he hears," I said, not sure where my bravery had come from.

"Do you two dumbasses want to suck face and joke, or do you want to stop that demon before he kills again? Besides, the quicker we get done, the quicker you guys can drop me back off at Hypnotic and can go literally fuck yourselves."

I couldn't argue with his reasoning, even if I didn't like his crude talk. "I saw the name of the school. It's Saint Brigid Academy. There are a lot of kids, teachers, and parents gathered outside the building for some reason when Orcal strikes."

"It's probably the last day of school for these kids. Maybe the school has something special planned for the kids and their families are attending also," D'Angelo replied. He whipped out his cell phone and looked up the location of the school, then looked at the time. "We better get over there and get into position. Where did this take coming from, man? I didn't ask you to come along. Lorcán *commanded* you to tag along with us." The car behind us started honking when the light changed green and we hadn't moved.

"Fuck you, asshole," Stephan said, then turned in his seat to flip the driver off. Of course, it was doubtful they saw the gesture through D's tinted windows. When he turned back around, I was happy to see the animosity was no longer on his face. "Hey, Angel, I'm sorry for what I just said. That was really unfair to you—to both of you," he amended, but I noticed his tone wasn't as friendly when he included D in the mix. "I don't know, D. I'm just really feeling out of sorts lately. I'm not sure where it's coming from. Nothing has changed, but the things that made me happy in the past just aren't cutting it any longer."

I nearly had whiplash from Stephan's sudden turnaround. One minute, he was snarly, and the next, he sounded like he was sitting on Dr. Phil's couch. D'Angelo glanced over at me long enough to roll his eyes. I was pretty sure that D would rather hiss, spit, and bicker with Stephan than listen to him unburden his troubles. D'Angelo only extended that broad shoulder to me, but I was his mate and he loved me.

"I didn't agree to listen to you whine about your love life," D'Angelo snarled. *Yep, that shoulder was just for me.* "Pull up your big boy briefs and focus on what we need to do. The sooner we kill the demon, the sooner you get back to doing… whatever it is you do for Lorcán." D'Angelo held up his hand. "No, don't enlighten me, either."

I turned around to look at Stephan, expecting him to be glaring at D, but he was grinning like a fool. I could tell he was dying to come back at D'Angelo with a snarky response, but he wisely kept his mouth shut.

I sat there beside D'Angelo riding into battle, but in a Jeep instead of on a horse, against a scary mofo demon with a goofy fucking grin on my face. It wasn't that I was under some misguided notion that I was a fearless warrior, because I was scared out of my damn mind, and I didn't know jack about killing a demon. The thing was, I lived my whole life in fear of something or other, so I was kind of used to it. The difference was that I no longer feared being unloved or feared loving someone else. I was truly loved and wanted for the first time in my life, and if it was my last day on earth, at least I knew what that felt like.

D'Angelo must've sensed my emotions through our bond because he reached over and cupped the back of my neck. His hand was warm and the weight of it kept me tethered to him. "We're going to kill that bastard and then we're going to go home—"

"Oh god, here we go again," Stephan groused.

"—and celebrate all night long. No one better knock on our door," D said, paying no attention to our guest. "I have many things to show you."

"Yeah?" Stephan asked, sounding interested for the first time. "Like what? Were you a virgin?" I turned to pin him with my meanest glare, but he wasn't scared of me. He grinned from ear to ear. "Oh, so now you remember that I'm back here and clam up when you get to the good shit."

"Shut your fucking mouth," D'Angelo said between gritted teeth. It was obvious he didn't like Stephan thinking or picturing anything intimate between us.

"Yes, Daddy," Stephan said playfully, ignoring D's dangerous tone.

"Eww, no," D'Angelo said. "Stop that."

"No daddy kink, huh?" Stephan asked.

"I'm going to twist your nuts off when this mission is over." D'Angelo had lost all traces of humor. I thought it was because Stephan crossed some kind of line, but I realized the real source when he spoke next. "We're here, so let's get our heads back on the mission and keep our eyes peeled for Regis."

"This isn't the entrance I saw," I told D'Angelo as he drove by the front of the school. "There were more trees and shade, so the sun was on the opposite side of the building." D'Angelo drove around the block so we could see the side entrance to the left and the rear of the building. "Nope, it must be the right side."

I sucked in a sharp breath when D made that final turn because it was identical to my vision. It still shocked me how accurate and detailed they were after several years of living with them. I had never been wrong, not once. There were minivans, SUVs, and sedans parked along both sides of the street. It looked like the parents, mostly moms with some dads mixed in, were milling around the outside of the building. Some of them looked happy that the end of the school year was minutes away, and others not so much, but they radiated vibes of expectancy, which told me we had showed up in the nick of time.

All talking ceased as the three of us searched the perimeter for Regis. There was nowhere to park on that side street, so D'Angelo circled the block again until he found one just around the corner at the rear of the building.

"It's time to suit up," D'Angelo said when he put the Jeep in park. He wasted no time getting out of the Jeep and circling around to the back. He had the hatch open and was sorting through his tools by the time Stephan and I joined him.

"Whoa," I said when I looked down at the wicked-looking weapon he picked out. It had a long blade that ended in a sharp point and two curved prongs projecting from the handle. "What the hell is that thing?"

"It's a sai," D'Angelo replied. "This one happens to be blessed, so all I need to do is get close enough to stab Regis with it in a vital place like the heart."

"So you think you're just going to walk up to an elementary school carrying that sword and no one is going to call the cops? You'll be shot dead before Regis shows, mi amigo," Stephan said. He had a good point, but I could tell by the arrogant lift to D's brows that there was more to his plan than he'd revealed so far.

D'Angelo snorted in derision. "It's cute how you think this is my first rodeo, Stephie."

"Do not call me that again," Stephan snarled.

"Don't insult my intelligence again," D countered. He pulled out a long black coat like the kind you'd see a hunter wear in a television show or movie. D'Angelo slipped it on and slid his wicked sai into a special holder on the inside of the left side.

Stephan snorted again and shook his head. "Yeah, you don't stand out like a sore thumb at all in that getup, Blade. No one wears a long black coat like that in June. It's like you're itching to get shot or something."

"Fellas, can we save the testosterone for the battle?" I turned to my mate then and said, "Tell us about the rest of your plan."

"I have a cloaking device," he replied.

"Like the rings we wore into the movie theater?" I questioned.

"No, this is more scientific than a spell," D replied. "Our group uses a combination of blessed skills, magic spells, and cutting-edge technology. Look, the rings worked great at the movie theater because we only wanted to slip in unnoticed. That won't work in this case unless we can somehow slip a ring on Regis' hand before we kill him." D'Angelo reached into a bag and pulled out a nondescript-looking black box with a crystal on top and toggle switch. "See, scientists have been trying to find a way to invent a real cloaking device since Star Trek. Angel, when I tell you to, I want you to push this button up to engage the cloaking device. You won't have to be too close to the crowd for it to work."

"Whoa," Stephan said. "I've heard of these, but I've never seen one up close."

"When engaged, the crystal on the top uses light to distort what people see. It's kind of like a shield so they won't see us killing the demon. Our military is developing something on a larger scale that uses magnifying glasses that alter light beams to distort people's vision as a means to cloak. This is similar but on a smaller scale and for a short period of time. This baby is only good for fifteen minutes, so we need to use our time wisely," D'Angelo replied. "It…" He stopped talking when the weird music from my dream began to play. "Is that the music you heard?"

"Yeah? What the hell is that?" I asked.

"It's an ice cream truck! What better way to draw a bunch of kids, parents, and teachers to you than with an ice cream truck when school lets out for the summer? Fuck, we've got to move!" D'Angelo reached into the back of the Jeep and grabbed something that looked like an ancient net. "Do either of you have good aim?"

"I was a pitcher on my high school baseball team," Stephan answered quickly in response to the urgency he heard in D's voice.

"Here." D'Angelo tossed the net at Stephan's chest. The ginger easily caught it in his hands, but looked unsure of what the hell he was supposed to do with it. Before he could ask, D said, "That's a holy net, and it will burn and weaken him enough, so I can move in with my sai and send that bastard back to hell where he belongs."

"Got it."

"Let's go!" D'Angelo told us, shutting the rear hatch of his Jeep. He set out on a quick-paced jog, but I had to flat-out run to keep up with his long-legged strides. "Fuck!" D'Angelo yelled when we rounded the corner of the school.

"Oh my god," I said in horror as I saw Regis come around the side of the ice cream truck with the *Stone of Astaroth* extended in front of him. At some point during our trip around the block, school had let out and the children made a mad dash to the ice cream truck. Regis used it as a distraction and now stood in front of the kids and adults. He began chanting and the relic sparked to life, emanating the eerie blue light I still saw in my nightmares. In my despair, I dropped the cloaking device and heard a sickening crunch as Stephan stepped on it as he ran behind us. "We're too late."

"No, we're not, baby," D assured me as he picked up his pace. "We just need to disrupt him before the last soul is captured. Remember how he repeats the same chant over and over?"

"Yeah."

"If we can disrupt his chant before the last soul is captured, then they'll all be saved," D'Angelo said.

"Jesus," Stephan said when he saw the bodies begin to writhe in pain as their essence was slowly ripped from them. It was a horrific sight that even the most hardened heart would have a difficult time watching.

Screams of fear and agony pierced the air and sent shivers down my spine. I had never been a physically active person, but it was obvious I would need to start working on my stamina immediately for the next battle. I didn't need a vision to know that we would live to fight another day, I just knew. I sucked air into my lungs as fast as I could through my open mouth and soon felt pressure in my chest like my lungs were about to explode, followed by a sharp, stabbing pain under the lower edge of my rib cage. I hadn't experienced a side stitch since the last time I had to run for gym class in high school.

I ignored the pain, pushed away any fear I felt, and sent up a silent prayer for the three of us. D'Angelo had Christ's blood in his tattoo that marked him as a blessed warrior. I refused to believe that he had lost favor because of his sexuality. D'Angelo was all that was good in the world and he was needed. Yes, I gave my best sales pitch to God like I'd done many times with my customers when questioned about an item on the menu at Martinelli's, but with more vigor because there was so much more on the line than someone's dining pleasure.

As we got closer, D'Angelo veered off the sidewalk onto the street, and used the parked cars as cover as we made our way closer. We crouched down so Regis couldn't see us, and I only caught a glimpse of his progress in the small gaps between cars. I felt the tears streaming down my face when I saw that the souls were ripping free and floating closer to the cross. The blue light glowed brighter the closer the souls got to the cross. We had to be careful to stay out of the relic's radius, but we couldn't hesitate long, or it would be too late.

"Throw the net," D'Angelo yelled as soon as we cleared the last car and came up behind the scene.

Stephan heaved the net as hard as he could at the demon on D's command. Regis moved to evade the net at the last minute, so it hit him but didn't cover him. Regis, or the meat suit formerly known as Regis, staggered and let out an evil hiss as soon as his flesh began to burn where the ropes of the blessed net touched his skin. I sucked putrid air that reeked of burning trash into my lungs and began choking. My eyes burned and tears slid down my face as I labored to pull fresh air into my lungs in between wracking coughs.

Stephan's toss didn't have the exact effect we wanted, but it was enough to break the chant. As soon as that happened, the blue light from the cross was snuffed out and the souls drifted back into their original hosts. It looked like something you expected to see in a sci-fi movie, not the middle of the day in a Chicago suburb. The children and adults fell to their knees, clutching their heads and crying for help.

The demon raised his hand and blasted Stephan hard enough to send him flying back through the air into the side of a shiny, black SUV. Stephan fell hard to the ground but he wasn't dead. In fact, he was already rising to his feet, though slowly, with a sadistic smile on his face. "Is that all you got?"

"I'm sending you back to hell, Orcal!" D'Angelo roared, holding the wicked-looking sai in his hand as he prepared to attack.

The net weakened the demon and slowed him down, but it didn't stop him from turning to face D'Angelo and begin chanting again. The cross shook in the demon's hand as it starting to spark to life again. The demon grinned evilly as he chanted louder and faster. The blue light began shimmering around the edges of the relic and it was only a matter of time before the soul-sucking rays captured the soul that meant the most to me.

I didn't have time to think; I only had time to react. I drove myself into the demon's side as hard as I could once again. I was too much of a lightweight to knock him to the ground, but I surprised him enough to stop him from chanting. He pushed me off him like I weighed nothing and I fell to the ground. Luckily for me, he didn't throw me ten feet like he had Stephan, because I wouldn't have been able to just shake that off.

D'Angelo took advantage of the demon's brief distraction and lunged forward with the sai, piercing the sword into the demon's chest. Regis had turned in just enough time to prevent the sai from stabbing his heart, so instead of killing him, D'Angelo only maimed him. Orcal threw back his head, emitting this ear-shattering scream that nearly shattered my eardrums. It felt like a thousand sharp knives were stabbing my brain all at once. I covered my ears to try to drown out the sound, but it barely dulled it. I fell to the ground and curled into a fetal position as something warm trickled from my nose.

I felt my consciousness fading and knew I was moments away from death. My only hope was that we injured the demon enough to save the kids that day. The screeching stopped as suddenly as it had started. I slowly uncurled from my tight ball and sat up even though my ears were still ringing painfully.

"Damn it!" D'Angelo spat out from where he sat beside me. "He got away with the relic. He's weakened, but not dead." He looked up to the sky in aggravation and blew out a frustrated breath. Then he looked at his wicked-looking weapon in his hand and smiled crookedly. "I know how we can find him. We need to get back to the girls."

D rose to his feet and slid his sai back inside his long coat. He offered his hand and helped me up. I saw that his nose had bled also, but his powers were helping him recover faster than me. I looked around and saw that all the kids and adults were coming out of their trances. They were dazed and injured, but they all survived. At least we were victorious in saving their lives.

Sirens blared in the distance, jolting D'Angelo into action. "Come on, Ansell. We need to get out of here fast. We have precious little time to locate Orcal before he heals and starts wreaking havoc again, and the last thing we need is to be impeded by an interview with the cops."

D grabbed my hand and turned in the direction of his Jeep. Stephan was lying unconscious on the sidewalk. The combination of the demon blast and sonic screech must have been too much for him. Lorcán's blood might've made him stronger, but he was still human, therefore, not invincible.

"Stephan," D said, shaking him.

"Just let me sleep five more minutes, Mom," Stephan said drowsily.

"Christ," D'Angelo said in disgust. "I'll grab one arm and you grab the other. We'll drag him to the Jeep."

The sirens were getting louder, and we were running out of time. I wasn't feeling too strong myself, but I knew we didn't have a choice. We couldn't leave Stephan behind. D and I each looped our arms beneath his shoulders and scooped him up enough to drag him. He was heavier than he looked, and we couldn't drag him fast enough.

"This isn't working," D'Angelo complained. He stopped and hoisted Stephan over his shoulder and took off running.

My lungs burned and my legs felt like limp noodles, but I did my best to keep up with him. I slowed down when I reached the shattered cloaking device. I had hoped that it was salvageable and Jinx could fix it, but I knew there was no hope for it.

"Leave it, Ansell. We don't have time."

I was ecstatic when we turned the corner and D's Jeep came into sight. D unlocked the doors with the fob as we approached. I opened the back door and D'Angelo unceremoniously dumped Stephan in the back seat.

"Careful," I told D.

"He's going to be fine, baby. I promise. His nose isn't bleeding enough for him to choke on it." My man definitely wasn't nurse material. "Let's get you cleaned up though." D'Angelo pulled out tissues from the center console between our seats. We each took a few and cleaned ourselves off.

"I'm sorry that I broke the cloaking device. I hope Jinx won't be too angry with me."

"Hey, you did great for your first battle."

"Yeah?" I asked, needing to hear that he believed I could share his life with him.

"You made a rookie mistake. We've all made them." D'Angelo touched his fingers to my cheek. "Give me a few months and you're going to be one hell of a warrior."

My heart was pounding wildly in my chest from both exertion and adrenaline from the battle as I strapped myself into the shotgun seat. We weren't completely victorious, but we saved hundreds of lives that day. The high emotion flowed through me like ants crawling beneath my skin. It made me fidgety and horny, but there was no time for fucking with that crazy demon on the loose.

I didn't think I took an easy breath until D'Angelo pulled the Jeep out into the street and turned down a road that took us away from the aftermath of the demon's attack. I was anxious to hear how the incident would be reported on the nightly news broadcast. What would the victims remember, if anything?

My relief was short lived because D'Angelo turned and looked at me with a sinister expression in his eyes once we were stopped at the next red light. "What is it with you and your body-tackling a demon, Ansell?" Clearly, D was too angry to be horny. "That makes twice now."

"He was about to suck my mate's soul out of his body," I countered, shrugging with a casualness I didn't feel. "I had no choice." Besides, I didn't have any other skills to speak of right then, but I knew that would change as soon as D'Angelo started training me.

"I don't like it," D'Angelo responded. He opened his mouth to say more but moaning from the back seat cut him off. It wasn't the kind of sound a person made from pain.

"Mmmmm, Alex." *Alex?* Stephan had clearly gone to his happy place. I wasn't the only one with post-battle horniness racing through their bodies.

I looked over at D'Angelo and he was grinning. "So, that's his problem."

"Who's Alex?" I asked. I thought the guy was hung up on Lorcán.

"Alex Renaud," D'Angelo replied as if that somehow explained it. "He's Lorcán's second-in-command."

"Oh, cozy," I chuckled. I glanced back and saw that Stephan was smiling in his sleep. "Are we going to tell him what he revealed?"

"Hell no," D'Angelo replied. "I don't want or need to know anything about his personal life. Getting chummy with supes or their humans is not on my to-do list. I only care about killing that demon and then locking myself in a room with you for two days."

"I thought you said one?" I asked, disbelieving that I could have a rational conversation after battling a demon. This wouldn't have been my reaction a week prior. So much had changed in my life—all of it for the better because of the man sitting beside me.

"I can smell your arousal, Ansell. There's no way I can burn through that in just a day. It's going to take at least two."

"Oh."

"Business first, though."

"Drive faster," I told him. D'Angelo snickered, but sped up to reach home quicker.

Stephan started to come to as we pulled into the underground private parking garage beneath the warehouse used for the antique store and our personal residence. "Did we get him?" I heard him sit up slowly.

"Not yet, but we at least saved those lives and weakened him," D'Angelo said proudly.

"Where are we?"

"We brought you back home with us," D told him. "You're going to stay on the main floor with our sales associate, Meggie, while my ladies work their magic."

"What kind of magic?" I asked D'Angelo.

"Why can't I go too?" Stephan asked groggily.

"We don't allow supes or their humans in our center," D'Angelo said firmly.

"Suspicious bastard," Stephan grumbled.

"I could've left your sorry ass behind but didn't, so I think you should be a little bit more appreciative," D said. He parked the Jeep and looked into his rearview mirror so he could see Stephan. "I'm even going to be nice and have Vixen fix a little something for you to drink that can help you revive even faster than Lorcán's blood will."

"No, thanks, man," Stephan said quickly. "I'll grind it out."

"Suit yourself," D'Angelo said with a shrug.

Meggie smiled when D asked her to hang out with our reluctant guest. I think she liked feeling like a part of the team. I dropped a kiss on her cheek as I followed D'Angelo upstairs to find Vixen and Jinx. The girls raptly listened as D and I told the story in tag team fashion.

"Can I see your sai?" Vixen asked. D'Angelo pulled the wicked blade from the coat he still wore. "Perfect! His blood is on the blade, so I can perform a locator spell to find him. It's doubtful he went too far before he decided to hide and heal." Vixen quickly set out what she needed to perform her magic. She put the ingredients in the center of a city map of Chicago.

"Let's hope this works." She began chanting as she dipped the sai into the clear potion. It turned a dark shade of red and thickened until it took on the consistency of blood. Vixen continued to chant as she poured the liquid at the top of the map.

The liquid thinned out until it ran in a rivulet across the map and stopped on the far eastern part of the city. Vixen continued to chant and placed a ring with a black stone on top of the spot. As soon as the ring touched the map, it absorbed the enchanted liquid and began to glow a light shade of red.

Vixen stopped chanting and picked up the rock. "The locator spell gives you a general location. This ring will glow a brighter shade of red as you near the demon."

D leaned over the table and studied the map. "I somehow doubt that Orcal is at the bus station," he replied calmly. "It's more likely that he's hiding in the rat-infested sewer system that runs beneath the bus station."

"Rat-infested?" I asked weakly.

"They'll scurry away from us. Besides, I won't let anything happen to you," D'Angelo said convincingly, then gave me a quick kiss. "I can't wait to tell Stephan where we're heading next. He's not going to want to get his snazzy clothes dirty." He returned the sai to his interior coat pocket and we returned to Meggie and Stephan.

"The fuck you say," Stephan replied when D told him we were heading to the sewer system. "Do you have any idea how much I paid for this outfit?" He might've been bitching, but he still followed us to the Jeep.

"I don't give a fuck," D answered.

"You're going to when you get my bill from the dry cleaners." He practically pissed and moaned the entire ride across town, which took forever since we were trying to maneuver through rush hour traffic by then.

Once again, all chattiness came to a standstill when we reached our destination. I felt the seriousness of the moment wash over the interior of the car. "Let's go kill this asshole demon once and for all."

D'Angelo expertly led us through a tunnel beneath the bus station until he reached a round manhole cover. He glanced down at the ring a few times and it had glowed darker with every step we took inside the tunnel. "This is the only entrance that I know about in this area and our best bet to find Orcal." He pulled a small flashlight out of his coat, turned it on, and put it inside his mouth so his hands could be free. The stench of raw sewage assaulted our noses as soon as he opened the cover. It was all I could do not to vomit. I wanted him to be wrong, but the ring glowed a dark red color that nearly looked black.

"Here, rub this beneath your nose and it will help with the smell." D'Angelo pulled out a small jar of something from another pocket.

"Magic?" I asked, accepting the jar.

"Vicks VapoRub. Cops use it a lot to combat the smell of decaying flesh at a crime scene."

"Fuck!" Stephan mumbled something about *Inspector Gadget's* coat before he smeared some under his nose. "Let's get this over with, asshole."

D'Angelo went first, then me, and Stephan brought up the rear of our trio. The climb down took so long, it felt like we were descending into hell—smelled like it too. That Vicks could only do so much.

I didn't even want to think about what was floating in the dark, stank water that we slogged through as we followed the ring. I heard the sounds of rats scurrying on both sides of us but kept my eyes looking forward. I had to be brave if I wanted to help my mate.

"Up ahead!" D yelled and started to run, splashing rancid water on me as he did. I shoved all thoughts out of my head as I followed him. "Damn it, we're too late again."

Regis' body was lying face first in the water. D'Angelo turned him over and the condition of the body startled me. I gasped and took a few steps back. I was no expert, but he looked as if he'd been down there for days instead of hours. His skin color had a bluish-white hue to it and his lips and eyes were so swollen, they looked like they could burst at any minute. There were huge chunks of flesh missing from his face, indicating that the rats were quick to take advantage of their gift.

"Orcal has left Regis' body," D'Angelo said. "Once he did, the host body began to decompose rapidly."

"Now what?" Stephan asked. "That fucker could be anywhere."

"We bring out the big guns," D responded.

"Big guns?" I asked.

"Yeah, wolves. They can track his evil ass so we can kill him and send him back to hell."

Chapter Nineteen

D'Angelo

I was so fucking pissed to see that rotting body instead of the demon. I was ready to end this shit once and for all. I hated having to drag my ass and Ansell's sexy ass into this horrible fucking sewer for nothing. Even worse, I was going to have to come back down there if I could get one of those werewolves to help us out. They were another bunch that liked to keep to themselves and didn't care for hunters. I'd never had to ask for their help before, but Vixen helped Warren a few weeks back when a witch cursed one of his wolves. I remembered the alpha being kind of pissed that he even had to ask for our help. The good thing was that his wolf member was alive today because of us and his ass owed us one. Time to cash in that chip.

I turned, looking at the disappointed and disgusted faces of my mate and the loudmouth bastard Lorcán had cursed us with. They looked how I felt. "We can go back up for now."

"Thank god! I thought you wanted to hang around here longer," Stephan said.

"The sewer isn't a place I like to visit, Stephan," I said as a rat scurried past my leg towards Ansell and Stephan.

"Oooh shit!" Ansell yelped and damn near leaped into my arms to get away from a big, fat rodent with its long, hairless tail.

Stephan moved out of the way, but shivered in disgust afterward.

"Okay, I'm ready to get out of here," Ansell said as he was still clinging to me.

"Sure, let's go." I led them back to the manhole opening and we all climbed out. We stunk like the sewer and I couldn't wait to take a shower, but all of that was going to have to wait. I pulled out my cell phone and called Vixen. I needed Warren Jackson's number. She gave it to me and I thanked her before hanging up.

"Let's hope he has the same number," Ansell said.

I looked at him. "Oh, please don't say that."

"Sorry," he said with a sweet smile.

"My outfit is fucking ruined. I'd be too embarrassed to even take this to the dry cleaners. Damn this whole situation," Stephan whined.

"Fuck your ugly-ass clothes, you damn fop," I snapped. I was so annoyed with his ass at this point. I'd take Lorcán over him right about now.

"Hey, I'm here, in the muck too, helping you," he retorted.

"Because you were ordered to. This is real shit, Stephan. If we don't kill this demon and prevent Astaroth from rising, all hell will break loose. I could care less about your flashy outfit," I said, hoping to put things into perspective for him. I didn't wait to hear anymore bullshit from him before dialing Warren's number. Luckily, Stephan decided to keep his comments to himself for once.

The alpha answered on the third ring. "Who's calling?" Warren asked. His voice was a deep baritone. You could just hear it rumbling through his chest. No doubt, it was intimidating to the wolves of his pack.

"Warren, it's D'Angelo. I'm calling because we need your help," I said.

He sighed. "Didn't take you long to cash in that favor I owe you, I see."

"That's because shit is about to hit the fan. Listen, Warren, I'm tracking a demon that just abandoned its human vessel and could be anyone anywhere right now."

"Don't you have like some freakishly strong senses? Can't you track him down?"

"I can't track a demon in its non-corporeal form. A wolf's sense of smell would be able to do that. Please, we need you now," I said, hoping I was pressing upon him how important it was that he come to our aid.

"Jesus Christ, I knew I was going to regret having to ask you for help. Where the fuck are you?" Warren groaned. I gave him our location and he groaned again. "And I was having such a good day. I'll be there in about ten minutes." He hung up and so did I.

"Is he coming?" Ansell asked.

I nodded. "He's not happy about it, but he'll be here." I was actually happy he didn't send one of his wolves. With him being the alpha, he was the strongest.

"I can't believe I'm about to meet a real-life werewolf," Ansell said in an excited tone.

"They're all right, I guess," Stephan said. "They tend to keep to themselves. They have their own bars, clubs, restaurants, stuff like that."

"Is there more than one pack?" Ansell asked.

"In this city, there are four packs. Northside, Westside, Eastside, and Southside packs. No, they don't really get along. They don't like to share territory, which is one of the reasons they keep to themselves, and they have their own businesses. Warren is the alpha of the Southside pack, known as the Warriors of Anarchy," I said, giving Ansell the 411.

"Like a gang?" he asked.

I nodded. "You could say that, yeah. Each pack does have their own names, cuts, and territory disputes, which we as hunters stay out of. As long as no humans are killed or injured in their wars, we leave it to them to handle."

"Why can't they get along if they're all wolves?" Ansell asked.

Stephan rolled his eyes and huffed. "I see your sweetie pie has like a thousand fucking questions. I'm going to go over there and sit down." With that, he walked over to the bus stop by the alley and took a seat on the bench. With one whiff of him, I was certain he wouldn't have to worry about anyone sitting down next to him.

I turned back to Ansell since we had time to kill and decided to break it all down for him. I wanted him informed as much as possible. He still had so much to learn, but I loved how quickly he was absorbing all of this in such a short time. I walked over to the side of a store and leaned against the wall. Ansell joined me.

"Werewolves are very much like their animal counterparts. They are extremely territorial. They aren't friendly to lone wolves that breech their territories, and it's up to the alpha if they kill that wolf or let him stay as one of them. They have their own ceremonies for induction too. They do turn on full moon nights, which they do on the property set aside for that. We can't have werewolves in animal form roaming all over the city freaking people out. So, they obey that part of our peace treaty. If they don't, we will hunt them down. It's not easy to kill a werewolf, as you'll need pure silver weapons like knives, swords, or bullets. Or, in our case, a blessed weapon." I looked down the street, waiting to see Warren pull up. Time seemed to be standing still or dragging its ass. Every second that passed, I knew Orcal was getting further away.

"Are they immortal like vampires?" Ansell asked.

"Nope, but they do live longer than humans. I think the oldest werewolf whose age was recorded in history was three hundred nineteen years old," I said. I heard the sound of a motorcycle approaching.

One whose engine roaring I clearly recognized. I stepped out of the alley to see Warren coming down the street about two blocks away on his *Harley Davidson* hog. "He's here. Thank god."

Warren pulled up and parked his bike. He was just as imposing as his voice, no doubt. He climbed off his cycle, wearing a pair of mirrored shades, black jeans, leather steel-toed boots, a white T-shirt, and a black leather cut with the insignia of his pack sewn on the back. The title on the front of his vest over his left peck said: Alpha. Under that was his nickname: "War Machine." He had over a dozen tattoos covering his dark brown skin, but none on his bald head, which was gleaming in the bright light of the summer sun. I did love his beard and mustache, neatly trimmed and just thick enough to be legit facial hair.

He walked over to me and removed his sunglasses, revealing gray eyes framed by long, dark lashes and arched eyebrows. Stunning, they were, and rare. "Okay, I'm here. Now what?"

Straight to business then. Just the way I liked it. "We need to go down into the sewer where the body is. That's the last place the demon was."

"The sewer? Son of a bitch. I would have worn my shit-kicking boots if I'd known I'd be going down into the fucking nasty-ass sewer," he complained.

"Preaching to the choir," Stephan chimed in as he approached our little huddle.

"Trust me, I wasn't happy about it either, but let's go."

"Do I have to go back down there too?" Ansell asked.

I looked at him, he was staring at Warren with a look of pure wonderment. The same way he looked at Lorcán when he'd first met him. I was also sure he was noting how handsome the man was because there was no denying that fact. But I didn't feel threatened. I knew Ansell only had eyes for me and me for him.

I answered his question. "No. Just Warren and I need to go. You two can stay up here."

"I wasn't going to go anyway," Stephan commented. Damn, I'd be glad to get him back to his precious vampires.

I led Warren back down into the sewer and to Regis' body.

"Ugh, shit… how long has he been down here?" Warren asked as he covered his nose.

"About two hours at the most."

He cocked his eyebrow. "Really? Looks like he's been down here for at least a month. Smells like it too. Shit, motherfucker, you may have to owe *me* a favor for this one. Damn, got me smelling this horrible-ass bullshit. Do you realize how sensitive my sense of smell is? Had I known this was the gig, I would have sent my omega."

"I'm glad you didn't. We need your stronger sense of smell, Warren. This is what happens to a human body when a demon vacates it. The flesh rots instantly. The longer the demon had been inhabiting the body, the faster it rots. I guess because the evil that inhabited was so corrupted. Now, take a big whiff and stop bitching," I said.

"Oh, I'm going to say some shit about this." Warren groaned, but stopped holding his nose. He walked to the body, leaned over it and inhaled deeply, then coughed. "Fuck, that stinks! That's not all rot I'm smelling, either. I can smell the demon. Strong scent of sulfur."

See, that was why we needed the wolf. I could smell just a hint of the sulfur, most of which had been washed away by the putrid sewer water. There were just too many scents for me to accurately distinguish one from the other. Not only that, but with Orcal in non-corporeal form, a wolf would be able to follow that trail.

Warren took several more deep inhales around the body and the area in general. "Okay, I've got his scent. What kind of demon is this I'm tracking?"

I started walking back towards the exit with Warren behind me sloshing through the murky water. "Its name is Orcal, and it's a servant of the demigod, Astaroth. We have to get to Orcal before he gets a thousand souls and opens the portal for Astaroth to enter this world."

"Jesus, do you even have normal fucking days in your life?" Warren asked.

"I wish I did. But this is my life," I said, then climbed out of the sewer. Warren followed me and I closed the manhole. It was best that I didn't alert the police to Regis' body. If I did, it would have to be anonymously. But that was going to have to wait for later if we survived whatever was coming next.

"Do you have his scent?" Ansell asked. I could tell by the way he was still looking at Warren that he was curious about the werewolf. I couldn't blame him, this had to be a total mindfuck for Ansell. It had only been a matter of days, yet he had been introduced to vampires, demons, werewolves, humans with special abilities, and witches. It was almost enough to make a person want to turn back time to a period where everything seemed normal. But not my baby, he was going full steam ahead.

Warren nodded. "Yeah, I got his nasty-ass, rotten egg-smelling scent. Won't be a problem to track."

"Good, we need to get a move on. If Astaroth rises…" I just left it at that. We all had an idea or at least a fear of what would happen if the demigod rose.

"Well, let's make sure that doesn't happen," Ansell said.

"Are you going to track him on your hog?" I asked Warren.

Warren shook his head. "If he was in a human form, I probably could have. I can barely smell his scent as it is. I need to go full wolf for this. Question is, can you keep up? Oh, I need cover," he said as he began removing his clothes.

The three of us huddled together, blocking the street view from Warren. This would be my first time seeing him full monty. Werewolves were not your bashful type, that was for sure. Especially not natural werewolves. The ones who were born werewolves instead of being turned. That was another thing we monitored. People who were bitten against their will. The offending werewolf needed to be held accountable for the crime. That was if we even learned about it.

Like I said, werewolves kept to themselves and handled that sort of thing internally.

We all watched as Warren stripped out of his black boxer briefs, freeing a long, meaty cock that looked happy to stretch its figurative legs, so to speak. Damn, the man had the body of an Adonis, no doubt. Holy shit, I thought I had rippling muscles! It was really adorable how Ansell turned away when the underwear came off. I could tell he wanted to peek, but he was being modest. Couldn't say the same for Stephan, though. By the way he was staring at Warren and his cock in particular, I was surprised he didn't take out his cell phone and snap a photo or drop to his knees.

Getting back to business. "I probably won't be able to keep up if you run your full speed. Remember, my Jeep only goes so fast."

"Then take my hog, but you better not hurt her," Warren said, then he leaned down, reaching into his jeans pocket for the keys to his motorcycle. Lucky for me, I knew how to ride one. Nice of him to assume, though. He tossed the keys at me and I caught them one-handed. "Not a fucking scratch."

"Yeah, yeah, I get it. Now, let's get to it." I pulled my Jeep keys from my pocket, giving them to Ansell. "Take the Jeep. I'll call you and give you my location if you get lost."

Ansell nodded and took the keys from me, then he walked over quickly, picking up Warren's clothes. He returned to his place beside me, blocking the public view, then watched another unnatural miracle take place. Of course, for Warren, it was very natural. He began to transform his body into that of a full wolf. It really was a sight to behold. It didn't take him long either as the fur began to cover his body. His bones broke and contorted at an alarming rate, forcing him to go down on all fours. His features distorted, his eyes grew narrow as the space between them widened. His mouth elongating until a full muzzle protruded from the middle of his face, complete with razor sharp canine teeth. The last thing to form was his long, fluffy gray tail. He was a majestic beast, indeed, and twice the size of a normal wolf… maybe even three times. Damn! He did have that alpha stare, too. Fierce silver eyes peered at us, giving me a chill. I may have a newfound respect for him and wolves in general. I mean, out of all the monsters that existed, they bothered me the least.

"That was so amazing. Oh my god, I can't believe I just saw that!" Ansell exclaimed.

"Calm down, baby. We don't want to draw attention over here," I warned. I understood his excitement. I'd seen a werewolf transform before, but the first time had me hyped too. You just didn't see that kind of shit every day.

"I'm sorry, I didn't mean to get so loud. It's just… oh my god." He was still in hyper mode.

"I know… I know. But right now, you need to get into the Jeep," I said.

He nodded. "That's right. Sorry. Okay." He ran to my Jeep, climbing in.

"It was pretty cool to see," Stephan said, then followed Ansell to my Jeep and climbed into the passenger seat. I guess he was trying to play it cool. I wondered if he'd ever seen a werewolf transform. Vampires and wolves didn't really bother each other, but sometimes they did frequent each other's businesses if they were bold enough. It wasn't common. But who was to say what Stephan knew or didn't know.

I ran over to Warren's motorcycle and started the engine. As soon as I did, Warren took off running northbound. I hoped that son of a bitch, Orcal, wasn't in the northern wolf territory, because that meant Warren could only help us so far. *Please, god, I need a win right now.* The wind was whipping me in the face as I pushed Warren's bike to the extreme in order to keep up with him on all fours. Werewolves were fast as hell; most could outrun most cars as their top speeds could exceed a hundred twenty miles per hour.

Warren didn't make it easy for me to keep up, either, but I didn't complain. He had to follow the trail of a demon and I had to follow him. He paused briefly at an alley behind a bar, took a few more sniffs, then he was off running again. I wondered if this bar called The Lagoon was the place where Orcal snatched up another body. He'd need flesh if he was going to release Astaroth. He needed a voice to chant the words. Things were really getting dire. I was praying that we'd get there before he could get the rest of the souls. I wished I could destroy that relic, but that would just be a mistake. It would trap the souls inside forever. If I could reverse the spell, maybe we could free the souls, and those who could be saved would be saved and those who couldn't... well, at least then their souls would be free to go to heaven or hell. After I freed the souls, then I would gladly destroy that damn relic, so it could never be used again and Astaroth could stay in hell.

I was right on Warren's tail when he stopped at the subway entrance. Oh shit, please don't tell me Orcal was in the subway... and during rush hour. I parked the bike and hopped off. I noticed that Ansell wasn't behind me, so I quickly texted him my location as I headed towards the entrance, but hit a repulsion barrier. At least, now I knew why this area was pretty vacant. Even I felt the urge to turn and walk away. Instead, I pushed through, fighting the nausea that threatened to break me down until I got past the barrier. Warren was beside me, he growled as he walked through the barrier, and together, we took to the stairs into the subway. I stopped when I got to the last step, because I could already see that we were too late.

Bodies littered the platform. Transit employees, civilians, teenagers, children.... all lay dead, their souls robbed from them. Behind me, I could hear Stephan and Ansell gagging but fighting it, and then running down the stairs, the sound of metal clinking. They reached us and stopped dead in their tracks.

"Oh my god... we're too late," Ansell cried, his chest heaving. I could hear the tears and shock in his voice. I turned to him, he was holding the net and holy water. Stephan was holding a knife and a can of gasoline. Warren began to transform back into his human form.

"He's still down here," Warren said once his transformation was complete.

"I know, I can hear him chanting. Let's go." I began running towards the sound of Orcal chanting in a female's voice. I knew I was probably running towards my death, but the threat of death was something I faced all of the time. Only this time, I was truly afraid of it, because now I had Ansell in my life. Would my death mean his? What would I do if I lived but he died? God, these were thoughts I couldn't entertain right now. I had to be focused on saving the world and all selfish thoughts had to be put aside. We hopped the turnstile and ran down another flight of stairs to the train platform where even more bodies lay on the ground and tracks. Two trains had been in the terminal at the time. With a quick look through the windows, I could tell the people inside were also dead.

"You're too late, hunter," Orcal said, stepping out from behind one of the columns.

He was wearing a female's skin: a blonde, Caucasian woman with red lipstick to match her red dress and heels. Demons didn't really care about matching their gender with whatever gender they were in hell. Shit, maybe they didn't have specific genders in hell. That was always a mystery. I wondered if the human was still inside. Most demons had to make deals with humans to let them in. But one as powerful as Orcal could just body snatch. Shit, I wished Regis had left this motherfucker in hell where he belonged. This was why humans shouldn't fuck with dark, evil forces.

"My master is rising and soon this world will belong to the demons."

As soon as he said that, the ground beneath us began to shake until a deep crack formed, splitting down the middle of the platform. I dodged to one side and Ansell had to leap to the other as the crack widened. You could actually see the fires of hell licking the surface; black smoke was belching sulfurous fumes into the air, choking me, Ansell, and Stephan. I looked around with watery eyes and didn't see

Warren, but I knew he was near.

"Yes! Yes! Rise, my master. Take your rightful place on this plane!" Orcal yelled as he approached the crack. His/her face was a mask of wicked glee as Orcal grinned from ear to ear.

He was distracted as his eyes remained glued to the thick black smoke that was coming up from the crack. Loud, screeching noises bellowed, the sound echoing off the walls and ringing my ears. I was discombobulated as I struggled to my feet. My equilibrium was completely thrown off. I stumbled towards Orcal, throwing my body at him. We tumbled to the floor, rolling until he ended up on top. He pinned me to the ground by my throat, cutting off my air supply.

"I'll give you this much, hunter. You were tenacious in your pursuit of me. I'm way out of your league, but you never stopped trying to take me down. I suppose one could be flattered, but not me. I was just annoyed that a flea like you dared to pester me so," he snarled.

I could see my vision blurring, which terrified me. I couldn't afford to lose consciousness right now. I reached up, grabbing the demon's hand that was wrapped around my neck with both hands, trying to free myself, which made Orcal laugh.

"Still trying? Give up, and maybe my master will take pity upon you and kill you quickly," he taunted. "You know you're no match for him, don't you? You have to know this. Hell, you're no match for me, and all of your pathetic training at your audacious little academy amounts to shit when you're facing true power."

I reached up, attempting to jab my thumb into his eye, but he laughed again as he took hold of my wrist and pinned it to the ground.

"I've been wanting to kill one of you arrogant hunters for a while now. You're not the one who sent me to hell, but you'll do," Orcal said, then I felt him increase the pressure around my neck.

Seconds felt like hours as I struggled to breathe and stay awake. "Ffffuuck…yyoouu," I managed to spit out as tears flowed from my eyes. The only reason I was still alive was sheer will at this point.

"Mmmm, maybe I will fuck you, hunter. Tell me, ever had sweet pussy before?" Orcal laughed, and right then, Warren jumped on him, all teeth and snarls. The force of the blow knocked Orcal off me and sent him and Warren rolling among the bodies covering the platform. I turned, coughing as air began to rush back into my lungs. I could now see what Ansell and Stephan had been doing while Orcal was whooping my ass. The place was lit up with the fumes of gasoline and Ansell was tossing the holy net on both Orcal and Warren as the werewolf ripped flesh from Orcal's arm and face.

Orcal screamed when the net trapped him. Warren howled, but I believed it was in frustration as it couldn't burn him, yet it weakened them both. I had to get back into the fight. The horrific howling coming from the crack portal to hell was distracting, but I couldn't let it stop me from doing what had to be done. I pulled my sai from my coat and ran over to them. Ansell was doing his best to hold Orcal down, having tossed his body on top of both of them. God, he was so brave right now. I was so proud of him, but I didn't have time to tell him just yet. I pushed Ansell to the side and plunged my sai into Orcal's heart with all of my supernatural strength. My blade pierced his flesh, splintered his bone, and sliced through his heart. Blood bubbled up from the wound as the demon released another ear-splitting scream that had us all clutching our ears and curling into a fetal position. Warren howled and whimpered as he got low, attempting to cover his ears with his paws.

We all watched as Orcal's black smoke seeped out of his body from the wound I created and burned itself out as it did. With the last puff of smoke went the death screech as Orcal died. Not returned to hell, but died. One less demon to worry about. In retrospect, I didn't mind being cannon fodder if it meant we could get the jump on his arrogant ass, and we did. But now we had an even bigger problem. Astaroth was coming and I had no way to prevent it. I needed to find my *Orb of Orleander* and pray that would be enough to trap Astaroth once he was fully on this plane.

I looked at Orcal's corpse. The female body was already decomposing, its skin turning pale and a little shriveled as if it had been dead for at least a week. Damn, I was so fucking happy we had Warren with us. Speaking of him, I had better get the net off him. I pulled my sai from Orcal's body and lifted the net off Warren, who shook himself all over.

"Thanks for saving my life. Looks like I owe you now," I said to him. He snorted in response. I guessed that meant "damn right" in wolf speak. I looked at Ansell. "Are you okay?"

He nodded. "Yeah, but what are we going to do? How do we stop this?" he asked, pointing to the black smoke that was starting to mold itself into a large, hulking form.

"I'll be back." I didn't have time to explain as I dashed as fast as I could past the many corpses, up the stairs, and to my Jeep that was parked illegally on the street. I did note that the spell that was blocking the entrance before was now gone. It died when Orcal did. That, of course, wasn't good news, because we needed to keep people out of this area. I didn't have any spell I could use to accomplish that, so I just had to hope nobody came down here. I got to my Jeep and saw that I already had one ticket on my window, but at this point, I didn't give a shit. I opened my trunk and very gently removed the *Orb of Orleander*, which looked like a black glass orb that fit into the palm of my hand. I ran back down the stairs, hopping over the turnstile, and hit the second set of stairs leading back to the platform to hell.

"What's that?" Stephan asked.

"The *Orb of Orleander*. I hope I can trap him in it," I said.

"Oh, that's great. Do it now!" Stephan urged.

"Bad news is, he has to be in solid form."

"If we wait for him to be in solid form, we're as good as dead, right? This is a fucking demigod we're talking about," Stephan shouted.

"I know that, but it's all we have right now. As soon as he takes solid form, Ansell, you throw the holy water at him. Stephan, you toss the net. Hopefully, it will weaken him and I can do the spell," I said, trying to come up with a battle strategy to take on a fucking demi-god. Something I'd never ever dealt with before and hoped I never would. Talk about a crash training course, and one I never asked for.

"What about the gasoline?" Ansell asked. "We poured it all around when Orcal had you and he was distracted."

"We are definitely going to light it. Where did you pour it?" I asked. I wanted to make sure we wouldn't get burned.

"All in that area by the smoke," Ansell said, pointing.

"Perfect, light it right now. Now, do it now," I yelled, seeing the black smoke finally opening its red eyes. Thank god his rising wasn't instantaneous. Already, we were out of time, and were the only beings standing between this demon and the end of the world as we knew it. I prayed again and could hear Astaroth laughing.

"God won't help you now, human," it said in a voice that sounded like many voices.

"Shit, the lighter won't work!" Stephan exclaimed as he and Ansell tried desperately to get a flame going. Damn, where was Lorcán when you needed his fire-conjuring ass. Too bad, Stephan didn't have that ability. I reached into my pocket, tossing them my lighter.

"Try that one, now!" I yelled.

"Yes, try it," Astaroth said as he took his final form. He looked like a normal human Caucasian man, complete with a black suit and hat. He was powerful enough to take whatever form he so chose, and that was the one he wanted. He stood about six-four and was grinning at us the entire time.

Ansell got my lighter to work and he tossed it on the bodies that surrounded Astaroth. Flames leaped into the air, licking at the demon, but never touching him. I began chanting the spell to activate the *Orb of Orleander*. Astaroth laughed louder as he began walking through the flames, coming out unscathed. Behind him, the flames began to peter out until the only thing left were smoldering corpses.

He looked at Ansell. "Did you think fire could kill me, boy? I was tortured in the flames of hell, foolish human. There *is* nothing hotter or more devastating." He turned to look at me, his glowing red eyes narrowing. "Ah, what do we have here? A trinket from the bitch angel, Orleander." He laughed. "His orb, or as I like to say, the one ball sac he used to have."

"It's enough to send you back to hell," I said, hoping to keep him distracted long enough for Ansell to toss the holy water on him.

He cocked his head to the side. "You think so?"

I nodded. "Worked before," I shot back, then started the chant. Right then, Ansell tossed the water and at the same time, Stephan tossed the net, but the demon teleported out of the way, stepping behind Ansell and swatting him like a fly. My heart literally stopped in my chest when I saw my mate flying high in the air, his body crashing into the stationary train. He landed with a hard thud and was knocked unconscious. I wanted to scream his name. I wanted to roar in a rage and run to his side, but I couldn't break the chant of the spell. This might be our only chance to trap the demon. I had to let the others sacrifice themselves to create the distraction I needed until I had Astaroth trapped again.

Stephan lunged at Astaroth, slicing his blades into empty air as the demon dodged every blow. His laughter was maniacal as he taunted us. "Fuck you, you demonic bastard!" Stephen yelled in his frustration as he turned, searching for the demon.

"Hahaha, your race is so weak. Conquering you will be easy, almost to the point of disappointing, I see," Astaroth said. The taunt seemed to come from the shadows, since the demon was nowhere in sight.

"Then why are you running, bitch?" Stephan yelled and Astaroth appeared behind him, raking his claws down his back. "Ahhh!" he cried out as he dropped to one knee, his blood now soaking the back of his clothes. Yeah, that outfit was ruined.

Astaroth grinned down at him. "Who's running?"

Warren came to Stephan's side and together, they tried to combine their efforts, a werewolf and a vampire's servant, both risking their lives to save the many. If we survived this ordeal, I would not forget this. The orb began to glow, finally. The spell was awakening it.

"I don't think so," Astaroth snarled and he lashed out, mentally knocking Warren and Stephan away from him as they tried to charge him. They were sent flying in two directions and landed with hard thuds on top of corpses. Astaroth teleported in front of me. "Fun and games are over."

I kicked at him, but he teleported, coming up behind me and punching me in the back of my head. The blow was so painful, I saw stars and the chanting I was doing came to a halt as the world spun around me.

"I'm done playing with you humans. It was cute at first, but now you've just pissed me off," Astaroth sneered, then he grabbed the orb from my hand and threw it against the wall, shattering it.

"No, fuck!" I snarled, then rammed Astaroth. He didn't move when my body slammed into his and it felt like I'd hit a brick wall. He grabbed me around the waist and tossed me into the air. I hit a column hard enough to break ribs and fell ten feet to the ground, nearly falling into the deep crack in the platform. I burned my arm on the edge where the flames of hell still flickered, causing me to snatch my limb back. "Shit," I groaned as I struggled to my feet.

"Well, you don't give up easily. I like that."

Astaroth walked towards me and stopped briefly to kick Warren, sending the wolf crashing through the window of a train, shattering it. I could smell canine blood and knew Warren was seriously hurt, but I didn't think he was dead as no silver was involved, not to say a decapitation wouldn't do the job. I looked to see Stephan also unconscious. The demonic blow he gave them with the force of his power probably would have killed a normal human. Lorcán's blood link was certainly doing the ginger favors right now.

I didn't have anything to use on him, really, except my other sai, and I wasn't even sure if that would be enough to take him out. But I was sure as hell going to try. I knew I had to let him get closer, so I pretended to be more injured than I was, even though I had several lacerations and broken ribs. When he reached for me, I let him lift me up. My lip and nose were both bleeding freely, as well as several wounds all over my body. I could feel blood trickling down the sides of my face. This really was the worse ass-whooping I'd ever taken.

Astaroth grinned, revealing razor-sharp teeth like something nightmares were made of. "I wonder how you taste?" he asked, then he bit my shoulder and I screamed, feeling all thirty-two of those razor-sharp teeth piercing my flesh. More blood gushed down my chest and back, but I forced myself to ignore the intense pain and use this opportunity to hurt him. I stabbed him in the back, piercing his body, but when the blade hit his heart, it felt like I'd hit solid steel. Astaroth released his bite on me to scream in agony, his face transforming from that of an average male to that of a demon complete with horns and snout. "HOW DARE YOU!" he roared, his putrid breath battering my face just as brutally as his fists did.

I tried to reach my weapon again, hoping to drive it deeper into his body, but he slammed me hard against the column, my head rattling in pain from the impact. He reached behind him, snatching my weapon from his back. He was terrifying in his appearance, a full demon. He stood at least eight feet tall, full of muscles, black scales, claws and fangs. I was used to seeing demon faces behind their human facades, but to see a full demon was another ballgame all together. The scent of sulfur grew thicker in the air, choking and blinding me with its fumes.

"I'm going to rip your guts out and watch you bleed a slow, painful death, fucker," the demon snarled and was on me faster than I could see. It plunged its clawed hand inside my stomach and I screamed in pain as I felt its scaly fingers wiggling inside my abdomen. I grimaced in agony as I grabbed its wrist with both hands in an attempt to keep it from disemboweling me, though I thought this was my end. "Ahhh, yeeessss, how does that feel? Can you feel your life slipping away?"

Not only did I feel my life draining from my body in streams of blood that poured from my numerous wounds, but I knew I'd given this demon everything I had and it wasn't enough. Not only was I going to die, but I was going to die a failure. I couldn't protect Ansell or the world. God, I hoped Christian could do what I couldn't, and killed this son of a bitch.

"You see now that you were never a match for me, human. The blood of Christ won't save you now," Astaroth taunted, and then dug his fingers deeper inside of me, pulling on my intestines. The pain I felt was excruciating and I was too weak to fight back. My head throbbed, my body was a wreck from being used as a crash test dummy. A part of me wanted this fucking demon to just make it quick and be done with it. The other part told me to keep fighting, so I did.

"Go… go… to hell," I spat out between feeble gasps.

"Not before you," he said, then I felt him slice through my intestines with his claws.

Oh god, I was really dying!

"Astaroth," a deep voice said from the shadows. It was a voice I recognized only because who it belonged to was so significant. Holy shit, I couldn't believe he was here!

Astaroth pulled his bloodied hand from my body and dropped me to the ground to turn around and address the new presence in our battle. I grabbed my stomach, putting pressure on my bleeding wounds and trying hard to keep my insides from spilling outside. I could feel myself starting to heal, now that I was given a break from being abused. Thank god I had some of Lorcán's blood inside of me. I think it really was helping me, even though I was still in very bad shape. Astaroth walked away from me, closer to the demon I knew had to be Damien, coming down the stairs.

"You should have stayed in hell," Damien said. Finally, he came into view, past the smoke, and I could see his glowing red eyes and the glowing red eyes of his hell hound that he always had with him, Seth.

"Do you think I fear you, demon knight? I am a demigod!" Astaroth declared with false bravado, because even I could hear the terror in his voice.

"I'm fully aware of what you are, Astaroth." Damien was wearing a royal-blue suit with a high collar and silver buttons. In his left hand was the leash to Seth's collar, and in his right, was a demonic sword. "Your being here disrupts the peace of the treaty."

"Peace!" Astaroth spat on the floor, and where his spit landed, the ground burned as if it had been hit with acid. "You dare speak to me about peace and treaties and call yourself a demon? Our rightful place is ruling these humans, not placating them, making deals with them. PROTECTING THEM FROM ME!" He roared the last part so loud, the foundation shook and dust from the cement sprinkled down onto us.

I wanted to go to Ansell, but this was no time to draw attention to me, and especially not to him. I sat quietly and watched Damien and Astaroth trade words and insults.

"Seth, be a good boy and help Daddy out," Damien said.

Oh, shit was about to get really real now. Seth looked like a normal Rottweiler, but he was anything but. In full demonic form, he was a Cerberus. Also known as a hell hound, a guardian of hell. Damien removed the collar from Seth's neck and the beast shook himself and began to transform into his full form, which forced Astaroth to take several steps back. Staring back at him now was a large monstrosity with three snarling, growling heads, all with red glowing eyes and mouths full of razor-sharp teeth and brightly glowing hellfire. The damned thing was frightening. The Cerberus charged toward Astaroth, as did Damien, who raised his sword above his head to deliver one hell of a blow.

Astaroth teleported before the dog could reach him, but when he appeared again, he slammed against some invisible force field and stumbled back, looking at the open space before him leading to the exit in bewilderment.

"Like I wouldn't have set up precautions before confronting you, Astaroth. You're not going anywhere but back to hell," Damien said, then he used his demonic magic to light his sword on fire.

I saw movement out of the corner of my eye coming from Ansell's direction and I turned to see him struggling to sit up. His head was bleeding from the blow he'd taken, and he was holding his side. He looked at the two demons, make that three, and I saw his mouth open to scream. I raised my hand, hoping to capture his attention. It worked. He looked at me, I could see the fear in his eyes, but I pressed my finger to my lips, motioning for him to remain silent. I held my hand out to caution him to stay where he was. He nodded and pressed himself as flat against the train as he could. The last thing we needed to do was distract Damien or Seth.

Stephan was coming to as well, and he crawled slowly towards where I was still recuperating. He was as quiet as a mouse, which was amazing, considering he had to crawl over dozens of dead bodies. Dead bodies that I hoped I could restore souls to if the relic hadn't been destroyed. I hated that we had to burn some of them, but we were trying to do our best to save lives. Hopefully, those people's bodies weren't too badly injured. But it all came down to this battle if they could be saved.

Astaroth roared in rage again as he failed to dodge the Cerberus' attack this time. All three sets of teeth managed to sink into parts of his body. You could see the hellfire in its mouth burning the wounds, weakening and hurting Astaroth, who swung his body around, trying to throw the hell hound off, but its grip was unyielding.

"What's going on?" Stephan asked once he reached me.

"We need to let Damien handle this," I whispered, and then motioned for him to remain silent. Let Astaroth be preoccupied with the demon knight, not us. That was my plan. So far, it was working. Damien was giving the demigod hell. They moved at speeds I had a hard time tracking. Every once in a while, I saw them come to blows, fists flying and claws slashing this way and that. The hell hound was a perfect tag team partner for Damien, as he was all over Astaroth every chance he could get. Astaroth finally managed to get Seth off him, but he lost his arm in the process, as the Cerberus' three heads had been biting his arm at the time. Black blood gushed from the wound as Astaroth howled in pain. Seth spit the severed arm out and lunged for Astaroth again, attacking his legs. With the demigod being double teamed by a demon knight and its hell hound, he was looking desperately for a way out.

He released a powerful demonic blast aimed at Damien, sending the knight crashing into the side of the train. The impact not only knocked the train off the rails and onto its side, but the imprint of Damien's body dented the side of one of the cars. The hell hound jumped on Astaroth's back, biting his skull, crushing it in its jaws as the other two heads each bit a shoulder. Damien pried himself from the crevice his body had made inside the train car and rushed towards Astaroth. I could tell he was injured as he ran with a limp and black blood oozed from several wounds. But he aimed his sword at Astaroth's heart, the flames burning red hot as he plunged the fiery blade into the demigod's chest.

"Ahhhhh," Damien screamed as he used all of his strength to push his blade all the way through until the tip of his sword pierced through Astaroth's back, barely missing Seth, who seemed to know where not to have his body.

The demigod yelled in pain as black blood bubbled up from its mouth, as well as smoke. The walls and platform shook again and I yelled for Ansell to come to me, and he came running as fast as he could, leaping over the crack and flames that licked at his feet as he jumped higher than I could have imagined. He fell into my arms and I held him as tightly as I could. We all turned and watched as Damien twisted the blade and said a chant that was meant to return Astaroth to hell. The demon thrashed about, trying to toss Seth off him and remove the blade, but it was all in vain. Astaroth's body seemed to collapse into itself as it formed into a cloud of black smoke. That smoke then returned to the crack it came from and the flames faded as the shaking stopped.

Damien fell to one knee, propping himself up by his sword. Seth transformed back into its normal dog form and trotted over to his master, licking his face. Damien said something else in their demon tongue that started to close the crack in the platform. Again, the subway shook with the power of the ground mending itself. Afterward, he sat back on his heel and looked in our direction.

"Fine mess…. you had here," he said between pants.

"Would have been worse had you not showed up. I'm… surprised you did," I said, wincing in pain as I struggled to adjust myself.

"Baby, are you okay?" Ansell asked as his eyes roamed over my body, examining me. "Oh my god, you're bleeding!"

"I'm healing, baby. I'm healing. I'm not dying, don't worry. It just hurts like a son of a bitch," I said. I didn't want him to worry. I already scared him enough as it was.

"We're all a bit worse for wear, I suppose," Damien said, rising to his feet. His eyes were now their normal crystal blue instead of demon red. He was handsome, the form he'd taken when he breached this world over two thousand years ago was a good-looking guy. I wasn't into demons, but he was nicer on the eyes than most. Couldn't say the same for his true demon face, which was as terrifying as Astaroth's.

The sound of metal scraping brought everyone's attention to the train and Warren as he pried the doors open and had to hop out because that was also the train that had been knocked over by Damien's body. The alpha looked like he'd seen better days, but at least he was fully healed.

"Please tell me this shit is over," he begged.

"No thanks to any of you, I see," Damien remarked.

Fucking demons. "If you'd been more diligent in your job,

monitoring who breaks out of hell, none of this would have happened. You should have been on this from the start," I shot back, since he wanted to get so high-and-mighty.

"If I did that, then I'd just be bored," Damien said.

"So sorry that saving billions of lives is boring to you. Aren't we all lucky you came," I snapped.

Damien chuckled. "Well, yes, you all were lucky. Lucky that my time was free," he shot back, then said another few words in his demonic language and a gust of wind passed through the platform.

"What the hell was that?" Stephan asked as he looked around nervously.

"I lowered the seal I had on this place. You have about ten minutes before the people start making their way down here, most likely the authorities," Damien replied, then he placed the collar back around Seth's neck and started walking toward the exit.

I knew it might not matter, because demons didn't seem to possess humility, but I felt like it needed to be said. "Thank you," I called out to Damien.

"Your gratitude isn't required," Damien said, then he left us down there. It was a response I was expecting, but I was hoping for something different.

"What the hell kind of demon was he?" Ansell asked.

"A demon knight, and the dog with him was a Cerberus, a hell hound. Next to an angel, they are the strongest supernatural beings that can take care of demigods," I explained.

"Shit, we could have used his ass earlier when we were getting our motherfucking asses kicked," Warren complained.

"I don't disagree, but demons are a petty lot and don't often honor the treaty. They must not have wanted Astaroth to reign and that's why they intervened. Whatever the case, I'm fucking grateful." I looked around at all of the dead bodies. "We need to find the relic."

"I already did," Stephan said, then pulled it from underneath his shirt and handed it to me.

"I could kiss you, but I won't. Maybe Alex could, though," I teased, remembering his little unconscious slip-up.

His eyes widened. "Huh, what? What are you talking about?"

I just smirked and didn't bother to answer him. Ansell chuckled a little, then groaned in pain as he held his side.

"I think my rib is broken," he said.

I didn't doubt it, Astaroth gave us one hell of a beating in spite of the fact that he was toying with us the whole time. That was until Damien showed up. Then that was the end of all his fun and games.

"When we get back to the girls, I'll have Vixen whip you up one of her healing potions. You'll be good in no time," I said. I looked down at my own wounds. The good thing was, the bleeding had stopped and the wounds were starting to close.

"Oh, baby, I hate that demon for what he did to you," Ansell said as he looked at my injuries.

"We're both alive, that's all I care about," I said, then leaned over a little, kissing him.

"Well, I'm alive too, motherfucker. You ain't happy about that?" Warren remarked. "Selfish bastard," he grumbled.

"I concur," Stephan added.

"I'm happy we're all alive, okay? Now, let's try to make sure we can bring these people back to life. I need you all to be quiet," I said. It was good that I already had my blessed blood on my hands, because this spell was going to require a blood donation. I held the cross in my hands and chanted the words to a restoration/resurrection spell that was specifically linked to Astaroth's relic. For some of the souls, it would be too late, but for everyone who died in the past couple of days, hopefully, it wouldn't be too late for them.

Warren, Ansell, and Stephan were as quiet as mice as I worked the magic necessary to restore life. It took a few minutes, but the cross began to glow blue and the souls started to flow out from the cross and towards the bodies on the ground and in the train. Other wispy souls flew out of the train station, returning to the vessels wherever they might be. I could see what the souls looked like because of my vision, I knew Ansell and the others couldn't. I was happy the spell was working. Sure, the Institute would have opted to let all of these people die as to not start a panic. And maybe that was the right thing to do, but it didn't feel like it to me. I had the power to help these people, so I did. Whatever happened next would be dealt with, even if a spell has to be cast to make people forget. At least, these people could go home tonight, or to the hospital.

The last soul left the cross and I sighed in relief. "Let's get the hell out of here before these people fully come to."

"Not to mention, I'm naked as fuck down here. Where are my clothes?" Warren asked.

"In the Jeep," Ansell said as he helped me to my feet.

"Good," Warren said.

We left out of the train station as fast as we could. Whatever interference the demons ran to keep the authorities away had worn off and I could hear the squad cars approaching. Ansell tossed Warren his clothes and he dashed into an alley to change. Luckily, I had parked his bike close to that alley. Stephan jumped in behind the wheel of my Jeep and I didn't complain. He was the only one between the three of us who was fully healed. Both Ansell and I climbed in and we were off. Out of the rearview mirror, I saw Warren heading off on his bike in the other direction just as a police car passed by him. We got out of there in the nick of time.

I still got one ticket. I guess it would have been more if Damien hadn't done a people-off on the area. Little blessings, I supposed. Stephan drove us to our headquarters and parked my Jeep in our underground garage.

"Well, this is the end of the line for me. I have a vampire to get to. It's been fun."

Ansell looked at him, a frown on his face. "Reall—"

"Not really," Stephan interjected. "Nearly dying twice wasn't fun. I was being... I don't know... sarcastic. You two love birds take care."

"Thank you, Stephan," I said. Ansell echoed me.

"You're welcome." Stephan climbed out of the Jeep and walked off toward the exit.

Both Ansell and I had to drag our injured asses inside where I was so happy to see the girls. I had called them ahead of time to let them know we were on our way and would need help. They took care of us right away, pampering us with potions and praise. Just what we both needed after the last couple of days we'd had.

"People are talking about a miracle happening all over the news. Although, some are calling it a gross sign of negligence. That some of the people killed in the diner and theater coming back to life means they were never dead in the first place and the medical examiner was wrong. They think it's some kind of gas that slows the heart down and makes you think someone is dead. There's all kinds of speculation," Jinx said, giving us updates.

"Let them think it was a mistake then. At least those people are alive now," I said, pleased with the choice I'd made.

"I'm so proud of you," Ansell said, and he leaned forward, kissing me.

I reached up, stroking his face. "I'm so proud of you. Your selfless sacrifice was breathtaking. I was trained for this life, but you jumped in with both feet and I can't tell you how extraordinary you really are, Ansell. Your mother may not have given you much, but she did give you a name worthy of your generous soul. Angel."

"Oh," he said before tears began trailing down his face. I sat up, kissing them away.

"I love you, Ansell."

He kissed me deeply, our lips locked in one of the most passionate embraces I'd ever experienced. When he pulled back, he was grinning wider than I think I'd ever seen him smile. "I love you, too, D'Angelo."

"Awwwww, you two are going to make me cry," Megan said, wiping tears from her eyes.

"Already ahead of you," Jinx said as she wiped tears from her eyes, then blew her nose into the tissue.

"I'm so happy you two finally found each other, and you kicked ass, so that's why I want to hear every detail," Vixen said.

I chuckled. "Fine. But before I get into that, did you hear back from Chris?"

Vixen nodded. "Yeah, he kicked ass, took some dings, but he's on his way home. Should be back by tomorrow, he said."

I sighed, relieved to hear that he had not only survived his mission, but that he was also successful. Dealing with a Nephilim wasn't any small task. I was worried about my boy, but with so much on my plate, I couldn't focus on him, just as I knew he couldn't focus on me. Not if we both wanted to save the world.

"I'm happy to hear he's all good and coming home. I've got so much to tell him," I said.

"Us first, details. Now," Vixen demanded playfully.

We were fully healed at this point, but exhausted. Still, I thought I could recite what the day had dealt us. The girls deserved to hear how lucky they had it back at headquarters. I had destroyed that damn relic once and for all. Let's see Astaroth bring his ass back to earth now. Not to say it couldn't happen, but it was going to be damn near impossible. That was all I was saying. After telling the girls what happened and answering a ton of their questions, both Ansell and I had to retire for the day. Didn't matter if it was only nine o'clock. We were exhausted, too tired to even make love, so you knew a motherfucker was done for the day. All I wanted to do was hold him in my arms and never let him go.

"I've been meaning to ask you something," I mumbled. It was hard to keep my eyes open by this point, but I needed this question answered.

"What?" Ansell replied in an equally mumbled voice.

"How in the hell did you get me out of Regis' mansion?"

Ansell giggled. "I told you that I was stronger than I looked."

I smiled at that, because he sure as hell did tell me that. "You sure are."

"I used the fireman's carry, by the way."

I squeezed him a little tighter. "I love you so much, Ansell," I said.

"I love you, too, D'Angelo," he said, then snuggled closer to me.

This was the very definition of happiness to me. Thank you, god.

✣

I was sitting in the living room, laptop on my... well... lap, and paying the bills. Boring and slightly painful as I was giving away my money to people I didn't even know just to live a decent life. Honestly, I'd rather fight demons than pay bills. Ansell was still sleeping soundly in our bedroom, because I'd put the dick to him good and proper for over two hours this morning. I think it was safe to say he learned the extent of my level of stamina. I could go for a few more rounds, but after the fourth orgasm, he threw in the towel and declared he needed a nap.

I finished paying the bills, then started looking up the information I really pulled my laptop out for. People Finder, I just needed to do a little bit of research. I was busy looking through a bunch of details when I heard the elevator open. I set my computer to the side and turned to see Christian stepping off the elevator, suitcase in hand.

"Welcome home, chump," I teased. A part of me got all excited to see him back safe and sound.

He chuckled as he placed his suitcase on the floor and walked over to the chair opposite me and plopped down. "Happy to be home. Shit, it was a long-ass flight."

"Which means you were the perfect man for the job," I said. I couldn't stand flying, hated heights and only did so when it couldn't be avoided. There wasn't much I was afraid of, but shit, you couldn't fight gravity. I guess that's where my fear stemmed from.

Chris half snorted, half chuckled. "Are you saying that just because a lot of flying was involved?"

"Yes. So, how was the mission?" I asked.

He cocked an eyebrow. "How was yours?"

"A literal pain in my ass," I said. That part was true, after the battle with Astaroth, I had a bruise on my ass. Of course, it healed, but still.

He snorted. "Mine was about the same. That fucking Nephilim had me globetrotting until I finally caught up to his ass in Beijing."

When he said that, his eyes stared forward like he had gone to some deep, dark place. "Hey, you okay?" I asked.

Christian blinked as if snapping out of some trance, then gave me a rueful smile, which caused me to worry. "Yeah, man… I'm good. Just… well, this one took a toll on me, is all. I think I'm just tired."

"Are you sure? You know, if you want to talk, you can tell me anything,"

He nodded. "Yeah, I know. It's just… that fucking Nephilim… he made me see things… stuff that, you know…"

I nodded, knowing full well what he meant. Shit that he liked to keep buried. "It was fucking with your head, man. That's what they do. They make you see shit that will trip your mind up, make you doubt your own sanity. I know for you—your ability—that it probably took a toll with all you've seen. Listen, I'm here for you, Chris, no matter what."

Having the ability to see a being's darkest secrets wasn't a gift, at least, that was what Chris once told me one night when we were teens. I knew he still felt that way, but he used it to do good. However, I knew he didn't always like having it. He didn't just see thoughts, he saw visions played out with Dolby digital sound and high-definition graphics. I've seen him actually upchuck after seeing a demon's darkest secret several times. I couldn't even imagine what the hell he saw, or just how bad it could have been to get that kind of reaction out of him. Chris was one of the toughest sons of bitches I knew. So, he didn't show weakness much, if at all.

Chris leaned over and patted my knee in a reassuring manner. "I know, D, and I love you for it, man. Really, I do. But enough about me. The mission was difficult, I took some major hits, had to work with a warlock, but in the end, we fucked that Nephilim up and saved the second kid he was trying to kill."

"Awesome, glad to hear it. Hey, which warlock did you have to work with?" I knew Chris really hated having to seek outside help. I didn't care for it either, because I didn't like owing favors, but sometimes it couldn't be avoided. Like with our recent missions.

Chris sneered. "That arrogant bastard, Silas."

"Oooh, him? Damn, I feel sorry for you. Yeah, he's powerful as fuck, but even being in his presence is enough to make you want to put a bullet in your head or better yet, his."

Chris laughed and I was happy to see it. "You're not wrong. But, I put our differences aside for the greater good."

"The greater good," I panned in a drone voice, mimicking a scene from one of our favorite movies, Hot Fuzz. Again, Chris laughed and this time, I joined him.

"But yeah, it was an ordeal. Hey, enough about me," he said again. "What about you? Vixen tells me that Ansell turned out to be your mate? Holy shit, man! I've been dying to talk to you about that," he beamed.

"Well, I had to work with not only my new partner, which turned out to be an amazing experience, but I also had to work with Lorcán, Stephan, and Warren. Then, believe it or not, Damien, the demon knight, actually saved our asses," I said.

"Fuck! Damn, shit was intense over here, I see. I'm surprised Damien showed up."

"Me too. I can't say that I wasn't happy to see him. I was dead if he hadn't showed up."

Chris sighed and nodded. "Then I'm VERY happy he showed up. With a demigod, you really did need a demon knight or an angel to defeat him. If we had one of those demon knight weapons... never mind."

I snorted. "Yeah, a demon knight weapon would do us no good without demonic power to wield it. Let's face it, there's a lot we can do, but demigods and hexigods are really out of our league. I don't like admitting it either. But facing one, weelll, that puts shit into perspective for a motherfucker, know what I mean?"

He nodded. "Yeah, it does. I'm glad you're alive. Too bad you had to work with Lorcán," he sneered. "Fucking hate vampires."

"I know. But he was tied in with my case. It just happened. Surprisingly, he was willing to help. I didn't think he would. Ansell helped a lot in convincing him," I said.

Chris huffed. "A decent being doesn't need convincing to do the right thing. Vampires aren't decent. Don't let that ever fool you just because he helped this once. I'm sure it was purely selfish on his part."

"I think he's different, though."

"If the world would be destroyed or taken over by demons, that's bad news for vampires. Purely selfish," Chris protested.

I held my hands up, not willing to debate it because I agreed. But, there was something about Lorcán that made me think he actually did want to help save the world, if only because he liked living in it. I mean, he was a tough regent and made sure humans didn't get killed and he punished vamps who broke the rules. I wasn't sure all regents were as diligent as he was. Anyway, that wasn't the only thing I wanted to tell Chris about Lorcán.

"One more thing about our regent vampire. He can conjure and control fire," I stated.

That seemed to catch Chris' attention. He arched both eyebrows. "Really? Did you see him?"

I shook my head. "I was... indisposed at the time... but Ansell saw him use fire to defend against Orcal, the demon."

"Now, that is interesting. I wonder how many vampires can do that, or is it just him? Have the vampires been honest about what they can or cannot do? I have more questions than answers and you know how I hate that," he said as he settled back in the chair.

"I know, I don't like the unsolved puzzle either. Regardless, he saved my life by doing that," I said.

Chris just looked at me when I said that. He stared so long, I started to get a bit concerned, and then finally, he made an off-handed gesture, as if dismissing that fact. "I'm happy you're alive. I just don't trust vampires. He probably wants to fuck you."

I snorted. "Feed on me, is more like it. He seemed waaay more interested in my blood than my body." I knew one of the reasons he didn't trust vampires was because he couldn't read their deepest, darkest secrets. The vampires we faced, he could never breach their minds to get that information. That only added to his level of distrust of them.

"Okay, tell me about Angel, did you feel the connection, is that how you knew?" he asked, completely changing the subject from the marvel Lorcán was, to the gift from God that Ansell was. Fortunately for him, I was willing to talk all day about my baby. I told Chris about everything Ansell and I went through. The attraction I felt burning inside of me, the pressure building until neither of us could take it any longer and we had to have sex. We had to feel that passion satisfied. Chris sat there, listening to every word I said like a kid listening to an engrossing bedtime story. He was grinning from ear to ear as he leaned forward.

"Wow, I can't believe it, but I'm so happy for you. Gives me hope that maybe one day, I might find my mate," he said after I brought him up to date.

I smiled. "You will." I hoped he did. He was such a good person, he deserved happiness, the same happiness that I had with Ansell. But whoever it was that becomes his mate, I hoped he could handle the monster cock that Chris had between his legs. The thought made me laugh and Chris looked at me in confusion.

I waved him away. "Don't mind me. My mind is in the gutter."

"Ahhh." Chris nodded. "In its normal habitat, then. I understand."

"Man, fuck you." I flipped him the bird and he laughed.

"Well, I'm sure we'll talk more—oh, I see we have a new employee," he said.

"Ansell's best friend. I sort of gave her a place to stay and a job. I hope you don't mind," I said sheepishly.

He shrugged. "It works out for us to have a third employee who can take over the store duties when we need Vixen or Jinx for missions. She seemed nice, I met her downstairs. Jinx and Vix are teaching her the ropes."

"She is nice, I like her a lot."

"I did catch the flirtatious looks, though."

I laughed. "She's barking up the wrong tree in this place. Everyone goes the same way."

He chuckled. "I'll try to let her off easy if she makes any moves."

I cocked an eyebrow. "She seems the saucy type. Might trap you in a corner. I'd expect for her to make a move."

"It'd be the most action I've had in months," he joked, although, he was telling the truth. I didn't know how Chris did it. My balls couldn't take the torture. But, I guess if you could read deep, dark thoughts, some might turn you off of sex.

"You need to get laid, man. Find a sweet piece of ass and fuck the hell out of him," I suggested.

Chris just shrugged it off. "I'm good. I'm sure I'll get to learn more about her and Angel later. Right now, I want to go to sleep and snooze for about two weeks."

"I hear you. Go on, I'm not going to hold you up. Rest easy."

Chris nodded, then took his suitcase upstairs to his bedroom. I went back to doing what it was I was doing, which was going to be a surprise for Ansell.

Chapter Twenty

ANGEL

Three months later...

Meggie stepped up beside me where I stood looking at my reflection in the mirror above the dresser in the bedroom I shared with D'Angelo. Our eyes connected and I smiled at the woman who would stand beside me on the biggest day of my life. "Angel, you look amazing." Her eyes welled with joyful tears and her lips trembled slightly.

I knew the day would be emotionally charged, but I was hoping to stall the water works until the ceremony, at least. "This tux is really something else, isn't it?" I thought the charcoal-gray color looked better with my skin tone than the stark-black one, and the white jacket I tried on made me look washed out. D'Angelo, on the other hand, looked remarkable in the white jacket he chose to wear for our special occasion. The light color acted as a blank canvas against his darker skin and allowed his beautiful ancestry to shine through.

"I wasn't talking about your tuxedo, but I must admit you made a stunning choice." Meggie rested her hand on my shoulder and tipped her head to the side as she studied my face in the mirror. "Love looks good on you, Angel. It's been a long time coming too."

I turned and kissed her temple. "Your time is coming too, love."

"Did you have a vision?" she asked excitedly. "When? I'm getting all kinds of impatient and feeling a little frustrated at having to watch sickening lovebirds day in and day out." She rolled her eyes dramatically. "Jinx and Vixen have one another and you have D'Angelo. I was hoping Christian might swing my way, because if there is a more beautiful man on the planet, I haven't met him. But noooooo, he's strictly dickly too. Some guy is going to be a lucky bastard because Christian's beard would feel amazing against a person's inner thigh or…"

"No, I didn't have a vision," I said, cutting her off. I didn't want to think about Christian's beard and how it would feel against any part of anyone's body. I'd been deprived of sex for a week and I was starting to feel very frustrated. "Damn purification rituals," I grumbled.

"Someone is feeling a little out of sorts, is he?" Meggie asked. It was obvious she was enjoying my displeasure. "Not digging the separate bedrooms and no sex part leading up to the big day, huh?"

"Not at all," I replied honestly. "I spent more than two decades without sleeping beside D'Angelo, but now I can't manage more than a few hours when he isn't next to me."

"That all ends today and you get your man back, sweetie," Meggie said soothingly. "I'm going to be honest with you, Angel. I wasn't thrilled when I found out that your bonding ceremony included bloodshed, but experiencing the rituals this past week has truly been a magical time. I have never felt more in tune with my own spirituality and I can only imagine what it will feel like once you guys are truly joined in every possible way."

D'Angelo and I had originally planned to sneak off to the

courthouse for a quick marriage, but I slipped up one morning at breakfast thinking we were alone and mentioned shopping for rings to D. I couldn't remember which one of our nosey ladies overheard us because they all converged on us at once.

"You can't just have a traditional wedding, D'Angelo," Jinx had said.

"Why not?" D'Angelo had asked.

Vixen had looked at him like he was crazy. "Because you don't have a traditional relationship, D, and quite honestly, a lame-ass marriage certificate from the state of Illinois is an insult to your lineage. Or were you going to fly off to Vegas for an Elvis-themed wedding?"

"Are you referring to the lineage that abandoned me because I refused to deny my attraction to men?" D'Angelo had asked bitterly. *So that was his reason for wanting a traditional marriage. The first time that rings were mentioned, it was in relation to a ceremonial bonding. Since then, D'Angelo only talked about a wedding. They were not the same thing at all. Even I knew that.*

"They can deny you until their final breath, but that doesn't mean you turn your back on who you are," Vixen had countered. "You refused to deny that you're gay, and it's time you stop denying the other parts of you also." She had pointed to his chest. "That tattoo above your heart isn't just for show. You can no more disavow the ink above your heart than you can loving Angel. It's who you are, and you can't pick and choose the parts you wish to acknowledge."

"Vix, I know damn well who I am. Don't I prove that every day?"

I had reached for D'Angelo's hand beneath the table because I could tell he was losing his cool. D had voiced his bitter feelings about his expulsion from the Institute community, and I thought his feelings were justified, but I thought Vixen might have a valid point. Acknowledging and accepting were not the same things. It was possible to know something and block the way it made you feel at the same time. D had buried his emotions and put his focus on ridding the world of evil.

"Yes, you risk your life every day for the good of the world," Vixen had said, "but that's not the same thing as fully embracing who you are." She had lowered herself in the chair across from D at the kitchen table. "You are a Genesis Circle member who happens to also be a former Institute member that has found his eternal mate. That requires something more special than a few brief lines in front of a magistrate, D'Angelo. There are time-honored traditions…"

"I don't want to talk about this anymore," D'Angelo had said, cutting her off.

"I do," I had gently added, squeezing D's hand. Just four months ago, I never would've had the courage to stand up to D'Angelo. My intimidation of him when he visited Martinelli's was a close second to the insane attraction. That all changed when I had a vision of him dying. I went from meek to fierce when it came to him. I always wanted what was best for him and I strongly felt that honoring his legacy would go a long way toward healing him.

D'Angelo had released a resigned breath. "I'll listen, but I'm not committing to anything."

I'd spent a lot of time the past week thinking about how amazing our bonding night would feel. Somewhere along the way, I'd stopped thinking about it as a wedding, even though our ceremony would be a combination of traditional and spiritual aspects performed by Vixen's friend who was both a high priestess and ordained through the state to conduct traditional marriages. I knew that Meggie was right, and I rejoiced in the knowledge that I was only hours away from being claimed again by my mate after a long week of physical separation.

Our week started out with a banishment ritual. D'Angelo and I wore matching simple robes made of white cotton and sat across from one another on plush cushions in a circle surrounded by pure white candles while Batya chanted and called upon the spirits to rid our souls of negative spirits, thoughts, and influences. At first, I didn't think it had worked very well because I spent a lot of time squinting hard to see a glimpse of D's sexy man parts through the small gap in his robe. We were instructed to wear nothing but the robes and my body yearned to at least see what I had to physically deny myself.

The smoke from her smoldering bundle of herbs permeated my nose, and I could honestly feel it invade my soul. As happy as D'Angelo made me, I still carried hurt and darkness inside my soul that not even his love could completely banish. I stopped thinking about sex and imagined the wispy, magical smoke circling the dark recesses of my soul until it formed a cyclone of pure light and love. The swirling light invaded the darkness and kept churning like a spin cycle on a washing machine until all signs of the stains of negativity were lifted from my soul. I felt lighter than I ever had in my life. When I reopened my eyes, I saw the same dawn of recognition in D'Angelo's eyes. I prayed that the light helped D'Angelo begin to fully heal as well.

The next phase was a purification ritual to cleanse our blood of toxins and other harmful components. This was accomplished by both magic and fasting, so that our blood would be at its purest state when we exchanged our blood vows. Vixen was given strict instructions on what we could eat and drink. As with the first ritual, I was so focused on the things I wasn't allowed to eat that I didn't recognize how good I felt with the absence of sugar, starches, and caffeine, to name a few. D'Angelo took a day or two longer to rebound on that one since he had a sweet tooth, but I recognized the moment he felt the difference inside him.

The final step was a special bath the afternoon of our ceremony, but not together for obvious reasons. No one trusted us alone and naked, which was why D moved into the room I had used my first night beneath his roof. Batya blessed the milky-looking water that had flower petals and herbs floating in it while I stood next to the deep tub in a terry cloth robe. Once she finished, she left the room so I could sink down into the water in private. I was happy when I learned that I would be trusted to wash myself rather than have strange hands on my body.

The water was the perfect temperature and I sank down lower so I could rest my head against the rim of the copper tub. I closed my eyes and inhaled the herbal aroma that was a heady mix of spice and flowers. I had never felt so relaxed in my entire life, and I wondered just what kind of herbs she had put in my bathwater. The same white candles from our banishing ritual stood on pillars around the bathroom, bathing the room in a romantic glow. In fact, the environment was so tranquil, I worried that I might fall asleep and drown on my bonding day. I reluctantly sat up and reached for the special soap Batya provided.

"Wash your body and hair only with this soap," she'd instructed before leaving the room. Apparently, fancy shampoos and hair products would ruin the purification. Or, the hair products were a fire hazard with as many candles that were likely to surround us throughout the ceremony. Not only were they pretty and smelled good, the burning flame represented the element of fire, which represented purification.

"Farmers have set fire to their fields for hundreds of years after a harvest to eliminate any impurities in the soil and to trigger regrowth," Batya had explained to us during our first meeting with her.

I washed myself thoroughly with the purification soap while the candle flames burned any remaining impurities that escaped my body. I had never felt so clean when I stepped out of the bathtub and dried off with the plush towel that waited for me. I wasn't just talking about my skin and hair, either; every part of me—inside and out—was free of negative burdens that had taxed my mind and spirit.

"Why did you guys decide to go with traditional tuxedos instead of ceremonial robes?" Meggie asked, pulling me from my memories of an incredible week.

I grinned wryly, then said, "It's D's way of bucking the system. There was no way he was going to conform a hundred percent. He figured we would wear ceremonial robes many times during the week leading up to the ceremony and a tuxedo would be a nice change of pace." He wasn't wrong, either. "Of course, Batya wasn't happy, but she compromised by blessing our tuxedos before we put them on." I looked at the clock and saw that it was time to meet my mate for our ceremony. "Are you ready to dazzle our friends in your dress?"

Meggie looked ravishing in a long dress in a shade of deep purple that should've clashed with her bright red hair, but instead, it made her look regal. "I sure am. Are you ready?"

"I sure am."

"Well then, I bet there's a beautiful man at the foot of the steps waiting to escort you inside the ceremonial circle."

I smiled because I had no doubt D'Angelo was waiting for me. I could feel his presence as surely as I felt my own beating heart.

Sure enough, D'Angelo was pacing at the foot of the grand staircase. He stopped when he sensed me approaching and turned slowly to look up at me. His eyes seemed to light from within when they connected to mine. My heart sped up when he smiled at me. I couldn't be sure what made me do it, but I was guessing it was pure joy that prompted me to hop onto the banister and slide down into D's waiting arms.

"I got you now," he said playfully.

"You're going to have me forever," I countered.

"It's not long enough, Ansell." The tenderness in his voice threatened to trigger the tears I was trying to hold at bay.

"The sooner we start, the sooner you two can sneak off to do your favorite kind of bonding," Meggie teased.

D'Angelo set me down and reached for my hand. We entered the living room together where our friends and Batya waited for us. I had to admit that Christian looked stunning in a tuxedo that matched D's. He would stand beside D'Angelo during the traditional wedding portion of our ceremony like Meggie would do for me.

We had moved the furniture out of the living room to convert the space into our ceremonial room for the week. Our friends would sit on the cushions that were placed in a semi-circle around the perimeter of the ceremonial circle. Batya waited at the top of the circle, smiling at us. I was once again struck by her statuesque, African beauty. She was almost as tall as D'Angelo and looked distinguished in her ivory ceremonial robe with golden embroidery. Her many braids were beautifully arranged on top of her head.

D'Angelo and I took our places inside the circle while Meggie and Christian stood beside us just outside of it, Meggie next to me and Christian next to D'Angelo.

"We are gathered today to witness the joining of these two men," Batya said in her rich voice. "It's my absolute honor to officiate both the traditional and the spiritual bonding ceremonies. May we begin?"

Vixen, Jinx, and Father Thomas, who was there as our honored guest, remained standing as the traditional vows and ring exchange took place, but sat on the cushions with Christian and Meggie when it was time to start the bonding ceremony. I glanced down at the shiny ring D'Angelo had slid on my finger while Batya lit the strategically placed candles. The rings had been blessed with holy water prior to the ceremony so they could be pure when exchanged.

"As this ring has no end, neither shall my love for you." The steady, deep timbre of D'Angelo's voice during his promise caused a delicious shiver to slither down my spine. In comparison, my voice shook with emotion, but not from a lack of conviction. I knew my place was beside him.

The tenor and pitch to Batya's voice changed when she began the spiritual bonding. "Today, D'Angelo and Angel, your spirits will join as one unbreakable bond. The air you breathe will be shared between your lungs, two hearts will beat as one, and the blood that flows through your veins will also flow through your mate's. A spiritual bonding once completed can never be broken—not even in death—and should never be entered lightly. Do both of you freely enter this ceremony committed to the love and health of the other?"

On cue, D'Angelo and I both said, "We do."

"Very well, gentlemen. Let us begin."

I kept my eyes locked on D'Angelo's as Batya chanted and prayed. "Our gods, I call upon thee to bless this union. Please give these two men your strength and vitality. Oh gods, bless them with a long life and a love that remains as pure as it is today." She continued with chants that evoked the elements of earth, air, water, and fire. "These two men enter this commitment unburdened by negativity and pure of souls. Lift them up, guide them, and blessed be their union for all eternity."

I felt the magic of her words enter and lift my soul. I felt so light and airy that I expected to levitate. D'Angelo felt it too; I saw the awareness in his eyes.

"Instead of hand fasting, D'Angelo and Angel will make a blood oath to one another," Batya explained. She handed the ceremonial knife to me first and I accepted it with a shaky hand. This was the part I dreaded the most. I would rather stab myself than cause D'Angelo a second of discomfort. He was a battle-hardened warrior and could take the pain—not to mention, he would most likely heal before the ceremony was over, but still…

"You won't hurt me, Ansell." D'Angelo opened the palm of his left hand that bore my ring. He nodded for me to continue. If I wanted to be bonded to him for eternity, then I needed to suck it up and prick his palm enough to get him to bleed. I wanted that bond more than air, so I pressed the blade to his flesh and sliced him. It wasn't deep enough though, because he healed right before my eyes. "A little deeper, baby."

"Show off," I grumbled, earning chuckles from our friends, but I did as he said.

D'Angelo took the knife from my hand and I presented my open left hand also. I saw the same hesitation in him that I felt and I prodded him along. "Quick, before you heal again. We have better things to do tonight," I whispered. D grinned sheepishly, then sliced quickly. The cut wasn't very deep, but I still had to bite my lip to keep the hiss from escaping me. I wasn't quite as badass as him yet.

Batya took the knife from D'Angelo and set it aside. "Join hands, gentlemen."

I gasped in surprise when our cut palms connected. Batya began another chant while I sat staring into my mate's eyes. I could literally feel our souls joining and fusing; our hearts and lungs began working in tandem.

"D'Angelo and Angel, you are now of one blood, spirit, and mind. Blessed be thy bond that ties you together for eternity."

Batya handed us a warm towel so we could wipe our hands clean. D'Angelo was nearly healed, but my palm still bled a little. He frowned as he looked at my wound until Batya spoke again. "You may now kiss your mate," she said, combining both traditions.

D'Angelo forgot about my minor cut the second his lips touched mine. Happiness and contentment flowed thickly through my body like warm honey as we shared our first kiss as husbands and spiritually bonded mates. By the time he pulled back, all pain was forgotten—at least, it was for me.

"Vixen, did you bring the salve?" D'Angelo asked when she greeted us after the ceremony.

She rolled her eyes as if to say, "duh," and smeared a tiny amount of magic healing salve on my cut.

We were embraced by our friends, and even Christian, who had seemed like a different person lately. He'd gone on several missions the past few months, and he grew more and more terse each time he returned. Of course, I worried that I was partially to blame. *Was Christian resentful of my presence? Did he not like me? Was he jealous he hadn't found his mate too? Was he secretly in love with D'Angelo?* That last one made D laugh out loud when I expressed my concerns. He assured me that Christian sometimes got in these moods because evil had hit him harder than most. I admit that I was curious about Christian's past, but I didn't feel right pumping D for information, so I let it pass.

So, I was pleased when he smiled at us genuinely for the first time in months and offered us congratulations. My relief was short-lived because his somber expression returned almost immediately. "D'Angelo, are you sure now is the right time to leave for a week?" he asked. "I feel like there are things at work in the universe right now…"

"Things you don't care to share with the rest of us," D nearly hissed in response. "I can't believe it's okay for you to disappear for months, but I can't take my husband and mate on a short honeymoon."

"We're going on a honeymoon?" I asked in surprise. Christian grimaced when he realized he'd caused D to tip his hand.

"It was a surprise," D'Angelo said. The glare he directed at Christian made it obvious how unhappy he was at his friend for ruining his plans. Tension had been building between them ever since Christian returned, but I sensed it was fast approaching the boiling point.

"Chris," I said, using the nickname that D frequently used during friendlier times. "Don't stress about it." I looked at my husband and mate. "I'm still surprised and thrilled."

"Man, I am sorry," Christian said. "Look, you're right. You guys get out of here and take a well-deserved honeymoon. We'll talk when you get back." He walked off without another word.

"I'm so worried about him," Jinx said. "I can't reach him no matter what I try." She shook her head and added, "Please try not to worry about us. We'll call you if we find ourselves in a dire situation. Come on, baby," Jinx said to Vixen, "let's go make sure all the food is set out on the buffet tables."

My stomach growled at the thought of eating whatever it wanted, but I wasn't going anywhere until D answered some questions. "So, where are you taking me?"

"San Francisco," D'Angelo calmly said, but I picked up undertones of nervousness.

"Why there?" I asked.

"There's a large group of people waiting to meet someone special that they thought was lost to them forever."

I swallowed hard to dislodge the lump in my throat. "Me?" I asked.

"Yes, you." D'Angelo cupped my face in his hands. "I knew they hadn't forgotten about you. Your mom carefully hid her trail and only took jobs that paid in cash once she got here. In fact, she paid cash for everything so they couldn't track her. They'd already given up hope by the time you entered the foster care system as a teen or they would've claimed you."

"But then I would never have met you," I told him. I was thrilled to learn that my father's family never forgot about me, but I couldn't regret the path that led me to my mate.

"Oh yes, you would've," D'Angelo countered. "You were meant to be mine, and I'm going to prove it to you once we get upstairs." He began leading me toward the stairs instead of the kitchen.

"Don't you want to eat the feast the girls prepared?" I asked.

"Special delivery," Jinx said as she re-entered the room. She held a large silver tray laden with plates of various foods, including the top tier of our wedding cake. "There's a little bit of everything for you guys."

"I love you." D took the tray from her and kissed her cheek.

"I know, and I love you too." She skipped back in search of her girlfriend.

"After you," D'Angelo said, nodding his head for me to walk up the steps.

I was rooted to the spot. "Some days I'm so overjoyed by what my life has become and others I'm terrified that I'm stuck in a dream and none of it's real. I just know that I'm not stuck in that circle of darkness my life had become before I met you, D."

"I'm real. Our love is real." D'Angelo leaned over and kissed my cheek affectionately. "We've only just begun, Ansell."

Epilogue

Lorcán

The blood I relished drinking flowed down my throat in a luscious stream. The human whom I fed on moaned in ecstasy as I gently sucked down his life fluid. Being a vampire was almost too easy, as people gravitated towards us for the pleasure we could give them. But at our core, we were predators, and even though I might have humans throwing themselves at my feet for a bite, I still enjoyed hunting every once in a while. Of course, I couldn't kill, per our treaty with the Institute, but the thrill of the hunt was enough to satisfy the predator in me.

I pulled back from my human before I'd taken too much. The last thing I wanted was to have him too weak to go home on his own. I looked down at his face, his half-lidded eyes, and smiled. "Did you enjoy that?" I asked.

I knew he did. His cock was as hard as a rock and it was pressed against my ass as I was straddling him. He wasn't quite my type, but if he was, I'd have given him a go.

The human gave me a goofy grin and nodded slowly. "Y—yes. It was… amazing. Bite me again," he begged. They always wanted you to drain them again, chasing that pleasure that used to come once in a lifetime in the old days. Mainly because humans rarely survived an encounter with a vampire.

I had tracked him down after he left work. I wanted him to know I was following him to get his blood pumping from fear. It always made the blood taste that much better. He ran and I chased him. He was running as fast as his human legs could take him, while I merely jogged, but with my speed, I caught up to him instantly. And that was after I had given him a three-block lead. The chase was fun and when I bit into his flesh… Ahhhhh, ambrosia.

For now, he knew there were things in the night that monster movies and nightmares were made of. I had two choices here. I could make him forget this ever happened. Or, I could leave my marks upon his neck that would give him a little reminder that this had taken place. I decided to go for the latter.

I leaned closer, looking him directly in his eyes, capturing his attention so I could work my magic. "You loved what happened just now and you want more of it, don't you?"

He stared at me blankly and nodded. "Y—yes."

"You will keep this a secret, but if you ever want to feel the pleasure you felt tonight, come to Hypnotic." With that little message, I left him there, moving so fast, to his human eyes, it would simply look as if I had disappeared. I climbed into the back of my Maserati that Stephan was driving. "Let's head back."

"You know, I could have fed you, Lorcán," Stephan said.

"I know." I looked at him. "But you know I love variety."

"My blood tastes different when I eat different things. That gives you variety."

I sighed. "Are you feeling jealous that I fed on someone else? We've discussed this, Stephan. We are not lovers, nor will we ever be.

You have your role in my life and that is all. Now, shut up and drive."

He didn't say anything else, although, I knew I'd pissed him off. He desired me sexually, I'd have to be blind if I didn't know that. But, like that human tonight, he wasn't my type. Shit, I couldn't even remember the last time I met a man I wanted to fuck. D'Angelo the hunter was probably the closest to someone tickling my fancy, but even he didn't really do it for me. Besides, it looked like he was all taken by the little Asian cherub at his side. Their love was almost sickening.

At least the nasty business with that demon was over with. I didn't like being involved with that nonsense, especially knowing I had almost lost Stephan. I was relieved that I hadn't. I may not love Stephan as he wants me to, but I did have feelings for him. Not to mention, I depended on him. We were about ten minutes away from my club when my cell phone started ringing. The number, face, and name on my screen revealed my child, and second-in-command, Alex. I answered.

"What's up?" I asked.

"I found another one. This time, I got here before the cops did," Alex said.

I groaned. It was days like this that being a regent was a pain in the ass. This was the second dead vampire in two weeks, and I didn't like shit like that going down on my watch. "Where are you? I'm on my way."

Alex gave me his location and I gave the directions to Stephan. "Looks like it's the same weapon that took him out, too."

A blessed weapon, one synonymous with the hunters of the Institute. The first time I found the dead vampire, I contacted my liaison with the Chasseur Institute and they swore up and down they didn't issue a contract on any vampires. Normally, they wouldn't have to, because I kept the vampires in my Regency in control. No killing, no turning humans without my permission. I followed the rules to a T, because I didn't have time for bullshit drama. What I was going through now was bullshit drama.

With this second vampire being killed by a blessed weapon, this could mean there was a rogue hunter out there. Or someone who found a blessed weapon and wanted to put an end to vampires. Either way, I wasn't going to let it continue.

"I'll be there shortly," I said before hanging up.

Stephan pulled up to the location and I climbed out of my car and walked over to Alex, who was examining the body of a shriveled vampire. His skin was black and dried out, the power of a blessed weapon sucked the lifesource out of him, leaving a husk. I hated those fucking weapons because they were so lethal. You get stabbed in the heart with one of them and it was over for you. It was definitely the same weapon, therefore, the same murderer.

A rogue hunter, maybe. The only hunter I knew rumored to have a grudge against vampires was D'Angelo's partner, Christian. I was sure they all had a bias, but his stood out more because of what had happened to his family. As for Christian and D'Angelo, both had been kicked out of the Institute, which made them rogues of a sort. I decided to give D'Angelo a call to see if he knew what his partner was up to.

"Lorcán? Why are you calling?" D'Angelo asked upon answering.

"I'm going to get right to the point. I have a second dead vampire lying at my feet in a dank alley in two weeks. He was killed with what looks like a blessed weapon. Know anything about that?"

There was a pause, but then he finally answered. "I don't, but what are you implying?"

"Well, your partner, what's he been up to lately? It's rumored that he doesn't really like our kind."

"So? Only people who do are fools who think it's trendy to be feedbags for bloodsucking monsters," D'Angelo said.

"Well, that was rude, and after I helped you." *Fucking hunters.*

"Hey, it's the truth. But to answer your question, we didn't have anything to do with your dead vampires."

"You're speaking for Christian as well? How can you account for what he's doing when you've got your cock in your boy toy?" I could be rude too.

"I know Christian. He wouldn't be out there killing vampires who didn't have it coming. Maybe they had it coming."

"If they did, treaty dictates you share intel with us. Breaking the rules are we?"

"I'll talk to him, but I'm sure he has nothing to do with your vampire problem. Now, if you'll excuse me, I'm on my honeymoon. You know what, better yet, why don't you ask Christian yourself. He's at our store, Things from the Past. Don't bother me, I want a week without monster bullshit."

His honeymoon, eh? How nice for him… whatever. "Fine." I hung up first, because I refused to be the one he hung up on. Looked like I was going to be paying Christian a visit. I didn't know anything about him, really, but if he was behind these killings, I was going to put him down personally.

Other Books

Other Books by Nicholas Bella and Aimee Nicole Walker

Undisputed

Other Books by Nicholas Bella

Cobra: The Gay Vigilante Series

The New Haven Series

Demon Gate Series

The Odin Chronicles

Gods and Slaves Series

Other Books by Aimee Nicole Walker

Only You

The Fated Hearts Series

Curl Up and Dye Mysteries Series

Road to Blissville Series

Acknowledgments

Nicholas and Aimee would like to thank Heidi Ryan and Judy Zweifel for working so hard to make the book shine. They'd also like to thank Jay Aheer, and Stacey Blake for making the exterior and interior of the book look so beautiful.

As always, they wanted to thank their readers for all the love and support they've given them over the years. Without you, this collaboration wouldn't have happened.

About
Nicholas Bella

About me? Hmmm, I'm just a person with a wild imagination and a love for words who was sitting around the house one day and said, "Why hasn't anyone written a book like this before?". As with every storyteller, I wanted to share mine with the world. I like my erotica dark, gritty, sexy… and even a little raunchy. I'm not afraid to go there and I hope you aren't afraid to go there with me. When I'm not writing, I love watching movies and TV shows, clubbing, biking, and hanging out with family and friends. I love life.

I'd love to hear from you, feel free to send me a shout out!

You can reach me at:

Twitter—twitter.com/AuthorNickBella

Facebook—facebook.com/authornickbella

Website—www.nicholasbella.com

About
Aimee Nicole Walker

I am a wife and mother to three kids, three dogs, and a cat. When I'm not dreaming up stories, I like to lose myself in a good book, cook or bake. I'm a girly tomboy who paints her fingernails while watching sports and yelling at the referees. I will always choose the book over the movie. I believe in happily-ever-after. Love inspires everything that I do. Music keeps me sane.

I'd love to hear from you.

You can reach me at:

Twitter—https://twitter.com/AimeeNWalker

Facebook—http://www.facebook.com/aimeenicole.walker

Blog—AimeeNicoleWalker.blogspot.com

Printed in Great Britain
by Amazon